THE SHIFT OF THE TIDE

UNCHARTED REALMS – BOOK 3

by

Jeffe Kennedy

Thank you for reading!

Credits
Content Editor: Peter Senftleben
Line and Copy Editor: Rebecca Cremonese
Back Cover Copy: Erin Nelsen Parekh
Cover Design: Ravven

A QUICKSILVER HEART

Released from the grip of a tyrant, the Twelve Kingdoms have thrown all that touch them into chaos. As the borders open, new enemies emerge to vie for their hard-won power—and old deceptions crumble under the strain...

The most talented shapeshifter of her generation, Zynda has one love in her life: freedom. The open air above her, the water before her, the sun on her skin or wings or fur—their sensual glories more than make up for her loneliness. She serves the High Queen's company well, but she can't trust her allies with her secrets, or the secrets of her people. Best that she should keep her distance, alone.

Except wherever she escapes, Marskal, the Queen's quiet lieutenant, seems to find her. Solid, stubborn, and disciplined, he's no more fluid than rock. Yet he knows what she likes, what thrills and unnerves her, when she's hiding something. His lithe warrior's body promises pleasure she has gone too long without. But no matter how careful, how tender, how incendiary he is, only Zynda can know the sacrifice she must make for her people's future—and the time is drawing near...

Dedication

Some of the themes and images in this story came from Patricia McKillip's *The Forgotten Beasts of Eld*, probably in ways that are invisible to anyone else. Still, I owe her a debt for lighting the magical green fire of this story in me.

Acknowledgements

A huge thank you goes out to Evergreen who not only gave me the insider's tour of Epcot but helped me without knowing it by giving me the idea for dolphins killing the shark.

Thanks to my long-suffering critique partners and beta readers Marcella Burnard and Carien Ubink. A special thank you to Anne Calhoun, who served as fresh-to-the-series reader and mostly commented "What the hell is going on in this book???"

Cherished writer friends Kelly Robson and Grace Draven gave support and advice many times as I was writing. Without their sanity checks I'd be lost.

Peter Senftleben has been the developmental editor for this entire series and I'm grateful he could continue freelance and work on this book, too. You helped me sort out a major mess! Likewise, Rebecca Cremonese extended her production editing skills to this book and made it so much better. The fact that I use "suicide" as a verb is entirely not her fault. She tried to talk me out of it. She really did.

Thanks to Lynne Facer for suggesting the nicknames for the twins. Love and appreciation, too, to all my readers and especially the crew in Jeffe's Closet on Facebook, for early feedback and eternal enthusiasm.

Much appreciation to my Santa Fe critique group for wine and conversation, along with insightful comments. Thanks to Sage Walker for a full read when I needed it most and making me put back what I took out. Also big thanks to Edward Khmara, M.T. Reiten, and Eric Wolf. Extra special gratitude to

Jim Sorenson, who cried foul on an anticlimactic battle to the dragon and made it SO much better.

I'm giving a special shout-out to Ravven for the absolutely incredible cover. I looked at it for inspiration while writing, it's that good.

I always thank David last, because he's the one who's there day-in and day-out for every phase of writing. This time, though, he went the extra mile—literally. I was finishing the draft of this as we, meaning he, drove through central Wyoming. He made a decision while I was immersed and he was *not allowed to talk to me*, pulled over at a lake and fished while I wrote the final scenes. It made all the difference and I'll always associate that peaceful spot with the happy ending of this book. An observant man, as the quiet ones often are.

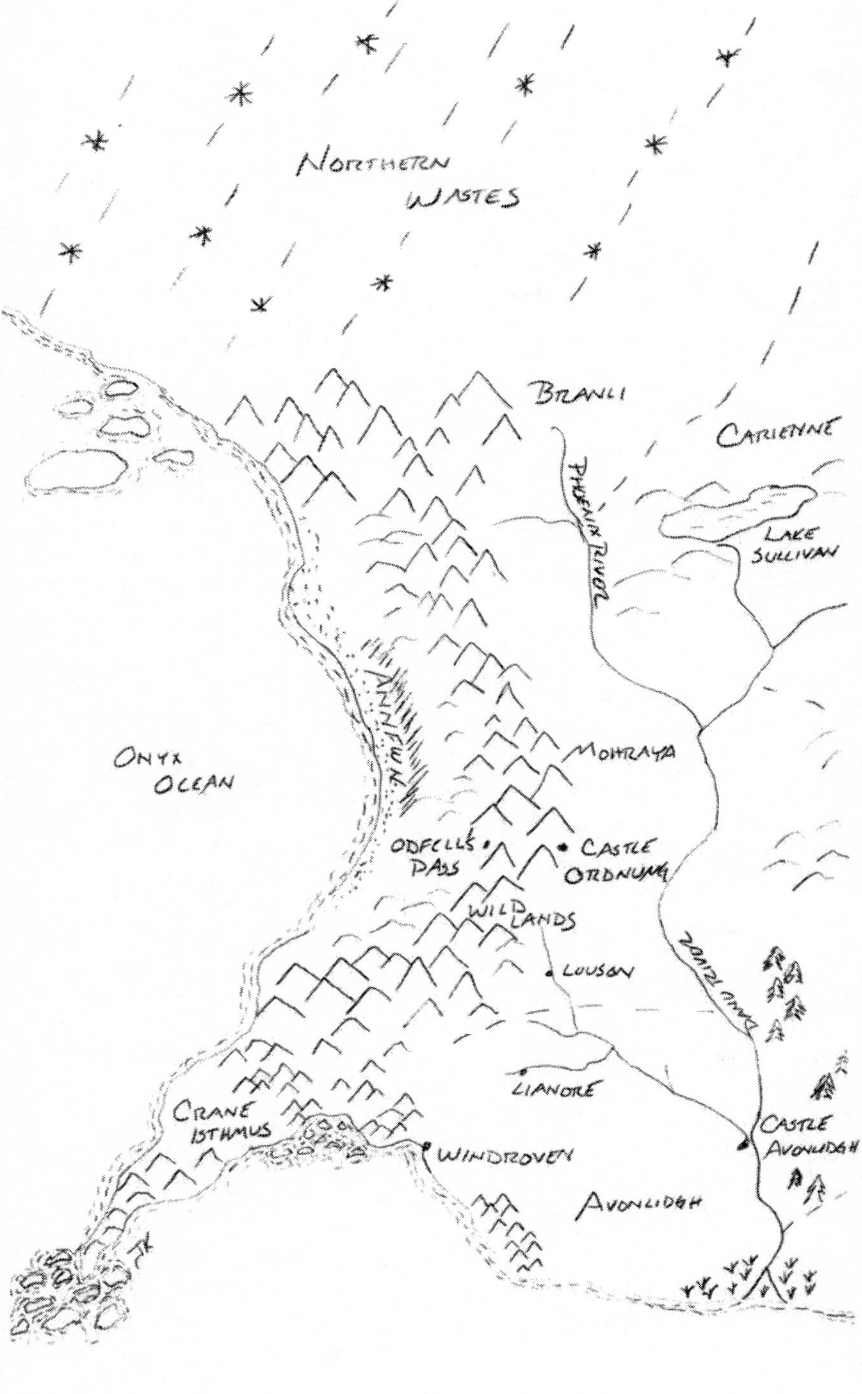
NORTHERN WASTES
BRANLI
CARIENNE
PHOENIX RIVER
LAKE SULLIVAN
ANNFWN
ONYX OCEAN
MOHRAYA
ODFELLS PASS
CASTLE ORDNUNG
WILD LANDS
LOUSON
DAVID RIVER
LIANORE
CRANE ISTHMUS
WINDROVEN
CASTLE AVONLIDGH
AVONLIDGH

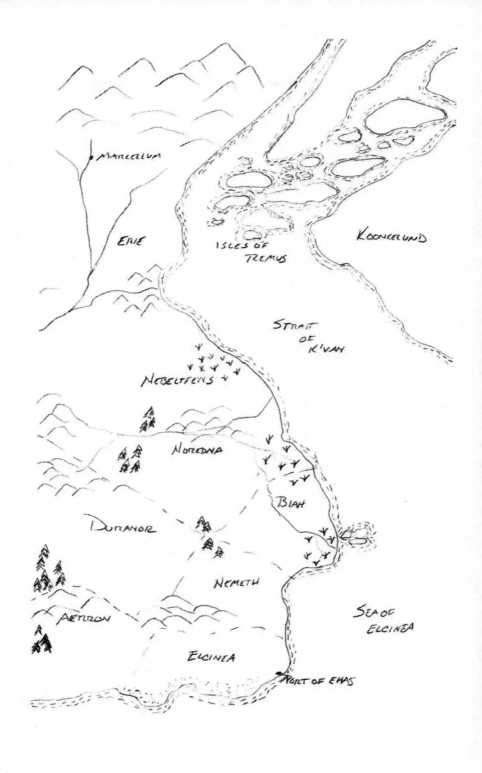

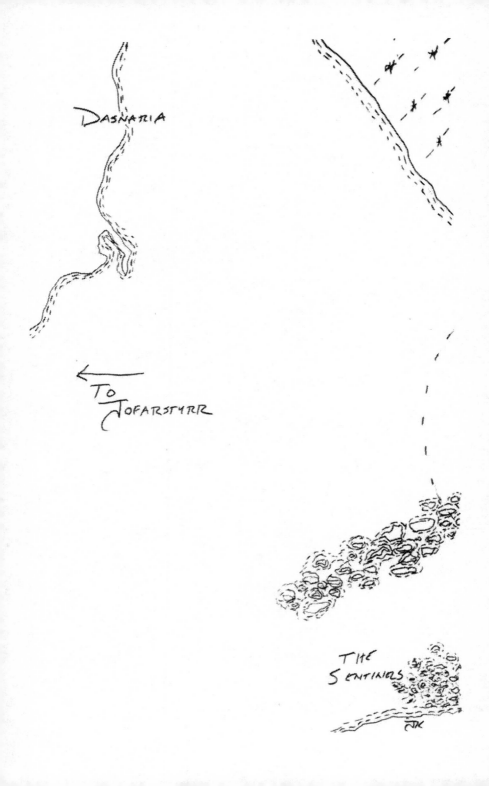

DASNARIA

TO JOFARSTYRR

THE SENTINELS

NORTHERN WASTES

THEORETICAL / PAST BARRIER PERIMETER

BRANLI

CARIENNE

LAKE SULLIVAN

ORIGINAL BARRIER PERIMETER

ONYX OCEAN

MOHRAYA

ODELL'S PASS

CASTLE ORDNUM

NAHANAU

WILD LANDS

LOUSON

LIANORE

CRANE ISTHMUS

WINDROVE

CASTLE AVONLIDGH

AVONLIDGH

WITH ADDITIONS BY DAFNE MAILLOUX KRUPO

THE SHIFT OF THE TIDE

by Jeffe Kennedy

~ 1 ~

W ATER STREAMED OVER my skin in a rush, responsive as it
enveloped me, like music following my dance.

Around me, the shapes of coral resonated with depth, shad-
ing moving beyond the visual and into other spectrums. That
was one reason I loved this form, where my echolocation gave
sound nuance like a rainbow of color. The crystal waters teemed
with sea life of all varieties, most of them quite tasty looking,
making my stomach tingle with animal anticipation.

I exercised enough conscious control, however, to refrain
from sampling the living buffet. Unless pressed into it in order
to survive—which had happened more often since I undertook
this quest than ever before in my life—I didn't eat as an animal.
It was one of those rules taught to Tala children early, one of the
tricks and habits to forestall the worst disaster imaginable for a
shapeshifter: being trapped forever in a non-human form.

With the great exception of Final Form. I'd accepted taking
that as my destiny, as the only way to save my people. I would
do it for my sister's dead babies, and for the ones I would never
have. I'd be lonely, perhaps, but my family was dying off one by
one regardless. My mother was gone along with all my siblings
but two. And if Anya kept trying to have babies, she'd soon go
with them. I would live my life alone, either way, and nothing
would change that.

One day, quite soon, I would become a dragon, and stay that way forever.

Though that day drew ever closer—if I succeeded in getting the invitation I sought—for the moment I savored one of my favorites of my many forms, swimming hard and working out the restlessness that plagued me. If I were given a choice of what form to be stuck in forever, I'd pick the dolphin. Its large, mammalian brain contained plenty of room to retain a good portion of reasoning and higher thought. Fast, agile, being a dolphin was simply fun. I'd learned it early and returned to it often.

Learning a new form is part instinct, part observation and study, and part gift from beyond. Some say those are the gifts of the three goddesses—knowledge of the heart from the goddess of love, dawn, and twilight, Glorianna; disciplined study from the warrior goddess of high noon, Danu; and the mysterious arcane touch of Moranu.

Most Tala look to Moranu first, and that's largely why, because we are shapeshifters—and each shift is a leap of faith in the goddess of the moon, night and shadows. But I needed more than Moranu's guidance to take Final Form. I needed a real dragon to teach me.

Our ancestors had found a way to shift into it, becoming the great, virtually immortal dragons of old. In that form they retained full consciousness—some said greater intelligence than human minds—along with all the magical gifts the shapeshifter had possessed. Most important, being a dragon came with the additional and priceless gift of modulating magic, something we needed desperately if the Tala, the magical and shapeshifting last remnants of the great races were to survive beyond another generation. We'd preserved so much—and yet not enough. So much knowledge the ancients had taken with them, that we failed to understand.

How it would feel to be the dragon... well, no one had been able to take Final Form in generations. So, no one could tell me if taking that irreversible final step felt like being trapped in an unyielding cage. Even if it would, much as the prospect revolted me, I would do it. And once there, I would be unable to turn back. But the reward would be worth it. I firmly believed that.

Taking Final Form was both the pinnacle of accomplishment for a shapeshifter and the ultimate sacrifice, but we'd lost the intangible path when the dragons disappeared from the world.

Now that my friend and scholar Dafne, now Queen Nakoa KauPo of Nahanau, had awakened the dragon Kiraka from hibernation beneath the volcano, I hoped to be the first Tala to take Final Form. But that required an invitation from the great dragon, and so far she'd only spoken to Dafne. I tried to be patient—after all I'd waited my entire life for this moment, and generations of Tala had lived and died without ever reaching it— but the sense of time slipping away rushed around me like the crystal warm waters.

A pod of actual dolphins sounded in the distance, their convivial feeding luring me to join them, to enjoy for a while longer the joy of freedom from responsibility. I swam in their direction. Paused when the alarm call went up.

Shark.

And they had calves in the family group. No question that they should be protected at all costs. Babies are the future. Without them we die the final death.

I shot past the group encircling the calves, joining those who attacked the shark. Finding my opening, I angled exactly and rammed its gills with my beak, exulting in the crunch of soft cartilage. It should have flinched—from my blow and from the other dolphins, attacking the gills on the other side, and its soft belly—but it swam on. Almost mindlessly.

I had a bad taste in my mouth, both literally and metaphorically. Like magic gone rotten.

A limitation of the dolphin form, however, is that I can't use my magical senses in it. Otherwise I would have probed for the source of the distasteful essence. As it was, the pod easily herded the shark away. It floundered in the water, slowing and sinking. It would be no threat to them or the precious calves.

The group sang to me, promising fish and fun. Very tempting to join them.

But I'd made promises, and I intended to keep them.

With a mental sigh, I headed back to shore. That had been enough of an exercise break to clear my mind and restore my sense of self. Mossbacks didn't seem to understand how shifting into animal form could be a kind of recentering, as it looked to them like the exact opposite of that—going further away from self, not more firmly into the center—but mutability anchors me in a way I can't easily explain. Or wouldn't, even if I found the words. The Tala have a reputation for keeping secrets, and it's well earned.

It's also a dodgy undertaking, full of fine lines and careful obfuscation. Especially as we have no hard and fast rules—the Tala rarely do—beyond making sure no one ever again has the power to destroy what we've so carefully preserved.

Though that too lay in our future. I don't have strong foresight, but the visions plagued even me. Oily shadows penetrating to soil the white cliffs of my home in Annfwn. Blood in the water. My cousin Ursula, the High Queen of the Thirteen Kingdoms, thought the Temple of *Deyrr*, with their unholy black magic and corrupt rituals to enslave the living dead was entirely her problem. But that ancient and lethal arrow pointed ultimately at the Heart of Annfwn. The beginning of this conflict, and the prophesied site of the end of it.

Not for me, however. My task had been set before the priestess of *Deyrr* showed up at the court of Ordnung, corrupting the former high king. Others would take up that battle. Though I'd helped my companions, doing my best to make sure the powerful jewel, the Star of Annfwn stayed out of the High Priestess of *Deyrr*'s fetid hands, ultimately protecting the thirteen—and the other realms inside the protective magical barrier—would fall to them. My allegiance belonged to the Tala and my personal mission, first and foremost. It would do us no good to turn back *Deyrr*, only for the Tala to wither and die.

As the dragon, at least, I'd be well situated to fight to defend my homeland of Annfwn.

Had that been the oddly familiar flavor of the shark? It didn't seem likely. Not here in the waters of Nahanau, a fair distance from the barrier. I'd never encountered *Deyrr*'s living dead at Ordnung—they'd all been burnt by the time I arrived—but I had tasted the High Priestess's magic when she attacked Ursula. They could be the same. Though why it would be in a mindless shark, I didn't know.

Troubling.

Once in the shallows, I shifted back to human form, swimming with a relaxed breast stroke until my feet found the bottom. While the Nahanauns had become more accustomed to my presence around the palace, they weren't accustomed to shapeshifting. After a few early displays to impress them with my abilities—at my companions' behest, mostly to demonstrate that we weren't captives to be underestimated—I preferred to shift discreetly. I rarely cared to make a show of it, regardless. It's a private thing. Intimate.

Also, swimming the short distance gave me a moment to settle back into my Birth Form. My muscles stretched out anchored to the longer, harder skeleton, articulating at different joints, the water now feeling cooler against my thinner human skin, with less subcutaneous fat insulation beneath. The fine sand sifted pleasantly against the soles of my feet—something a dolphin never experienced. Compared to the dolphin form, being human felt less powerful in the water, but also more sensitive to sensation. My light gown swirled in the water, too, clinging here and trailing there, my usual dress that I manifested with my human form out of long habit. As I waded to the shallows, it clung wetly to my upper body, but the thin silk would dry quickly enough, if stiff with residual salt.

My friend Jepp, a warrior woman, loved to natter at me about trying to return to human form with different kinds of clothing, and even with an arsenal of weaponry. Trust her agile fighter's mind to come up with such schemes. That's how she thought. A very mossback way of seeing the world, too. All focused on *things*. The Tala didn't care much for material objects, giving us a tendency to forget about ones the mossbacks regarded as precious—something that distressed them no end.

Beyond that, though, I didn't discuss with Jepp how critical habit could be for returning to my Birth Form. You'd think it would be the easiest to attain, as it's our natural form, the one we have before we consciously understand that we even have bodies, much less that they're mutable. In fact, we don't tell children—or adults learning to shapeshift late in life like my cousin the Tala queen Andromeda—how fraught with danger the return to human shape can be. Better to maintain that perfect confidence.

We find out soon enough on our own how perilous it can be.

For most of us, having a standard, very simple, garment as part of our return to Birth Form is a key part of that confidence.

Some shapeshifters have to return to human form naked, but that can be problematic for many reasons. We drill in having something to wear, just in case. Personally, I'd also fixed a habit of including a pin for my hair in a little pocket along one hem. Getting the sometimes wild locks out of my face counted as more than convenience.

For the moment I left the pin where it was, wringing the water out of my long hair as I waded, shaking it out again to dry, and wiping the dampness from my face—then glimpsed someone standing on the sand.

Waiting for me?

I had to reorient my senses to the human focus on vision. No echolocation in this form, and the sudden lack felt as if I'd left a hand behind. One of the many reasons settling into human form again can be fraught. For all that we have opposable thumbs and busy brains, human senses are sadly dull compared to other animals. I'm forever reaching for the more acute senses of my other forms. Recognizing people when I've recently shifted back can be a strange experience. I often want to sniff them, which is really not appropriate in most any human culture, but particularly among mossbacks. The man's face finally hit the correct memory.

"Lieutenant Marskal," I said, by way of greeting. The water caressed my ankles as I moved through the last of the shallows, then stepped onto the packed damp sand where the waves gently lapped.

He dipped his chin in a nod. The Hawks lieutenant was a man of few words, which I appreciated. Most mossbacks seemed inclined to extensive conversation. Not that the Tala weren't effusive and fond of company, but I think the time we spend in animal forms makes us more comfortable with not speaking every thought in our minds. Or even to not having thoughts in our minds in the first place.

I raked my wet hair back from my face so the water from it dripped down my back. Marskal gazed, not at me, but just past my face, as if at the sea. With some amusement, I realized he was determinedly averting his gaze, out of politeness or embarrassment.

I didn't think he was one of those who found the Tala revolting and thus avoided looking at me for that reason. More likely the wet silk clung to my body enough to leave little to the imagination, something the islander Nahanauns didn't mind, but the men of the original twelve kingdoms sometimes did. The mischievous Tala trickster in me wanted to see if I could make him look, but I hadn't come on this journey to cause trouble. Quite the opposite—I'd done my best to preserve my secrets and keep from undue notice.

"Were you waiting for me?" I asked, to put him out of his misery. I'd begun to get the trick of asking the questions with obvious answers—another mossback courtesy—rather than the actual questions, which they seemed to regard as invasive. Better to let them volunteer information on their own terms, rather than feeling interrogated. I, myself, didn't quite understand why they felt that being asked a question demanded they answer it, but that's the onus many of the twelve labored under and I tried to be respectful of it.

Marskal's eyes—brown as earth, not Tala blue, green, or gray—flicked to mine, and back to that point over my shoulder. "Yes, Lady Zynda. My apologies for intruding on you, but Her Majesty Queen Ursula and Her Highness Queen Dafne Nakoa KauPo request your presence in the library." He put his fist on his heart in the Hawks salute, and inclined his upper body in a slight bow.

Ursula and Dafne had been in the library with their heads

together for days trying to discover how to thwart the High Priestess of *Deyrr*, and whether locating the lost civilization of N'andana could help. The dragon Kiraka had been N'andanan, a shapeshifter and scholar before she'd taken Final Form. She'd been teaching Dafne the N'andanan language, but tended to be less helpful on answering direct questions. Apparently Tala, as their far descendants, came by our caginess naturally. It fascinated me that, even though they knew Kiraka had once been human, they all seemed to think of her as a dragon only, fixed in that shape. I'd tried to warn my friends about Kiraka's nature—a shapeshifter didn't change her spots by taking Final Form—but true to both of their obstinate characters, they persisted to a point that exhausted me.

I'd needed the break, to quiet my mind, but I'd clearly been gone too long if Ursula had sent her lieutenant after me. I turned my feet in the direction of the palace, the damp sand warm against my bare soles. "Calling me plain 'Zynda' is fine, as I know I've told you before."

"I know." Marskal fell in beside me, matching his pace to my amble, and folding his arms behind his back. He'd prefer a brisker march, I imagined, more his usual speed, but conveyed no impatience with me. That quality went with his quiet reserve. "It would be overly familiar, however, to address you without a proper title."

I shook out my gown, holding it away from my body so it would catch the air and dry faster, then glanced at him. He stared steadfastly ahead, scanning the long, white-sand beach with that same relaxed alertness Jepp always displayed. No surprise, as long as they'd worked and fought together. "I'm not royalty," I pointed out. "I have no title."

"You're related to royalty." His firm mouth, bracketed by deep lines, quirked at some wry internal thought. "In at least two realms."

"In Annfwn such things aren't as… regimented." I settled on that word, though I wasn't sure it was the one I wanted. I'd learned Common Tongue as a girl, part of my training to follow in the footsteps of my celebrated aunt, the sorceress Salena, who'd been Queen of the Tala and the most proficient shapeshifter of her generation. Her path had taken her beyond the magical barrier that once shielded Annfwn from the world, to be high queen of the Twelve Kingdoms. I knew mine would also take me out of Annfwn, as no one there had been able to find the key to Final Form.

"Ah," Marskal replied, not asking more. He'd never been to Annfwn and couldn't know what it was like there. We walked in silence and it occurred to me that he might consider it my turn to say something. The mossbacks could be particular about that sort of thing.

"How did you come to be at Ordnung?" I asked. "Or were you raised there?"

Marskal tilted his head, sliding me an opaque glance. "Why do you ask?"

I had to smile—both for his evasion and that I'd made the attempt at conversing with the man, against my natural inclination—then gestured at the expanse of beach, the palace on the point in the far distance. "We've a bit of a walk ahead of us."

"And yet, you've never struck me as someone to make idle conversation for the sake of killing time."

I considered him. An observant man, as the quiet ones often were. I'd never thought he'd paid all that much attention to my nature. "How did you know where to find me, anyway?"

"I didn't find you. I waited for you to emerge from the water."

"Yes, but at the exact spot."

He studied a tree we passed, eyes narrowed in concentration, but I doubted he contemplated the heavy fruit or the strawberry colored Nahanaun bees partaking of the sweetly overripe juice, crawling over the fallen smashed pieces. "You routinely go to that beach when you shapeshift into aquatic forms."

That startled me, and not in an entirely comfortable way. "You follow me every time?"

Glancing at me, he pressed his lips together, considering the words he'd let squeak through. "Not I, personally, but I am a scout, first and foremost—I recognize signs. It's also my responsibility to ensure the safety of the High Queen and her retinue."

"You have spies." I said it lightly, but my skin crawled. How unsettling that I'd been observed. Though my movements wouldn't have revealed to a casual observer that I'd been attempting to draw Kiraka's attention and invitation, I still should have noticed.

"That bothers you." He turned his head more fully to study me now. Exactly as if I were another exotic bit of fauna to assess and track, which I supposed I was.

"I'm not accustomed to being watched." Or treated with suspicion.

"If something were to happen, I need to know where everyone is, so they can be retrieved and confirmed safe."

"I can take care of myself." Irritation prickled inside me, my fingertips tingling with the desire to extend claws I didn't own in my present form. Just as well.

"Oh, of that I'm well aware."

We walked in silence. He didn't seem to be about to say anything more. It rankled that I should be the one to initiate the dialog, yet again, but I wanted an answer. "In that case, why would I need to be confirmed safe?"

A slight smile twitched the corner of his mouth, making me think he'd deliberately drawn me out. "Maybe I meant I'd potentially need your help."

Ah. I resisted asking more, ignoring the dangling "maybe," no doubt intended as more bait. This time, he relented first.

"You weren't watched so much as checked up on. You're fairly regular in your habits. So I only ask my people to verify that you've gone to your usual beach—and that you returned. It's a lovely cove. Private. I can see why you chose it."

"And yet you claim you've never followed me there."

"I didn't say 'never.' Just not every time." He gave me a serious look. "And only to verify where you go. I wouldn't otherwise invade your privacy."

I considered his studiously averted gaze and reassessed my assumptions. A learned skill, to both spy on people and give them privacy. "And it comes in useful when Ursula and Dafne suddenly decide I'm urgently needed."

"They did wait some time for you to return, but I understand something urgent has come up. Her Majesty asked me to retrieve you as quickly as possible."

"Would you have plunged in to swim after me?"

He shook his head, not smiling at the joke. "It's a real problem that we have no way to reach you when you're… away, like that. Were you anyone else, I'd ask you to take measures."

Away. A euphemism for *not-human.* Perhaps Marskal, like many of his mossback brethren, did harbor a deep dislike for my shapeshifter nature. No surprise there, as the Tala had been at war with the Twelve Kingdoms until relatively recently. Normally I didn't give such prejudices—or the people who harbored them—much attention. This time, however, I had to poke at him.

"'Anyone else.' Does that mean someone who isn't a

shapeshifter—or someone who isn't the High Queen's cousin?"

He gave me a long, steady look. No ire or amusement in it. Considering his answer. It might be interesting sometime to see if I could goad him into speaking without thinking about it first. But that's the trickster in me, and I'd resolved to leave such childish games behind when I undertook this mission. The Shaman had sworn me to both secrecy and discretion. I wouldn't fail either charge.

"Someone who would be amenable to such requests," Marskal finally said.

Had I fur, I would have bristled. "You're saying I'm difficult."

"I'm saying that, if I asked you to report in regularly, to inform me or someone I designated of your plans—how long you'd be gone, what form you planned to shift into, what medium you'd employ and in which direction you'd go—that you would be unlikely to take that well."

Just the thought had me wanting to claw. Which meant the mossback understood much more about me—or about the Tala in general, though he'd never been to Annfwn—than I'd suspected. He'd out-tricked me.

I burst out laughing, and Marskal's eyes widened slightly, a slight flare of his nostrils and flex of his fingers, though he didn't reach for any of his weapons. Too controlled for that. His mouth quirked uncertainly.

"I'm surprised you didn't suggest tying a long rope to me."

He pursed his lips, as if contemplating the idea. "Difficult to fasten a rope on a fish. Perhaps a string to hold in your mouth?"

Well, look who had a sense of humor after all. I liked humor. "I rarely take fish forms."

"Can you?"

"Of course." I made the answer offhand, breezy.

"Because you can take any form."

"Not *any*."

"How many forms can you take?" He had a rhythm to the questions, but more determined people than he had attempted this kind of interrogation. Nothing like being ship-bound in a storm with someone as curious and relentless as Jepp.

I gave Marskal my sunniest smile. "Several."

He made a sound of disapproval, flattening his mouth, all humor fled. "It would be helpful to know."

"Why?" I was genuinely curious.

"To plan strategy. A good commander knows the abilities of everyone who serves with him."

"But I am not one of your Hawks."

"No—you have your own agenda, don't you?"

I shook out my gown, then my hair, pretending that sally hadn't struck exactly on target. How had the cursed mossback discerned as much? We neared the palace and I looked mostly presentable. Sticky with saltwater, but not dripping wet or covered in sand.

"Not going to reply to that?" Marskal asked, grit in his tone.

I shrugged with an easy smile. "I'm not sure what you're asking me."

"That doesn't reassure me."

"I wasn't aware reassurance was necessary."

"Let's try this—why did you come on this journey, Lady Zynda?"

"I accompanied Ursula to Annfwn, and thence to Nahanau to aid in Dafne's rescue. Then I went with Queen Andromeda to assist with moving the Dasnarian ship through the magical barrier. After that, I helped Ursula look for Jepp, then returned here with her."

"You're very helpful, aren't you?"

"Indeed." No need to mention that staying the vicinity of Nahanau and Kiraka suited my needs.

"Though none of that explains why you left Annfwn in the first place, and haven't yet returned," he added, as if reading my mind. "I understand few Tala care to be away from their homeland."

"Maybe I wanted to see the world." Two could play the "maybe" game.

He frowned at me. Opened his mouth, but I spoke before he could.

"Maybe I thought you'd potentially need my help." I patted his cheek, moving faster than he could react, tempted to scrape my nails in the slight stubble. He jerked back, startled. Mossbacks forget how fast shapeshifters can move, if we wish to. I usually keep my movements deliberately languid around them, so as not to be upsetting.

But every once in a while, it's good to remind them of who—and what—they're dealing with. I smiled at the lieutenant, his hand now on the sword he'd never draw in time if I truly wanted to do him harm.

"It's my duty to protect Her Majesty," he ground out, jaw tight. "From all threats."

"Don't fret yourself," I said. "Those of Salena's line protect their own." I turned and walked up the broad steps of the palace.

"That still doesn't answer my question," Marskal called after me.

I tossed a pleasant smile over my shoulder, adding a bit of sashay to my hips. And didn't reply.

~ 2 ~

I LIKE THE palace at Nahanau. It's intended to be beautiful, to reflect the grace of the natural world, and to be accessible to the people—all aesthetics that work for me. In many ways, it reminds me of Annfwn. Enough to make me a little less homesick and nostalgic. The open archways and balconies offer views of the outside from every room, and egress is always possible, though getting out requires me to take wing on occasion.

As long as I can get out quickly, I'm happy.

I suppose it's different for mossbacks. As far as I can tell, they never seem to feel trapped in places like Castle Ordnung, where the walls and stone and heavy doors are there to close danger out and allow them to snuggle inside in safety. For me, safety has always meant being able to escape.

Various palace denizens bowed as I passed, and I smiled at them. They knew me as the companion and confidante of their queen, Dafne, and of the enigmatic High Queen Ursula laying claim to their islands. I didn't mind being unclassifiable to them or to the Lieutenant Marskals of the world. He hadn't followed me, apparently trusting my motives enough to believe I'd go to the library as requested.

Or some other of his spies watched me.

The wood floors had complex patterns, but they'd been

sanded smooth, first by craftsmen, then by time and the passage of many feet, so they felt like the finest fabric on bare feet.

In places like Nahanau, where the tropical weather allows people to go barefoot year round, they paid attention to such textures. Not like at Ordnung where I'd finally had to accede to wearing slippers on those cold, uncomfortable floors. The scent of salt from the sea and the heavy sweetness of tropical blossoms wafted in on the warm breeze that caressed my skin. The sensitivity of human skin was one sense that exceeded all other forms, with their protective fur, scales, and feathers. Even the human half of the mermaid bore fine scales instead of actual skin.

I have a mermaid form, but I don't care for it. I grant that it's more useful than being a dolphin because it combines the swimming power of an aquatic form with humanoid arms and those very handy opposable thumbs. The best of both worlds, in theory. Not in my experience, however. Even though a mermaid technically has a humanoid mind, it still doesn't feel like my human brain. Far from it. And the fish half always gives me this strange aggressiveness. Asexual, but in a ferocious way. Not at all peaceful.

In the legends of mermaids, they lured and seduced sailors, then drowned them. I suspected this violent behavior came from that strange sexual frustration. In that form, I understood the urge—they killed what they couldn't have. The intelligent desire for intercourse from the human half battles with the non-contact reproduction of the fish portion. Fish, naturally, reproduce by the male ejaculating milt over eggs the female laid—no intimacy there at all. So with mermaids, even if the human part longs for sexual contact, it's physically impossible beyond a certain point. Endured long enough, it could drive a person insane.

I'm not driven by sexual urges, in general, certainly not to the exclusion of all else. It did say something about me, though, that I'd rather forgo having human hands than subject myself to the warring frustration of a mermaid's dual nature.

And yet, at the moment, it felt as if I'd become the metaphorical mermaid, similarly armored. I'd dallied with lovers, but since my vow to take Final Form I'd eschewed such intimate pleasures. It wouldn't be fair to a lover who might become attached, then left behind when I abandoned human form.

Also, I had selfish reasons. Once a dragon, I'd be isolated from intimate relationships. As with my shapeshifting and magic spells, I thought it best to practice at being alone, too. It might make that transition less wrenching. It's a piece of the magic I don't quite understand, that maybe is beyond our limited comprehension as mortal beings, that I can become a mermaid though I've never encountered a real life mermaid. Though I believe they must exist if I can assume the form.

There's debate about this in the Tala scholarly circles. Some argue that if we can imagine a form, a gifted shapeshifter can create it—or Moranu can, passing it along to us. Others say that if a form has ever existed in the history of the world, it lies within our racial memory. No one can quite explain why we can imagine a dragon and yet the form remains beyond anyone's reach. The racial-memory contingent of shapeshifting theorists tend to align themselves opposite the gift-from-Moranu ones.

I fall somewhere in the middle and, like most shapeshifters able to assume multiple forms, I prefer to leave the debates and parsing to the scholars. Overthinking something as instinctual as shifting can mean disaster.

I smiled at the Nahanaun guards keeping watch at the library doors. They opened them for me with sunny courtesy. Another reason the islands reminded me of home—the Tala also tended to be relaxed and playful, though we did it more deliberately, to shed from our backs the eternal dread of ceasing to exist.

Dafne and Ursula had set up at a long table in the library, scattered with tomes and scrolls, and sat at opposite ends of it. This room, alone of all in the palace, had no open arches to the outdoors. The high windows showed the sky, but through thick glass, so one couldn't fly out. Dafne had explained that this was deliberate design, to create a consistent environment to protect the documents contained within. I believed her, though it didn't make me like it any better. If the stories are memorized, then told and sung, then there's no need for all this preservation. I avoided the place when possible—too much like a cage—but she loved it.

Neither of them wore court garb. Instead they were in casual wear for their day of study. Ursula's bloodred hair stood up in spikes from running her hands through it, her crown no doubt left back in her room. Dafne looked more composed, as she naturally did, though she frowned at whatever she read, deep in thought while absently rubbing her swollen belly. She wasn't that far along, but the Nahanaun customarily scanty dress of halter and low-slung skirt revealed her tanned midsection, and the growing bulge within.

Uncoiling just a tendril of magic, I reached out to the babe within her, sending affection and welcome. The old grief and longing wanted to well up, but I refused it. I hadn't been able to save Anya's daughter. I wouldn't have my own. My destiny lay elsewhere and I would be at peace with that. I had no room for sorrow.

"You sent for me?" I asked, as neither of them seemed inclined to notice my presence.

Ursula held up a hand with a raised finger, an implicit command to wait, while Dafne didn't even move. I sighed lightly. So intense, these two, so focused on the interred words of the long dead. If Jepp were here, she'd roll her eyes and shake her head. But she was off on the *Hákyrling* with Kral, former prince of Dasnaria, trolling the edge of the magical barrier.

Once the field that sealed Annfwn from the rest of the world, the barrier had hugely expanded—one of their ongoing projects was mapping the exact boundaries—preventing people from crossing, unless they had magical or Tala assistance. Jepp now had one of those magical tools—the Star of Annfwn, and Ursula had tasked her and Kral to help those stranded on the wrong side to cross over. Those who posed no threat, that is.

The High Priestess of *Deyrr* and her minions had to be kept firmly outside the barrier, lest they pursue their voracious hunger for the magic inside.

At last Ursula looked up at me, her gray eyes unfogging from abstract thought and going to sharp steel, focusing on me. Though she couldn't shift, she had more predator in her than most mossbacks. If she could shift, I'd expect her First Form to be a wolf. Sometimes I glimpsed the she-wolf in her eyes.

"Sorry to send Marskal to fetch you," she said. "We weren't sure when you'd be back and two time-sensitive tasks have come up for you, if you're willing."

It occurred to me that she'd known Marskal could find me, which meant she also knew that he and his people watched me—likely at her order. My cousin was no fool. She wondered at my agenda also.

"Why would you apologize?" I asked, with more irritation than I'd realized brewed in me. "Your Majesty commands my obedience."

She sat back slightly, considering me with raised brows.

"My turn to apologize," I added, going for a convenient half-truth, "I meant to tease you only, but it came out wrong."

"Nakoa tells me that it's the dragon in me speaking when

I'm unintentionally waspish," Dafne said. She'd straightened from her bookish bend, pressing hands to the small of her back and stretching. Then she grinned. "He doesn't comment on the intentionally waspish ones."

"Harlan doesn't comment at all," Ursula said in a dry tone. "He just gives me that eternally patient *look*."

"Do you think that's a real phenomenon?" Dafne asked me, more seriously, picking up her ink pen out of habit. She wouldn't write down what I told her, unless I gave express permission, but she itched to regardless. "I'm obviously not a shapeshifter and I don't completely understand what it is that lets me talk with Kiraka mind-to-mind, but do real shapeshifters experience that—the animal within having its own emotions and motivations?"

"Can we perhaps postpone the academic discussion on shapeshifting until we ask Zynda to do what I had Marskal drag her back for?" Ursula asked in a dry tone.

Dafne put down her pen, abashed and nodding, then reached for a wooden box and a small scroll. She got up and set both before Ursula, tacitly deferring the decision to her.

"He didn't exactly drag me," I said, amused by them, and letting go of my irritation. "He made for good company on the walk back."

Ursula snorted. "You had a conversation? I never can get five words out of him strung together."

"That's because you're scary," Dafne muttered.

"Is it? Harlan isn't afraid of me."

I smiled at the thought of her muscle-bound, former mercenary Dasnarian consort being afraid of anything.

"That's why you love him," Dafne retorted. "Which first, Your Majesty?"

Ursula shot her a sharp glance. "We've been arguing priorities," she explained to me, handing me the wooden box. "Start here."

I took it and peered inside. It was full of what looked like small pieces of driftwood, worn smooth by water. "May I touch?"

"We have and nothing bad has come of it," Dafne said, and Ursula nodded, watching me with keen interest.

Just to be cautious, I caressed them with a tendril of magic. Another sense I didn't have in animal form, and one I at times greatly missed. Magically inert, the wooden pieces seemed to be not much at all. If I'd found the box, I'd have discarded it as no more than a child's collection of "treasures." Ursula and Dafne, however, must perceive something more about them. I set down the box and took one piece out, turning it in my fingers. Small enough to fit in the palm of my hand. Mostly flat, with series of indentations, both rounded and sharp, on each vertical side, like a double-bladed knife with notches might have. But these were clearly not sharp enough to be a weapon. Like most inanimate objects used by people for a long time, the one I held hummed with deep remanence, impressions of many different hands, along with sun, sea, and wind.

And a stronger memory, embedded by someone more like me, with shapeshifter blood running strong and clear in his veins. His hand with long, brown fingers, holding the wood and comparing it to a coastline, the feeling of waves buoying the moment. One of the ancients? Excitement coursed through me.

"A map?" I asked that man, forgetting in the strength of the image where I truly stood and why.

"Ha!" Ursula smacked a palm on the table and pointed at Dafne. "I win that one, librarian."

"I don't see how it's a fair test for her to simply *hold* it," Dafne grumbled. Then she narrowed her pretty brown eyes at me, the caramel shine sharpening with acute insight. "Unless you have other ways of knowing?"

"Simply a guess." I shrugged, then set the piece back in its box, rubbing my palms together to shed any remanence that clung to me. Dafne noted that gesture, too, though I'd never explained the significance of the practice. Truly only another magic user should know. Hard to say what Kiraka had been teaching her, however. "Is that what they are—maps?"

"I think so." Ursula leaned forward and plucked one of the pieces out of the box, holding it up to the light and tracing the edge with a bony finger. "Inlets, coves and peninsulas. Perhaps showing the route between chains of islands. I could wish we had Kral's shipmaster Jens here. I bet he'd confirm it."

"You're hoping these are a map to N'andana," I said. Which would be something. All we knew, from fragments of tales and records—and a few hints dropped by the High Priestess of *Deyrr* herself—was that *Deyrr* wanted what the N'andanans had died to protect. Dafne wanted to find their forgotten islands because she believed knowledge would save them. Ursula wanted to find them because she reflexively considered everything inside the barrier—and the N'andanan islands now would be, almost certainly—her responsibility.

"Without Jens, unless Zynda can confirm, we're simply speculating," Dafne countered. "They might simply be pretty objects. Driftwood carved by idle hands."

"The fact that they were kept in the library indicates deeper meaning," Ursula replied.

"Why bother to carve a map into small pieces like this?" Dafne scowled, though she plucked out another piece, rapidly sketching the shape onto paper. "It makes no sense to me."

"Maps are bulkier," I pointed out. While such a small carved piece would be easy to carry in one's talons or mouth. Very interesting solution.

"And paper gets wet," Ursula agreed. "Ink and paints smear. Hides rot in the humid conditions aboard ship. Sea salt is abrasive. This makes sense to me as a durable, portable guide."

Dafne glanced between us. "Two of a kind, you adventurous types. They still don't match anything. Look at this." She stood, taking a moment to stretch again, grimacing. "Ugh. I feel like I ate an enormous steak and it's sitting on my bladder—is this going to get worse?"

Ursula looked mildly horrified, holding up her palms to ward off the suggestion. "Don't ask me."

I shrugged, my horror coming from another place. I could survive many things, but I doubted I could live through holding another infant while she died. Certainly not my own. It didn't bear considering. "No help here."

"Figures." Dafne arranged sketches from the pile in front of her, then pulled over a large map—an illustrated one on paper— of the extensive Nahanaun archipelago. I'd seen mossback maps of this style before, at Ordnung, and had used them to orient my journey as a hummingbird to spy for Ursula. An even smaller carved piece that showed the edges of land features, that I could've carried tucked up against my body, would have been far more useful. The hummingbird brain had been good for remembering direction—and worked perfectly for returning home—but I'd been forced to periodically stop and shift back to human, simply to remember the map I'd memorized.

Would I have to do the same with the map-stick? It would be interesting to test if a bird brain could analyze the symbology. Hummingbirds understood shape and color quite well, so it was possible. If not, a corvid form certainly would, as they comprehended and even invented tools to solve problems. That wasn't a form with the same speed and endurance for extended journeys as a hummingbird was, but the trade-off of not having to stop and expend energy to shift forms and back again might make it worthwhile.

The more I thought about it, the more likely it seemed that a shapeshifter had crafted this mapping method. That feeling of restlessness prickled at me. The sense of that hand, cupping the stick, waves moving me up and down in a gentle sea, the feel of salt spray on my face and... something in the distance? It felt like a vision of the future, but also not. Perhaps the sense of a greater mind moving over my own. Could this be Kiraka noticing me—my invitation, at last?

"Zynda?" Dafne had her brows raised, a line between them for my inattention. "Do you see an overlap between my sketches and the map?"

I shook my hair back, then wound it into a coiled rope, pulled the pin out of its pocket and fixed it up off my neck. The library was too close, overwarm with no cooling breezes. I took a moment to master the instinctive urge to flee, gentling the bird inside that wanted to batter itself against the glazed windows.

"Are you all right, cousin?" Ursula asked. She rarely called me that, and it helped to ground me as myself again. I gave her a grateful smile, wondering if she understood that. Of all of Salena's daughters, Ursula had known her mother the best. She'd been ten when Salena died, and so must have witnessed the sorceress's decline—and perhaps devised ways, as daughters do, of bringing her mother back from the lands without borders.

"I think so," I told her.

"Is there something... tainted in these wooden pieces after all?" Dafne rubbed her hands together, imitating me, consciously or not.

"Not like you mean," I replied. "But they are potent, and somewhat unsettling. Also," I laid a finger on the map of one of

Nahanau's neighboring islands. "I think this could match this notch, here." I indicated one of the sketches, where the bottom tapered to a point.

They both cocked their heads, studying.

"I don't see it," Dafne muttered, sounding irritated. She never liked when she couldn't immediately grasp something. Probably she tried to understand the sticks as she did language, breaking them into parts and pitches, instead of seeing them as one piece.

"Unfocus your gaze," I suggested. "Look as if you were a bird in the air—and remember that the wood represents the spaces between—the ocean—not the land masses."

"May I?" Ursula asked and Dafne handed her the pen. With a deft hand, Ursula shaded in the areas outside the lines of Dafne's sketch, adding shadows that made those parts look like forests and mountains, while in the part between—which would be the wood—she drew small waves. An enviable skill. I nodded in affirmation, glad she'd been able to do it. Though I'd tried to learn to use Dafne's scribing tools, they never felt right in my hands. Perhaps I was too Tala. Still, King Rayfe had learned, and he was as pureblood as any of us.

But he had been determined to become king, to take control of deteriorating Annfwn by waging war to make Andromeda our queen. She'd at least been able to step into her mother's shoes to use the Heart to manage the permeability of the barrier, putting us better off than we'd been a few years ago. We all have our roles to play. It was coming time to play mine.

"All right." Dafne lined up Ursula's colored-in drawing with the map. "I can be convinced, but I still think we need one more test before we send ships to look for N'andana." She glanced at the fading light. "But she can hardly do it in the dark."

"You want me to fly and see if I can navigate according to

the map-stick?"

"Exactly," Ursula replied. "Though it can wait until morning if the light is too low."

"But—" Dafne started, and Ursula flicked a steely glance to stop her.

"Zynda's safety is more important. Jepp can wait a day."

"Has something happened at the barrier?" I asked.

Ursula sighed, tapping a piece of paper small enough to fit around a crow's leg. "Jepp sent a message via one of Ove's crows. They believe our old friend is alive and attempting to cross the barrier." A ghost of pain edged the corners of her eyes at mentioning the High Priestess of *Deyrr*, and she passed a hand over her belly. Not like Dafne, with her maternal habit of checking the child, but in memory of being gutted by the foul woman in her attempts to steal the Star of Annfwn. Ursula had aged since the nearly mortal blow. Not obviously, but in the thin skin around her eyes and mouth.

"It would have been too much to hope that she'd died," I said. None of us knew the priestess's name—or if she even had one. I'd expected them to try again, though not this soon. No wonder the visions of death had increased. That shark... could it have been part of this incursion? A strange way to attack, if so.

Ursula glanced at me with a wry lack of amusement. "And yet hope for it, I did."

"Are they sure?"

"Of course they're not sure," she snapped, her irritation for the lack of certainty obvious. "I would give a great deal for the simplicity of someone telling me that an army is marching or besieging me. Not this ..." She waved both hands, wiggling her fingers like worms. "Magic."

"The missive came a few hours ago," Dafne explained. "She didn't have much room, obviously, and she used the Hawks' cryptic language, so it's not a lot of information—"

"Even for that and knowing Jepp, it's terse," Ursula broke in. "She wants you to come see—by ship, she recommends, not swimming or flying, and I agree—but to come soon. She used codes for danger and *Deyrr*, with immediacy but not emergency. I'd go myself, but—"

"But you're High Queen of the Thirteen and you can't," Dafne interrupted in turn. "I'll point out that you should be back in Ordnung, ruling, not chasing ways to stop *Deyrr* from invading."

"If they invade I may end up with nothing to rule," Ursula snapped back and Dafne held up her hands in peace.

"I'm only saying you're needed there—for many reasons. Should I remind you of Ami's message of a few days ago? The volcano beneath Windroven is no more restive, but they've had strange encounters with odd beasts that she thinks are related to the dragon's presence. We need to make a decision about how to deal with *that*. Who's to liberate that dragon?"

"If we even should," Ursula countered darkly.

Dafne looked aghast. "You'd leave it to die in there—one of your own subjects?"

"These dragons are no more mine than Zynda and her Tala ilk are, as she so adroitly teased me with just now."

"I apologize."

"Don't." She said it sharply, but her mouth twitched in a slight smile. "You're good for my humility. Besides," she returned to the argument with Dafne, "you still don't understand Kiraka and what she wants. Loosing more of her people on the world could be irresponsible."

"We also don't know what *not* releasing the dragon will do. What if it means the volcano will erupt? That would mean the destruction of Windroven and likely most of Avonlidgh."

"Does that mean you're volunteering? You and Nakoa will sail there and free another dragon?"

Dafne shook her head, almost absently, rubbing her belly and staring at the bookshelves as if they might provide answers. "That's not an option. Even if it were, I think it wouldn't work. Kiraka was ours to awaken. The Windroven dragon will answer to someone else." Her gaze slid off the books and onto me. "What do you think, Zynda?"

I shrugged. "I am not the one to ask about dragons." There. A neat dodge.

Ursula narrowed her eyes at me, then tapped Jepp's scroll, returning to the immediate question. "Jepp asked for Zynda specifically for a reason. The map-sticks can wait until she returns."

"Kiraka asked for Zynda specifically, too."

It had been on the tip of my tongue to mention the shark, but a zing went up my spine at that, the excitement crowding out all else. "She did?"

"When I asked Kiraka about N'andana, she agreed that finding their forgotten islands would be helpful in thwarting *Deyrr*, and she told me to find this box," Dafne continued, "that the contents would be helpful. She said to see if you knew what to do with them."

My invitation at last—preceded by a test. The time had come.

"You're not surprised," Ursula noted, sniffing out trouble, as seemed to be one of her gifts.

"Did she call me by name?" I asked Dafne, dancing the line of truthfulness by not answering.

Dafne frowned at me. "She said, 'your shapeshifter friend.' I assumed she meant you."

"I can test the map-sticks tonight," I declared. Kiraka had

summoned me at last—if more obliquely than I'd anticipated—and I wouldn't fail to answer.

Both of them glanced at the windows, now violet with dusk.

Ursula shook her head. "We've nattered too long. I'll not send you out to fly at night. I know it's dangerous for birds."

"Not for an owl," I answered.

Dafne frowned, picking up her ink pen. "I didn't know you had an owl form." She must have a list, somewhere, of my forms. The ones she knew about. I couldn't very well stop her from writing down what she observed, but I didn't need to reveal more than necessary. Among people who remember everything that's said, you learn early to watch your words. Probably another reason Tala avoid garrulousness.

"Which stick matches this sketch?" I asked, instead of addressing her question that hadn't exactly been one.

She sorted through the box, and Ursula narrowed her eyes at me in speculation. "How many forms do you have?"

"Several," I answered, and smiled when her frown deepened. I took the stick Dafne offered, dropped it to the floor, and shifted into owl shape—no need for privacy among friends and family—and grasped the map-stick in my talons. A perfect fit. I flew up to the windows, irresistibly drawn, a more distant part of me belatedly remembering they weren't true exits.

"Zynda!"

I followed Ursula's voice to the open doors and swept through the palace and out into the twilight. Free under the open sky.

Much better.

~ 3 ~

M ORANU'S MOON SHONE silver, beneficent, and just
rounding from full as she gathered her shroud again to
wane toward her dark face. Those who don't follow Moranu, or
who know little of her worship, believe she's at her peak when
her bright face is full. This is a misconception, born of a bias for
daytime and thus bright light. Danu is at full strength at her
brightest—high noon—and Glorianna at the crepuscular verges
of the day, sunrise and sunset. Moranu is at the opposite pole
from Danu, strongest at the dark of the moon.

For all that Ursula followed Danu's path and adhered to the
warrior goddess's strict discipline of the sharp blade and clear-
eyed justice, she never seemed to note that I was her own
opposite, her dark shadow. Of Salena's three daughters, Andi
belonged most to Moranu, bearing the mark of the Tala, but she
still remained a child of both worlds.

I might not be Salena's daughter, but I embraced her legacy
of sacrifice and would serve my role as the dark face. No matter
the dragon's test, I'd make sure to pass it, and prove my
worthiness to take Final Form. I would not allow myself to fail.

Another advantage of animal forms was that, as the owl, any
regrets or apprehension I might harbor floated a distance away.
Animals simply weren't equipped to worry about the future or
chew over the past as humans did. Sharper, more alert than

some others, my brain in owl form allowed for a fair amount of calculation. It was, however, somewhat more driven by the predatory instincts than the dolphin. I had to exert considerable willpower to keep myself on task. No chasing after the enticing rustles of prey. Instead, I turned away from land and the drive of hunger—I should have eaten when I stopped in at the palace; would have, had I not been so eager to answer Kiraka's summons—and winged up and over the sea, the sky full of dusky violets, indigos, and all shades of shimmering grayscale. And so much more full of light than my human eyes had perceived.

Thermals spiraled up as the cooling night air sank, as easily perceptible to my owl senses as if I saw them, though it wasn't exactly the same as using vision. Catching one, I curved my wings into a relaxed arch, not unlike surfing a muscular wave, and practiced bringing the talon holding the map-stick far enough forward for me to look at it while still in flight.

I bobbled the maneuver the first time, losing the thermal and plummeting through the air ungracefully. If I'd been in the water, I'd be like an erstwhile surfer ignominiously dunked by the wave and tumbled. A real owl would have been able to ride the air currents with practiced ease, and would never do so badly. Recovering, I pumped my wings hard to regain the spiraling current—glad that none of my brethren, either shapeshifter or true owl, had witnessed my clumsiness—and settled in again.

Owls can look at their talons, but do it mainly when perching or stooping on prey, which are both different body alignments. Being a shapeshifter means sometimes contorting the animal form, which is exquisitely tailored to perform like a champion athlete, into something far less efficient to serve an entirely different purpose. We rely on the instinct laid into the muscles, sinews, and nerves of the forms we assume, to perform in ways our human bodies cannot understand—like using wings to fly—and then, if we're proficient enough, we bend the shape to follow our will, also. To do things it would never occur to the actual animal to try.

I am of Salena's line, and a proficient shapeshifter. Surely demonstrating that proficiency was part of the dragon's test.

It worked, just as I'd suspected. I was able to hold the map-stick against the coastlines of the darkening islands dotting the sea below, and match it up as if it had been designed for this express purpose.

A shapeshifter had created this map, and Kiraka had known it. Had she only wanted to test if I could take a form, manipulate it to grasp the map, and think through the symbolism of map to land? Seemed too easy.

"Such arrogance."

The acerbic alien voice thundering through my mind with the power of centuries sent my avian heart pounding with the atavistic urge to fight or flee. At least I retained enough self-possession not to bobble in my flight this time. Though I'd known Dafne could hear the dragon's thoughts as clearly as speech, I'd never experienced such a thing—actual words, rather than feelings and images—though the old tales spoke of powerful sorcerers having the ability. Did Final Form convey the ability, or had the sorceress possessed it before she transitioned?

"Lady Kiraka." I formed the thought carefully, adding a mental genuflection of the kind I'd give to the Shaman.

"Hmm. Your mental discipline is quite muddy. Are you truly the prodigy chosen to apprentice to me?"

The indignation stiffening my wings might be residual from the day. First Marskal taking me off guard with his suspicions and now this … dismissive questioning of my abilities. I was the best of my generation—and the one before and after. I might not match Salena's powers, but I was—

"Immature yet. So I perceive." A mental sigh, like scales coursing over hot rocks. *"But you were chosen?"*

The way she used the term "chosen" implied extensive testing and competition. That, of course, had not happened. Though I had more years than Ursula, High Queen of at least fourteen kingdoms, and was of an age with Dafne and Jepp, both accomplished in their respective fields, it could well have been my immaturity that made me mulishly dig in my heels and balk at the dragon's dismissive tone. Attempting to clear my mind, I tried to reply with the proper deference.

"I volunteered."

A long pause, along with the eerie sensation of sinuous scales snaking through my thoughts and memories.

"Soooo…." Her mind-voice sounded like a hiss. *"Not chosen, after all."*

Had I teeth, I would have set them. Instead, I turned more fully into the headwind, using the exertion of pumping my wings to gain ground against it to vent my turbulent emotions. I *had* been chosen, in a way—albeit from a paltry few candidates. And I'd been the only one willing to make the ultimate sacrifice. That hadn't been an easy choice, but I'd made it—and persevered this far.

"Foolish youngling. Sacrifice is only the beginning." Kiraka's voice had become a wisp of regretful sorrow, a trail of thin smoke from an extinguished fire. *"When I took the sleep, I expected to wake to a changed world. But I did not imagine I'd find my people so diminished, the blood so thinned and so much lost."*

My owl form couldn't handle these emotions generated by my conscious, tangible self. The sense of failure—not only my own, but extending into some kind of collective memory well of grief—nearly swamped me. I struggled to form a reply. *"Much has been lost, yes, which is why I'm coming in the name of my people to ask for your help. I am a proficient shapeshifter and I can learn."*

"You don't know what proficient means. And your control is easily shaken."

Kiraka's mind clamped down on mine, and I plummeted through the air.

For the first time since I'd been a green child, when I'd whimsically shifted according to mood rather than by design, I felt my control of the form I wore falter. Warning tremors shuddered through me even as I strained to regain my position in the air. Even though I'd long since turned back for the main island and the palace, if I wavered any more, I'd be plunging into the sea.

At least if I died this way, neither my teachers nor any of my people would know of my catastrophic failure.

"I would." Kiraka's voice was smug, taunting. *"And I'd tell."*

Fuck you, you withered bitch. I didn't channel the thought at her. It sprang unbidden to my mind—another indication I was losing control—but she heard it anyway.

"Temper, child. Here's your invitation. Come and see me. If you can make it. Hurry back to land, little groundling. You're losing form."

At least land was in sight. My muscles wept with exhaustion, all of my mental energy going to sustaining the winged form. I briefly considered going into the sea and shifting to dolphin or fish—but I wasn't confident I could execute the change with the precision required for going from animal to animal without returning to my Birth Form in between. And then I'd have to evade predators, along with Kiraka stripping at my control. Either way, I'd drown, like that mindless shark. No, better to keep on the wing and strive for land.

The quiescent volcano loomed, a fiery orange glow against

the moonlit sky. Kiraka's lair would be there. I'd nearly made it. Dread filled me at the prospect of facing her in my current state. Much of that came from owl instincts to avoid such a large and lethal predator, but a great deal of it was mine. And I couldn't not go. Another test, perhaps.

In my mind, the dragon's laugh scraped over stone. *"If you work up the courage—and if you decide you can show me better than you have thus far—come see me in the morning. My Daughter will need to attend, and she needs her rest, broody as she is."*

I welcomed the reprieve with relief, though there would be no going to find out what Jepp wanted me to see. I'd be disappointing Ursula, which had never bothered me before, and yet…

"Tell your queen she can wait on my convenience." Kiraka was all smug, imperious indifference. *"She can try her sword against me if she cares to make the challenge. See me in the morning, or never."*

She blessedly released her crippling hold on my mind, and I found it in me to home in on the lights of the palace. I landed on a palm tree frond in a shadowed clump not far from the perimeter of the spilling torchlight. Taking only a moment to rest, lest I become too tired to shift back—and that way lay disaster—I plopped to the sand, taking back my human form with a rush of gratitude that I was able to.

Moranu seemed to gaze down on me, and I made an elaborate gesture of thankfulness, the deep bow taking me to my knees in the sand. To my surprise, hot tears spilled down my cheeks. At least Kiraka was leaving me alone for the moment. I needed time to recover.

"Are you all right?"

The voice had me leaping to my feet, spinning, ready to lash out with the razor sharp beak and talons I no longer possessed.

Marskal jumped back, stumbling a little in the sand and

drawing his sword out of reflex. Then lowered it, his face still contorted with astonishment. "Danu! I've never seen anyone move so fast."

"You haven't spent much time with shapeshifters then," I said, my voice a caustic echo of Kiraka's, my mind still disoriented from my precipitous shift, physical exhaustion along with that of mental sparring with my ancestress, not to mention the dull ache of guilt.

"I've spent time with you," he returned evenly, sheathing his blade.

"And I'm usually careful not to alarm you mossbacks," I replied. More than I should have said, but I was not yet fully myself. The ravenous predator in me combined precariously with my physical body's hunger. I wanted to snap and rend.

"All right." Marskal sounded wary, but not alarmed. "How can I assist you?"

"Why are you even out here?"

"I was watching for your safe return."

"And you are suddenly my keeper."

"I am. Her Majesty assigned me the duty."

I'd known that, and yet I'd been asking unnecessary questions. I blinked, reassessing. The night grew no brighter. *Human eyes. Get a grip on yourself.* "I need a moment."

"Take what you need."

Stepping a few paces away, I breathed deeply, reorienting. Upright spine, soft feet on the sand, hands, no claws, no beak. Weak. So hungry. I finally turned back to Marskal.

"Better now?" he asked, staying a careful distance back.

His caution tweaked my sense of humor. Happy to feel something other than fear and failure, I laughed. "I'm not as likely to eat you now."

He surveyed me, his quiet face serious. "In truth, for a moment there, I thought you might."

"I'm very hungry," I confessed. "Can we discuss these orders of Ursula's later?"

"I'll do you one step better," he said, offering me a crooked elbow. "Let me feed you."

I eyed his arm, bent in such a strange way. "What am I meant to do?"

"Take my arm, Zynda," he replied. All seriousness, no teasing in it. "You're weaving on your feet."

I'd thought it was the soft sand. Or the lingering twin sensations of swimming and flying. Too much shifting, too many forms, too fast, fighting a mental battle with the dragon with not enough rest, not enough nutrition. I should have known better. I'd grown arrogant in my time among the mossbacks, thinking myself so invincible. All along I'd known I might fail to find a dragon, then when Kiraka miraculously awoke, I had to face that I'd perhaps fail to gain an audience. It had never occurred to me that I wouldn't measure up. My will and legs weakened, the sand beckoning.

"Zynda," Marskal urged softly, "let me help you."

"I don't need help." Rather, I didn't want to need it. Another failure.

"Of course you don't. Think of me as a servant. A handmaid assigned to brush your hair and empty your chamber pot."

I snorted at that image, but found myself taking his arm. The contact immediately bolstered me, his masculine strength speaking to something in me. I leaned into him, surprised to find that I wanted his warmth, the solid feel of human flesh. Some shapeshifters needed this, the reconnection with human form through sex, especially after shifting through several shapes, but I never had before. Of course, I'd never before taxed myself quite so severely.

And I wouldn't contemplate it now. I could be within a day of taking Final Form—if I passed tomorrow's tests—there would be no more lovers for me. I edged away, but he tightened his arm, lightly pinning my hand against his side. "Don't pull back—I've got you."

We'd reached the steps where they plunged into the sand, and I vaguely wondered how deep they went. Better than surveying the long climb up. I retained too much owl instinct still, because the bright lights repelled me. I wanted to flee again into the dark.

That's another complication and peril of shifting through too many forms or tiring oneself in the doing. To the stranger's eye, we appear to shift completely from one form to another. In reality, assuming a different body involves many layers, not all of them tangible. Otherwise I wouldn't gain owl instincts along with the form. Imagine a human in a bird body with no idea how to work it. We'd be no more coordinated than we were in our infant bodies.

Lying there, waving our limbs while our senses struggle to make sense of the world is hardly useful—and not too far from how I felt just then.

Shifting back too rapidly, without the proper buffering time and energy to realign myself to human form meant that impulses intended to work an owl body stayed with me. I could no more climb those steps than an owl could.

"On second thought," I said, keeping my words relaxed and easy, "I think I'll stay on the beach. Such a lovely night."

Marskal studied the steps, not looking at me. "And food?"

"I'll get some later."

"I'll get some for you while you rest." He settled into his usual quiet, bolstering me while I held myself together enough to make it to the shadows behind the curve of the steps, which felt infinitely safer. Sitting there in the cool dark, I let my mind relax.

Moranu's nourishing gaze helped, her reflected light and shadows filling me, realigning my thoughts with my bones. Kiraka might scorn who the Tala had become, but we were still Moranu's children, the last of them to carry the goddess's blood in our bodies, her sacred vessels, and she rekindled the vitality in me with generosity and palpable love. I floated on the nourishment from the great mother.

"Here, drink this."

I mustered the will—and aggravation—to turn my head and give Marskal a baleful glare. "I thought you were leaving."

His mouth quirked without humor, the soft torchlight casting his face with oblique shadows, the deep lines catching them to runnel down his face like water down bark. "I did leave. And now I have returned. The fact that you didn't mark my absence is something that even a stubborn shapeshifter should recognize as a problem. I don't know what's wrong with you, except that you said you're hungry and you're clearly exhausted. So drink this or I'll sit on you and pour it down your throat."

"And here I'd thought of you as a man of few words."

"Depends on the need." He held my gaze, pushing the tall mug at me.

Because it smelled enticingly good—and made my stomach lunge with all the greed of a starving predator—I took it and drank. A hearty broth, well salted and full of the dense strength of marrow, slid into my empty gut. I eyed Marskal over the rim, watching him for sudden movements.

He chuckled, relaxing his crouch to sit back in the sand. "You look like the owl still, your eyes huge and catching the light."

Finished with the broth, I set the mug aside. "Were you so close, to note the appearance of the owl's eyes?"

"No." He reached into a basket such as those the Naha-nauns used to gather fruit and pulled out a cloth, laying it on the sand, then setting items on it. A tall flask of water and another of wine. A packet of roast meat. Several pieces of fruit. Bread, butter, and honey.

Because the owl lingered, though only in memory, I hoped, I took a piece of meat, doing my best not to tear into it. My body hummed, singing a song of need and gratitude, the nourishment following the broth into my blood and weeping muscles.

Marskal watched me without comment, though I likely looked like a wild thing, giving up on decorum, heavily buttering a slice of bread—it was warm and fresh and fragrant, the butter soft, salty, and smelling sweetly of green grass and sunshine, the honey bright with tropical nectar—and devouring that also. I alternated voracious bites of meat with that. When I'd finished it, I ate the fruit he'd brought, then drank the wine and water.

At last it felt as if I could draw a measured breath, then an-other. And I stopped licking my fingers clean, using the cloth to dry them. Belatedly I realized I hadn't offered Marskal any of it, not even a taste of the wine. *Just because you can be an animal doesn't mean you are one.* My mother would have been disappointed in me.

"My apologies," I said.

"For what?" Marskal rummaged in the basket. "I can get more food, if you like. I'm afraid I didn't bring enough to sate you."

"No need. I'm fine for now. I apologize for my rudeness."

He shrugged that off, shaking the sand out of the cloth. "You're far from the first royal to snap at me."

"I told you I'm not royal. And I meant for my greed, for not offering to share."

"I already ate. This was for you. Though I feel sure I've never seen a woman eat so much at one sitting. I don't know how you can be so slight, eating as you do."

"Shapeshifting burns a great deal of energy." I paused. It wasn't a large admission. Hardly a useful piece of information. But that I'd admitted as much went against long habit of not discussing the details of being a shapeshifter. Anything could be a weapon in the hands of the enemy. Marskal might not be the actual enemy, but he clearly harbored suspicions and I had no doubt he wouldn't hesitate to use any information against me, should things come to that. Ursula owned his loyalty, no question. If all went well, I wouldn't be arrayed against her, but my own loyalty to the Tala and Annfwn came first.

"You've shapeshifted before without suffering such profound effects," Marskal noted, torchlight glimmering a moment in his eyes as he studied me. "What happened out there?"

A dragon spoke in my mind, tested my control, and nearly broke me. I shook my head, the heaviness of my hair moving over my shoulders. "Nothing noteworthy. I got a ... cramp."

He made a noncommittal sound as he packed the flasks back into the basket.

"Thank you for the food," I said. It sounded awkward, coming so late. *You're far from the first royal to snap at me.*

"Doing my job."

"Your job?"

"Her Majesty," he said, "has assigned me to guard you, to accompany you on your journeys, whatever they may lead you, and to assure that no harm comes to you."

Of course she had, but what about the spying? "When did she task you thusly?"

"After Jepp's message arrived."

"Then you are absolved of duty for the time being," I told him, "as I will not yet be going to see Jepp."

He stood, tucking the basket under one arm and holding out

a hand to help me up. "Are you able to climb the steps now?"

"Of course." I hoped.

"If you say so."

We gazed at each other a moment, engaged in a silent battle of wills I didn't quite know how I'd gotten involved in. He still held out a hand. I still ignored it.

"I'll escort you inside then," he finally said. "We sail early. You need rest."

Such a mossback, to think that rest could only be had indoors. But that reminded me that I had a change of plans to communicate, my responsibilities not yet discharged. So I took his hand, using his strength to pull myself to my feet, my body responding reasonably well, though I might not have been so graceful without the help. It brought us too close, certainly for my peace of mind, so I hastened to drop his hand, stepping back again.

"We don't sail early," I informed him.

He cocked his head. "Oh?"

"I'm sure Ursula will inform you of what you need to know." I moved past him, but he edged into my path. Not blatantly blocking me, but enough that I'd have to make an exaggerated effort to go around him. It brought us close again, his face too near mine. I borrowed his trick, gazing off over his shoulder, though no endless horizon engaged my eye. Instead I looked at the palace, still not wanting to be within even its open walls. I could always come back outside after I talked to Ursula. Did, most nights, unless I had obligations.

"I'll be ready to accompany you in the morning, whatever your plans," Marskal said.

"Do as you like, though I doubt you'll be needed before midday at the earliest."

"What changed that we're not leaving?"

I turned my head to look him in the eye. "I thought good soldiers take orders and don't question them."

"Keeping me ignorant serves no one well. And I *will* do my job." The warmth of his breath tickled my cheek. "We are not enemies, Lady Zynda."

"Nor are we allies. Nor are you my keeper. I come and go as I please, and not even Ursula may command me."

"What about your king and queen—don't you bow to them?"

"It depends. The Tala are different."

"This has not escaped my notice," he muttered, stepping out of my way.

At least he acknowledged the fact. I continued up the steps, glad for the easy response of my legs now. How disconcerting that Marskal had seen through me so easily, had discerned my earlier weakness. Salena would have done better. I needed to do better, if I was to withstand Kiraka's tests and convince her to teach me Final Form.

At the moment, doing so seemed as insurmountable as the long flight of steps had before I rested and ate. A good analogy, though—a bit of rest, nourishing food, the benevolence of Moranu's gifts, and I was ascending with vigor. Perhaps my eventual task would fall out the same.

"You only wish, little changeling."

Kiraka's dry warning sifted through my consciousness, nearly as startling as before. I "heard" it differently now, my human brain processing it as more alien, oddly enough, but also without as much of the instinctive need to hide from a greater predator.

Still, something in me quailed, and I doubted I'd sleep quietly with her slinking about in my mind.

~ 4 ~

THE NEXT MORNING, Dafne and I met in the outer courtyard to venture up the volcano for my interview with the
dragon. To my surprise, Ursula had deferred to the change of
plans without protest, though she'd had a thoughtful look. She
only commented that Jepp knew how to reach us if urgent
became emergency, and that one didn't antagonize a dragon
lightly. I felt a bit of guilt that she assumed I'd be asking about
using the map-sticks to find allies or assistance in N'Andana. I
could ask about that, too, while still pursuing my primary aim.

I had told Ursula about the strange encounter with the shark,
and she'd listened, asking me a few questions. It clearly troubled
her, but she had no more idea what to think about it than I did.
Even if I did go see what Jepp had to show me right away, that
wouldn't necessarily give us any more answers.

Dafne gave me a radiant smile as I approached. She did
everything with that radiance these days, the glow of pregnancy
and the happiness of love giving her a beauty that lightened my
mood, despite my misgivings. No, I should be honest in the
privacy of my own mind, which was no longer private. Despite
the fear of failure that gave a brittle feel to my bones, I needed
to face those emotions, not deny them.

Change was coming and a shapeshifter should never fear
change.

"So I'm to bring you for a conversation with Kiraka?" Dafne said, as if we were going on a stroll along a beach. "That's a first. She hasn't wanted to talk to anyone else before."

"Apparently so." I shrugged as if it weren't a matter of critical importance. Tropical flowers glowed in the morning light, no longer dewy. Dafne had slept long. Mindful of both Kiraka's directive and her husband Nakoa's glowering and protective presence, I'd waited her out.

Even Ursula had displayed unusual patience. Of course, she'd worked off her steam in the usual way, training with Harlan and the other Hawks she'd brought with her. At least that had occupied Marskal as well. Normally I would have engaged in my own style of morning exercise, which on Nahanau meant shifting to an aquatic form to enjoy the tropical waters while I could.

For today, however, I'd thought it wiser to conserve my shifting strength. Moranu knew what Kiraka's further tests would involve. Hopefully I'd do better, now that I'd rested and eaten heartily.

"I'm ready to go." Dafne indicated her satchel of scribing materials, and a basket of food and drink like the one Marskal had brought me the night before. Perhaps the palace kept a store of them on hand, for picnicking queens and exhausted shapeshifters.

"Shall we walk?" I asked, glancing dubiously at her bare feet, remembering how she'd once walked them raw enough to lay her up for days. "Or, would you prefer if I—"

I broke off as Ursula strode out, Marskal at her left flank, a step behind as if he expected to guard her from attack. His sharp brown gaze rested on me, assessing. He moved with unusual grace for a mossback, born of warrior training, lithe and athletic. Even in rest, those deep lines bracketed his mouth, part of the weathered complexion of a mossback who'd spent most of his life outdoors, and in often harsh conditions. Mossbacks never renewed their skin, and so it showed the passage of trial and time. Why those lines suddenly attracted me, why I wanted to run my lips along them, I didn't know. Irritated, I pulled out the jeweled pin I'd tucked in my sleeve and wound up my hair, the knot keeping it out of my face.

"I promised King Nakoa you'd carry Dafne as you did before, if that's not a problem," Ursula said, having caught the tail of my question.

I nodded, though the mountain pony form would prevent me from trying to extract information from Dafne about Kiraka along the way. Perhaps just as well. The dragon would tell me what she wished me to know. I waited for her dry mental commentary on that thought, but she remained silent, as she had since her parting challenge the night before.

"And Marskal will go with you, in case of problems," she added, gesturing him forward.

"He wasn't invited," I said, not mincing the words. The man's presence irritated me, making me feel like that dual-natured mermaid, both wanting and unable to have.

Ursula raised her brows at me, her lean face chilling slightly at being thwarted. In those moments, she reminded me keenly of Salena, how my aunt's storm-gray eyes would go thunderous and the air crackle about her with magic. Ursula was no sorceress, but she had plenty of latent shapeshifter in her, and of the alpha female variety, just like her mother. I didn't tuck my metaphorical tail between my legs, but the wolf in me felt the urge.

"It's true that he can't come with us," Dafne surprised me by saying. "Kiraka is most particular about who meets with her. Asking to see Zynda is a first, though I'm surprised she hadn't wanted to talk to her by now, seeing as how the Tala are descended from the N'andanans."

Marskal's expression didn't change, but I felt his attention sharpen, his quiet brown eyes studying me.

"I don't like you two going unguarded." Ursula had her jaw set, which made me think of Kiraka's taunt that she could try her sword against the dragon.

Dafne pursed her lips, acting puzzled. "I go by myself all the time, Your Majesty."

Ursula's gaze flashed steel. "Oh, stop that. I know full well what you're about when you trot out the titles, Queen Dafne Nakoa KauPo, and I am not distracted. If Jepp's warning proves true and *Deyrr* has found a way through the barrier, no one is safe from harm. Zynda, I don't have to remind you of this after your odd encounter yesterday. You'll need your full attention on Kiraka, not worrying about strange animals that taste of *Deyrr* coming at your back."

Dafne flicked a glance at me, looking thoughtful. Of course Ursula would have filled her in. "So noted. But I cannot vouch for Kiraka's tolerance."

I opened my mouth to add to the argument when Kiraka's voice slid into my head.

"The warrior may attend, as long as he watches from a respectful distance. He might come in useful. You never know. I might need a snack." Dry amusement threaded through her mental voice, giving me a bad feeling.

From the look on Dafne's face, the dragon had spoken to us both at once. Nice trick, that. As was her apparent ability to eavesdrop at will. Dafne relayed Kiraka's permission, leaving out the bit about the snack—though maybe she'd added that only to me—and Ursula nodded crisply, mollified. "Convey my thanks to the dragon," she said.

Dafne got a peculiar expression, but only inclined her head, not passing along the dragon's tart reply that our queen's thanks were unnecessary and irrelevant. "But, seriously, my feet are tough now." She lifted a foot, canting it over her knee to show me with some pride. "I can walk."

Ursula set her jaw, and I intervened, lest we be arguing all day. "Might as well take advantage of my presence," I said, and shifted into pony form. Another advantage of being an animal: mossbacks don't argue with you, because they tend to forget you can still understand them just fine, even if you can't talk back. Well, *I* can understand them. And a few other purebloods can, depending on the form they take. Some retain just enough wit to remember they have a different Birth Form and to revert to it before it's too late.

Becoming the pony was my first shift of the new day, and the first since I'd nearly bobbled the owl form. To my relieved delight, it went cleanly, with no shadows of other animal layers. It felt good and strong to be the sturdy horse. Four solid legs upon the earth. I tossed my mane and bit Dafne's coppery skirt, tugging at it, and she laughed, scratching me between the ears.

"Who's a pretty pony?" she teased, mischievous and delighted.

"Allow me, Queen Dafne Nakoa KauPo," Marskal said, going to one knee and cupping his hands for her foot. Showy and over the top. I bobbed my head in the pony version of an eye roll. Something he seemed to understand because he narrowed his eyes at me.

"You can call me Dafne, you know." She stepped into his hand and swung a leg over my back, then settled the satchels so they draped evenly behind her. "Is that good, Zynda?"

I nickered an affirmative, adjusting to her weight more than to the inert bags. Carrying inanimate things rarely felt odd in animal form, because I was accustomed to doing so as a human. Very few of my forms, however, had the size or conformation that allowed for a rider. Jepp had ridden my back twice while I was a mermaid, but with her athletic ability—and despite her non-swimmer's aversion to water—she'd adjusted to my movements with an ease that made her a joy to carry. Dafne wasn't as bad as some, and she'd ridden horses on long journeys, but riding without a saddle or reins took adjusting.

Also, the feel of her sun-warmed skin against my back, the clasp of her legs—something about the contact reminded me of leaning against Marskal the night before. Perhaps the nearing possibility of taking Final Form had me feeling the imminent loss of human touch. Too late to mourn that.

Ursula sent us off, admirably refraining from reiterating any warnings, and I set a brisk pace, my hooves clattering on the marble esplanade. Hitting the dirt of the path felt much nicer. It would be lovely to trot to work off these nerves, or even canter or full-out gallop up the winding trail draped with paniculate blossoms in pastel shades. But, much as I might enjoy demonstrating just how not-weak I was to Marskal, it wouldn't be fair to tax his human form that way—or to make Dafne uncomfortable. My brisk walk should be a slow jog for him—which proved to be the case—so good enough.

"Have you been up the volcano before?" Dafne asked Marskal.

"No, Queen Dafne Nakoa KauPo." He didn't sound at all out of breath. I could likely go faster. Even a smooth trot would jostle my pregnant rider, however.

"I told you." She sounded crisply annoyed. "Plain Dafne is fine."

I snorted for our similarity there.

Marskal shook his head. "It wouldn't be appropriate, Your

Highness."

"You called me Dafne just fine on that hard journey from Windroven," she reminded him. "In fact, I recall you threatening to leave me behind if I didn't get my lazy ass up and—"

"I apologize for that, Your Highness."

Horse forms make for excellent 360 degree vision, with the exception of small slices dead ahead and exactly behind, so I easily observed the chagrined flush beneath the tanned skin of Marskal's face. Had I been able to, I would have chuckled. As it was, I blew out a sound between my thick pony lips, and he slid me one of those narrow glares.

"Well, I was a soft librarian commoner and an unwelcome burden back then. I knew that very well," Dafne said. "My point is that I'm no more a queen now than I was then, just because I married well. I put up with the titles in the palace because I have to, but when it's just us, you'd be doing me a favor by—oh, Zynda. Can you slow a bit? We're not in a hurry and you're making poor Marskal jog uphill."

He looked fine to me, but I slowed to an exaggerated stroll.

"That's not necessary," he said, as much to me as her. "I'm perfectly able to sustain that pace, even go faster."

I quirked my ears forward. A challenge? My pony instincts loved the sound of that. I quickened again.

"Oh, Goddesses, no," Dafne groaned. "Curse my pride, I'll admit it. Zynda, you're making me queasy. If you don't want me to barf on your pretty white hide, go slowly."

"Perhaps you *would* be better walking," Marskal said, all solicitous gallantry.

"You wouldn't tell on me?" Dafne sounded hopeful.

"Not at all. I have five sisters, all with at least two kids—one with seven—so I'm familiar with the tolls of pregnancy. Walking is almost always better for them than riding, no matter what overprotective husbands think."

Dafne's laugh was full of relief. I stopped and Marskal helped her down. "I can carry the satchels, Lady Zynda," he said, once again addressing me directly, despite my animal form. "If you'd prefer to shift back and join the conversation."

I wagged my head in a no, and started walking again.

"It's better for her if she doesn't shift too often," Dafne told him.

Had I been human, I would have shot her a warning glare. The librarian paid attention to detail, and was ever curious about my abilities. Generally, however, she remembered to be discreet.

"Oh?" Marskal laid a hand on my neck, combing his fingers through my mane as they walked on either side of me. It felt nice, making me want more just when I couldn't have more. "You met Zynda in Annfwn, yes?"

He knew that. He'd been in charge of the base camp when Ursula, Harlan, and Dafne had climbed Odfell's Pass and crossed the barrier. He had to be digging for information on me. If I weren't meeting a dragon shifter intent on putting me in my place, I'd shift back to forestall further confidences.

"Yes," Dafne agreed. "So, do your sisters live near Ordnung, that you've observed so much of their pregnancies?"

I lipped at her skirt in a thank you and she stroked my nose. Yes, I should have trusted her discretion.

"I grew up in the township outside the walls," Marskal told her. "With the exception of one brother who moved to Carienne with his wife, my family is all still there."

"Has your family been in the region a long time?" Dafne asked it casually, but I had to work to keep my ears from pricking.

"Since it was Castle Columba, yes," he confirmed quietly. "We had farmland in the region and swore loyalty to your family."

"Ah," she breathed, though her stride didn't falter. "I'm surprised your family survived—though glad they did."

"My grandfather was a renowned coward," Marskal said wryly. "He handed over everything to the Duranor armies and fled. When we returned initially, it was to the township, because Uorsin had taken over the old manor house and lands."

He sounded diffident, but his fingers tugged at my mane in hidden distress. I didn't know the details of the history, but Dafne had been a daughter of the ruling family in Castle Columba, which fell early on to Uorsin's pillaging. Not strange, I supposed, that she and Marskal should share this old commonality. Odd to me was that they hadn't known it until now. But the mossbacks didn't meticulously trace and memorize family connections the way the Tala did. They didn't have to, as they didn't have our problems with inbreeding and the malformed babies it produced.

Dafne had been orphaned as a child, and Marskal had to be somewhat older than she, so he'd remember those days. They didn't speak of it further, dropping the painful topic by mutual accord and instead discussing the lush flora of the island, Dafne giving us the Nahanaun names of the flowers and trees we passed, when she knew them, picking specimens to tuck in her satchels on my back when she didn't.

Before long, even at Dafne's slower pace, we reached one of the lower meadows—which was still well above most everything else on the island. With Kiraka's emergence, the volcano itself had quieted, though it was far from cool and dormant. It didn't rumble, belching smoke, flame and ash, as it had on our first trip up. Where there had been bare rock, coals and layers of ash before, green foliage flourished. Lush ferns arched with lacy grace and a kind of blooming moss formed a cushion so deep and soft that my hooves made no sound.

I hadn't been there since then, when I'd watched the legendary dragon take life before my very eyes, knowing in my heart that Final Form was within my reach at last.

Dafne paused, looking around—as if the dragon could possibly be missed. "Usually she's here when I arrive."

I smelled Kiraka before Marskal called the warning, pointing at the sky. Ponies apparently also retained an atavistic terror of dragons, and I had to clamp down on the instinct to flee. Having learned my lesson there the night before, I didn't try to fight the animal. Instead I reverted to human form, shouldering the satchel and basket, watching Kiraka's wheeling flight.

She glittered bright gold, like a second sun in the sky, only far eclipsing it in size—and growing larger as she descended at high speed, then braked with a booming snap of her great wings. The first time I saw her perform that maneuver, my heart had leapt in instinctual horror. Not afraid of her, but in terrible, sympathetic fear that she'd shatter her wings. They must be stronger and more resilient than any I'd ever had, because they held, the dreadful dive converting into a soundless glide. Light as a petal drifting on water, she landed on the far side of the meadow, wrapping her tail around herself and settling her wings as fastidiously as a cat arranging itself for a nap in the sun.

"Well? I hope you don't plan to dawdle all day. Unless you're afraid. Come here, little pony."

I started forward, definitely afraid, but obeying automatically, when Dafne told Marskal, "She's reminding us that you have to stay here."

Interesting—had the dragon been able to speak to both of us at once, saying different things?

"I am capable of a great deal. But we're here to discover what you can do. Hopefully in this millennium. I may be immortal but my time is yet

valuable. To me, at least."

"I can be closer and still be respectful," Marskal argued. Something tugged my hair, and I glanced back, absently pulling at whatever had snarled it—only to find he had ahold of it. Had he kept his fingers tangled in my mane when I shifted and thus had them still in my hair? Rarely was anyone ever so close to be able do that when I shifted. I would have said it wasn't possible—a mane might be somewhat equivalent to the hair of my human form, but these things weren't exact. It wasn't as if I converted my hair to a mane and back again. The magic didn't work that way. I frowned, both for the puzzle and the man's presumption. I didn't care to be tethered.

Marskal was giving me an intent stare full of some sort of wordless communication.

"I have to go," I told him, trying to be gentle. Moranu knew, if Kiraka's immense and world-shattering presence threw me off, it must be that much worse for a mossback.

"It's dangerous," he said with quiet force, still saying something else beneath the words.

I shrugged, giving him an easy smile I didn't feel, and extracted my hair from his grip. He seemed surprised that he'd been holding it. "The dragon is dangerous whether you stand here or close enough to be reduced to ash by one sneeze."

"I can't protect you from here."

"You can't protect me there either."

"That doesn't reassure me." He spaced out the words, still keeping his usual quiet tone, but a frustrated snarl coiled beneath.

"If you hadn't insisted on coming along, you wouldn't be so concerned."

"Completely untrue."

"Kiraka has never harmed me in any way," Dafne inserted,

and we both glanced at her, having somewhat forgotten in our private battle that she stood right there. She gave me a strange look, then laid a hand on Marskal's arm. "You're here to make sure no one else disturbs or harms us, and we greatly appreciate your service."

"I do swear I'm aging during this endless delay."

"The dragon summons us," I informed Marskal, who still looked as if he might lunge out of his skin. Relenting, I touched him, a pat of reassurance, the contact with his muscled shoulder making my fingers itch to feel more. I snatched my hand away. *Focus.* "Thank you for guarding our backs."

His lip curled, his eyes dark with frustration and some longing that echoed the one that stirred in me. For a moment I searched for other words that might soothe his ire, but came up empty. Instead I looked to Dafne and she and I turned to walk across the meadow together. Kiraka watched us, her chin resting on one great taloned foot, eyes glowing. I risked a glance back, to be sure that Marskal had stayed put. He inclined his head, a wry twist to his mouth.

"What was *that* all about?" Dafne asked in a voice that wouldn't carry.

"He's a stubborn mossback soldier with delusions of grandeur," I replied. "I can't imagine what he's thinking."

"Can't you?"

Well, I could—but he'd picked the wrong woman to be interested in, and his timing was terrible. Kiraka loomed larger, the very air growing hotter and drier as we approached. "Let me rephrase. I have no interest in trying to puzzle out what his thoughts might be."

"I've heard you call non-shapeshifters 'mossbacks' before, but never as an insult," she remarked, as if we were out for a stroll.

"I'll be hard-pressed to keep him from getting his fool self killed."

"That's harsh."

"Is it?" I couldn't worry about the man's well-being. I had my task to think about, what Kiraka would demand of me and whether I'd be able to do it.

"I can honestly say I've never heard you be so dismissive of anyone before," Dafne replied.

"You are accustomed to the ways of mossback men—and they are accustomed to being the protectors, physically stronger and larger than the women in general. Among Tala, among shapeshifters in particular, we have no such distinctions. Your mossback men see themselves as heroes, forever seeking a helpless damsel to rescue. I have no patience for it."

"I think that's a dramatically unfair assessment of Marskal."

"Regardless, the man gets under my skin." That human skin twitched with irritation. "He asked me why I left Annfwn and all but accused me of harboring an agenda of my own."

"Are you?"

I took my eyes off the dragon for a moment to find Dafne scrutinizing me with her keen gaze. For all that she was no warrior, her intelligence made her formidable in her own way. I thrust aside the guilt. I wanted to help my friends, but my mission took priority.

"That's up to Kiraka," I replied, and turned my attention back to the dragon.

~ 5 ~

THE DRAGON'S RUBY eyes shone—not reflecting or refracting, but with their own light which shouldn't be possible—mesmerizing me. The dragon's nostrils, tall enough for me to walk into standing, flared as she drew in my scent. Was that her primary sense?

"All senses are acute in this form," she replied. *"It's one of the many reasons it's the ultimate form."*

That could be hyperbole. Or calculated propaganda on her part. I had a snake form and the taste/scent sense was excellent, along with fine-tuned proprioception for vibrations and infrared heat sensations. But sight and auditory other than body-felt long wave sounds fell short. Not to mention the loss of sensitive skin with all those scales. A dragon should be like a snake with legs and wings. Four legs and two wings, though, which was two more appendages than any other creature besides the arthropods. And the wings looked like a bat's, which was mixing mammal with reptile, where avian would have been a closer relative and more likely. As likely as such things went, anyway.

But then, I'd been a mermaid, and I knew full well the "maid" half of that combination had little to do with being human. Or the other half with true fishes.

Dafne stepped far closer to Kiraka than I would have, seeming completely unconcerned, greeting the dragon with affection and taking the satchel and basket from me. She unpacked them, shaking out a blanket on the brightly flowering moss, relating greetings from King Nakoa and speaking of how the babe progressed.

I felt as if Dafne and I occupied two different worlds. I'd used that metaphor with Ursula once, to explain shapeshifting. Magic allows many things to exist at once, I'd said. Some Tala groups believe shapeshifting isn't truly changing forms at all, but rather exchanging a form we exist in, in this world, for one in another. Those who subscribe to this theory suggest that, for example, in a parallel realm I am *always* the pony. When I shift here, I trade places and my human body goes there. I don't subscribe to that belief system, because that's not how shifting has ever felt to me.

And yet...

And yet, this close to Kiraka, I could almost sense a kind of... echo. A sensation that she simultaneously existed in several worlds at once. And that the dragon Dafne knew and trusted, who called her daughter and taught her to read ancient N'andanan, wasn't quite the same as the shapeshifter whose immense presence studied me, weighing me on an insubstantial level according to her own arcane measure. I felt as if I stood under the merciless scrutiny of the goddess Moranu, Herself.

And that I came up far short of expectation.

"It's true that you're much too young," Kiraka said, though she sounded less caustic than she had the night before.

"So you mentioned, Lady Dragon," I replied, shaping my address carefully.

"No more with the 'withered bitch'?"

"I apologize, Lady Dragon. I was overwrought and failed to show you the proper honor and respect."

"Amazing how you ornery younglings remember such things when you

are within reach of my flame." She snorted, twin clouds of smoke billowing out of her nose, hot enough to make my breath sear my lungs when I took a breath.

Impossibly, Dafne seemed not to notice, seated on the blanket with her quill and paper out, apparently also conducting a conversation with the dragon. I wondered what Marskal saw from his vantage, but dared not look.

"They see what I want them to. My Daughter loves you and need not be distressed by this meeting between us. This is the realm of shapeshifters, not hers."

"Why have her involved at all?"

"She is my... anchor. The one who reminds me of my humanity still, just as her mate cools my fire. Be glad of her presence. Without it, I might forget myself and kill you in a fit of draconic irritation."

Forgetting her humanity and losing herself to dragon instinct. It's what we all feared from being trapped in one of our forms. I'd thought, however, that the ancients settled on the dragon form for immortality in part because it retained the human mind best of any.

"Yes and no. All is relative. Stay as a fish for more than a day and that will extinguish cerebral comprehension. Stay as a dragon for tens of centuries and the same might occur. Or rather, you become more dragon and less human with each passing decade."

An appalling thought, to be trapped in a single form and feel your very sanity erode. A wave of nausea rolled through me. In my mind, absurdly, Kiraka laughed.

"I shouldn't worry, if I were you. You're highly unlikely to face the problem."

"Why is that?" I pushed back the persistent sense of imminent failure. For years I'd trained for this moment. I'd sacrificed, given up my home, companionship, so much.

"Sacrificing such minor worldly things isn't enough," Kiraka

snapped. *"Goddesses save me from petulant children. It's not enough to want a thing, or even to work hard for a thing. Anyone can do that. You haven't done enough."*

"What do I need to do?"

"I wish I knew. I only know you're not ready. Not even close to ready. No—you won't do."

"My people need someone to take Final Form. We need you to teach us. To teach me."

"What is this Final Form?"

"Like you. I want to learn to be the dragon."

"This is not a simple thing."

"I know. This is why I need you to teach me. I'm willing to do whatever it takes."

"Younglings always think that, but they don't understand what's required. Better to send another."

I swallowed down my hurt pride. Later I would feel sorry for my inadequate self. Making sure my mental tone stayed even, I replied to her calmly. *"There is no other to send."*

"Then wait until there is."

"We cannot wait. Our need is urgent. And it's unlikely anyone else will eclipse my abilities."

Smoke wisped black from her nostrils, a scorched scent rising with it, her eyes glowing hotter as she looked into me, as if she suspected I lied. *"There must be someone better. Who is your queen—who holds the Heart?"*

"Andromeda is queen. She holds the Heart."

"Then she is the one. Send her and I'll find out." Kiraka flipped her wings, dismissing me, and even Dafne looked up in surprise at the movement.

"Lady Dragon, I don't wish to contradict you—"

"Then don't."

"But," I gritted my mental teeth and continued, *"she is not a*

pureblood. She bears the Mark, but she came to shapeshifting late in life, and so has only three or four forms."

"How can that be?" Kiraka sounded plaintive enough that my heart softened for the irascible old bitch.

"A great deal has happened while you slept—surely Dafne has explained."

"My Daughter is clever, but understands only one face of the world. You explain."

I gathered my wits, certain I only understood a different face and not the whole thing, but I'd try. *"When the ancients—"*

"Watch who you call ancient, child."

The tart rejoinder made me pause, and I relaxed some that she retained a bit of humor. *"Apologies. When our ancestors created the Heart and sealed magic within the barrier, aspects of the world outside began to wither for lack of magic."*

"I know this part. I was one of those that withered."

"Do you want me to tell the story as I know it or not?"

"So impetuous. You have arrogance in plenty, but it has not been tempered by true trials. I imagine you've been celebrated among your pitifully gifted folk, certainly treated as something special among the mossbacks. You haven't learned the iron will of one who's endured the worst and survived through her own efforts. This is part of why you're not good enough to learn how to be a dragon."

"I'm the best my people have," I snapped back, growing tired of hearing the litany of my inadequacy. *"Do you want the rest of the history?"*

"I said so."

"As I understand it, those of you outside the barrier who relied on magic began to starve for it."

"Yes. Many who'd taken dragon form died. A few of us, the strongest and most enduring, put ourselves in hibernation."

I nodded to myself. Dafne had told me as much. *"Inside the barrier, in Annfwn, we have very old tales of dragons, of the Final Form and what it can do, but they are legends only. History became tales that were embroidered.*" Dafne would likely argue that this was the drawback of oral histories, rather than her precious documents. "*If we ever knew why the barrier was established, we lost the reason for it.*"

Kiraka said nothing, so I continued. "*The Tala, as we came to call ourselves, lived in prosperity for a very long time. Annfwn is bountiful, warm, protected, and we flourished there. But, trapped inside the barrier, the magic seemed to intensify.*"

The dragon mentally snorted, but offered nothing further, so I ignored the growing sense of anger from her.

"*The magic turned back on us, corrosive in a way. Babies were born with too many limbs, extra heads, sometimes animal parts. Those that survived birth didn't live long. The wizards and priestesses worked to teach these misbegotten children to shift, in the hope that they could make themselves whole, but they went wrong. Dreadfully wrong.*"

"*We could have told you that would happen.*"

"*Well, you weren't there, were you?*" I retorted, my nails biting into my palms. Easy for her to be distantly superior. She hadn't held her own niece, soothing the poor babe with her misshapen face and crabbed claws, giving her love the few hours she'd lived, so she'd at least die with someone holding her. My sister, Anya, hadn't been able to bear to even look at her daughter. "*We did the best we could and it wasn't enough. A few generations back, some Tala tried leaving Annfwn. They went out into the neighboring kingdoms and found mates to make whole and healthy children with.*"

"*Diluting the blood.*"

"*Surviving.*"

"*No, I survived. Your bastardized race is slowly dying.*"

I couldn't argue that. It was, after all, why I'd been sent. "*We did make babies with the mossbacks, but only some could return through the barrier. Some pairings worked and others did not, though no one knows why. Those who could not remained outside and made lives the best they could. Depending on how strongly the old blood, how deeply the old magic marked them, these children were drawn to each other and sometimes their children possessed enough ability to return through the barrier. Many of them did, as they felt the call of the Heart in their bones, their longing bringing them back to Annfwn. A blessing, as these brought fresh blood back to us, making the birth of viable children more possible again."*

"*But not enough, I'm sure,*" Kiraka observed, not so caustic. But still angry, though I didn't understand why.

"*Not enough. We were fortunate, however, to have Andromeda ascend to the throne. Salena was of the old blood, very pure. She is Andromeda's mother and my aunt.*"

"*Dead, though?*"

"*Long since.*" I paused to send a blessing after Salena, may she look upon us and send good fortune for my effort here. "*Over twenty-five years.*"

"*Barely a blink. I just missed her.*"

Many of us would have Salena back, but she'd left us and Annfwn long before she died. "*Salena possessed powerful foresight. She saw the rise of one of our outcast children, a mossback but with a bastard mix of shapeshifter blood—and a lust for power, along with his consuming need for Annfwn. Though she confided in no one, it's believed she went through the barrier to be his queen in the outside world in order to divert him from Annfwn, to prevent him from consuming us in his hunger. She helped him conquer the various kingdoms, calling on us and her own magic to win the wars for him. Then she bore him three daughters, and died. The middle daughter was Andromeda, who grew up without magic, but then came home to wed our king.*"

"*Powerful blood, that she learned to shapeshift as an adult,*" Kiraka commented thoughtfully. "*Has she children?*"

"*Not yet.*" I didn't know if she and Rayfe had managed to conceive or not. Many Tala women lost the babies early on in pregnancy, a grief just slightly preferable to carrying the babes to full term only to have the hope they'd tried not to nourish be so brutally shattered.

"And the other two daughters?"

"One of them is Ursula, here on Nahanau, who you invited to test her sword with you."

"Ah. I knew she shone brightly in my mind. Not enough of the blood, however."

"No. She is not a shapeshifter, and has no sorcery. As such. She is the one who finally slew Uorsin and caused the barrier to move. The three sisters wrought some spell with the spilling of his blood, a magic jewel, and expanded the barrier outward. The return of magic wakened you and your brethren."

"Yes. That makes sense." Kiraka dismissed that tidbit as uninteresting, though I'd have dearly loved to learn more about it. *"The third daughter contributed to the working?"*

"The youngest daughter, Amelia, is the same as Ursula, but has borne twins, one of them a daughter with the Mark. Both have already shapeshifted."

Kiraka's attention leapt like a flame. *"How old is this one?"*

"She is but a toddler."

"Young enough to be trained up properly," Kiraka mused, a trickle of smoke making it clear she thought I hadn't been. *"But you say you haven't enough time for her to grow up. What of your sisters, brothers, cousins? Have any of them more proficiency?"*

"No." Weary of this, I sighed. Never mind that I had only one sister and one brother left. *"I am the best. And I might not be trained properly, but I can learn."*

"How do you know?" Kiraka looked into me, the glow of her eyes turning my skin pink.

"I've trained hard all my life. I have many forms, am still gaining more, and my magical skills are excellent—and also growing."

"Yes, yes, yes. But how do you know you're capable of learning what you need to, that you have the force of will to become the dragon and sustain the form? That you and your people even deserve this knowledge?"

"How can I know that?"

"Exactly."

We fumed at each other, Kiraka literally. *"Tell me,"* she finally said, in a mental whisper licking with hissing flames, *"what you imagine I want of you."*

"I imagine you'll tell me. I'm prepared to pay whatever price is needed."

"Do you even understand the stakes?"

Once again I held Anya's dying baby in my arms, her forked tongue darting out to taste the tears that fell on her face, before it went still and pale, lolling out of her lipless mouth.

"More than that," Kiraka said without compassion or remorse. *"The scale is far larger than you comprehend."*

"Then tell me," I asked, trying to sound humble. *"I seek to understand."*

"You are not good enough." Kiraka sounded infinitely weary, terribly resigned. *"And the* gelyneinioes *approach. They have grown stronger over time while my children have grown weak and scattered on the one side, twisted and infertile on the other, all the while feeding the enemy through their selfishness. Perhaps it is all for naught. We lost the battle long ago and all of this has been spitting into the wind while we writhe in our dying throes."*

"Who are the gelyneinioes?*"* I didn't even recognize the word.

"The ancient enemy who broke us and drove us to ground. The followers of a cruel god of permanent yet undying death. They took the brightest and best of us and made them into monsters, enslaved to be their puppets. We fought, but they won every battle. We faced the ultimate defeat. The only way to stop them was to take magic from the world. But if you understand anything at all about the universe you will know that nothing can disappear completely."

"It can only be reduced, grown, or converted," I replied.

"You are not a complete idiot. We couldn't destroy magic utterly, so we condensed it. It was meant to be only in the Heart, buried in the depths of the sea, sealed away from all living beings."

"But…"

"Yesssss." Kiraka hissed her displeasure. *"But some—your people—couldn't bear to give up their precious spells, the freedom of changing forms at will. Even as the greatest of us resigned ourselves to the end of immortality, to the final sleep of infinite death, a few stole into the Heart and created an echo of it."*

"The barrier around Annfwn."

"Was never meant to be. And thus your foolish people planted the seed and watered it, allowing magic to grow outside the heart. Your children should not flourish. They should all die, as they were never meant to exist in the first place."

The ruthlessness took my breath away. *"Regardless of what my ancestors did, we do exist. And we are innocent of such crimes. Certainly the Tala today don't deserve such a punishment."*

"Does the world deserve to be subsumed to the gelyneinioes? *You sprouted from a selfish seed and that is all you're capable of sprouting in turn. Because of you, magic survived. Because of you, it spread. Because of you, the* gelyneinioes *are awake and growing by the moment. And now you come to me and ask that I help you?"* Her scorn scorched my soul. *"When I awoke and felt the presence of the* gelyneinioes, *I despaired. Then my Daughter came and I dared hope. She spoke to me of your kind, of shapeshifters and sorceresses such as my gallant comrades at arms had been, and I nurtured that hope. Perhaps we could yet win the war. When you came back, I watched you, listening to your thoughts while you played at taking forms and discarding them again. And I've realized there is no hope."*

I was weeping, I realized, overcome with her ancient despair and my fresh and final failure. *"Then why even summon me here today?"*

She chuckled, not in humor, but the wry, self-deprecating hiss of dry scales over rock, of flesh seared by fire. *"If you live long enough, baby changeling, you will discover someday that there is a freedom in the final loss of hope. Because in the ultimate despair, you'll try something you'd never thought to attempt."*

It made a certain sense, but I didn't know what response she wanted from me. She waited, too, saying nothing, the burning scarlet flame of her eyes lighting every dark corner of my soul.

"What will you attempt?" I finally asked.

"A trial by fire."

The hairs rose on my neck and absurdly I wished that I hadn't made Marskal stay so far back. A ridiculous thought, as he couldn't help me. I was alone in this. *"What does that mean?"*

"We'll burn away the weakness and see what's left. You said you were prepared to pay the price, any price. Are you really? I'll give you a gift—if you can learn how to use it, perhaps there is cause to hope."

Despite the fear that tried to throttle me, I had my answer ready for that one. Long since memorized. My mantra whenever my resolve flagged. *"I'm prepared to learn whatever I need to. I'll pay whatever price is needed."*

"Careful, youngling." Again a wisp of compassion, of shared humanity in that inhuman mind voice. *"Don't simply parrot those words your elders ground into your mind. They are not here, but you are. You offer to pay with yourself. And it will take everything you have. Perhaps forever. And even then you may yet fail."*

"Yes." As Salena had before me. She'd given her life, her happiness, her entire future, to save our people and the greater world. I would do no less. *"I will pay."*

"I lied," Kiraka mused with a hint of surprise. *"It seems I retain a grain of hope, after all. I find myself hoping I'll see you on the other side of this. I didn't expect to like you."*

If the dragon liked me, I'd hate to see how she behaved toward those she hated.

"What is your name, little changeling?"

"Zynda. I am Zynda."

"I shall remember your name, Zynda, and ask Moranu guide you. You might add your own prayer. You'll want to take the easy path. If you truly want this, don't take it. Choose pain."

"Pain?"

"Yes. More than you think you can endure."

And the dragon opened her mouth, a wash of flame roaring over me. The agony rent me, my skin firing and hair going to ash.

As I died, I sent up a last plea to the goddess of the moon, and the darkness. And regeneration.

～ 6 ～

S OMEONE WAS SCREAMING, but it wasn't me. Someone else was shouting. Also not me.

A dragon roaring. Definitely not me.

But who was I?

I was all burning agony. Fire upon fire. Pain wracked me, and the sense of *not being* became almost worse than even that.

Form. I needed form, but there was none to be had.

I'd had a body once. A human one. The memory of it rippled in the distance, a sweet beacon that glimmered then faded as it receded. Unable to reach it, I cast about, seeking others. All my possible forms offered themselves—the dolphin, the falcon, the great heron, the tiger, the pony, the hummingbird, the snake, the owl, the wolf, the mermaid—and more. Ones I'd attempted and hadn't grasped, or hadn't cared to revisit. Others it had never occurred to me to try.

Desperate, I grabbed for them as they danced past, gazing back at me with my own eyes. Accusing and compassionate at once. Despite their sympathy for my plight, none would stop long enough for me to slide inside their skin.

And it hurt. Oh, it hurt so much.

I couldn't bear to hold on anymore, so I let go.

I began to dissolve—the agony blessedly releasing me from its savage grip—spreading thin, becoming mist. The screams thinned in the distance and I welcomed that surcease, as well.

The quiet, the lack of feeling. All so much better.

After a timeless lapse, doorways appeared, opening into what seemed like long hallways. Each portal offered a fresh form. Human bodies for me. Not the one I'd had, but the seeds of new ones. Beginnings of new life. A fresh start.

Eager, spurred by an odd sense of urgency, I surveyed them. So many options. They beckoned to me, welcoming. I could be anyone. Easiest to simply pick one, then perhaps this prickling need to take action would ease.

"The easy choice," someone said.

Nothing and no one there.

No, that wasn't right. *She* was there. The absence of light. The dark of the moon.

"Goddess?" I asked. *I shall remember your name, Zynda, and ask Moranu guide you.* But I didn't remember who said that or who Zynda was. Or maybe I did, vaguely. I'd been her once.

"I am the dark, the absence that is the beginning. From the richness of this void we are born and grow, waxing again into full brightness, before waning into death. Vanishing, only to begin again."

Those words tugged at a memory, also formless and without substance. It didn't matter. The way lay before me. From the dark and the absence, I would go from this nothing to the fullness of life again.

"The easy path," She repeated. "A right, but also a gift."

I didn't want to listen. I wanted a life again. A body to be mine. My birthright, She'd said as much.

"But for an accident of chance, others will not have that gift."

I hesitated, not wanting to hear, but something in me turning to listen anyway. The moon goddess was there. All around and invisible. In Her formlessness, She was all forms. I caught glimpses of Her, curling horns, a sweep of wings, snaking tail, pumping gills. In Her shifting face, Her eyes alone remained constant, the color of moonlight at full, the dark centers the depthless dark of the new moon.

"Do you want to see?" She asked me, a simple question without judgment or expectation. Up to me to decide.

"No," I said. I didn't want anything but to go on my way, to my fresh start.

"I understand," She replied with gentle compassion. "Go with My blessing, Daughter."

Daughter. That caught me, a fish in a net, the silver cords of it pricking me. "But I *should* look," I said, turning away from the feast of lives.

"There are no 'shoulds.' Only if you want to see. Only if you want to consider a different choice."

Flickers came back to me. Standing before an altar, making a vow, promising to give my life to a different path. I'd believed in those promises, once. Back in the pain. In another life. And yet... it wasn't in me to simply turn away from it.

"I ask to see it, Goddess."

She turned, and I turned with Her, drawn into Her subtle vortex of shifting forms. They played over and through me, eddying currents, different and same, like the spectrum of colors in a rainbow, shimmering from one into the next.

"You may recognize these," She said, showing me an endless array of portals, but with truncated or missing hallways. Already some were misshapen, straining to change and grow, but unable to. "They cannot thrive." Her voice held a universe of sorrow.

"I know." I remembered the grief of it and wanted to reach out to those countless babes and comfort them. The Goddess kept me wrapped in Her embrace.

"It's all right. They're Mine," She murmured through me. "I hold them close to Me for the time they live, and then they go on their way again."

There was one I'd held, in another life, her little tongue licking up my tears.

"I was with you," the Goddess hummed, rocking me, as if I'd been that babe. "And the little one came away with Me."

"Is she here?"

"No." The Goddess sounded pleased. "She has gone on again. Will you, too, go on?" Both the dark and the bright of Her eyes were luminous with remorseless compassion. I didn't want to leave the sanctuary of Her embrace, but I agreed, turning to the array of portals, those young bodies, fresh with potential.

"Not those. You would have to grow up again, and there isn't time for that." She directed my gaze back, along the way I'd come. A glittering trail followed me, full of pain and deteriorating bits of mortality. A broken body lay in a hallway, one that extended forward as with the young bodies, but only partly resolved. Wavering. Dissolving.

There was nothing to that form. A pile of ash and shards of burnt bone.

"How?" I asked.

"You have My gift. Find the shape again."

"Will it hurt?" The agony blared harsh in the distance, coming closer. I winced, though it had nothing to do with light or sound. "Yes," I answered my own question.

"Yes," the goddess said with me, in harmony.

Moranu and I said it together. Though She held me still, the pain of my old body reverberated through me again. Fire. Agony. Death.

"I died," I said, trying to understand.

"Yes and no. My presence was invoked, so I lent your

73

body—already strong with the gift of My blood—more of My strength. That form may yet be reshaped by you. If your will is strong enough."

How?? The question howled through me, the pitiful pile of my remains revolting and terrifying.

"Only you can find the way," Moranu said, insistent, but without reproach. "I shared My gifts with you, but only you can know how you will use them."

"And if I fail?"

"Then you fail. But if you do not go back, then you have already failed. This is your choice."

"Send me back." I said it with resolve, ignoring the brass warnings of suffering to come.

"It doesn't work that way." Moranu swirled around me, then moved back, leaving me uncovered as if I'd lost a warm cloak in winter. An old memory, from many lifetimes. "It's your choice. You go on your own or not."

I was so afraid. But I couldn't let that stop me.

"Will I remember this?" I asked, but She didn't answer. She'd returned to the dark form, hugely present, but unseen. My focus narrowed on that broken pile of abandoned flesh left behind me.

I moved toward it, and it seemed I swam against a strong current. I bent my will to it, trying harder, flying against a headwind. Pushing against my own terror. I needed to get back into my dead—no, dying—body, but I didn't want to. I thought of those suffering souls. It wasn't enough.

Fire and death. Pain. The animal in me clamored to flee, to escape this terrible captivity.

"I'm not strong enough," I confessed. "Will you help me, Moranu?"

"Remember who awaits you," Moranu murmured through

me. "It won't be all pain. There also is joy. There is being loved. I promise you that. There is loving and being loved."

Who? My mother had loved me, but she'd been gone for so long. Anya, yes. My brother Zyr. Oh, and my friends. Jepp. Dafne. Ursula. Marskal. It confused me, that last. Not my friend. But the sensation of his fingers tangled in my hair. *It's dangerous.* I remembered his words and how they'd seemed to say something else.

As if it had anchored and drawn me still, the memory of that touch drew me in and down.

Into seared flesh.

Into unbearable agony.

~ 7 ~

I T TOOK MORE will than I'd ever thought to muster, just to stay in that body. The flesh kicked at me, resisting my efforts to shape it. It felt like those early days of intense study, trying to control a shift and direct it with my conscious will, rather childishly letting whatever form take me with it. That formless time with Moranu had distanced me somehow, too, and I couldn't quite recall how to *make* my body anymore. Hair, nails, limbs, brain. No. Too much.

I billowed out of it, banging against that corridor of time. In the one direction all those memories reeled out. Dancing on the beach. Playing with Anya and Zyr. Holding Anya's baby. Zyr's homecoming. Meeting Andi. Annfwn. The joy of completing a new form. Swimming. Flying. Seizing the Star from the priestess of Deyrr, the taste of Ursula's blood in my mouth, fear in my heart. Nahanau. Marskal feeding me.

That last one was so new. Just a bit down the hall. His fingers, tangled in my mane, in my hair. No reason that it should loom so vividly.

The human body felt too big to wrestle, too much to shape. And there wasn't enough of my former body left to work with. Desperate, losing my grip, I condensed as I tried to hold on. Not to Birth Form—that was beyond me—but to First Form. Almost as natural as Birth Form, and so much easier, so much

76

less of it to wrestle. Small and simple. I curled into it, drawing the meager bits of flesh together. They formed around me. Heart beating. Lungs drawing air. Mind working but quiet. All there.

I hoped.

I'd done my best, given all I had.

Exhausted, I slept.

I WAS CUPPED in a warm embrace, comforting and solid. Moranu's arms? The Goddess held me once again, which meant I'd failed. But no—flesh held me. A strong rough hand. And pain—pain ran through me. Physical trauma wracked me, the nerves singing with it, heart struggling to pump blood through my small body. Too fast. Too much obstruction in the blood vessels, the tissues not healed or made well enough.

And weakness. I couldn't move, even to lift my head or open my eyes.

Someone spoke to me, sweetness flowing down my throat. That helped. Energy sang into my blood, good and strong. I shifted. Not to a new form, but again into a solider First Form.

Better. Less pain. Healthier body. Blood flowing. Feathers growing.

Blessed relief. I let go, drifting away again.

BRIGHT FLOWERS CATCH my eye. *Want.* I flutter, trying to reach them.

"Soon. Not yet," a warm voice soothes. "Drink this, Zynda."

Zynda. I'd been that name. Once upon a time. I drink the sweetness, cuddle into the warmth. Bright flowers. *Want.*

"She keeps trying to fly to the blossoms."

"Can she?"

"I don't know. She has all her feathers, but I don't know if she can fly."

"We don't know if *she* is even in there anymore."

Voices voices voices.

Bright flowers. *Want.*

"Here, give her this."

Bright flowers. I look. Bright bright bright. No nectar. My beak finds nothing. Must fly! Can't. Try harder. *Must fly.*

"Just let her go."

"What if she falls?"

"Then she falls. She'll burst her heart from the stress if you keep restraining her."

Freedom! Wings stretch and buzz. Bright flowers. Want. Yes.

Full at last, I go back to my nest. Warm. Safe.

"WE'LL HAVE TO face that she may never shift out of this form again."

"How can you be so callous?"

"I'm being realistic. We have no idea how to help her. Dafne refuses to speak to Kiraka—"

"Absolutely."

"—even if Nakoa would allow it, so—"

"It's my choice, not his."

"*So*, the only people who might help her are in Annfwn. We have to take her there. As soon as possible. Tomorrow."

Annfwn. That name is like bright flowers. Like sunshine. Like home. *Want.*

"She's awake."

Faces. Those faces that give me the sweet. Something more bothers me. A greater recognition. I need. Reach. Stretch the wings. I fly, but I hadn't always flown.

"Zynda," someone says, insistent, gentle. Drawn, I land on the finger.

"She responded to her name."

"Instinct. She's going for the food."

"You don't know that."

"I know she's implied that a shapeshifter stuck in animal form for very long loses her human ability for higher thought."

"Implied isn't—"

"It makes sense."

"*None* of this makes sense!"

"Enough. Arguing with each other solves nothing."

Quiet. A bright bowl. Delicious sweetness to sip. The words around me mean something something something. I almost understand.

"She's so beautiful."

"Yes. I've seen this form before. Back at Ordnung."

"Same coloration, too, so maybe it's a familiar form, one she knows well. Maybe that's a good sign."

"How long do hummingbirds live?"

Quiet. Quiet. Quiet.

SUN IS RISING. Time to fly! Bright flowers. Sweet. Good.

Replete, I sit to rest. Someone is there. The bringer of the bright bowl and the sweet. Not moving though. There is a thing that needs doing. More flowers? No—too full. What then?

Niggle niggle. I am restless.

Who am I?

I am... supposed to be and do and... something.

I fly down to the someone. I know this someone. More than just the bringer of the bright bowl. More more more. Eyes open and I fly up. Not away. Hovering. Watching. Maybe there is the more here.

"Zynda."

It means something, this sound. I fly closer.

"Zynda. You have to come back now. Shift back to human. We need you. I need you."

A finger, so I light on it. It's like a warm branch. Safe. Feeder of food.

"Please shift back. I love you. I never said, because you never even saw me and it makes no sense, not even to me. Especially not to me. So I won't bother you with it. But you need to come back to us. You are loved."

There is being loved.

The many-faced goddess with eyes of moonlight and darkness. I don't know how to want it, but the want is there, all around me. Pulling at me. Fingers tangled in my hair.

The niggling niggles. Something to do. To be.

I reach. Reach through. It hurts and I pull back.

But the wanting is stronger.

Zynda.

There is being loved.

The pain pulls me apart. I shatter. I'm dying. I'm born.

"Zynda! Thank the Three. Zynda, can you hear me? Wake up. Look at me."

I open my eyes. The light is too bright. My wings are broken. I cannot fly.

I am also held, hands running over me. Remember this. Skin on skin. A scent I know. A light slap on my face, and it hurts, oh, it hurts, my skin like new born. I whimper and he shushes me. Comforts me. Safe.

"It's all right. You're all right. You're alive. You're you again. Zynda. My Zynda."

The chanted words anchor and comfort me. Safe. Safe but wingless.

"Zynda? Can you talk. Are you in there? Say something. Anything."

Brown eyes. Intent and serious. I know this man.

"It's dangerous," I say.

I fall asleep to the sound of his ragged laughter.

I AWOKE TO the sound of the sea and sun on my face. Sheets against my skin. A vase of bright flowers on the table beside the bed. Smelling so sweet, looking so tempting. I lifted a hand to touch one. Too far.

"Here." Someone lifted the flower and put it in my hand, wrapping my fingers around it. So fragrant. And bright. I licked it, not sure why.

"Not that. Have this." An arm behind me and then something against my mouth. Water, cool and fresh ran down my throat. I discarded the blossom, seizing the glass. My clumsy hands bobbled it, splashing me, but the woman put her hand over mine, steadying me so I could drink it down. I was parched. Mutely I held out the empty glass and the lovely woman signaled, another someone pouring more water into the glass. I drank it, too, and the woman laid her fingers against my wrist. "Careful. Go slow. Much sick."

My mind felt sluggish, not quite understanding her words. "I am sick?" I asked her.

She pursed her lips and shook her head. "Common tongue, please. Remember that language, Zynda?"

Zynda. Me. I'd spoken in Tala and she was... Inoa. Nakoa's sister. On Nahanau. And I had... I dropped the glass, water splashing across the bed, the glass tumbling to the floor and shattering. Pain. I'd shattered, too.

Ladies were speaking to me, words like Tala and not, someone holding my wrists. Then hard arms wrapping around me. "Hush, Zynda, shh. You're all right. You're safe."

"Safe?" I repeated the word, tasting it on my tongue. So harsh and strange. The Tala word came to my mind and I said that instead. Better.

"Safe," Marskal echoed, holding me, stroking my back.

Marskal? Why was he here? I pushed at him and he let me go, turning his face away, lines carving around his mouth, lips fluttering before he compressed them. He dashed the heel of his hand against his face.

"When did she wake up?" he was asking. He spoke faster than Inoa, and she scowled at him.

"Told you I'd send a girl when she awoke. I just sent, yes?"

"Marskal?" I looked at him, Inoa, and a cluster of Nahanaun

ladies—one sweeping up the broken glass—then around the room. Netting hung over the windows, tied down all around, puffing slightly in the breeze off the ocean.

"Yes." He smiled at me, an odd look on his face, lightly stroking hands up and down my arms. I flinched and he lightened the touch even more. "Sorry. Your skin is still so sensitive. I'm sorry I wasn't here when you woke up. I only laid down for a bit…" He trailed off, the strange smile dimming. He looked terrible, with deep circles dark under his eyes, his color sallow and those lines around his mouth carved in deeper than before, his jaw sharp, face gaunt.

"Why are you here at all?" I wondered, not understanding, and he dropped his hands, then stood, stiff and awkward.

"I—," he began. "I, ah—"

"Zynda!" Dafne burst through the doors, a whirlwind of copper hair and tears. She flung herself at me, but Marskal caught her.

"Careful, Your Highness. She's tender yet."

Ursula strode in on Dafne's heels, her consort Harlan behind her. The names came easier now. My cousin looked strained, too, though not as bad as Marskal. What in the Three had happened? I tried to think, mushy as my brain felt. Pain. No, don't go there. My eyes kept going to the flower lying beside me. So bright. *Want.* I picked it up, then couldn't remember why I'd wanted to.

"Zynda." Someone clicked fingers in front of my eyes. Dafne, her brow crinkled. "Can you hear me? Do we know if her mind is all there?"

"How many fingers am I holding up?" Ursula asked, holding up three.

"She doesn't have a concussion," Dafne snapped.

"It's a test for brain damage," Ursula shot back in the same tone. Marskal, grave and silent, simply watched me. He looked dead on his feet, swaying slightly.

"If I may?" Harlan rumbled, his words mild but the question cutting through. Dafne moved away and the big Dasnarian sat next to me, the bed sinking under his weight. His pale gray eyes stared seriously into mine. "Welcome back to us, Zynda."

"Thank you, Harlan," I replied in the same tone, though I couldn't match the deep baritone. Why that made me want to laugh, I didn't know. But it felt good to want to.

He lifted a finger to my chin, touching it lightly, then turning my head side to side. I kept my eyes on him. He asked me to stick out my tongue, and—after a moment to remember how—I did, curling and wiggling it as he instructed. I pressed back on the palms he held up, curling my fingers to tug back, repeating similar movements when he turned back the light blanket to do the same with my feet. Someone had put a white silk bed gown on me and I plucked at the soft texture in wonder.

"What do you remember, Zynda?" Harlan asked.

Remember? For some reason an image of a long hallway came to mind, stretching forward and back, crowded with memories in both directions.

"She gets—" Marskal started to say, stepping forward, then stopping when Harlan held up a finger. Ursula put a hand on his shoulder, drawing him back and speaking quietly into his ear. He shrugged her off, irritably, and that struck me as being as strange as his smile before, though I had no reason to think so.

"Zynda?" Harlan called me back to the question, gentle and insistent. He took my hand, massaging my finger bones, then pressing into my palms, my wrist bones. "It's a beautiful day," he said conversationally.

"Yes," I replied, though it was hard to tell, with the windows screened. I'd like to be outside. Flying in the blue sky.

"Do you know where you are?"

He possessed healing skills. I remembered that suddenly, like a bubble popping. Not magical, but for warriors, for helping the wounded. I'd been wounded in battle. Whatever he was doing helped center me. Grounded me in my body. My human body, which had... I gasped, the room spinning. Harlan held firm.

"Steady," he said in exactly that way. "You are Zynda, a Tala woman. You are in a human body and it is healthy and whole. You are here with people who love you and you are safe."

Safe. I looked to Marskal. His mouth was set in a fierce line, but he nodded at me.

"How long was I a hummingbird?" I asked.

Ursula's set grimace broke and she rubbed a hand over her face. Dafne began weeping silent tears, which she pushed away impatiently. "Three days," she said.

"Nearly four," Marskal corrected.

Too long. Much too long. And I'd eaten for days in that form. I shouldn't have returned from that.

They all stared at me, expressions stricken, except for Harlan who still worked his subtle massage, now on my other hand. I realized I'd spoken that last aloud.

"You did return," Marskal said, his sharp jaw set in a stubborn line. "And you're fine."

Was I? "I feel very strange."

Dafne coughed out a laugh that was mostly a sob. "You look amazing for someone who was reduced to a pile of ash."

My head throbbed suddenly at the memory and I put a hand to my temple. Harlan followed the gesture, stroking finger pads into the spot that hurt, then over my jaw, behind my ears, and over my scalp to the back of my neck. Working. Spreading ease and surcease. So much gentleness in such a big man. No wonder Ursula loved him so.

There is also being loved.

Inexplicably, that made my throat tighten. I knew with deep certainty that Moranu had spoken those words to me. I'd come back for that. Had somehow scraped together enough of the shards of my body to shapeshift it into the body of a hummingbird.

I shuddered and Harlan braced the back of my neck with one hand, the other against my forehead. It felt ridiculously good.

"I don't know much about shapeshifters," Harlan continued, moving his hands to press thumbs into points at my collar bone, "but I understand human bodies, at least. You are like a warrior who's been so badly wounded that she's no longer a perfect fit in her skin."

For some reason that analogy made me smile. Which felt good, too. I liked to smile, and to laugh. That was part of me.

"This will help," he continued. "Then rest. Trust yourself to find the fit again."

We were quiet for a bit while he worked. Marskal leaned against a window frame, his back tense as he gazed out at the sea through the tacked-down curtains.

"Why are the curtains drawn and tied down?"

"We couldn't risk having you fly out, lest we lose you forever," Marskal explained, his voice oddly strained.

That made sense. But I thought my skin might never fit again. I might have lost my self anyway.

~ 8 ~

A S RECOMMENDED, I rested for a while, but I grew restless. Even after I'd persuaded Inoa's ladies that I was no longer a flight risk and that I wanted the curtains removed, I couldn't bear the trapped feeling. They'd all left me alone to sleep, so it was relatively easy to make my escape.

I reached for a bird form, ready to fly out the window. Some time in the clear sky, stretching my wings, would help clear the muddiness in my mind. When I came back to human, my body would feel right to me again.

I reached—and slammed into a wall headfirst. Pain radiated through every nerve, oozing out my pores in a cold, stinking sweat. I lay there, dazed, staring at the blue sky that mocked me through the open window. I'd never been unable to shift. Except in that nightmarish haze of black and red agony, when I'd tried over and over to find a form again and failed.

It made my stomach turn to remember it, intensifying my need to flee.

Deeply unsettled, I escaped the confines of the palace on foot to walk on the beach. I needed to make a plan, to come to terms with what had happened, but I had trouble concentrating. The flowers distracted me with their bright colors, and the sky beckoned. The worst of my fears hovered all around me—that I'd never shed the hummingbird brain.

Though the weakness and clumsiness plagued me, I determinedly continued down the beach. The more I moved in this body—my body, I really needed to think of it that way—the more I'd settle into it. Then I'd be ready to shift again. It had just been too soon, for whatever reason. Contemplating anything else made me feel ill.

"Should you be walking so far?"

Marskal paced beside me, and I glanced at him, surprised to find myself grateful for his presence.

"I can walk. There's nothing wrong with me physically."

He nodded, clearly humoring me, not in agreement. He also kept walking with me, not seeming to mind his boots sinking into the soft sand while I waded ankle-deep in gentle, cooling waves. If I'd been myself, I would have shifted into a fish or a dolphin, to better enjoy the water, and to let my worries drift. But I didn't dare try that again yet. Instead, I turned my feet and determinedly continued down the beach on foot.

What if I'd lost the ability forever? Or what if I pushed past that astonishing pain and bungled it, a horrifying death. I'd seen a Tala woman suicide that way to avoid interrogation. Though she'd been an enemy and my animal selves hadn't mourned her death a moment, the grim memory stuck with all of us who witnessed it. Especially the shapeshifters.

I'd have to be able to shift again. Not only because that was who I was, but to take Final Form. Surely I'd know when I'd be ready to shift again. If only I could ask the Shaman. Or my brother Zyr, who taught the children, and had a talent for the difficult cases. I felt like that again, a youngling of few years—except that I'd never felt anything like that pain or terror in trying to shift.

"I've never seen anyone manage to make a stroll on the beach feel like a forced march," Marskal observed.

Had I felt grateful for his presence? Now I only wanted to be left alone in my misery.

"Why are you here?" I hadn't meant the question to sound so harsh, but he didn't seem to note it.

Instead, he squinted at the sky, contemplating. "A question for the ages. Why are any of us here?"

Great. Now he was a philosopher. I stopped and waded into the water again, though I couldn't go far enough to escape him. The sea cooled and tempted me, my borrowed Nahanaun shift floating up to swirl around me. If only I could. Fish didn't have conversations.

"You know that's not what I meant," I finally said, when it became clear he wouldn't respond further.

"Do I?" He pursed his lips, then toed off his boots. "I'd think someone who just had a near-death experience would be interested in such questions."

I wasn't discussing that. "Go back and tell Ursula I don't need a thriced babysitter."

He chuckled, bending over to roll up the cuffs of his pants to the knee, revealing strong calves, lightly furred with brown hair. His bare feet were surprisingly long, even graceful. Keeping on his sword, he waded in. "Not to insult your considerable skills of intimidation, but I'm more afraid of Her Majesty than I am of you."

Once I would have shifted into a tiger and quickly changed his mind. Instead I dug my toes into the sand. My own feet looked pale in the water, like something that didn't quite belong to me.

"Zynda."

I glanced at Marskal, who had a strange expression on his face. He stood quite close, near enough to reach out and pick up a long strand of my hair, rubbing it between his fingers. It triggered a sense of nostalgia in me, that kind where you long for something you never had.

"Zynda." Marskal studied the hair, then my face, searching for something. "Are you all right?"

He posed the question so seriously, with such a wealth of unspoken meaning behind it, that I couldn't brush him off. I wanted to lean on him, have him tell me that everything would be fine, that I would be fine. But he was a mossback who could never understand. Still...

"I don't know," I told him honestly, surprising myself. "I don't feel all right."

He dipped his chin, acknowledging that as some kind of profound truth. "Maybe that's not a bad thing."

Now he surprised me. "What do you mean?"

He gazed back at me, intent, a world of thoughts behind his careful brown eyes. "You survived a terrible event. It's not surprising that you're having to adjust to it." He tore his gaze from mine, instead winding the lock of my hair around his finger. "You've lost your tan, you know. You should be careful in the sun."

I resisted looking at my arm. That hadn't occurred to me, but I didn't want him to know that. "I'm careful."

"You should give yourself time to recover."

My habitual response rose in my throat, to tell him I didn't need time to recover. I'd never been seriously ill, never had an injury shapeshifting couldn't heal. "I don't think I know how to do that."

He studied me. "You don't feel like yourself."

I didn't know how he knew that, but I nodded, my throat too tight for words.

He gave my hair a little tug, a sad cant to his mouth. "Want to hear a story?"

"A story?"

"Yes, come into the shade and I'll tell you. It might help."

Bemused, I let him lead me out of the water and into the deep shade of a graceful tree with fernlike fronds that draped nearly to the sand, bright with slender green leaves and tiny white blossoms. It felt surprisingly good to sit, and it bothered me not to know that I'd needed to. Marskal stretched out his long legs, leaned back on his elbows, and gazed out at the water.

"Long ago, before the Great War, before the twelve kingdoms found a common tongue, there lived a mighty warrior called Morvared. He lived a good life, but when war came to his kingdom, he went to battle and fought bravely."

"As all good warriors do," I put in, and Marskal flicked a glance at me, amused but continuing with the thread of the story.

"Of course. But on this day, Morvared took a blow from the enemy that knocked him from his horse. He lay, bleeding, amidst a pile of bodies while the fight moved on, certain that he'd met his death, that help would never come to him in time. He recalled leaving his body and seeing the battle as if from a high vantage. He knew he was dying, but he had family he longed for, a sweet wife who awaited his return and would be crushed by his death, and children—children who wouldn't fare so well without his protection and care.

"So he resolved to get back to his body, to live if he could manage it. He searched and found it, wedging himself back in, willing the wounded body to continue to live. He lay there for hours, but was eventually found, and nursed back to health."

I shifted, uncomfortable with the parallels and Marskal gave me a concerned look. "And then?" I prompted, uncomfortable, too, with that concern.

"He returned to his wife and children, but they weren't as he remembered them. They, in turn, found him terribly changed. Though he regained his strength enough to protect and care for his family, the love he'd once felt for them seemed to have died on that battlefield."

"Perhaps he didn't truly love his wife. The Tala have such tales, too, of those who face life-changing events and discover the relationships before to be like those of the very young— formed on shallow things and no longer relevant to their changed selves."

Marskal considered that, his gaze searching my face for something. "That could be the case," he agreed, "though that's not how this legend goes. Morvared grew restless and unhappy, unable to shake the feeling that he missed his wife and children, worrying for them, though they were right in front of him. He took on riskier jobs, invested in business ventures, thinking that if he amassed enough wealth, the feeling that he'd failed them, that he couldn't reach or protect them, would eventually ease."

An unsettled feeling grew in my heart. "And did it?"

"One day, he rode in a part of the realm that seemed oddly familiar to him, though his men assured him he'd never been there. He passed a small estate, then turned back, driven by an urge to investigate. The place had fallen into disrepair, but it nevertheless seemed beautiful to him. It seemed that, everywhere he looked, he could see the potential for it to be so much more. It felt like coming home to a place he'd been seeking all this time. He rode with his men up to the house, and a young woman with two children came out. They were too thin, in ill health, and clearly afraid of the men. The boy, though, carried a sword he could barely lift, and stood before his sisters, bravely defending them."

"Tell me Morvared didn't kill them."

Marskal chuckled. "You have a soft heart guarded by those

fierce claws. No—the warrior recognized the sword. It was his own, the one he'd died holding on the battlefield."

It twisted my brain too much. Part of me, however, understood and trembled. "What does that mean?"

"Morvared had been at that battle, fought in it, and died, just as he'd thought. But when he'd fought his way back to his body, he found someone else's. Another warrior whose spirit had fled following a near-mortal wound. He'd taken over Morvared's body and his life, but the man he'd been, his own body, had truly died in that battle. That body had long-since been buried, his sword sent home to his family."

"And so he hadn't returned to his family at all," I whispered. "He'd gone and saved someone else's while his own..."

"Fell apart, as he'd feared. His wife had died of heartbreak, and his oldest daughter had struggled to keep the estate going, with his young son laboring to learn to lift his dead father's sword."

"Marskal. This is a terrible story!"

He gave me a somber look, sitting up, then tucking a lock of hair behind my ear. "I didn't mean to distress you."

Something of the tenderness in the gesture stopped my breath. "Tell me he saved them."

"He did. He purchased the estate and took the children into his household. The son grew up to be a great warrior in his own right, which is another tale." He fell silent, tearing his gaze from mine and looking out at the sea again.

"And Morvared?" I prompted.

"What about him?"

"Did he find happiness—did the feeling of seeking ease?"

"Ah. Hmm." Marskal rubbed a hand over his face.

Figured. "Just tell me."

"After he ensured the children were all well, and his former

estate restored to good working order, he killed himself."
Marskal spoke the words slowly, as if regretting having to say
so." Then he turned his head, staring at me intently, mouth
firmed. "That's not why I wanted to tell you this story. Morvared
felt that his life had been a borrowed one, that he'd been meant
to die on that battlefield. So he put both families in order, then
went to the death he decided was overdue. But it doesn't have to
be that way for you. Though you might feel something of the
same way, this is your body. You are you, however altered."

"I died up there," I said, very quietly. It felt like confessing a
shameful secret.

"I know," he said, equally quiet. "I was there."

"Don't tell the others."

He hesitated, then nodded reluctantly. "I don't see how it's
relevant strategically anyway. You're safe now. I hope you
learned what you needed to from the dragon."

"I didn't," I replied. "I have to go back." Perhaps this would
be enough, Kiraka's final test. I'd died and managed to survive.
She said she'd hoped I would, didn't she? Dread at the thought
of facing her again made me feel ill. But I'd made the choice. I'd
come back to see my mission through. Moranu wouldn't have
helped me only to deny me shapeshifting. The ability would
come back and I'd take Final Form as even the goddess
intended.

Marskal was staring at me, jaw so clenched the muscles there
rippled and his throat worked with the words he fought. "You
will not."

"You are not my keeper!" I fired back. Anger felt much
better than terror. "I'm going and you can't stop me."

"Understood." He released a breath. "If that's how it has to
be, then that's how it is. But I'm by your side for all of it. No
debating or arguing."

"Excuse me?"

"You heard me."

"I heard, but I must have missed the part where we were bargaining."

He cracked a slight smile. "That sounds more like your usual self. Let me lay out the terms then. You agree to cheerfully suffer my company and protection, and in return I won't tell Her Majesty how tenuous your health is."

"I never said that."

"Not in so many words, but you and I both know it's true."

I regretted that lapse, confiding in him. Why had I? "I'll deny it."

"You died, Zynda!" Marskal didn't raise his voice, but the words came out with the force of an accusation, harsh with anguish. "I stood on the far side of that thrice-cursed meadow and watched, helpless, as that dragon burned you to ash. Don't ask me to go through that again."

"I never asked you to go through any of it!" I flung back at him. "You weren't even supposed to be there."

He set his lean jaw, stubborn. "Yes, I was. And if you insist on going, I won't stay behind."

I threw up my hands. "If you'd been beside me, you would have died. And *you* can't shapeshift to save yourself."

"Is that what it comes down to?"

"What?" I'd lost the thread of the argument. *Hummingbird brain.*

"I'm only a mossback. I've heard you say that, and I don't miss your meaning—or the implicit condescension. Basically I'm a rock to you, so inert that plants grow on me. You don't even see me as a man. I might as well be dirt."

I swallowed back asking "what?" again, though it perfectly fit my stunned confusion. I had no idea how we'd reached this point. Finally my feeble thought process grabbed onto one piece of that. "I don't think you're dirt, Marskal."

He stared at me, as if equally confounded. With a hoarse, unamused laugh, he scrubbed his hands over his face, then ran them over his scalp. "I'm exhausted and have no idea if I've won the argument or lost it."

He did look terrible. Haggard. Hummingbird memories nudged my brain, then flicked away again. Surely he hadn't stayed awake, tending me all those days. Even Ursula wouldn't command so much. But his ragged state tugged at my sympathy. I reached out and laid a hand on his cheek, thick with stubble. He stilled, like a mouse when I flew over in owl form.

"I don't even know what we're arguing about, much less who's won or lost," I said, then smiled, not at all sure what was funny. "You need to rest."

Slowly, as if afraid of startling me, he put his hand over mine. It felt oddly familiar, comforting. Safe. "I will if you will."

Uncomfortable with the strange intimacy, I dropped my hand. He let it go, but not without brushing his fingers over my skin in a way that sent a shiver through me. "I'm not sure I can," I told him. I'd slept for days.

"Nakoa is holding a formal dinner tonight. That's what I came to tell you. The topic of Kiraka and the safety of the island will be discussed. If you want to confront the dragon again," he focused over my shoulder, that long-distance stare, "then you'll have to be in top form, to convince him."

I would see Kiraka again whether Nakoa allowed it or not, but best not to jeopardize my cousin's peace. "All right." To my surprise, a yawn overtook me. Perhaps I could nap. "We can go back."

Marskal laughed softly, shaking his head. I slanted a questioning look at him.

"I'm a doomed man," he explained. "Whether you argue with me or when you're unexpectedly docile, I have no idea what you're thinking."

I gave him a radiant smile, though it felt like a shadow of my old one. "I *am* Tala."

He muttered something under his breath I didn't catch.

"What was that?"

"Nothing I care to repeat. We don't have to go back to the palace yet, you know."

"What do you mean?"

"To rest. I know you don't want to be inside again so soon."

And he claimed he didn't know what I was thinking. "You're willing to sleep outside?"

He raised his brows at me. "I'm a soldier, as you've pointed out. I've probably slept more nights outside than in, at least in the last twenty-five years."

"All right. Here—in the shade?" Funny that I felt hesitant. This negotiating was new to me.

"Perfect." He lay back, his body immediately relaxed, a groan sighing out of him, but he kept one eye cracked, fixed on me. He held out a hand, wiggling his fingers.

I frowned at it. "What am I meant to do?"

"Lie down and take my hand."

"Why?" But I did as he bade me, lying back and lacing my fingers with his. That felt good, too. Skin on skin. His hand warm and steady, like his presence.

"So I'll wake up if you move." He squeezed my hand gently and closed his eyes.

"You don't trust me," I said softly. He'd gone so still he might already be asleep. But his lips curved in a slight smile.

"That's not the reason, quicksilver girl."

~ 9 ~

INOA'S LADIES ARRIVED in full force to bathe and dress me for my formal appearance. Fortunately Marskal conceded to modesty—of which I had little, but I was willing to play on his scruples—and let me out of his sight long enough to tend to his own hygiene.

I had fallen asleep, deep and dreamless, and had awakened with my hand still in Marskal's. A strange emotion rolled through me—along with a long-ago memory of sleeping with my siblings, curled together like puppies. Safe and warm. How odd to feel that again, especially now. His eyes flicked open the moment I turned my head to look at him, and he'd assessed the light, sat up and pronounced that we should get back to the palace to clean up. No moment of sleepiness. No hesitation in pulling me to my feet and putting us on task. The man confounded me.

It felt good to get clean, though. The ladies chatted quietly to each other in Nahanaun, which let me ignore their conversation. I'd never been tended to much in my life—not a Tala custom, so much—but in my heart of hearts I enjoyed the pampering. They washed my hair with gentle thoroughness, bathing and oiling my skin with tender care.

Because they'd been so kind, I let them braid my hair into one of their intricate styles, and apply their makeup. Apparently none of my clothes met their approval, for they presented me with a new gown. Made of deep blue silk that hung off the shoulders with fine silver chains, the loose drape came close to my usual style. Not so much the middle part. After a swath that covered my breasts, more silver chains held up the skirt, skimming low on my hips and falling in angular panels that parted around my legs as I moved.

In the mirror they wheeled in—from Dafne's rooms, I was certain—I examined myself. My skin gleamed pale. Some of that was in contrast to the intense blue, dark as the sapphire depths of the sea. But Marskal was right that I'd lost my tan. My belly showed white as the cliffs of Annfwn, while my shoulders and cheeks glowed pink from the sun.

The ladies added silver jewelry—bands for my upper arms in the shape of hummingbirds, which wrapped around to dip slim beaks into stylized flowers tucked into their tails, and a similar torque around my neck. I watched their faces for signs of irony, but they seemed reverent. More small silver hummingbirds decorated my braids, and with a pang I realized my usual jeweled pin had been lost to dragon breath. It had been a gift from my mother, and the first *thing* I'd learned to take with me when I shifted—and bring back successfully. Perhaps it still existed out there somewhere, wherever my other forms lived, and when I shifted again and came back to human, I'd have it again. I had no idea how else to retrieve it.

Too much there to contemplate.

Marskal arrived, dressed in the formal uniform of Ursula's elite guard. I'd seen him dressed so for court at Ordnung once or twice, but had never paid attention. The Hawks had adopted Ursula's sigil as high queen, a gold and silver hawk stooping on a field of ruby red, a sun and crescent moon on either side, Danu's star at the peak. He'd shaved clean and trimmed his already too-short hair. Perhaps I could convince him to grow it long, though I didn't know where that impulse came from. I had no business wishing anything about him. Now that I'd survived Kiraka's test, I would almost certainly become the dragon. No sense reneging on my resolution to eschew lovers now.

Though, for the first time in a long time, I regretted it. I had a need to be petted. And I'd felt good waking up beside him. Not so alone. But I would be alone. I needed to learn to embrace that.

Marskal clicked his heels together in the glossy black boots, and put his fist over his heart in the Hawks' style, bowing low. "I stand ready to escort you, Lady Zynda."

I didn't bother to correct him that time, instead taking the arm he offered. I was learning to save my arguments with him. "Did you pack a formal uniform and fancy boots, to drag all over the Nahanaun archipelago, just in case?"

He slid me a look, then returned to scanning the shadows. "I accompanied my queen on a mission that could require war or diplomacy. I came prepared for both, of course."

"Of course," I agreed with a smile.

We moved through the open hallways, the evening breeze bringing the scent of sea, night-blooming jasmine, and hints of the feast to come. His boots made a light clicking on the wood, while my bare feet made no sound.

He cleared his throat. "You look very beautiful tonight."

Surprised at the curl of pleasure at the compliment, I plucked at the skirt with my free hand. "Not my idea."

"I wondered if the hummingbird jewelry had been yours. You could remove it and I'll keep it for you, if it makes you uncomfortable."

I blinked at the sting of tears. How fragile I'd become. How strange that this moss—this man saw it in my heart. "It's all right. That's my First Form, so I have affection for it beyond... recent events."

"What does that mean—First Form?"

And how glib with Tala secrets I'd become. Still, I'd already said it and I found myself unwilling to shut the door I'd opened. "All shapeshifters have a First Form, the one we intuitively take on the first time we shift. For most shapeshifters, it's also their only form."

"Because it's your favorite?"

"It's difficult to say. Probably not, because the first shift usually happens very young, even in the cradle, and infants are unlikely to have seen the animal they shift into, much less have formed a favorite."

He nodded. "That explains why Willy and Nilly took early forms that they couldn't have seen."

"Willy and Nilly?" I searched my brain, appalled at the possible memory loss.

"Apologies." He broke his vigilance a moment to give me an abashed smile. "Ash calls Astar and Stella that, because they're forever dashing about and shapeshifting willy-nilly."

I laughed at the image. Ami's shapeshifter toddlers were running merry rings around them. "I forgot you would have spent time around shapeshifter children. They can be a handful."

The hall opened onto the grand esplanade, incandescent with torches and teeming with people. The previous formal dinner we'd attended on Nahanau had been a tense and unhappy occasion, the night before we were forced to abandon Dafne to Nakoa's doubtful intentions. I'd been especially torn, wanting to stay near the dragon but unable to refuse Dafne's implicit plea— and Jepp's explicit demands—that I be the one to fetch help. Just like that night, music played and dancers entertained. Dafne, arrayed in dazzling copper and decked in dragon jewelry, sat next to Nakoa on a living throne the twin of his. The vines trained into chair shape bloomed with blossoms of all colors.

Nakoa wore similar colors and his habitual frown. A large and imposing man covered in tattoos that mimicked dragon scales, he sported wildly curling hair that fell to his shoulders, streaked with white, reminiscent of lighting racing through black thunderclouds. His dark eyes fixed on me, assessing with a keen intelligence that reminded me uncannily of Kiraka. We'd somewhat cavalierly dubbed him the dragon king when we'd first arrived on his island. In retrospect, the joke had been entirely too prescient.

"Cold?" Marskal asked, and I darted him a wry look.

"In this heat with torches everywhere, I don't see how that would be possible."

"You shivered. And you've been… unwell."

That understatement made me laugh, catching Dafne's attention. She smiled at me, clearly happy to see me on my feet and more my usual self. On her other side, seated on a throne of equal size, though less elaborate, Ursula looked over, also. She and Marskal exchanged some set of signals I'd never quite deciphered. Hopefully the message had to do with security and not me.

She had a more careworn, tight expression. Though she'd left King Groningen in charge back at Ordnung, she had a massive and varied realm to govern. Between that—and the ongoing issues and conflicts that entailed—and her recent, near-mortal collision with the High Priestess of *Deyrr*, she carried a heavy burden. No wonder Harlan wanted to get her home again. Standing next to her chair and just behind, Harlan kept an eye on her and all comers. Ever vigilant.

Speaking of, Marskal led me to my seat at a table near the royal dais. He handed me into the chair, and I let him, since it was easier than arguing that I was perfectly capable of bending my knees. However, when he remained standing behind my chair and signaled a server to bring me food, I drew the line.

"The rest of the Hawks are sitting over there." I pointed to the next table over, where several of his cohorts looked to be enjoying the wine and telling stories.

"I'm fine here."

"You'd be a few paces away."

"I thought we were done arguing about this."

So did I. "I'm not a queen to have a guard standing at hand. At least sit."

"As my lady commands." He sounded wryly amused, though why my irritable poking at him should do that, I didn't know. Taking the seat beside me, he still solicitously passed me every dish, holding it for me and extolling its charms, as if I were a youngling needing enticement to eat. In truth the food all seemed wrong. Too dense, too rich. The bright flowers, redolent of nectar, kept catching my eye. With his newly acquired knack, Marskal seemed to see it in me. "You need to eat, Zynda," he murmured when I poked at a piece of meat. "You're much thinner now."

I'd made an entire body out of ash—what miracles did they expect? Though shapeshifting obviously wasn't a direct process, with equal mass converting to the same, I still hadn't had much strength to draw on. I choked back the words, though, grimly forcing myself to eat, however much my gut roiled.

"Here." Marskal took my plate away and set something else in its place. A bowl of honey, with fruit and slices of fresh bread. I stared at the change, bemused. He tore off a piece of bread, dipped it in the honey and held it out to me.

I met his determined gaze. "Will you make chirping noises so I can pretend I'm a baby bird in the nest needing to be fed?"

He didn't crack a smile. "With my nephews and nieces, we play hungry horsey and fork-loads of hay. Whatever metaphor gets it done."

That tickled my humor enough, the image of the weathered warrior pretending to fork up hay for a recalcitrant child—along with the surprising warmth at his thoughtfulness in figuring out that the honey would be more appealing to the hummingbird still in me—that I opened my mouth, challenging him to finish out his promise. His brown eyes deepened in color, intent as Nakoa's ever could be, and with infinite care, Marskal placed the honey-soaked bread on my tongue. I closed my lips over his fingers as he withdrew, holding his gaze. A high flush touched his tanned cheekbones and his hand hovered there, as if he'd forgotten what he was doing.

"Delicious," I said, unable to resist teasing him further. I'm not often a flirt. Especially not since I'd given up lovers, and even before that I'd been nothing like my brother, Zyr, who is both incorrigible and irresistible. But something about the lovely night and the party brought it out in me. Torchlight, flowers, and music. It reminded me of home. I'd escaped death and I hadn't had a lover in forever. For very good reasons, but they seemed less important now. Perhaps I should give this stalwart moss-back a try.

"More," I suggested.

Marskal's eyes narrowed, going suspicious. He reached for the finger bowl, briefly washed his hands and attacked his own plate. "I think you can handle the rest yourself, baby bird."

"Let's dance."

He gave me a surprised look, glancing at the open-air esplanade, where dancers—professional and otherwise—leapt and swirled with the music. "I don't dance."

"How disappointingly mossback of you."

His jaw tightened. "Fine. Eat everything on your plate and I'll dance with you."

"Is this another gambit you use with your nieces and nephews?"

Unexpectedly, his serious face cracked into a full grin. "Absolutely."

I found myself grinning back, delighted with this playful side of my serious soldier. "Deal." Applying myself to the fruit, bread and honey—and the goblet of fruit juice Marskal set beside my plate with a brow raised, daring me to challenge the addition—I found that sort of thing did go down easier than the meat. We sat with a group of Nahanaun nobles, all who conversed in their native tongue, leaving us out, which suited me fine.

"There." I showed Marskal my clean plate. "Now you have to—"

A gong rung, and the musicians went silent. Nakoa rose to his feet, offering a hand to Dafne to bring her up beside him. A petite woman regardless, the top of her head barely reached the level of his dark nipples. He put a protective arm around her and she looked up with a smile full of love. For a moment, his face softened, gazing down on her with a reverent joy that made my heart catch. *There is also being loved.*

"Saved by the gong," Marskal wryly observed, turning in his seat.

"I wonder how they manage to have sex," I whispered to him, needing to taunt him just a bit more. "She's half his size. The logistics must be daunting."

If I'd expected to fluster him again, I missed my target. Instead he met my sally with an intent and level gaze. One that oddly brewed the heat in my belly. "The rewards are no doubt worth the effort."

This time it was me who looked away, grateful that Nakoa

began speaking.

My relief lasted only moments, because the news was not good.

Not that I could understand all that he said. I picked out a word here and there, particularly *mo'o*, which meant dragon. But the tone and his grave mien, the way he held his war staff and banged it for emphasis, gave me warning. Dafne leaned against him, not looking in my direction. Ursula did, but revealed nothing in her lean, hawkish face.

Nakoa finished delivering his decision and the crowd stood, made obeisance, and began to disperse. So much for dancing. The group of royals descended from the dais and Dafne beckoned to me. Marskal and I fell in behind Harlan and Ursula, Dafne and Nakoa decorously leading the way. I declined Marskal's arm, pretending to be adjusting my arm bands. Despite my earlier flirtation, it wouldn't do to echo the couples. Time to get down to business. Which did not include dallying with anyone, no matter how intriguing, I reminded myself.

Our group made for a table set up on the edge of the esplanade, privacy guaranteed by a wide outposting of guards and waiting servants. Ursula, Nakoa, and Dafne sat at the table, lit with more gentle lantern light, and bearing carafes of wine and glass goblets. Harlan, naturally, remained standing behind Ursula's chair after seating her, though he accepted a glass of wine. I refused Marskal's offer to pour me some. My poor hummingbird brain had enough to deal with.

"Sit, Marskal." Ursula pointed to the empty chair beside me. "I can't convince this boulder to do so, but you I can order. And you're part of this conversation."

Marskal gave her the Hawks' salute, obeying with an alacrity that belied the hesitation I sensed in him. He'd rather follow Harlan's example, but I was just as happy not to have him hovering behind me. An interesting choice of words on Ursula's part, since as High Queen, she *could* command Harlan's obedience, but she clearly made a point of not doing so. Such were the diplomacies between lovers—another caution for me.

"Allow me to translate," Dafne began, laying a hand on Nakoa's arm and glancing at him for permission. He nodded, sitting back in his chair with folded arms, and studying me with that unrelenting dragon gaze. "Lieutenant Marskal has conveyed your request to visit Kiraka again."

I threw a hard and accusing look at him, which he returned with bland unconcern.

"However," Dafne said, "King Nakoa KauPo has officially decreed that no one is to go up the volcano until he lifts the ban." She held up a hand when I straightened. "Let me tell you the whole thing. This is done already, so arguing is trying to change a book that's already written."

I relaxed into my chair, trying to appear languid and unconcerned. The king could issue his edicts, but he didn't own my fealty. The needs of the Tala race exceeded politics.

"Kiraka has been silent since the ... incident, and I have not tried to speak with her, but I will if she shows any inclination to visit. Or further aggressive behavior."

Marskal and Ursula exchanged flinty glances at that, but remained quiet.

Dafne sighed and Nakoa ran a big hand over her hair, surprisingly tender for such a warlike man. She leaned into it. "That said, we don't believe anything of that sort is likely to recur. Kiraka has been nothing but careful with us. She's tutored me for weeks without expressing any harmful intent. We believe this was a unique event, somehow triggered by you, Zynda, and that without your presence, it won't happen again." She met my gaze, no longer my quiet librarian friend, but fully a queen, resolute in the protection of her realm. "King Nakoa KauPo has tasked me to ask you what happened up there and why."

Apparently taking the mention of his name as a cue, Nakoa leaned his elbows on the table, lacing his fingers together, and focusing all of his intent on me, reinforcing that the demand came from him.

I returned his intimidating stare, giving up all pretense of being languid. Salena would not have been afraid of this man. He might have considerable strength, and the magic to bring rain, but I possessed greater skills of sorcery. I shrugged carelessly, meeting Nakoa's rigidity with Tala indifference. "Kiraka and I spoke at some length about private matters. She decided to incinerate me."

"Private matters?" Ursula asked sharply, then belatedly nodded to Nakoa who lifted a finger, allowing her intrusion. Likely he regarded me as more her problem than his.

She was not, however, my monarch, so I gave her a lazy smile. "Obscure are the ways of dragons."

"This is not the time to play cagey shapeshifter, cousin," she warned. "You gave us to believe you conferred with her about the map-sticks."

"Shapeshifters are cagey by nature," I replied, "and the private matters are private, thus none of your business. Cousin."

Her face grew lethally taut, and—though Dafne hadn't yet translated for him—Nakoa glared at me. Dafne tapped her fingers on his arm, murmuring something to him, then to Ursula. Then she gave me a long, considering look. "Zynda. I know the Tala ways are not ours. Of everyone here, besides you, I've spent the most time in Annfwn, and I know how things are done—and *not* done there. But here you are in *our* realm, by King Nakoa KauPo's sufferance."

"I know that," I replied, feeling unexpectedly defensive.

Under the table, Marskal's knee brushed mine.

Dafne softened. "I know you do. But you are also our friend, and I think I speak for everyone in saying that we've believed we are your friends. If you can't confide in us, who would you then?"

She said it gently, but that last was a direct—and deliberate, I felt sure—quote, flinging my own words back at me from when Jepp and I had teased her about her love life. Entirely different, and yet... I shifted, uncomfortable in the chair, bored of sitting with the night-dark beach calling, wanting to flee entirely. It occurred to me that they'd moved this little meeting into the open air out of consideration for me. They were my friends, indeed, and deserved consideration for that. As much as I could give.

Telling them would change nothing at this point. I looked around the table. "I believe Kiraka intended it as a test."

Ursula closed her eyes and rubbed a hand over her face, while Dafne recovered, translating for Nakoa, who absorbed the information, then gave me a long, slow nod.

"A test of what?" Ursula asked in a reasonably even tone.

"Her abilities, I'm guessing," Dafne supplied when I didn't immediately reply, interrupting her low-voiced conversation with Nakoa. "Only a shapeshifter of surpassing skill could have done what Zynda did. I knew shapeshifters could accomplish some healing by changing form, but not to that degree."

Not without a goddess's intervention, anyway.

"So you passed the dragon's test." Ursula tapped her fingers on the table in satisfaction. "Salena would be proud."

I smiled at her for that, not caring to disabuse her of the assumption—in either case.

"Now what?" she asked.

"Now I need to go back to Kiraka."

"You can't," Dafne said, darting me a look and returning to her conversation with Nakoa.

"I have to." I said it loudly and firmly enough to gain their undivided attention. "Begging your pardon, King Nakoa. You may own this island and this archipelago, but you do not own Kiraka." *And you do not own me.*

Pinning me with his dark stare, he replied, speaking directly to me. Dafne hastened to translate. "He says that you're wrong. That he does not own these islands, no more than he owns the dragon. That he simply guards what belongs to all. He will not stop you from seeing Kiraka."

He added something pointed to Dafne and she replied, color high. Finally she cut him off. "We'll finish that argument in private."

"He's forbidding *you* to go?" I guessed.

"He thinks he can." She darted a mean look at her husband, which bounced off his impervious hide. "But this is mine to know." She tapped her breastbone for emphasis, directing that remark at him. I swear a smile twitched his stern mouth.

"Besides," I put in, "Kiraka would never harm you because you are the Dragon's Daughter, and you carry the child she's waited for."

"The first of many," she murmured, her eyes unfocusing on something only she could see. At least the pang I felt at that sat small in the turbulence of my greater pain.

"*We*, however, are not finished," Ursula inserted crisply, pulling my attention. "I can forbid you to go, and I can enforce my edict as *you* are my subject, Zynda. Annfwn is under my domain by agreement with King Rayfe and Queen Andromeda. They'll back my actions, particularly as your well-being is so obviously in danger. You barely survived this *test*, and—you may not want to acknowledge it, but it's obvious to everyone here—

you're greatly weakened. What guarantee is there that you could survive another attack? I won't condone another meeting with the dragon without more information. Especially regarding whatever it is you're keeping from me."

~ 10 ~

"I DON'T NEED your permission," I replied as evenly as I could, resisting a glance at Marskal. If she thought to use the warrior to physically prevent me...

"Perhaps you believe that, but you do need to convince me not to tie you up and lock you in a cabin on the first outbound ship. Don't even think to push me on this!"

I fumed, but withdrew my planned retort in the face of her steely resolve. We'd never truly tested the hierarchy between us. I would win, no matter what she believed, but I had no desire for such a battle to come to pass.

"The security of the realm is absolutely my business," she continued, iron in her voice. "How dare you jeopardize information we need to defeat *Deyrr*? I want to know what you thought so important that you'd commit this sort of deception."

The glint of betrayed grief in her eyes bled my anger away. She was right that I'd deceived them. I'd have to tell them at least some of it.

Starting to run my hands through my hair, I encountered the elaborate braids. That, I could do something about. So, I began plucking the silver hummingbirds from their nests, making a little pile in front of me, undoing the braids as I spoke.

"I am not being deliberately difficult," I told them. "And I did not act counter to your interests—just in parallel. There is much that is… private. The Tala are a cloistered people and we do not share our pain, or weaknesses, easily."

"Then this is not political," Ursula interrupted. "Nothing to do with orders you might have from the King and Queen of Annfwn."

I shook my head, smiling at her relief. She and her sister Andi had been too much at odds in the past. I could resolve that concern. "This is not political, at least not within the Thirteen Kingdoms"—I nodded to Nakoa—"or however you're counting all of your subsidiary kingdoms these days."

She returned the smile without humor, gesturing me to continue.

"Dafne, I'm asking you to be judicious in what and how you translate. Consider this more of your diplomatic dancing."

She wrinkled her nose at me, and I shook out my hair, finally free of the braids, my scalp tingling as I rubbed it. "I did talk to Kiraka about about N'andana, too, and can give you some information there. We've known all along—or some of you suspected from events—that *Deyrr* has sought the Star of Annfwn." Harlan's eyes glinted at that painful mention. "You also have discovered that the Star has certain properties that affect the barrier, which tie into what we refer to as the Heart of Annfwn."

Ursula's gaze sharpened, a hawk focusing on prey, and Dafne looked fascinated, even as she translated.

"I remember discussing some of this before," Ursula said, partly in question, and I nodded in confirmation. Andi had told her some of it when Ursula and Harlan came to Annfwn to rescue Ami and the twins.

"I don't," Dafne inserted, giving Ursula an accusing look. "You didn't tell me."

Ursula raised her brows. "I had to swear that what they told me would be information I held secret and would use only for the greatest good."

Those had been almost her exact words at the time. No matter how my cousin might aggravate me with her pushy ways, she clearly memorized and held inviolate the vows she made.

"None of that has changed. In truth, I shouldn't be discussing it now." I glanced at Marskal, who regarded me opaquely. "But you're all sworn to secrecy, for better or ill. Besides, I have no intention of telling you more about it than that the Heart, the Star and the barrier—which is an extension of those two—were originally developed by Kiraka's people, the N'andanans in an effort to fight *Deyrr*. Only she referred to them as *gelyneinioes*. From context, however, I believe that's who she meant. Bending it a little, in Talal that would mean essentially enemies of life."

Dafne held up a finger to Nakoa, so excited by the new information that she couldn't stand it. "The N'andanans deliberately pulled the magic into Annfwn, to what—starve the practitioners of *Deyrr*?"

"So we believe, though we've had little evidence until recently." I considered how to proceed while Dafne caught Nakoa up. "It was so long ago, and even then the effort was shrouded in secrecy. Plus tales change over time, fluctuating with the teller. *Even*," I said pointedly to Dafne, "if they're written down." She gave me a distracted grimace.

"But yes, they were losing to *Deyrr*—Kiraka did confirm some of this—so the ancient N'andanans worked a spell to pull all the magic to a center point, and they walled away some of their people behind it, to create a bubble in space where their race could continue." An equivocation, but I still hesitated to damn the Tala in their eyes.

"And locked themselves out," Dafne inserted, "killing off the dragons along with everything else that subsisted on magic.

Why didn't they go inside the barrier, too?"

I shook my head. "I don't know." Ugh—this was the trouble with equivocations and untruths of all kinds. Too easy to get stuck in the net of them. Also, Dafne had gotten a thoughtful look like she did when she'd nearly resolved a puzzle. I doubted she believed me.

"It didn't work, not completely." Ursula shared a look with Harlan. "A poor strategy that stranded their most powerful shapeshifters outside and yet allowed *Deyrr* to continue to thrive."

"I wouldn't say they thrived," Harlan said in his deep voice. "They found refuge in Dasnaria at some point, perhaps coming from elsewhere, but they only gained power in recent decades."

"Right around the same time Uorsin grew to power and Salena left Annfwn," Dafne said, her fingers twitching to make notes. Nakoa gestured to a servant standing well out of earshot, the young woman returning with paper and ink so quickly they must have had it ready nearby.

Dafne flashed her husband a grateful smile, sketching something on the paper. "Just when I want to kill him…" she said to us with a wry grimace. Though he shouldn't have understood, Nakoa stroked a hand over her hair again, saying something in Nahanaun that had her blushing.

Funny this, to be openly discussing these secrets, these ancient terrors, with my friends, trading inside jokes and affectionate digs. *There is also being loved.* Was this what Moranu had meant? My friends did love me, and letting them inside my own barrier of secrets did help ease some of the burden.

"Here's the timeline." Dafne turned the paper for us to see. "Uorsin rose from simple captain in Duranor's losing war to be general of their armies at this point in time. That's the siege of Castle Columba, a battle they were losing until then." Nakoa rubbed a hand down her back, and she gave him a look blazing with emotion. Not the kind I'd expected, though. Dafne had been a child and the lone survivor of the fall of Columba. Something had happened that she now looked happy about that horrible event that orphaned her. How interesting. "We can assume this also marks the moment Salena left Annfwn and made her bargain with Uorsin."

She glanced at me and Ursula for confirmation, and we didn't disagree.

"So, Salena throws in with Uorsin,"—she held up a hand as Ursula opened her mouth—"I know that's an oversimplification, just to save time, all right? We know this because suddenly Duranor starts winning, and can't be defeated. Columba falls and tales emerge around this time of shapeshifters, wizards—and a half-wild sorceress wife assisting Uorsin. Harlan, do you know when *Deyrr* first appeared in Dasnaria?"

He sipped his wine, pondering. "I don't have your memory for history. And *Deyrr* himself is a very old god of the hunt. The salient change came when the Practitioners of *Deyrr* rose as a new sect emphasizing one of *Deyrr*'s more obscure faces—that of transmutation of the living animal into death and death recycling back into life through consumption of the meat. That happened... maybe four decades ago, at a guess."

Ursula snorted. "Your guesses are better than most people's histories."

Harlan smiled and tipped two fingers to his forehead in his private salute to her.

"There are Dasnarian histories in the library," Dafne observed, frowning at her timeline, "so I can verify. Still, the timing is coincidental. It makes sense that these *gelyneinioes* appropriated the Dasnarian god for their purposes. The question is, were these Practitioners able to work actual magic outside the barrier?"

"Illyria did, at Ordnung," Ursula pointed out, "before the barrier moved."

Nobody spoke up to correct that to "before Ursula moved it," which would be more accurate. Only Ami or Andi would have that much spine, as Ursula steadfastly maintained she possessed no magical ability, despite having the same blood as her sisters. It made me wonder, however, about these Tala ancestors who expanded the original barrier around the Heart to the much larger one. Tied to the Star and tied to Ursula—which implicated Salena's line.

"Though Salena's decline during her tenure at Ordnung has been solidly blamed on her starving for magic," Ursula was saying.

"That and a broken heart," Dafne muttered, then glanced at Ursula in chagrin, but the High Queen only nodded. "So," Dafne continued in a brighter tone, "the question is: did the barrier start leaking magic?"

They all looked at me, and I shrugged. "I was inside. No idea."

"All right," Ursula said, "finish your tale, Zynda. I know that's not all of it."

I grimaced and she smiled, in her thin-lipped predatory way. "The Star and the Heart," she prompted. "The N'andanans implementing the barrier to starve *Deyrr* when they could not defeat them. Centuries or more elapse. We come to recent days, and...?"

And she accused Harlan of remembering everything. I laced my fingers together and laid my hands on the table. "You called it a poor strategy, and we could debate that all night. We can't deny, however, that the Practitioners of *Deyrr*—Harlan is correct that we should differentiate between the god and this sect that twisted one facet of his being—failed to take over the world. In that, the gambit was a rousing success."

"Take over the world," Ursula echoed, stricken. "Was that their goal?"

I held up my palms for her naivete, Dafne's translation for Nakoa a low-voiced murmur in the background. "What else? And it still is, as evidenced by their collusion with the Dasnarian emperor." Jepp had brought back that much information from her spying mission. "And with your High Priest Kir," I added.

"Not mine, nor of Glorianna's Church," Ursula replied absently, thoughts elsewhere. "Ami had him excommunicated. He moved against her, and against the Tala, which was triggered by Andi's marriage to Rayfe. That's what brought *Deyrr*—the sect, that is—their attention to my realm."

"Surely you don't hold that against her." I tensed, ready to engage in that argument. We'd needed Queen Andromeda badly in Annfwn, and her arrival had been the first step toward saving the Tala.

"No." Ursula brushed that off. "It's ancient history at this point, regardless. Though I can't help but wonder—if Salena foresaw all of this, why did she leave Annfwn and sire her daughters with Uorsin? If she hadn't, I might not have moved the barrier." She met my eyes, bleak guilt in hers. I'd been wrong. She knew very well what she'd done, consciously or not. "The Practitioners of *Deyrr* might have remained asleep. I don't understand how Salena could have seen and still knowingly loosed such a terror on the world."

"It's possible," Dafne said slowly, "that Salena didn't see that far ahead, to awakening *Deyrr* and the sect's practitioners. It could have been an unintended consequence. Everything I've read about the gift of prognostication indicates that it's an uncertain tool."

"One that can be affected by the intentions of people around you," Ursula confirmed, "we ran into that in the search for Ami."

"That's true," I agreed. "And each small change in response to a glimpse of the future ripples through in thousands, millions or billions of unpredictable ways."

"Andi says that some events are more certain than others," Ursula said, a grim set to her jaw.

Kiraka's words came back to me, damning my people for their selfishness. It must have shown on my face, because they all looked at me, waiting for the answer. Expectant silence fell, Dafne having finished translating Ursula's last words.

I stared at my hands, unable to meet their eyes, guilt coiling in my belly. A tug at my hair and I looked down to see Marskal's fingers tangled in one of the long locks under the table. I raised my gaze to his, finding only his quiet brown eyes, free of judgment, offering his strength.

No more equivocating. I'd have to come out with it.

"I think she would have done anything to save the Tala because we were dying," I said, laying it out there simply, but the grief sighed out of me. "That's the flip side of the questionable strategy." Harlan returned my wry glance with grave sympathy. "We were never meant to be inside the barrier. All magic was supposed to be contained in the Heart, and only in the Heart, but the original Tala expanded the barrier enough to encompass Annfwn, so we could continue to live and grow there. It's our fault that Deyrr has had enough magic to survive and grow strong again."

They all sat in silence, assimilating that. Harlan picked up the wine jug and refilled for everyone.

"You can't accept the guilt for this," Dafne finally said. "Salena, you, all the Tala—you acted to save your people and your land. Annfwn and the Tala are bountiful and magical treasures of our world. There is no crime, no guilt in trying to preserve that."

"Thank you for that," I told her sincerely, "though others may disagree. Including Kiraka. Still—it may be important to remember that the barrier was probably never intentionally planned to have specific boundaries." I nodded to Ursula who acknowledged that with a dip of her chin.

"There's something to that. Something important, yes." Dafne frowned at her timeline. "The pieces are all there, but I can't quite see the whole picture." She made a thoughtful sound, reaching for more paper.

"It's a question of geography," she said, almost more to herself than to us. "The barrier corresponds to geography, what it covers, what it doesn't. Who was inside, who was out." She drew a map on a clean sheet of paper, Nakoa watching over her shoulder with interest. The Annfwn coastline, the rest of the continent with the original twelve kingdoms, the span of the Onyx Ocean and the sprawl of the Nahanaun Archipelago. Sketching in an arc with dotted lines, she spoke absently, "we know the original barrier—the one we all knew for most of our lives—went through here, at Odfell's Pass."

Ursula leaned in, too, tracing with a broken-nailed finger. "Here in Branli, down to here, and through Avonlidgh, thus." She caught my surprised stare. "I traveled most of it."

Marskal tapped the impromptu map. "Not quite. It cut through in this range, and then somewhere in the middle of this chain of lakes. This is a rough drawing, but the lakes are up in this part of Branli. If you want to be precise."

"I need to sit you down with a better version," Dafne said.

Marskal dipped his chin. "My first assignment is to the Lady Zynda, but otherwise I'm happy to oblige. Or Her Majesty can show you."

"Marskal knows it more precisely." Ursula waved that off. "He kept the maps and notes on our journeys."

I raised my brows, looking between them. She shrugged, denying the significance, but he met my gaze. "Looking for a way in," he said quietly, letting me sit with that.

Of course they had. We'd been in enemy camps then. But I still felt strangely exposed.

"So, if you extrapolate that it's a circle, spreading concentrically from the Heart," Ursula said, "that puts the Heart about here and the rest of the barrier out to here."

"Or a sphere," Dafne replied, putting in the dotted lines and a star where Ursula had almost uncannily pinpointed the location of the Heart.

"How did you guess this?" I demanded, feeling my native territoriality in the growl rising in my throat, and Ursula gave me a half smile with some of that warrior fierceness in it.

"I know how to read a map and respect enemy borders," she answered.

I might have been certain I'd win any contest between us, but in that moment I was glad the Tala were no longer her enemy.

"This will be better on the big map," Dafne said, breaking the tension, "but we know the barrier now extends approximately here, keeping it as a sphere intersecting the surface of land and water as a circle." She drew another line of dots through the Nahanaun archipelago, Nakoa taking the pen to correct her in places. "Extrapolating to something about like this."

It was a big circle. Ursula nodded, confirming her part of the world. Harlan frowned, putting a hand on her shoulder. "May I?"

"I love it when you pretend to ask for permission." She

waved a hand at the map.

He flicked her an opaque look. "You've left out Dasnaria," he said to Dafne.

"Well, it's a small rendering and the empire is well out of..." she trailed off, frowning.

"Except for this peninsula," Harlan said, finishing the thought.

"I need to get to the big maps." Dafne's face burned with excitement and she popped out of her chair. An abbreviated movement, as Nakoa pressed her into it again with a big hand and zero effort. She argued with him, which he received with stoic silence, replying in one word to her dozen.

Finally she turned back to us. "I'm reliably informed I'll be doing it in the morning."

"The morning is soon enough." Ursula looked amused, exchanging a look with Nakoa. "Rest is good for you."

"I'm pregnant, not made of glass," she muttered, then yawned mightily. Nakoa set his hand on her belly, speaking to her warmly and quietly, her glare softening.

"I hate to interrupt," I said, "but where were you going with this, Dafne?"

She frowned at me, then at the circles. "It's the answer... to the riddle I've been working on."

Marskal breathed what might have been a laugh and Ursula and I exchanged puzzled looks. "Perhaps you'll explain to us dull kids, oh wise tutor," Ursula suggested.

Dafne rolled her eyes, a gesture worthy of someone a quarter her age. She indicated the space in between the two sets of dotted lines. "Look, we've wondered—or I have, Nakoa never wonders about anything—" She threw him an affectionate glance and he smiled broadly, an astonishing expression on his normally brooding visage. He must understand more Common

Tongue than he let on. "I've wondered how it could be that Nakoa and I were connected. Fated, if you like that word, to be mates and to free Kiraka. My family was here at Columba." She put a finger on Ordnung. "And Nakoa was here. See?" She traced a finger along the arc, following it from Ordnung down and around to Nahanau. "If I drew another circle..."

"You and Nakoa would have been on the same arc." I couldn't quite assimilate it.

She nodded at me. "It will be easier to see on the big map, with Marskal's help, I hope." She gave him a sunny smile. "The point is, what if the barrier was bigger at one point, so we were both included inside, along with the Tala. It would explain a great deal about why some cross-breeding works better than others, and how these connections were forged. How can a girl at Castle Columba be connected to a dragon in Nahanau?" She sketched the arc again and beamed at us. "Circles and spheres. And look what else is along that arc." She tapped Windroven, raising her brows at Ursula who scowled.

"I thought it was a bad idea to wake that dragon *before* Kiraka tried to kill Zynda. I'm certainly not authorizing it now."

"I'm just saying it's a line of connection," Dafne explained mildly.

"And a tangent from the current discussion," Ursula replied with a thin smile. "I know some geometry. From circles to lines to the point at hand, which is Zynda and her true reason for visiting the dragon. Something to do with continuing Salena's quest to save the Tala. Out with it."

I had to give my cousin credit. She perceived patterns very well.

"Wherever the boundaries of the barrier were," I explained, "they ended up around enough land to live on, but a relatively small area. And we were trapped inside of it for a very long time.

Over the centuries the magic intensified, turning back on itself, warping the land and the people. It exacerbated the toll of inbreeding, changing our babies in the womb." I had to stop, the image of Anya's doomed babe rising in my mind, making me want to weep all over again.

"Salena's babies died," Ursula said into the hush. "Her first husband suicided over it."

"Yes." I wiped away the tears I'd hoped to restrain. "Many did. We had...no hope, you see. If Salena hadn't left, hadn't seduced Uorsin and made her devil's bargain to gain a new queen for the Tala, we would have died out in another generation. And that hasn't changed enough. We still face that final death."

"We saw children in Annfwn." Ursula held up a hand to Harlan, who took it, wrapping her bony fingers in his big fist. "They showed us the tunnel slides, the shortcut to the beach from the cliffs."

I laughed, but it came out watery. "Then you saw all of our children. They're all in the cliff city, to be taught and protected." Even now, even knowing I was among friends, it made me feel vulnerable to admit that, to show our soft underbelly.

Ursula sobered, mentally counting, then inclined her head. She'd been trained well as a monarch, understanding what a population required to remain viable.

Dafne had a hand on her belly, sorrow in her eyes. "You're too far gone in numbers. Even with the barrier expanded and Tala partbloods returning home to have children, there's not enough time."

"So our scholars have determined. And with every outbreeding of purebloods with partbloods, we lose more of who we are. We're still doomed." I scrubbed my hands through my hair, catching on the tug of Marskal's fingers. He only twitched a smile in response to my inquiring look. Strange man. "The Tala face extinction and it's my job to prevent that."

They all stared at me for a moment in silence. Marskal's gaze felt especially hot on my face.

"*Prevent* it," Ursula repeated, while Dafne stared at me with a strange expression on her face. "Do you mean to somehow save the Tala race?"

"Thus you sought help from Kiraka, thinking she might have answers, since her people set up the problem to begin with." Ursula frowned. "This is why you left Annfwn?"

"What help?" Dafne asked, eyes narrowed and brain clearly working furiously at the puzzle. "What information did you think Kiraka could give you?"

I took a deep breath. "I would do that by taking what we call Final Form. I've asked Kiraka to teach me, as only a dragon can teach how to become a dragon."

I'd stunned them beyond silent, the air growing thick with their shock and tangled emotions.

"Danu save us," Ursula breathed.

"A dragon?" Dafne demanded. "You want to become a thriced dragon?"

"Yes. Virtually immortal. Good for maintaining the consciousness and thought process of being human. Capable of hibernation and... particular magical gifts, especially magic-dampening properties and encouragement of fertility." I pointed a meaningful look at her swollen belly, the growing child inside the womb she'd thought too aged to bear children.

"So, you'd take dragon form to encourage conception, then dampen the magic around Tala mothers, in the hopes that the babies will be born whole and healthy." Dafne's agile brain had raced far ahead.

"Yes."

"How do you even know that will work?" She patted her belly. "Besides this, of course."

"Our oldest tales have suggested as much."

"And you can't shift back from the dragon?" Marskal asked, a hitch in his voice.

"It's called Final Form for a reason. Something about the magic dampening prevents shapeshifting out of it again."

"When would you do this?" Ursula asked, her face a neutral mask, though her eyes glittered.

"As soon as possible. Tomorrow, if Kiraka is willing." And if I could shift. I set that anguished uncertainty aside.

"All along this has been your aim." Dafne looked pale. "You knew about the dragon."

I inclined my head, not really a nod of agreement, unable to look Dafne in the eye. "When we heard rumors of volcanoes quickening with the possibility of dragons beneath, we connected that to the old stories, yes."

"And you didn't tell us," Dafne accused. "You let me go through all of this and said nothing."

I accepted the guilt of that, too. "All I had were wisps of old myths, knowing no more than any of us about the dragons. There was nothing solid to tell. Also, we had no evidence Kiraka was anything but a mute beast until you brought her out of her reptile brain."

"How did you know that part?" Dafne asked, paling. "I hadn't told anyone about that."

I tossed her a hummingbird charm by way of explanation and her eyes widened. Then she threw it back at me, unusual anger from her. I caught it, but my heart hurt.

"You said she tested you," Ursula said after a moment, the pause making me wonder if she'd noted my loss of composure and given me time to get it back. "For what purpose of hers?"

"I'm not sure," I admitted. "Maybe to test if I could manage that extreme level of shapeshifting. She didn't explain." *We'll burn away the weakness and see what's left.* What if all I had left was this weakness? Marskal poured me wine and wrapped my hand around the stem. I drank without acknowledging the gesture, though I was profoundly grateful.

Ursula narrowed her eyes. "If that's the case, if you confront the dragon, she might choose to immolate you again."

"If she does, she does. I won't get her help by not asking. None of you can stop me." I reached down and pulled my hair from where it was wound around Marskal's finger, throwing him a defiant look that he returned with no sign of emotion.

"You don't even know that taking this Final Form will work," Dafne bit out.

This time I met her gaze, letting her see my sorrow that I might have destroyed our friendship, but also my resolve. The need was greater than all of that. "Do you have an alternate suggestion for saving the Tala babies?"

She opened her mouth. Closed it.

I stood, and Marskal rose with me. "Thank you, all. I'm truly sorry if I've caused hurt or damaged the effort to stop *Deyrr*. If you still want me to, and I've not yet taken Final Form, I'll go see Jepp tomorrow, after I meet with Kiraka."

Ursula nodded crisply, clearly deep in thought. Then exchanged a signal with Marskal. Subtle, but I caught it. She met my gaze. "Marskal will, of course, go with you."

I glanced at him and, catching the obstinate set of his jaw, didn't bother to argue.

~ 11 ~

MARSKAL AND I went up the volcano in the morning, in the still misty pre-dawn, quiet of human activity and chorusing with bird song and the peeping of the tropical frogs who clung to the trees like living jewels.

Marskal fairly bristled with weapons, which I found laughable as none of them would work against Kiraka's least incendiary hiccup. But I tolerated his presence in silence, if not with good grace. In my current state, mossback politeness was beyond me.

I wouldn't let on, but each step up the mountain intensified my nerves and reminded me of my weakened state—physically and emotionally. Certainly I couldn't reveal either to Marskal, as he already had developed the habit of assessing me every few minutes.

"I need to stop and rest a moment," he said, after about an hour of walking.

"You do?" He hadn't needed to on the previous trip.

"Some of us are not magically gifted shapeshifters." He sat on a boulder of solidified lava, looping in blacks and grays, studded with silvery lichen, and opened his pack. "Besides, I missed breakfast."

I stretched, then lowered myself next to him. Might as well rest while he did. He handed me a flask of water and I drank, but my suspicions sharpened when he offered me a flaky pastry slathered in honey. "No, thank you," I told him.

"It's what you liked last night."

"I don't need to be coddled, Marskal."

"All right." He shrugged and set the bread down on a cloth, digging something else out of his pack. "Meatroll?"

Just the smell of the cooked meat turned my stomach. I snatched up the honeyed bread and took a bite, just to shut him up. More gracious than I, he didn't comment, eating the meatroll while thoughtfully scanning the landscape. From this vantage, the smooth aqua sea of the Nahanaun islands spread out to the horizon where it melded with no discernible line into the arc of the sky.

"It's understandable to be nervous," he said, after a while. "You wouldn't be human if you weren't."

I raised a brow at him. "I'm not human. I'm Tala."

He made a scoffing sound. "Surely you don't believe that."

"That I'm Tala?"

"That Tala aren't humans."

"Of course I do. Can humans shapeshift?"

"Tala interbreed with humans," he pointed out, "thus we're the same species. Don't laugh like that. On the farm, that's the definition—if you can crossbreed two animals then they're the same, no matter the minor details."

"I've seen dogs humping pillows, which appears to be sexually satisfying, but that doesn't make them the same species," I retorted.

Marskal gave me a slow grin. "But that doesn't produce viable offspring. It's all rubbing with nothing to show for it."

"The dogs might disagree. The lack of pillow-puppies doesn't seem to deter them."

"True. But then, there's a lot to be said for pleasurable rubbing." He stroked a brown finger down my arm, the sensation sending a hot shiver through me. When I looked up, his serious brown eyes burned into mine. "Wouldn't you agree?"

"I don't know," I replied. A silly answer, but coherent thought—something not reliable since the extended humming-bird phase regardless—seemed to have fled the moment he touched me. Along with my breath.

"You don't know?" He searched my face. "Surely you're not a virgin."

That made me laugh. A good, from-the-belly laugh. Though I remembered the campfire discussion with Jepp and Dafne, when we drank that excellent Branlian whiskey and Dafne confessed to that very thing. I leaned closer to Marskal, who seemed both pleased and confounded by my amusement. Flirting took my mind off the trial ahead.

"No, darling mossback man, I am most decidedly *not* a virgin. The Tala don't trouble themselves much over such conditions."

His lips quirked in a slight smile, the movement drawing my attention. He had quite a nice mouth, really, sensuously curved when he wasn't being so serious. "Ever had a mossback lover?"

"Why?" I brushed his cheek with my lips, delighted to hear him catch his breath in turn. "Are you volunteering?"

"Yes." He said it so immediately with such conviction that he took me by surprise. His hand came up to thread through my hair and cup my head, his mouth capturing mine at the same moment. Startled, I didn't think to push him away. The feel of his lips on mine turned me inside out in some odd way. He tasted of sunshine and exertion, different than any Tala man I'd kissed. Not quite definable. Harder. Edged. Perhaps a residual of that essential immutability. He was like a rock. No, like the earth. Solid and grounded. A stable point to hold onto.

Experimentally I opened to him, allowing him in, and he

made an incoherent sound, deepening the kiss, wrapping his other arm around my waist to pull me close. Arousal flooded me in a sweet wave and I felt singingly alive for the first time since I'd awakened, fascinated by those flowers and not understanding why. Heat pulsed through me, full of sweet and bright. Safe and loved. Human.

I pulled back a little—not all the way—but enough to break the kiss and stare into his eyes. They'd darkened with desire, his mouth stern with it.

"Were you the one that fed me, all those days that I was a hummingbird?"

He gazed back at me, his expression unreadable. "Not all of them," he finally said. "Only at first, when you were too weak to fly. After that you fed yourself."

"All that experience from the farm."

A dip of his chin. "I've rescued a baby bird or two before."

"I'm not a baby bird in need of rescue, Marskal."

He relaxed the arm around my waist, I thought to let me go, but he used both hands to comb his fingers through my hair, pushing it back from my face, expression rapt. A sense memory came with it, of his hands cupping me while I fluttered to escape. My heartbeat quickened. "No, you're a beautiful woman, and I want to be your lover."

Taken aback, I didn't reply. The feel of his hands in my hair, the admiration in his eyes, it was like warm sun on my skin, making me want to purr and be petted. Marskal leaned in and brushed a kiss over my lips, sweeter than honey. "Say yes," he murmured.

"Maybe," I replied, unable to resist teasing him, but I deepened the kiss, flicking my tongue against his, just to hear him groan. "Right now I have a dragon to meet."

My own words penetrated and I pulled away in truth, disentangling myself. I had a dragon to meet. In another hour, I might *be* a dragon—and I'd been seriously considering taking him as a lover. "We need to get going. Moranu knows what I was thinking."

Marskal shrugged a little, packing up the remains of breakfast. "You were resting and taking your mind off your cares. And if you're not too stubborn to admit it, you're better for it. Your eyes are brighter and your color is better now."

No doubt due to that humming sweet desire he'd sparked in me. "You did that on purpose, to distract me."

"I kissed you because I wanted to—and because you dared me."

"I didn't!"

"Not in so many words."

"You always claim to hear words I don't speak. Besides, I can't be your lover. I'm taking Final Form."

"I haven't forgotten."

"You act as if you have. In another hour I might be a dragon."

"Or she might set you another task. Why not enjoy the last days of being human?"

"It wouldn't be fair to either of us."

"You weren't thinking that when you were kissing me."

I growled in frustration. "You made me lose my head."

He looked thoughtful, rising to his feet, and shouldering the pack, then touching his hands to each of his weapons in obvious long habit that came without thought. "Let's walk and talk, since you're in such a hurry to risk your life again."

I hastened to catch up with his long-legged stride.

"I might point out," he continued, "that there is no actual rush. You could have taken some days to get stronger."

He had a point, but I wouldn't confess my fear that if I

thought too long about what might happen up there, I'd succumb to the temptation to flee and fly far away, never to return. "If I find out the next steps from Kiraka, I can go see what Jepp wants."

He gave me an incredulous look. "Now you pretend to care about that?"

"I do care," I insisted. "Thwarting *Deyrr* is important, too."

"But this Final Form thing is more important."

"Yes. We all have our roles to play."

He made a derisive sound, putting my back up.

"If I'd flown, I could have been there already," I said. "I should have."

"Why didn't you?"

Those warrior instincts. He'd zeroed right in on my bleeding wound. Just had to poke at it. Two could play that game. "Because I had to bring you along."

"You could have become the pony and let me ride. Much faster."

The thought of Marskal riding me blazed through my mind. The strong clasp of his legs, fingers in my mane. Oh no, that would not be a good idea. Though, now that it was in my head, I couldn't shake it.

"Are you worried about shifting?" he finally asked, quietly and without censure. Neutral, the way he'd offered me breakfast.

I couldn't think of a reply that wouldn't be giving voice to the terrible truth and didn't sound tart or downright nasty, so I didn't say anything.

"Because you haven't," he persisted, "since you shifted back to human form."

"You don't know that. And, besides, it's hardly been a full day since then."

"Three. You were a hummingbird for nearly four, shifted

back to human form, then were unconscious another two."

The silence stretched out, not comfortable because his expectation of an answer hung in the air. It made my skin itch.

"I've never known you to go longer than a full day and night without shifting, if only for a brief swim or flight," he finally said. "And that's when you were pressed. If you have the time, you do it more often." Not pushing, exactly, but making it clear he wouldn't let the subject drop. I should turn into a pony. Except even then he likely wouldn't shut up. He would have to be the exception, treating me as myself no matter what form I wore, and would take the opportunity to lecture me when I couldn't argue. Unless I bucked him off, which could be entertaining. The thought would've made me smile, if I weren't so uncomfortable with his prying. How long had the cursed man been observing my habits?

"It seems to me," he continued, after another long and pregnant silence—how long did this hike take anyway? It had not seemed so far before—"that if you're not certain you can shift, then—"

"I can shift," I interrupted.

"Ah." He didn't say more.

I should have enjoyed the peace and quiet, been grateful that he'd quit badgering me. But my lie refused to dissipate, clinging to me. Or, not exactly a lie, as I hadn't tried again. He didn't accuse me of the untruth, which only made it worse. My hair hung hot and heavy on my neck and I really wished I'd thought to find another pin to put it up with. No, I *really* wished I could get my old one back, that I could quickly shift and come back again to the familiar pin in its sleeve.

Just do it. Prove to both of you that you can.

But the thought of trying again made me queasy. Sharp memory fragments cut at me of that endless time of trying, the agony ripping me, the shapes just out of reach, losing my self.

My chest went tight with a kind of grief and dread, sweat popping out on my forehead, weirdly cold in the heat. More sweat ran down my ribs, which felt rigid, making it hard to draw breath. The edges of my vision went black and the honeyed bread rose in my throat, bitter with bile.

I had to stop, feeling dizzy enough to lean a hand on the smooth, golden bark of a tree. Her limbs draped over the trail, lacy green with lush violet flowers, so pretty and untroubled. Marskal handed me the flask of water and I drank it gratefully. Even more grateful that he said nothing. Gradually the constriction in my chest eased, and I could breathe better.

Giving the flask back, I made myself meet his quiet gaze. "I tried once, couldn't, and haven't tried again," I admitted.

He nodded, unsurprised.

"But I have to talk to Kiraka." I kept my voice reasonable, the tremble in it barely audible.

"Do you?" Marskal cocked his head slightly. "We could sail to find out what Jepp and Kral know. Then we can come back to talk to the dragon when you're stronger. More yourself. We'd have to come back past the archipelago anyway."

I was shaking my head. If I delayed, I might never work up the courage again. I made myself stand on my own again. And start walking uphill.

"There's tomorrow," Marskal said, easily pacing me. "We could go back down. Have a nap, some lunch—"

"You're obsessed with food."

"It's useful for keeping strong and healthy. We could take a swim, that would be refreshing."

It annoyed me that he'd noticed me sweating. "Not if I can't shift."

"People swim, too," he replied without rancor.

Neither of us said anything about what I'd just admitted. But it was out there now, and he clearly wouldn't leave it alone. The doubt rode cold in my chest.

"What if I can't shift again?" I asked the question of the overhanging trees, the birds flitting musically among the branches. Of the glimpses of sky between the leaves, fringed palms and deep green head-sized paddles. Of the sea beyond, beautiful and unconcerned with the problems of mortals.

"Is that something that happens to shapeshifters who are injured?" Marskal asked. I imagined him having this conversation with one of his subordinates who'd sprained an ankle or some such.

"If it did, they wouldn't talk about it." I had to laugh, just imagining.

Marskal slid me a look. "Is it such a point of pride then?"

I opened my mouth to scoff, then closed it again. How odd that he wouldn't see that. No Tala would ask that.

"Yes," I said simply.

He mulled that over.

"The thing is," I finally said, then had to take a breath. "The thing is that I don't know of anyone—any shapeshifter, but I guess that's obvious—who's done what I did. I should have died. I did die, and Moranu intervened. I don't think I would have been able to come back as much as I had without her help."

He nodded. We walked on in silence, the trees beginning to thin. Finally we neared the meadow, and now I wished we weren't so close. *We could go back down. Have a nap, some lunch.* It sounded so tempting. But I couldn't. I had to go through with this.

"Nothing to say to that?" I asked.

Marskal glanced at me and held out a hand. Surprised, I took it, and he laced his fingers with mine, the contact comforting, bolstering me.

"I'm glad Moranu intervened," he said, in that quiet tone. "I'll have to take up her worship. What is her preferred sacrifice?"

I laughed. Not at all what I'd expected from him. He smiled at me, a bare twitch of the lips, his eyes warm, but he wasn't joking. He did believe me. Just like that.

"It seems to me," he said, "that you're like any warrior recovering from injury. Even Ursula, who is easily one of the best fighters I've ever had the pleasure to spar with, still isn't up to her former strength since she nearly died—and she had the benefit of magical healing. I'd think shapeshifting is like any physical skill, like having an excellent sword arm. If you injure that arm, it takes time and gradual practice to get yourself up to your previous skill levels."

Such a strange perspective, and yet, it made an odd kind of sense. Still… "Except the wounded warrior doesn't dread trying to use that arm again and failing."

Marskal stopped and turned me to face him, holding my shoulders and staring into my eyes very seriously. "Yes. Yes, they absolutely do."

My lips parted, my insides quaking, though I didn't understand why.

"There's nothing wrong with you, Zynda," he continued, holding me steady. "Nothing that countless warriors before you haven't experienced, man or woman, mossback or Tala." His lips twitched slightly in amusement before he sobered again. "The fear and the dread is natural. Give yourself a break."

"It really hurt," I whispered, afraid to even say it too loudly. "So much." Impossible to put words to it.

He winced, eyes full of sympathy, as if he felt it, too. "I can only imagine. And that's part of it. Facing the possibility of that kind of pain again is one of the worst parts of recovering."

Strangely, that helped. "All right," I said. And took a deep breath. Let it out. "All right."

But he didn't move. "Zynda." He squeezed my shoulders a little. "What if the dragon attacks again? If you're still recovering and can't shift with your previous power, can you rely on Moranu's intervention?"

I appreciated the faith in me implicit in his phrasing, that I would be able to shift again, that my power would build. "It doesn't matter."

His brows drew together. "How can you—"

"It doesn't matter," I repeated, putting my hands on his, squeezing them a little before shrugging out of his grip. "I have to do this. If there's another test and I can't pass it, then I don't deserve to continue on this task."

He shook his head. "I don't understand you."

"You could wait here. You don't have to watch."

"Oh no." He set his jaw in grim determination. "I'm not leaving your side. If you burn, I'm going down with you this time."

"That makes absolutely no sense! If I burn, I can maybe recover. You can't."

He slanted me a cocky look, mouth turning up into a one-sided smile. "Consider it blackmail, then. Make sure that thrice-cursed dragon keeps her flame to herself."

Kiraka waited in the meadow, as if she'd never moved from the spot. Perhaps she hadn't. For the first time it occurred to me to wonder at my conviction that she'd be there, without arranging it through Dafne. But there she was, taking up the entire far end, like a mountain of gold, ruby eyes burning into me, and tail flicking idly.

"I wonder if the tales of dragons hoarding treasure come from the fact that they *look* like a thriced big pile of it," Marskal murmured to me as we crossed the meadow.

I laughed at his irreverence, which felt good. Far better than dwelling on whether I might die soon. Again. Or if he would. I took his hand and laced my fingers with his, giving him a smile. He smiled back, his gaze steady.

"You can do this," he said. "And I'm right here with you."

I didn't even want to protest that I didn't need him there. I was just so glad he was.

We stopped a decorous distance from Kiraka. Not so far that she couldn't immolate me again, but I suspected she could have done that as soon as we were in sight. Marskal gave my hand a squeeze, then dropped back half a step. Guarding my flank, ready to draw weapons to protect me. Foolish, in the face of this behemoth, but it warmed my heart nonetheless.

"Lady Dragon," I said, as Kiraka seemed disinclined to say anything. I bowed to her. "I've returned."

"So I discern. I'm a dragon, not a witless lump of metal as the mossback implied." Despite her caustic words, her tone wasn't unkind.

"I've grown accustomed to the mossback ways of idle greetings," I explained mentally, as much to see if I could as to spare Marskal's feelings. But not an apology. Moranu take me if I was going to apologize to this ancient and cantankerous shapeshifter ever again.

"Allow me then to return an idle observation. You appear to have survived your lesson."

The heat of anger helped burn away the frost of fear. *"Is that what you call it?"*

"Lesson. Test. Recall that I can and do listen in on your conversations. I know you explained it to your mossback companions as such. Playing games with me makes little sense at this juncture."

"You hadn't said anything." To me or to Dafne.

"You, I was waiting to see if you had the spine to approach me again. My Daughter…" The dragon sighed in a mental gust, hot wind over coals. *"I suppose, too, that I'm waiting to see if she forgives me."* The plaintive tone took me aback. The loneliness in it. Her immortality came with the steep price of utter aloneness. Dafne had been her sole companion.

"Well, who else am I going to talk to? The grass, the rain, the stars— Moranu?"

I startled at that, making Marskal twitch, so I waved a hand to tell him to stand down.

"Your lover is most protective. Handsome, too—as best as I can recall such things."

Now chit-chat and gossip? *"He's not my lover."*

"Pity. Perhaps you should change that. Second chances and all. Might as well indulge yourself now as lovemaking will be something forever lost to you as a dragon."

"Does that mean you'll help me?" I almost didn't dare hope.

"You survived, didn't you? I hardly dared hope you might. You didn't seem to have it in you. But I'm happy to be proven wrong. Perhaps you will find it in you to become the dragon."

Even her faint praise filled me with pride. Not such an immature weakling after all.

"How many forms do you have?" she asked.

I tensed. Not only because I didn't dare give her my usual coy answer, but because if she asked me to demonstrate… I wanted to weep. If only she'd asked this of me a week ago.

"Show me," she demanded.

Steeling myself, I reached past the pain, past the fear. Reached for just one of those other forms I'd once taken so blithely, with such easy joy.

Nothing. My flesh remained a lump of clay. I'd become a mossback.

"You can't, can you?" The impatience in her tone stiffened my spine. *"Why are you here if you can't shift? You do understand that becoming a dragon requires, oh, I don't know, shapeshifting?"*

"I thought I should come find out what you require of me," I thought at her, reaching for excuses. *"Tasks to work on for you while I recover my abilities."*

"If you recover them."

I had to. I was a shapeshifter. I didn't know how to be anything else. Even if I failed to take Final Form, I couldn't live my life trapped in this weathering skin.

She gave an irritable huff of steam. *"Perhaps you are correct that you could be spending this time profitably. What do you offer me?"*

What could a dragon want? My thoughts wheeled, breaking apart and reassembling. Part of me yearned for nectar, but I tamped it down. I could eat after. Marskal probably had enough food for seven hungry shapeshifters in that pack of his. It made me smile to think of it. And centered me.

"You want to make it up with Dafne? Help her find N'andana. Help her with the map-sticks." Perhaps that would go some small way to making things up with Dafne, too.

Kiraka contemplated that. *"Why does finding those forgotten lands matter so much?"*

"She has her theories, from books, and calculations. She thinks it will help thwart the gelyneinioes, *who we call* Deyrr. *Isn't that what you want?*

"There is nothing there. If N'andana could have stopped the gelyneinioes, *we would have."*

"Let her try. She's smart about this sort of thing. Isn't that part of why she's your daughter, born to be joined with you?"

"There are many reasons for that."

"But you do want to reassure her that you're not dangerous. You can do that by helping her, by helping us."

Kiraka's thoughts hissed, burning brighter, like coals when turned over. *"She wants you to consult with these travelers of yours? See whatever it is they've discovered about this new incarnation of the* gelyneinioes, *these Practitioners of* Deyrr. *This is important work, yes. But not my gift. I shall think on that. You will go now?"*

"Yes. We plan to sail in the morning and—"

"Too slow. You should fly."

That stung, but I was spared a tart, possibly impolitic reply, when she continued.

"I'll give you a ride. Climb on. Your stalwart protector, too, if you must." She sounded wryly amused, for my consternation or at herself, I wasn't sure. I couldn't spare a thought for it anyway, the way my mind fluttered from thing to thing.

"Now?"

"Of course now. I'm anxious to please my Daughter. Climb on. I'm aging as you dither and Deyrr *grows in power."*

I blew out a breath. Turned to look at Marskal, who waited without expression, a neutral stance that somehow conveyed perfect readiness. "Care to fly on dragonback?"

Even his stoic composure cracked, astonishment transforming him into slack-jawed incredulity, as he looked from me to the dragon. "On her?" His voice even squeaked and he swallowed it down. "Are you fucking kidding me?"

I laughed. I couldn't help it. How strange my life had become. "She's willing to help—and she'll take us to see Jepp and Kral, to save time. To make it up to us. To Dafne." He'd gone so pale—no, actually green—that I put a hand on his arm. "You don't have to. I'll go and be back in a few hours."

His jaw firmed. "I'm not leaving you. I'll go."

I squeezed his arm, my turn to be comforting. "She promises not to drop us in the ocean."

"I never promised any such thing." Kiraka put out a leg and snaked her neck down. *"It will be up to you to hold on."*

~ 12 ~

WE SURGED INTO the morning sky, the sun still fairly low for as long as the climb up the volcano had felt. Marskal perched behind me, one-arm wrapped around my waist in a death grip, the other no doubt free to draw his sword. We sat where Kiraka's broad shoulders narrowed into her neck, forward of her powerful wings. I held one thick spine—as she'd suggested, more helpfully than I'd expected—and we both squeezed tight with our thighs.

Marskal muttered a low litany, something I couldn't quite make out over the roar of the air. We flew high, much higher than I'd ever gone, even as a falcon. The air sang cold on my skin and it would have been unbearable if riding Kiraka hadn't been like straddling a furnace.

Her powerful wings pumped behind us, accelerating to amazing speed. I bent closer to her neck to get my face out of the wind. That helped so I lay to one side of her dorsal ridges, tugging Marskal to follow. He obliged, laying his body over mine and pressing his head into the nook of my shoulder. My hair whipped in the wind—probably nice not to have that lashing him in the face. I reaped the lion's share of benefit, as his warm body made a shell over me.

Below us, the ocean and islands spread out like one of Dafne's maps. I felt the change in Kiraka's muscles, recognizing her preparation for the dive, and turned to give Marskal warning. His face was right there, so I kissed him, hard and impulsively, loving that I'd surprised him.

"Hold on!" I shouted.

He frowned and opened his mouth—and the bottom dropped out from under us. Kiraka dove at such speed that we lifted from contact with her. I held on with all my might, my jubilant scream blending with Marskal's long shout. From experience, I could predict what would happen next. A small dot on the ocean below grew in size. The *Hákyrling*.

"Big stop!" I yelled as loud as I could. Marskal nodded, capitulating and reaching around me to fasten his free hand over mine on the dorsal scale. Just in time. Kiraka flexed her wings and caught the air with a massive *whoompf*, like a ship's sails bellying with the wind. My head snapped into Marskal's forehead and he grunted. But we managed to stay on, with my stomach even catching up, now that we spiraled down in lazy circles.

A few of Ove's crows rose up to meet us, and I realized that alarm calls clanged up from below, sailors scrambling over the rigging. Kiraka tracked the flight of one of the crows.

"Don't eat it," I told her. *"They already think you might be attacking."*

"As if they can hurt me," she grumbled, but obeyed. Sure enough, a volley of arrows whizzed through the air, Kiraka neatly dodging them with shapeshifter speed.

"We need to let them know we're friendly," I shouted to Marskal, who nodded, a grim set to his mouth. The arrows might not pierce Kiraka's scaled hide, but they'd surely kill us easily.

"Suggestions?" he shouted back, a thread of sarcasm in it, I was sure.

Moranu take it, if I could, I'd shapeshift and fly down myself. But I couldn't, and the crushing sorrow of that made my stomach and heart constrict, the cold sweat on my brow chill even at these lower altitudes. *Focus.* We needed a way to signal Jepp, like Marskal and Ursula transmitted information, but…

"The Hawks' signals—is there one to tell her it's you and to stand down?"

Marskal put his mouth against my ear. "Yes, but no way for her to see it from this far up."

"Leave that to me. What is it?"

He lifted his hand from the dorsal spine, flexing and folding it in a series of movements. Another set of arrows whistled past. Too close. "Again," I demanded anyway. I needed to make sure I had it exactly.

Unquestioning, he obliged. I nodded, then focused my magic. It flowed as easily as ever, unconnected to that impenetrable wall around the thought of shifting. I shaped it into a visible blue light. Picturing Jepp, I sent the bubble of magic to her and waited. One. Two. Three.

The arrows stopped. Orders rang out below, but with a different tenor. Standing down. I sat up, Marskal straightening with me. "How in Moranu did you do that?" he asked, turning his head as Kiraka circled, keeping his eye on the *Hákyrling.*

"Just a little thing—I sent Jepp an image of your hands giving the signal."

"Just a little thing." He had an odd look on his face. Not revolted, though. Still getting used to the idea. But also… proud of me? "You *can* do magic."

I shrugged that off. "Some."

He narrowed his gaze on me. "You know I have to kill you now. No one can know the Hawks' secret signals."

A week ago that suspicious tone would have put my back up. Now I knew better. Knew him and his dry, subtle humor better.

And I could repay him in kind. "You said you wanted to take a swim, right?"

"Yes. Why do—"

Kiraka tilted, dumping us in the ocean.

"YOU MIGHT HAVE warned me," Marskal groused as we swam for the ship in waters much cooler than nearer the islands. Despite his complaints, he handled the exercise as athletically as he did everything—with plenty of breath left over to natter at me.

"I can predict her intentions only moments before she does something," I replied, trying not to pant. Swimming as a dolphin, fish or mermaid was *much* easier.

Marskal, of course, noticed. "Loop your arms around my neck and lay over my back."

"I don't want to drown you."

He grinned, full of male confidence. "You couldn't if you tried. Trust me. Save your strength."

Because the *Hákyrling* looked impossibly far, I complied, my turn to lay over his back, holding onto his shoulders. The powerful muscles there flexed as he swam to the ship with mighty strokes. It made me imagine being under him and feeling that play of muscle while he stroked inside me. A distracting thought, but he *had* volunteered.

And I was not yet a dragon.

We reached the ship, a rope ladder thrown down for us. Marskal treaded water with apparent ease, helping me grab ahold and steadying it as I climbed. Hands reached down from above, helping me over the rail. Then Jepp had me in a fierce hug, her compact, vital body hard against me. She was laughing and cursing, rocking me from side to side, then pulled back and kissed me hard on the mouth.

A man's big hand tugged her back. "None of that now." Kral, fully outfitted in his shining black Dasnarian armor, though with the faceplate up, winked at me. "I have to watch her every second."

Jepp made a face at him. "You liked the idea well enough when we invited—"

"Shut up, Jepp," Kral cut her off pleasantly and she grinned at him, then snapped to attention, giving Marskal the Hawks' salute.

"Lieutenant!"

A dripping Marskal shook his head at her with a wry smile. "You don't report to me any longer, remember?"

Jepp dropped her fist with an abashed grin. "Old habits, don't you know." She looked between us. "So that's how you knew the signal. I recognized your sparkly blue magic globe thingy, but couldn't figure out the rest." She eyed Marskal. "You're going to have to kill her now, you know."

He returned her sally with a very serious nod. "So I've already informed her."

"Just make me a Hawk already then," I told them.

Jepp got a speculative expression and Marskal looked me up and down as if guessing my weight. "We don't have any Tala. A shapeshifter and sorceress could come in handy."

"She's a terrible soldier, though," Jepp pointed out. "Never follows orders. Might as well conscript a cat."

"True." Marskal rubbed his chin. "Plus she'd never make it through the initiation."

"Guess it's death then," Jepp agreed cheerfully, making to

draw her big bladed knife. She'd tied a scarf to the end of it, crimson ends fluttering in the breeze that matched the rest of her silk and leather outfit. With her short hair, dark skin and the exotic clothing, she looked even more a pirate now than when we found her fleeing the Dasnarians on the stolen *Hákyrling*.

"Not on the deck," Kral cautioned. "You'll stain the wood."

Jepp made a rueful moue and resheathed her blade. "I want to hear about why you're here on Kiraka anyway. Unless there are more dragons now? Maybe you can strangle her in her sleep, Lieutenant."

"Now there's a thought." Marskal's normally quiet eyes gleamed as if the prospect appealed to him. As if I'd asked him to dash himself to frustration following me around.

"Are you two done?" I finally said, having wrung all the sea water out of my hair that I could. I added an accusing glare for Kral. "You three. I expected better of you, General Kral."

"I don't know why—you've spent time with Harlan." Kral pulled off his helm and ran a hand through sweat-dampened white-blond hair. A leaner, sharper version of his brother, Kral was all shark with none of Harlan's gentler nature. Still, he'd given up the chance of being emperor of Dasnaria, though Jepp insisted it wasn't out of love for her. Something had changed them both during their sojourn to the Imperial Palace. I didn't really want to know what could put shadows like that in Jepp's carefree, insouciant soul. Kral pointed his naked sword at Kiraka, casting her vast shadow over the sailing ship like a menacing thunderhead as she circled above. "Is *that* going to remain?"

"No, she was just waiting for us to get on board." I sent a mental thank you to Kiraka, leaving out my irritation at her dumping us in the sea like that.

I thought you might get hurt if I dropped you on the deck. That float-

ing splinter couldn't hold my weight," she replied anyway, sounding miffed. *"I was trying to be considerate of your frail human bodies."*

I might believe that if she hadn't incinerated me. *"I understand, and we're fine. Would you please tell Dafne where we are?"*

She didn't reply, though I felt her banked-coal presence in my mind. Uncertain? Odd to feel the ancient bitch hesitate.

"Kiraka. If you wish to win Dafne's confidence again, give her that message and then help her with her study of the maps."

A long, smoke-filled pause. *"I would never harm her, or the babe."* She sounded wistful.

"I told her as much, but she knew it anyway."

"Hmm." It wasn't a thank you, but it might be as close as she came to it. *"I shall think on what else you can do to earn the gift of learning dragon form."*

"I look forward to it," I told her. She wheeled and flew up, a vanishing golden dot in the sky.

I lowered my gaze to find the three of them watching me. Jepp widened her eyes. "Apparently you plan to swim back? I didn't know the mermaid form was good for that kind of distance."

"A ride would be nice," I replied, ducking her leading question. Jepp picked up on subtle clues far too easily. "In fact, it would be good to head back to Nahanau immediately and you can explain along the way. We came to get more detail on whatever you sent the cryptic message about."

"I figured that's why *you* were here." Jepp eyed me, then Marskal, speculation in her keen gaze.

"Her Majesty sent me along to assist," Marskal explained. "As Zynda was recently injured,"

"You were?" Jepp lost all hint of playfulness, dark eyes spitting fire, body coiled to attack, eyes scanning for both aggressors and my health. "What happened? Who hurt you? They better be dead already."

"Down, girl," I said, wanting to kick Marskal. "It's a long story and not important. I'm fine now. What have you discovered?"

"Let's discuss all of this over a meal," Marskal suggested, eyes daring me to protest.

"But you're not obsessed," I said lightly.

"Not with food," he replied, letting that hang.

"Food is an excellent idea, regardless, as it's well past midday. Captain's dining cabin then," Kral declared, giving orders that sent people running. Marskal bent his ear, no doubt telling him my current food preferences.

Jepp looked between us with bright interest, but slid an arm around my waist, hugging me close. "You need to see what we have to show you."

"Do we have to *see* it—you can't just tell us?"

Jepp, uncharacteristically somber, dipped her chin. "Yeah. You should see it. We're keeping our distance, but we've been staying in the general area. Just in case. With this thing... well, we've suspended helping people cross the barrier for the time being."

Meeting her gaze, Kral had a similarly dark expression. This couldn't be good.

"Anyway," Jepp added, "it'll take only an hour to sail there and then we can head straight for Nahanau to take you back. Want to clean up and dry off? I still have some of your things that you left on board, so you can change, too. Kral will see to the lieutenant."

"Fine," I agreed, letting her lead me below. Exhaustion crept over me. That last swim had nearly done me in. Without Marskal to carry me... Ugh, I hated thinking about that.

Instead of leading me to the room we'd shared when Jepp,

Dafne, and I had sailed together on the *Hákyrling*, she turned the other way, to the captain's cabin. Of course, she'd share that with Kral now. A big space, it sat forward under the prow, a row of windows over the big bed that took up one end of the room. Jepp busied herself opening cabinets inset in the walls, so I gave into the tired, folded my knees and sat on the floor.

Jepp glanced at me. "Lie on the bed if you like. Kral has this thing about chairs." She got that sly smile that meant his "thing" was sexual. Once I would have teased her about it, drawn out the details, but I didn't want to open the door to questions about Marskal. With her scout's instincts, Jepp already perceived far too much, and I wasn't up for fending off her curiosity. Especially since I hadn't decided what to do about his offer yet. Though I must be seriously considering it, since my thoughts kept returning to prurient images.

"I'm too damp yet," I replied. "This is fine." Too fine, because I felt like I could stretch out and sleep.

Two Dasnarian sailors hauled in a tub and filled it with hot water. Dasnarian-sized, it would be big enough for me to soak in. Jepp folded down a platform and set towels, soaps, and oils on it. Then came over to me once they left. "Let me help you in," she said holding her hands down to me.

I took them, knowing she'd give me grief if I refused, and my pride would take a worse hit if I staggered trying to stand. She helped me shimmy out of my gown and steadied me while I climbed over the high rim. I settled into the hot water with a sigh, my tired body relaxing, and tried to ignore my craving for sugar.

"How badly were you hurt?" Jepp asked, eyeing me critically.

"Enough to set me back," I replied, closing my eyes to her.

"Uh huh. Dunk your head and I'll wash your hair for you."

"I'm not that bad off."

"I've gotten good at it." She had that too-pleased tone in her voice. "Kral has a thing for me playing handmaiden."

"Kral has a lot of 'things.'"

"Yes. Yes, he does, Danu bless the man." She set into scrubbing my hair, massaging my scalp with considerable skill. "Speaking of things, how long has the lieutenant had one for you?"

"Shut up, Jepp."

"That long, huh? And are you reciprocating the thing?"

"If I did, it wouldn't be any of your business."

"That's a yes."

"That's a 'none of your business.'"

"In-terr-est-ing." She rinsed my hair, added more shampoo, and massaged some more. "Not like him, you know."

I didn't want to know. But maybe I should. Moranu knew the man didn't talk about himself much. "Isn't it?"

"Well, you know, like any of us, he gets around just fine. Village girls and such, but never anyone important."

"And I'm important?"

She was quiet a moment. "Of course you are. For a lot of reasons, and you know that."

"Hmm," I replied, then realized I sounded like Kiraka. "To answer your question, no, there's nothing going on besides some mild flirtation, a few kisses. I've been busy not dying."

"Ah, now we get to it." She did a final rinse of my hair, draped it outside the tub, and set to combing and oiling it. "Spill."

Kicking myself for letting that slip—a measure of how much the topic of Marskal flustered me, when this sort of conversation had never unsettled me before—I searched for a reply that would satisfy the ever-inquisitive Jepp. "It was a near thing, but I'm fine now."

"Zynda, honey, that's a lie. You know I've always thought you were hot, but you're much too skinny."

I cracked an eye open at her. "Is this tender care a ruse to ogle me?"

She grinned cheerfully. "You know me. But I'm not allowed to act on it. I promised Kral exclusivity, Danu kill me now."

I laughed. I had missed her twisted humor and unrepentant verve for life. "That bad, huh?"

"Actually…" she trailed off, thoughtful. "It's not. I never thought I'd be the monogamous type, but it's good. Different." I felt her shrug. "It helps that he's hung like a stallion and committed to making sure I don't get restless."

When I finished laughing, she stroked my forehead. "Now, tell Auntie Jepp what happened."

So, I did. One thing about Jepp, for all her irreverence, she listened to reports well, filing away the information and not getting stuck in the gory details. She whistled low and long once I brought her up to speed, then helped me out of the tub, insisting on drying me.

"I don't know how you did it." She looked me over, not with lust, but as if trying to see the secret in my flesh. "No wonder you don't want to try shifting again."

"I have tried. I just … can't."

"Ah." She studied me thoughtfully. "Your trunk of things is right there. We've been dragging them all over hither and yon."

"I'd forgotten about them." With some delight, I extracted a gown I'd brought from Annfwn, a lovely hand-embroidered silk that Anya had given me. Shapeshifters tend to be hard on clothes, and I had literally forgotten I'd left these here when I first swam away from the *Hákyrling* on an urgent errand to inform Ursula of Dafne's abduction. Aha! And one of my other long pins. Happily, I twisted my damp hair—smelling of some

Dasnarian spice—into a rope and fastened it there. The old habit grounded me. I *was* fine. I would be fully myself.

"What can I do to help?" Jepp asked, unexpectedly gentle.

"With what?"

"Don't fuck with me, shapeshifter." Jepp's gaze had gone flinty, no more gentleness. "I recognize a trauma case when I see one. I think you probably can shift, but you're sabotaging yourself. You've lost your nerve."

"I have not," I snapped. "You're as bad as Marskal."

"Aha!" She nodded in satisfaction. "He's noted it, too. Good."

"It's not good. He's driving me crazy with the hovering, making me eat all the time, going on about how fear of the pain is the hardest thing to get over and I don't know what all."

Jepp just nodded again. "Perfect. He's a good man. Ready for lunch?"

"You're just dropping the topic?" This had to be some trick of hers.

She only smiled cheerfully and kissed my cheek. "Oh yes, honey. With the lieutenant on the job, I know you'll be fine. He's quiet, but tenacious as a mountain cat on the hunt."

"Great," I muttered. "Just wonderful."

Jepp slid an arm around my waist and squeezed. "I know."

~ 13 ~

AFTER A REASONABLY convivial meal—one where I ate all the fruit and honeyed breads available and no one commented—we gathered on deck. The barrier shimmered off to my left, a good distance away still, but so brightly full of magic that I couldn't mistake it for anything else.

I lifted my face into the breeze, sensing something strange, like the fetid odor of death though I didn't actually smell anything but sea. It reminded me of that oddly mindless shark.

"What is it?" Marskal asked quietly.

"I don't know. A wrongness." I frowned at him. He'd cleaned up, too, though he hadn't shaved, and wore borrowed Dasnarian clothing. With the shirt open at his collar, the laces hanging and loose sleeves billowing, he looked less the weary, hard-edged soldier. A tangle of chest hair showed through the opening and, tempted to touch it, I did, enjoying the catch of his breath when I tugged, and the way his eyes darkened. "I like you in this shirt."

"And you look even more lovely than usual in that Tala gown," he returned.

"I've been having a hard time deciding who I should warn not to break the other's heart or I'd have to kill them," Jepp announced, "so I'm just telling you both."

I let go of Marskal and smiled at her. "This from the woman

who bedded most of the Vervaldr, and with delight for new meat because she'd run through the population of Ordnung already?"

On the other side of her, Kral's jaw clenched and he growled. Jepp turned her back to him, cocked a hip, and rolled her eyes. "So, you've heard the stories. But I never did Marskal." She flashed her former lieutenant a winning smile. "Just so you know."

"Because I convinced you it would be bad for discipline," Marskal returned evenly.

She shrugged that off. "Stick to that story, but it's just as well, given how things have developed."

"Things, I might remind you," I said lightly, "that are none of your business. But you needn't worry. No hearts are or will be broken, as none are involved."

Jepp's gaze flicked to Marskal, and back to me. "If you say so."

"I see something in the water." Marskal was staring intently into the distance, holding onto the ship's rail as he leaned out to get a better perspective. Trust him to be all business, which I needed to emulate. Jepp, as always, was a bad influence.

I peered past him, the not-smell stronger now. "I don't see what you're looking at."

"We could climb to the crow's nest," Jepp said to Kral, though she sounded uncharacteristically subdued. "That way we wouldn't have to sail as close."

Kral, who'd shed his armor in favor of light pants and shirt, shook his head. "Too many of us to fit and I'd rather keep an experienced lookout up there, despite your excellent long sight."

"Best in the Hawks," Marskal commented quietly, and she gave him a brilliant smile.

"We're staying on this side of the barrier?" I asked, and Jepp sobered, frowning.

"Yes. I have the Star, of course, so we *could* cross." She patted the crimson leather over her breastbone. "But it's not a good idea in this area."

"What happens?" Marskal wanted to know, his attention sharpening.

"Inevitable attack, often within minutes," Jepp replied, falling into her pattern of reporting to her former lieutenant. "Animals of all types. The fish-birds that Zynda will recall from her previous voyage, seabirds, ocean mammals, but not alive. Not exactly."

"Like the animated dead Illyria created at Ordnung?" Marskal showed no expression or revulsion. But then, he'd dealt with dispatching and burning them, many of them former friends. Speaking of having nerve, I had no idea how one came through that kind of horror unscathed.

"Like, but not exactly," Jepp explained. "They can be dealt with by dismembering them enough to make them harmless, but otherwise no."

But exactly like that mindless shark. A chill raised the small hairs on my arms.

"Animals should be able to cross the barrier without magical assistance," I inserted. That had ever been the case, even when the barrier surrounded only Annfwn. It worked to keep out people.

Jepp gave me a shrewd look. "That's partly how we know these are unnatural. These animals can't cross, which is one of the things I wanted to ask you about, but hesitated to put in the missive. I lose track of which Tala secrets I'm not supposed to know."

I shook my head at her, frowning, not so much for her big mouth by for my mind not fastening on an answer. How did the shark cross, if it came from *Deyrr*? "It makes no sense."

"It doesn't have to make sense," Kral said, all practicality. "Suffice to say that your queen's barrier is protecting us from creatures animated by the Temple of *Deyrr*, which is a good thing because we have bigger problems than that."

"What?" Marskal demanded.

"This isn't something I have words to describe," Jepp retorted. "And why bother, when you can look?"

She pointed and I followed the line of her finger, Marskal squinting beside me. The sun was lowering quickly to the horizon, running ahead of the early tropical twilight, and at first I didn't see it through the glinting rays. Then, I did, and leaned forward, gripping the rail.

"Moranu preserve us," Marskal breathed beside me, and Jepp, on the other side of him, gave him an odd look.

Black matter oozed through the water, like fingers of flowing lava, but matte dark. Shipmaster Jens kept the *Hákyrling* well back, running parallel to the bulk of the ichor. For there was more, stretching back in a solid mat to a jutting shadow of land on the horizon. The shimmer of the barrier danced through the land. Beyond, the landscape seemed even more decomposed and corrupt.

"Can I borrow that glass of yours?" I asked Jepp and she nodded, handing it to me with a wry smile.

"My spare, because I knew you'd ask."

"I'd love to fly over it, get a better look," I said, holding the scope up to my eye and focusing it, remembering belatedly, with a stab of grief, that I couldn't.

"I won't allow it," Kral said. "The stuff has odd properties. We lost a man and one of Ove's crows to it. No one else is going near on my watch."

"What is that land mass?" I asked, the feeling of foreboding growing stronger. "Is it part of Dasnaria?"

"I'm surprised you recognize it. Kral replied. "A remote peninsula, but still Dasnaria."

"Dafne is way ahead of you," I told him absently, scanning the barrier and the land on either side. "All those maps in her library. She'd already determined the barrier likely went through a piece of Dasnaria."

He grunted, in irritation or amusement. "That *nyrri* is clever."

I sent a magical tendril to assay it better, despite the bad taste it left behind, as I hadn't been able to in dolphin form. I recognized that flavor, the sapping feel of it, twisted magic like the kind that High Priestess of *Deyrr* had wielded when she tried to steal the Star of Annfwn from us. She wanted it still. And was finding a way through the barrier to get it.

"Population?" I asked.

"Sparse. Mostly sheepherders." Kral's voice had an underlying tension.

"What do you see, Zynda?" Jepp demanded, cutting through the niceties. "You know perfectly well I wanted you to look at this because you can see through the barrier and we can't. Cursed thing is still mostly a big mirror to me, even with the Star—but it's going right through that peninsula, yes?"

I nodded reluctantly, handing her the spyglass. Then rubbed my eyes. "It is. And this ... ooze in the water is coming from the rocks there."

"What is it?" Marskal asked, terse, reading something in me, as he seemed to be gaining the knack of doing.

"Let's postpone the analysis," Kral said. "Have you seen enough? I'd like to put some distance between us and it—and you want to get back to Nahanau."

"Yes. Let's get out of here." And get the Star out of here. I nodded gratefully to Kral, who turned immediately to give the orders to come about. The sails snapped, ropes and timbers creaking as the ship responded to the sailors climbing the rigging. My temples throbbed and I rubbed them, closing my eyes against the too-bright sun.

"Zynda." Marskal put a hand on my back. "Come and sit down."

"No, I'm fine." I opened my eyes to their concerned faces. "This isn't a health thing—it's reaction to that stuff out there."

"What is it?" Jepp asked, even her irrepressible attitude subdued.

"I don't know exactly. I understand now why you didn't want to try to explain it." Moranu knew I didn't want to try. "The best I can say is that it's an aspect of the death magic the Practitioners of *Deyrr* wield. It's a waste product, what remains after they've digested life."

"You're saying it's literally shit." Kral's hand flexed on his sword.

I laughed and he frowned at me. It felt good to laugh. Merriment was the antidote to death, to so much of what *Deyrr* hoped to do. *There is also loving and being loved.* Maybe that's what Moranu meant. "Leave it to a Dasnarian to put something so crudely, if accurately," I said.

Needing the freedom, I pulled the pin from the coil and stuck it in my sleeve, shaking my hair out and scratching my fingers over my scalp. My skin itched, too. Marskal was right— I'd never gone this long without shifting, and the constraints of my human form made me restless. If I had to stay human forever, I might go insane. No wonder Salena had. *Don't think about it.*

"This is guessing," I continued, "but I think the high priestess is fully aware of that land incursion through the barrier— might have been since the barrier moved and the magical storms occurred—and they're exploiting it. *Deyrr* is using it as a kind of lever against the barrier, to attempt to dissolve it or punch a hole through. Your people there are lost to you," I told Kral, levelly, and he accepted it in the same way, with a brusque nod. "The undead animals…" I hated to speak it aloud.

"Just say it." Marskal's expression was set, tense, his jaw tight. I considered kissing him to soften those unhappy lines around his mouth. And to give myself the pleasure of something good and right.

"I think they were humans once," I said quietly. "Dasnarians, most likely, though they could be Nahanauns or…" I hated to give voice to it. "Well, no way to know now. We do know *Deyrr*'s magic is targeted at human beings, not animals, and we know the ones observed here aren't real animals because they can't cross the barrier. So they must be people forced into animal form in an attempt to trick the barrier."

"But shapeshifters in animal form could cross the barrier into Annfwn before," Marskal said, searching my face as if he might find more truth there.

"You and Ursula discovered far too many of our Tala secrets." I had to smile, and—because I needed the contact, even if he didn't—I stroked his cheek, lightly scraping my nails over his late-day stubble. I'd like to dig my claws into more than that. "That's true. I think, therefore, that these must not be true shapeshifters, but people—maybe partblood mossbacks—forced into animal form via unnatural magic."

"To what purpose?" Kral demanded, but Jepp understood.

"Scouts," she said. "And spies. Testing our defenses. They're experimenting, adjusting the magic until they can get someone through."

I nodded. "That's my guess."

"It's a good guess," Kral breathed, sounding as close to

horrified as I'd ever heard him. "It's good strategy. If I wanted to invade a land behind a barrier, that's what I'd want to do."

"And when they do find a way through..." Jepp trailed off, fingering her own blade.

I nodded. "I think some already have." And I told them about the shark I'd encountered, so near Nahanau. Jepp's expression turned ferocious.

"We need to get back with all speed," she told Kral. "Danu only knows how far those creatures have infiltrated."

As if her words had summoned the attack, the lookout shouted from above—a Dasnarian word I didn't know, but that galvanized the entire crew. Jepp whirled and drew her daggers, putting herself between me and the rail, while Kral seemed to grow a foot taller. He drew his sword in one hand, a huge knife in the other, striding back and forth, calling orders.

"Shapeshift into a defensive form already," Jepp tossed at me, frowning.

I shook my head, steeling myself for the admission. "Can't. Still recovering."

"Then get below," Jepp ordered me, but I ignored her, trying to see what had everyone so excited.

"Too late to get everyone into armor," Kral said, returning. Then scowled at me. "You were told to get below."

"I can't shift, but I'm not defenseless," I replied in a mild tone, "and you may need me."

He made a disgusted sound. "I know you and your missish *qualms* about using magic. If you're not willing to do that, batting your pretty blue eyes at these things won't make any difference."

"I've got her covered," Marskal said, with quiet assurance. I glanced at him, to find he'd also drawn a sword and a short dagger. He met my gaze equably. "But if *I* tell you to get below, you do."

I rolled my pretty blue eyes at him, then pushed past Jepp to the rail, following her line of sight. A black cloud rose out of the sludge covering the sea. Wishing for enhanced long sight or the spy glass again, I strained to see. Then Jepp cursed, and an arrow whizzed past my head, neatly nailing something zooming toward the ship and dropping it from the sky.

Glancing back, I saw the archer was a pretty woman—she had to be Dasnarian, with that height and coloring, her blonde hair in a long braid down her back—wielding a bow with impressive skill. Clearly she was the woman who'd nearly taken us out of the sky. Though several of Kral's men had joined her, none matched her cool speed and calm aim as she loosed several more arrows in succession.

"Kral's ex-wife," Jepp explained. "Long story."

"Annulled," Kral growled. "Incoming."

"Behind me," Marskal instructed, cool as ever, neatly maneuvering so that I stood inside a triangular shield of the three warriors. The creatures pinpointed and dropped by the archers had been the advance, their numbers intensifying. Yes, I certainly did remember these fish-birds, but these had that same wrongness, that not-smell. It was, I suddenly realized, the smell of something not alive and yet not decaying. I really wanted a closer look at one.

Jepp spun in a whirl of blades, pieces of fish birds dropping to the deck, black ichor spraying in a foul mist. On her left, protecting her weaker side—though with Jepp it hardly counted as "weak"—Kral bellowed, swinging his huge sword with devastating skill and speed. And Marskal—well, I'd seen him spar, but never fight full-out. As he did in everything, he fought with neat economy. No dramatics, no elaborate tricks with the blade. He simply picked off each comer, with sword or knife, his face as calm as if he drilled against a practice dummy. Moranu knew why, but the sight aroused me beyond reason.

A fish-bird, wounded but still twitching, dropped to the deck at my feet, oozing unnatural black fluids, and I crouched to examine it. Leery of touching it, I caressed it with a light magical tendril. Foul. Dead and not dead. This wasn't the bright green, vibrant, if mutated creature we'd encountered before. Its life force had gone elsewhere—and it had become a statically preserved carcass, mindless, animated from elsewhere.

Making sure I could, ignoring the increasing frenetic fighting around me, I manifested a very small globe of magic. Applied it to the carcass as a test—and it vanished. Good enough.

Marskal yanked me to my feet. "I said, get below, *now.*"

"Cover me," I replied. "I need to see."

His jaw tightened, his brown eyes molten in his otherwise impassive face, splattered with blood, both red and black, and I thought I'd have to fight through him. But he came to a decision, nodded crisply. "Fast. I can't protect you for long."

I'd already pulled hard on the magic. It's not a physical thing, so it doesn't need time. Like shapeshifting, it's there or it's not. At least I had that. "Get me to the rail."

He cursed but moved, spinning me to the rail, somehow getting me past Jepp's whirlwind of knives. I didn't hesitate, but released the magic in a sparkling blast.

Instantly, the sky was empty.

I almost laughed at the way they all faltered in mid swing, stumbling into a halt as their targets vanished, their deadly rhythm interrupted. Kral and Jepp swung on me with astonished expressions. Marskal only looked at me, shook his head with a soft laugh, and began cleaning his blades. Kral wasn't nearly so amused.

"*This* is what you can do?" he thundered. A deep scratch from a fish-bird talon bled profusely under one eye, giving him a decidedly dramatic mien. Otherwise the ichor had vanished along with the carcasses. "All this time?"

I shrugged, pushing my hair out of my face. "Sometimes." One benefit of rarely using my magic was it built up nicely. And that hadn't been a difficult task.

He swelled as if he might explode. "If you were my woman, I'd—"

"Ho-kay," Jepp said, inserting herself between us. "Let's not annoy the powerful sorceress. Come on below, baby, and I'll kiss those wounds to make them better." She tossed me an opaque look, nodding in agreement with whatever Kral muttered at her, drilling me with angry glares as she led him away.

"How do you feel?" Marskal asked me. He looked me up and down. "Are you wounded at all?"

"With such brilliant warriors to protect me?" I smiled easily. "Not a bit. You?"

"Miraculously, given what I'd heard about the speed of those creatures, I'm fine. Only a few scratches."

"They were slow," I replied, reviewing the brief attack in my mind.

He laughed. "That was slow?"

"Compared to when they were alive, yes."

His expression changed, and he glanced over the water, as if he might see them still. "Those were animated by *Deyrr*?"

I wrapped my arms around myself and nodded, feeling a bit sick now that the fever of fight had fled my body. "I examined one."

"Then they made it through the barrier."

"Small things pass more easily."

"I'd better tell Kral to make all speed then. You rest. I'll find you."

NEEDING NO FURTHER urging, I did as he suggested. If I could have, I'd have shifted to the form of a small cat to take advantage of the easy dozing. I almost felt the little claws and satisfying relaxed resilience of the form just a thought away. So easy to fit into that one, but the rime of fear held me back. It made no sense, but I didn't want to try again and not be able to. *You've lost your nerve.* I didn't think that was true. Not entirely. But no need to test my ability when I was so tired.

As it was, I curled up in the shady nook at the prow of the ship—up top, thank you, as I had no wish to be trapped inside.

The freshening air streamed over me as the *Hákyrling* flew before the wind, headed to the harbor at Nahanau, and I slept deeply, thankfully without dreams.

When I awoke, Marskal sat near my feet. He had his back against the gunwale and long legs stretched out in front of him, crossed at his booted ankles, hands folded in his lap. His chin lolled down to his chest as he, too, slept, but he sat in such a way that his outstretched legs blocked my egress, and I'd have to tiptoe over him to get by. I was tempted to try, just to see if I could. I bet I could, and it would be so satisfying to see his face when he figured out I'd outfoxed him.

Then I noticed he held a piece of my hem twined between his fingers. Not my hair this time, but still. Torn between affection for his foibles and irritation at being leashed, I took a moment to gaze up at the brilliant array of stars. Full night had fallen, but Moranu's moon was out of sight. She'd be at three-quarters, waning to new. Out on that wretched and dying peninsula of land, the priests and priestesses of *Deyrr* had to be watching it, too, waiting to exploit the power of shadows and change.

Marskal stirred, then snapped up his head, scanning for danger.

"Always guarding me," I said. "Even in his sleep." I tugged my hem from his grasp and he gave me a slow smile, not at all bothered by my tart tone.

"Call it a habit at this point," he said. "I feel better knowing I'm keeping an eye on you."

Hmm. The way he'd come to calm alert reminded me of how he'd looked fighting, and something about that quiet precision led my mind to how it would feel to have that meticulous focus on pleasuring me. And I felt better. Restless enough to shift, but with nowhere to put that energy. *You've lost your nerve.* I was not thinking about it. I needed something to take my mind off worrying, and he *had* volunteered.

"Hungry?" he asked, cocking his head to read my face.

"Yes." I slid over to climb onto his lap, straddling him and cradling his rough cheeks between my palms. Kissing him deeply, showing him the depth of my need. This felt good and right. Human. Skin to skin.

He recovered from his initial surprise—I might have moved too fast in the blaze of desire—and stroked his hands up my back under my hair, holding me close and escalating the kiss with even more intense desire. I hummed with delight and he groaned a harmonious counterpoint. Through my thin dress, against my heating sex, I felt him hard and ready. I reached down, but he grabbed my wrist, stopping me and breaking the kiss.

"Not so fast," he breathed.

I considered him. "You've changed your mind?" The turnabout had to be what bothered me, the true reason for the sense of crushing disappointment. Like Zyr, I'd always had my choice of lovers, back when I'd taken them. I hadn't expected for Marskal to refuse me now.

"Never," he said, still holding my hand away from his groin, but straightening and combing his fingers up through my hair to cup my skull, then kissing me deeply and fervently. I squirmed a little, gasping for the breath he'd stolen, but in all the intensity of his grip made me feel safe, rather than trapped. Finally, he withdrew, backing out of the kiss slowly, enticing me to follow, and he laughed, a warm, dark sound. "But not here, where anyone can see."

"The Tala don't care for such things," I said, though it wasn't entirely true.

"This mossback does. The things I want to do to you need privacy."

"Indoors?" I asked, dubiously, though his words heated my blood.

"Unless you want to swim or fly us to a private island." He didn't exactly dare me, but I felt the inherent testing of my nerve in the suggestion. "Have you tried to shift again?"

I crawled off of him, standing, and shaking out my gown and hair. "Even if I wanted to try, I don't know this part of the ocean. I suppose we'll have to postpone to another time."

He rose to his feet, fast enough to surprise me, and pulled me against him, fisting his hands in my hair, just tight enough to tip my chin up for him to study my face. He brushed my lips with his, soft, searching, with a gentleness belied by the ferocity of his grip. "Is that what you want—to wait?"

"No," I breathed. "Who knows what tomorrow will bring? I want to follow the impulse of the moment."

"Is that all this is to you? An impulse of the moment. A passing fancy." He kissed the corner of my mouth, then the underside of my jaw. I slipped my hands inside his open shirt, splaying them against his excellent musculature.

"It can't be more than that," I said, making myself think through the sweet, swirling arousal. "You know that. You have to remember it. This can't be more than right now. Sex only. Because I'll be—"

"I know. The dragon. That's in the future, not tonight." He trailed his lips down my throat and I arched for him, the pull on my hair relaxing as he murmured approval. "Besides—I don't believe you're so cavalier. You talked about me with Jepp."

"There is no talking *with* Jepp—she talks and the other person is left to confirm or deny."

"And yet, you didn't deny."

Hadn't I? I couldn't recall exactly what I'd said. It didn't matter. "What I want is irrelevant." I pushed out of his delightfully strong hold, gripping his shoulders to make him look at me. "My life is not my own. We can have this, for now, if you're willing to accept that, but long term..." I let go of him and shrugged for the inevitability of fate. "How I feel doesn't matter."

"There's a particular style to that Tala shrug of yours," he said. "Elaborate, languid, and full of lies."

"Lies?" I raised my brows. I'd expected anger from him, but not this.

"I've seen you in action, shapeshifter." He picked up a lock of my hair, winding it around his finger and tugging me closer. "You are powerfully in charge of your destiny. Nothing stops you from taking what you want."

I laughed, liking that image of myself. "Hmm. I do want you."

"Then take." He'd eased us close enough together again that my peaked nipples brushed against his chest, the silk a lovely tease of things to come.

"Tonight might be all we have," I warned him.

"I'm a soldier. I live with that reality every day."

"All right then." I kissed him, the feeling oddly like feeding from a flower, the sweetness and life flowing into me. "Take me inside."

~ 14 ~

I MIGHT'VE LAUGHED that his private indoor place turned out
to be the old cabin I'd shared with Jepp and Dafne. Except
that it seemed fitting. Someone had taken away the three
hammocks and put in a largish bed, but Dafne's desk still stood
in the same place. I could imagine her working there while Jepp
and I paced the floor in our shared restlessness. Always during a
storm. Otherwise I'd be out swimming or flying.

Odd to feel a nostalgia for the time I didn't spend with them.
Opening one of the desk drawers, I found it stocked with
scribing supplies, as if Dafne might return to use them at any
moment. Jepp's thought, no doubt, and it made me smile that
she might feel the same fondness for that shared journey. They'd
both completed their assignments, while I'd continued on by
myself, always keeping mine secret. Had that been the wrong
choice?

Marskal finished opening the portholes, a row of three that
let in the night air and occasional sea spray, and came up behind
me, moving my hair aside and kissing the back of my neck. I
hummed an encouragement, fitting my bottom against his
crotch, the fire between us flaring to life as if we'd never banked
it for the short trip below.

"Still alright?" he asked against my skin.

"Of course. Why?"

"You seem sad."

I laughed. "No, I don't. I'm not ever sad." Not that I liked to show.

"Because you're Tala, not human." He kissed the hollow at the juncture of my neck and shoulder, then licked it and I purred my approval, leaning my weight into him.

"Exactly," I replied, my voice throaty. "We live in the moment. No regrets for the past; no worries about the future."

"Lies." He spanned my waist with his long-fingered hands, then slid them up to cup my breasts. At the same time, he sank his teeth into that tender juncture at my neck, making me gasp and writhe in truth. Oh yes. My mossback lover might do just fine.

He held me there, teasing my breasts and nipples, alternately biting, licking, and kissing that spot that drove me wild. My fingers tingled with the desire to grow claws, to bite in turn. Instead I dug them into his forearms where he'd rolled up his cuffs, the tanned skin wiry with dark hair, corded and hard from his warrior ways. His hands tightened on my breasts, rough now with his desire, and I arched in his arms, making him work to hold me.

He laughed again, that same dark, drunken sound, and it went to my core. "Wild thing," he muttered, and spun me around, lifting me up onto the desk, and pushing between my spread thighs. I wrapped my legs around his lean hips, vising him, holding him tight against me, so I could rub against him for my pleasure. He leaned a hand against the desk, bracing himself, and recaptured my hair, winding it around his fist and dragging my head back so my breasts thrust into the air. His avid mouth took them, hot through the silk, the scrape of his teeth so keen I cried out the savage need.

"Shh," he urged. "People will hear."

"So proper." I laughed, which became a moan when he lightly bit my nipple, then sucked hard. "So private, my moss-back lover."

"Yes." He lifted his head to stare fiercely into my eyes. Letting go of my hair, he picked me up and set me on my feet. Then gathered my loose gown and pulled it over my head, tossing it to the floor. His normally quiet eyes burned with an almost savage hunger as he took me in. I let him look his fill, arrested by the way he arranged my long hair over my shoulders, reverently tracing the lines of my body. "Private, yes," he murmured, more to himself than to me. "At least with this. Here, in this place and time, I have you to myself." His gaze flicked up to mine. "Is it mossback of me to be so selfish?"

"Yes," I whispered.

"It's not in me to share."

"Mossback ways, not Tala."

"Let me guess: the Tala don't care for such things." He feathered his fingertips over my breasts, tracing my belly and the flare of my hips.

"Some couples are exclusive," I told him, a strange catch in my throat. Something about the way he touched me. That tenderness. I almost preferred the savage side. I knew how to handle that. "But it's rare. And frowned upon."

He hmmd thoughtfully, kissed the round of my shoulder. "Rayfe is possessive of Andi—I've seen it. And she of him. I was there that day, when she threw herself in front of him, to save his life."

"Caring about someone, wanting to save his life, isn't the same as mating for the duration of it."

"But they have."

"They're different. And it doesn't matter because you agreed this is only tonight."

"I'll take what I can have," he replied, hands tightening on me.

I moved under those hands, restless, unsure of the meaning there. "I want to undress you."

He smiled at me, a small lift of his mouth, a wryness behind it that made him think he saw through me. "Far be it from me to stand between you and what you want."

Just for that I should claw him. He brought out the ornery side of me, and I couldn't help showing off, just a little. I took his shirt in my fists and ripped it down the middle, using my shapeshifter strength to part the thick cloth as easily as one of Dafne's papers. He reacted to the shock quickly, hands seizing my wrists before I finished pushing the shirt off his shoulders. We stood like that for an endless moment, locked in place. Then he chuckled, shaking his head, fingers flexing to slide down my arms.

"Wild thing," he said again.

Yes," I replied. I scratched my nails over his chest in demonstration. Not hard, just enough to leave faint lines.

"What would it take to tame you?" he wondered.

I licked the hollow of his throat and up to the bulge of his larynx. He caught his breath, muscles flexing under my palms. "Is that what you want?" I asked, nipping at him, then laving the spot with my tongue so he shuddered. "A tame pet on a leash. Go find a mossback girl for that."

He laughed, wound his fingers in my hair and pulled me into a drowning kiss, my naked breasts crushed against his bare chest. The contact blew all my thoughts away. I had to have him.

I dragged my hands down to undo his sword belt. Once it gave, the too-big borrowed pants slid off his narrow hips. I started to toss the belt aside, but he firmly took it from me, setting it on the desk with precise care, then toeing off his boots and kicking off the pants.

He turned, and I took him by the cock and the mouth both at once, filled with the furious need he'd stirred in me. He picked me up, lifting me easily for the few steps to the bed, then fell on top of me. I worked his shaft, hard, hot, and long. "Inside me," I demanded.

"But you—" he started and I bit his lower lip, then pulled his hand between my thighs, into the slick tissues, swollen with wanting.

"Now," I told him. "It's not in me to wait."

He stroked me there, watching my face, working his clever fingers until I gasped and threw back my head. I clutched those strong shoulders, hanging onto him. "Please, Marskal."

A smile curved the tight line of his mouth, eyes burning into mine. "I like that, the way you said my name. Say it again." He slipped a finger inside me, curling it so I convulsed and cried out. He captured the sound with a kiss, then let me go. "Say it again," he urged.

I scratched my nails down his back, not being gentle this time. "Marskal," I growled.

He arched, hissing, and reached down to lift my knee, pushing my thigh back and opening me, then settled between my legs, leaning on one elbow, face taut with desire. "Next time is slow."

"If there is a next time," I cautioned.

"There's all of tonight, at least."

"Maybe."

"Maybe?" His cock nudged my entrance, easing in, so I moaned and closed my eyes, anticipating, craving that first deep thrust. He stopped there. Leaving me hanging, he waited until I opened my eyes to glare at him. "Maybe?" he demanded.

I tried to give him a fierce stare back, but it was driving me crazy, having him almost inside me. I wriggled, to no avail. The man had iron control and my leverage was all wrong, unless I changed that. "Maybe," I spat at him.

"Then this time is slow." He eased himself into me, bit by bit, stretching and filling, but depriving me of the powerful thrust and ensuing frenzy. I thrashed against him, lifting my hips, but he stared me down, burying himself to the hilt in me, then slowly drawing back. Almost entirely, leaving just enough inside me to obliterate my control.

"Marskal!" I snarled at him.

Infuriatingly, he laughed, a rolling of breath, soft thunder backing the storm in his eyes. "I like that, too."

I considered throwing him off me and reversing positions, pinning him so I could ride him to my satisfaction, but he spotted it in me. "Don't do it," he warned. "Or I won't play at all."

He eased into me, so slowly it was torture. I threw my head back and wailed my frustration. Buried in me, he easily caught my mouth, kissing me with such sweetness it didn't seem possible that he was the same man tormenting me. "Shh," he murmured, pressing my hands palm up beside my head, lacing his fingers with mine. "Relax. Calm. Feel that?"

His skin slid against mine, warm, hard edged, our legs and fingers tangled together. Brushing my lips with his, coaxing, soothing, breathing my breath, he rocked in me. No, the ship rocked around us, the pitching and creaking taking us up one side and down the other. He moved in me and I clung to the waves of pleasure as they built, suspended between him and the ship, and the ocean. It was like flying and swimming both. Animal, with our bodies joined and the sweat slicking us together.

More than that. I felt like I had when I was wrapped in Moranu's arms. Safe and loved. I whimpered and Marskal soothed me murmuring my name.

"Zynda. My Zynda." He kissed me in between, chanting my name and setting it on my tongue. Somewhere in there I let go, unfurling and going with it, letting myself be held and penetrated and wrapped up. He accelerated the thrusts, slipping a hand under my hips to adjust the angle, pushing deeply into me.

I'd lost all track of everything except his skin under my hands, the play of his muscles, and the sharply sweet merging of our bodies. Just as in the moment of shifting from one form to another, I blurred, no longer bound to flesh, but freed... and the climax took me in a rush, flinging me out of myself and into a starry realm where we were one person and many. Shifting faces of all things together.

I cried out, clinging to him, an anchor in the storm, my mouth feeding on his, on the sweet words he gave me, full of the love I'd been promised and never expected to have. It was wrong, and yet I soaked it up. Just that once.

I MIGHT HAVE dozed. Or fainted a bit, from the intensity of our joining. It shouldn't have been possible to sleep, pinned under his rangy body, my hair tangled under me. Though he'd softened, he was still buried inside me, our pelvises fused, my legs wound around him. He stirred, moving to withdraw and I tightened my legs, preventing him.

He breathed a laugh, kissed my temple and raised his head. "I should get off of you."

"Not yet." I drew him into a kiss, and he relaxed into it,

leisurely and thorough, now that we'd taken the edge off. We moved too much, though, and he slid out of me, a gush of fluid following. I sighed for it. "All right, fine."

He cocked a grin at me. "Allow me to fetch a cloth for my lady."

Levering himself up with considerable vitality given how we'd expended ourselves, he strode the short distance to a stack of towels on a small table bolted to the wall. I turned on my side, enjoying the view, feeling languid as a well-petted cat. "You're well prepared."

He handed me one, then sat on the side of the bed, using another to clean himself. "Part of the job."

I raised a brow at him. "Bodyguard, scout, lover, and hand-maid. So many facets to your profession."

He bent over and kissed me, lingering over it. "I like 'lover' best."

"You're good at it, too," I told him, sliding my hand up his lean back. His breath escaped in a hiss and he frowned. "I'm afraid I scratched you. Drew blood in a few places."

"Did you now." He sounded aroused and amused, tracing a finger down my throat to my breast.

"Surely I didn't need to warn you to be wary of my claws."

"And here I was so careful not to mar your pretty skin."

"Don't be careful," I told him. "I don't need it."

"But you do." He watched my face, cupping my breast and brushing his thumb over it. "You're so beautiful, Zynda. I meant to tell you before, in the proper order." He stroked down over my belly, and I turned on my back, letting him explore. "Your skin is like a newborn's. Flawless and soft as new cream."

"It's the shapeshifting," I said, not sure why I felt like con-fiding. Something about the way he looked at me made me want to. "We don't scar. Even the light tan I had before is as dark as I ever get. It's a kind of rejuvenation, every time we shift." Except I'd lost that. And I wasn't going to think about it.

"That sounds like a recipe for a long life." He looked somber at that.

I nodded. "If we don't get ourselves killed. That's another reason shapeshifters rarely form permanent relationships, except with maybe another shapeshifter."

"That's why you said Rayfe and Andi are different."

"I wasn't sure you were listening then."

"I always listen to you." He told me that very seriously, though he seemed to be watching the movement of his hand down my thigh. Then his gaze flicked up to mine. "Though I also know you don't always tell me the truth."

He bent and pressed a kiss to the inside of my thigh, just above the knee, and I sighed for the sweet pleasure of it. The man possessed a talented mouth.

"I don't exactly lie, either. Truth and lies aren't either-or things," I murmured, floating on the sensation. His hand smoothed down my calf, his mouth following with such exquisite caresses that I didn't mind that he laughed at me.

"How very Tala of you," he said, encircling my ankle with his fingers. "You're so strong and yet your bones are so delicate, like a bird's." He lifted my foot, stretching my leg up and scooting more onto the bed, holding me by the ankle with one hand so he could trace the line of my leg with the other.

I folded my hands under my head so I could watch him and his explorations. "Ever been bitten by a goose or scored by a raptor's talons?"

He flashed me a distracted smile, pressing his lips experimentally to the hollow by my ankle bone, sending warm currents straight to my groin. My lids fluttered closed and I shifted my free leg, opening my thighs to him. He looked. Oh yes, he took a good long look, his heated gaze crawling up my body to meet my eyes, full of renewed hunger.

"Why don't you come up here and do that?" I invited.

"Eventually." He returned his attention to my foot, pressing a thumb into the sole of it, biting lightly at the tendon at the back of my ankle, intensifying my growing arousal. I lifted my free foot, bracing it on his shoulder. He gave me an inquiring glance, his muscles flexing under my toes. "Can't tough it out?" he asked, a definite taunt in his tone.

"The first time was slow. No more of this…" I trailed off on a hiss when he bit me on the arch of my foot, grasp firm on my captured ankle, other fingers caressing the tender underside of my knee, in an amplifying counterpoint. I dug my toes into his shoulder, but he ignored me, continuing his game. "Marskal," I said, for lack of a better argument.

He chuckled in that dark, sensuous way. "There was no deal. You wouldn't promise all night, so for as long as I have you, I'm doing this my way."

I eyed his muscular body. "I'm strong enough to pin you, I bet."

"You could try," he agreed without looking at me, intent on following the line of my calf muscle with his tongue, up to the back of my knee. I could have braced against his approach with my other foot, but I liked the feel of his skin under my toes. "But that would be cheating."

"So many rules," I complained, the words coming out on a breathy sigh. I arched my back, instinctively tugging away from the excruciating teasing, but he held my ankle in an iron grip that aroused me as much as the tender kisses.

"Only one rule," he corrected. "You let me do what I like to you." He released my ankle, setting my foot on his shoulder, then captured the other, beginning all over by kissing the hollow by my ankle. My laugh became a moan of pleasure.

"That's hardly fair," I got out.

"Sure it is." He sounded perfectly reasonable, as if he didn't have me writhing at his least caress. "If my lady decides to grace me with another opportunity in her bed, then she may be the one to do whatever she likes."

"What if there's no bed? We might not have such a cozy, *private* spot again."

"Lady's choice, then."

"You might live to regret this bargain." I couldn't hold still, the desire burning a hole through me. Restless, needy, I undulated, and his hot gaze slid up my leg to my spread sex. Not nearly so detached as he liked to pretend. I lowered my hands, cupping my breasts and arching again. "Work with me here and I think we can come to mutual satisfaction."

"Oh, I think that's guaranteed." He nipped the back of my knee then sucked the spot, making me lose the thread of the debate entirely. Moving more fully between my upraised knees, he edged up, kissing and tonguing the inside of my thigh. "Your skin is more than soft. Luscious. And you smell good."

"Dasnarian bath oil."

"Not what I mean." His lean face went wolfish as he gazed at me, so close to my groin my lower legs draped down his back. If he were a shapeshifter, perhaps wolf would be his First Form. It made sense on many levels. He inhaled, then flicked his gaze up to me. "You smell like flowers. You always do. As if you have tropical petals worked into your skin."

I wound my fingers in his short hair, crossing my ankles behind his neck. "Marskal, darling," I purred.

"Yes, my lady?"

"If you don't put your mouth on me immediately, I will kill

and eat you."

He gave me that slow, certain smile. "Other way around, quicksilver girl."

~ 15 ~

A LONG TIME later, I lay half-dozing in his arms. I liked it. Wrapped up safe and skin-to-skin. Not something I'd ever much cared for. I'd always been the one to get up and move— just as Zyr's women always complained he did. We weren't cuddlers in our family. At least, not since childhood.

How much of this sudden attachment came from Marskal's tending me when I was the hummingbird? Animals imprinted like that and I'd been the animal for far too long. It hadn't been the disaster the tales made it out to be, with the shapeshifter never able to return to human form—or, worse, shifting back to their Birth Form, but with the animal mind. Not unlike *Deyrr*'s living dead.

I shuddered to imagine what that might be like.

"Cold?" Marskal asked and drew the blanket up around us. I wasn't, but I liked him doing it, so I didn't protest. Instead I snuggled closer, our legs entangled together, and my head comfortable in the fold of his shoulder. He kissed my forehead. I hummed a little and lifted my mouth for a real kiss, so sweet, quickly turning hot. Laughing quietly, he drew away and kissed my nose instead. "You should rest."

"I am resting. Besides, you've already kept me up most of the night, as promised," I replied. "It's only a few hours to dawn."

He stilled, listening. "How can you tell?"

"I feel it."

"Shapeshifter trick, or sorceress magic?"

"Hard to say. I always know where the sun is, the phase of the moon. The knowing is just there."

He was quiet a moment. He'd spread my hair over his chest and threaded his fingers through it, like children do, playing games with ribbons. "Why don't you use your magic?"

"I do use it. I used it today. Twice."

"The only times I've seen you use it."

"You don't see everything I do. Especially magic, because a great deal of that isn't visible. Not obvious like shapeshifting."

He mulled that over. "So, you use it rarely."

Such curiosity. "I wouldn't say that. Just not often."

"Because?"

"It upsets the balance of things."

"What things?"

I leaned up on my elbow, studying his face. "Why are you so interested?"

He smiled, a slight softening of his chiseled mouth. "I thought I'd made it clear that I'm interested in everything about you."

"Yes." I traced the line of one eyebrow, then the other. Not bushy, but thick, the same brown as his hair, but without the sun streaks. "But you've never explained why."

"Dodging the question or looking to be petted?"

"I do love to be petted." I kissed him, then traced the curve of his lips with my fingertip, and the brackets around his mouth, while I thought about how to explain it. "The world has a particular balance. The cycles of the sun and the moon, light and dark, life and death. One animal grazes, the predator eats the herbivore, then the predator dies and its body feeds the soil that grows the grass again. It's a balance. A circle." I set the tip of my finger in the divot below his lower lip and sought his gaze. "Does that make sense?"

"Yes." He reached up and tucked a spilling lock of my hair behind my ear. "Keep going."

I shrugged a little. "Well, that's it. Magic isn't part of that balance. If I use a spell to kill a flock of living fish-birds, for example, I haven't eaten them. They maybe haven't returned to feed anything at all. So, I've created a hole in the world. That can't be good. Now the circle is lopsided."

"But killing the fish-birds today?"

"I couldn't kill them because they were already dead. They were already unnatural, outside the circle of life. Once I determined that, I felt no *qualms* about vanishing them." I smiled for Kral's irritable jibes.

He returned my smile. "But isn't magic part of the balance, too, a natural thing?"

I frowned. "I don't know. It's an interesting question. Maybe not? Perhaps that's why the N'andanans locked it away. Could be it was never meant to be part of this world in the first place."

"I thought Kiraka told you they locked it away to defeat *Deyrr*."

"Yes, well—you know shapeshifters." I gave him a brilliant smile. "We lie a lot."

"Because truth and lies aren't an either-or thing."

"You do listen, even in the throes of passion."

"I'm a man of many skills."

"So I've discovered." I feathered my fingers over his hard-edged jaw, over the strong column of his throat. "True or false: am I a woman?"

"True."

"Am I a hummingbird?"

"Not at the moment, you're not."

I tugged at his chest hair. "You have to answer true or false."

He captured my hand and brought it to his lips, kissing my fingers. "Why do you get to make the rules?"

"My game and I'm making a point."

"Fine. False. You are not a hummingbird."

"Am I an owl?"

"False."

"Am I a dolphin?"

"False."

"See? But I have been those things, so that means that truth changes over time, therefore it's not an either-or thing. There is no such thing as truth."

He studied me, mouth pursed, a line between his brows. "I'm sure there's a flaw in that logic."

"You're thinking like a mossback." I tugged my hand away and pushed down the blanket, admiring the carved muscles of his chest, the flat plane of his abdomen, trailing my fingers along each masculine line of him. "Reality is more fluid than your people like to believe. Nothing stays exactly the same, even for the blink of a moment, thus truth is ever changing, thus there's no such thing as truth and lies. What was true a moment ago may be untrue now. What was once a lie might become true once the sun rises."

To my great pleasure, I found he'd hardened again, and wrapped my fingers around his cock, savoring the very soft skin at the head. He flexed his hips, pushing through the circle of my fingers with a groan. "You should rest," he murmured. "Sleep, I mean."

"But you keep asking me questions." I kissed the tip of his cock, then tasted him, and he hissed something, burying his hands in my hair. Taking that as an invitation, I pulled him deeper into my mouth, pleasuring him and enjoying the way he moved under my ministrations. Not so in control now. I drove him to the edge, then backed off, laughing when he cursed at me, ignoring his impatient pulling at my hair.

Instead I tormented him as he'd done me, kissing, licking and nipping at his thighs, the hollow of his groin and the hard line of his hip bones. Once he'd settled into resignation, I took him into my mouth again, deeper, working him hard and fast, until he was gasping my name. This time when I backed off to tease him more, he surprised me by sitting up and pulling me onto his lap.

He lifted me under my thighs and settled me onto his cock, face ridged with concentration. Happy enough, I flexed, riding him, loving the depth of him inside me. He seized my hips, holding me still. "Wait."

"No," I breathed, and squeezed my internal muscles around him. He gasped, a choking laugh and threw back his head, throat straining. Such a gorgeous man. I kissed the underside of his jaw, biting into the corded muscle of his neck, sucking hard as if I might feed on him. He groaned, hands digging into my hips, but without the same focus, so I pumped, riding him.

He let go with a shout, forgetting his quiet privacy, face contorted with the pleasure-pain of yet another climax. I slowed, letting him come down gently from it, showering his face with kisses. He sagged back and I followed, nestling against him.

Finally he breathed a laugh, hands running up my back. "You might kill me after all."

I propped my chin on his chest. "I did warn you."

He smoothed the hair back from my face, eyes warm with deep emotion. "It would be worth it."

Uneasy at what I saw in him, at the fervency in his voice, I rose. The mermaid, wanting what she couldn't have, poised instead to destroy it. "My turn to play handmaiden." I fetched a cloth, giving it to him, and using one on myself. The phrase reminded me of Jepp's remarks, including her one on hearts being involved. I knew mine wasn't, but if Marskal's was…. My hair had tangled hopelessly and I tried finger combing it. I'd grown so lazy with shifting, going to another form and coming back clean, my hair unsnarled. Marskal watched me, an arrested expression on his face.

"You're so beautiful," he said, almost to himself, "but that's not the only reason I—that I'm interested in you. You're magical, and wild, and free. You remind me of being deep in the forest or high on a mountain, far away from the business of civilization. Places where the very air feels full and fraught with something pure and wonderful. You're unlike any other woman I've ever known."

"Because I am unlike mossback women."

His mouth twisted in a wry smile. "You don't have to keep reminding me."

"I think I do."

He sobered at my serious tone. "Why's that?"

"A question for you."

He raised his brows in inquiry, a flicker of his old suspicion in his eyes. Good.

"True or false: are you in love with me?"

If I'd expected him to deny it or prevaricate, he proved that, even in this, he wouldn't flinch. "True," he said slowly. "How did you know?"

I shook my head at him. "You said so. I remember it from when I was a hummingbird."

"I didn't think you'd remember much of being a hummingbird."

"Some. Impressions, feelings. That." I shrugged a little,

those memories an irritating reminder. "Also I could feel it in you when we had sex, and it evoked those memories. It was in your eyes. It's there now."

He lowered his gaze slightly, lowering a hood over that vulnerability, though it was far too late.

"How long have you felt this way?" I asked.

"Why does that matter?" He met my gaze again, but his expression had gone remote, the reserved warrior.

I huffed out an impatient breath. "It matters because this is supposed to be about sex, not love. You led me to believe it could be only that."

"No," he said carefully. "I made it clear that I'm willing to take whatever I can have. And that I don't expect anything of you."

I sat on the bed beside him, laid a hand on his chest, which he covered with his, though his gaze remained wary. "It's not a good idea."

One side of his mouth lifted, not exactly a smile. "People don't fall in love because it's a good idea."

"No? Why do you think they fall in love?" I was genuinely curious what his answer would be. I'd never quite understood it myself. I loved my family, and I cared deeply about my friends. That little unnamed daughter of Anya's—I'd loved her with crippling intensity, which made no sense as she'd barely lived long enough for me to know her at all. But I'd always known I'd take Final Form, that falling in love with someone, having that kind of relationship would never happen for me. In my heart, I'd already become the dragon.

Marskal was watching me, a curious line between his brows. "That's a strange question to ask."

"Does that mean you don't have an answer?"

"I'm not sure there is an answer. Besides—you're a 'people,' too."

"I don't think that's necessarily true. I'm not the same, anyway. But I want to know what *you* think the reason is."

"Maybe it's like your spectrum of truth and lies—people fall in love for lots of reasons, and those reasons change from moment to moment, day to day."

"Waxing and waning." I nodded. "And sometimes it's a lie. People deceive themselves all the time, wanting to be in love when they really aren't."

"Or," he said, giving me an intent stare, "pretending they don't feel anything when they do."

I waved that off. "The point is that what you feel now could be an emotion of the moment—or rather, of this shared time together, since you won't tell me how long you've nursed this idea. You might get over it."

Now he frowned in truth. "It's not a stomach illness, Zynda. I'm in love with you, not suffering a disease or traumatic disorder I need to recover from."

"I think it would be better if you did," I told him, trying to make him understand. "I'm not the right woman for you. Loving me will only bring you pain in the end."

"Your opinion is noted," he replied evenly.

"But disregarded?"

In response, he wound a lock of my hair around his finger and tugged me down for a long kiss. It felt questioning and reassuring at the same time. I wasn't sure what answer he sought, but he seemed satisfied. "Lie down with me and sleep a bit," he murmured against my lips.

"This is your way of avoiding the argument."

"There's nothing to argue. This is my way of getting some sleep, which you need, too. Let's rest a while."

Because I felt sleepy, I did as he asked, snuggling up against his warmth, liking the way his arm curved around me as I found my spot, fitting exactly into his shoulder. He pulled the cover up around us. "We should have doused the lantern," he said, sounding far away.

A small thing, so I reached out a tendril of magic and suffocated the flame. He laughed a little, and kissed my forehead. "And you ask me not to find you miraculous," he said.

I was too far into falling asleep to argue.

BRIGHT LIGHT AND shouting awakened me. Not of alarm, but of sailors calling orders, relaying information. The ship creaked, changing speed and direction. We must be nearing Nahanau. I stretched, remarkably sated, but alone in the bed—and surprised that Marskal had managed to leave without waking me and that he'd left me at all. And at the ensuing tinge of disappointment. I should be delighted to have some time alone at last.

When the door opened and he entered, carrying a tray of food and other things, it all made sense. He gave me a crooked grin and set the tray on the desk. "Good morning, lovely lady," he said.

I raked back my snarled hair, not feeling particularly lovely, but replete and relaxed enough to return the smile. "Tell me you have water to wash with."

He set out a bowl and filled it from a pitcher of water, setting a bar of soap beside it. Then, with a flourish, he presented me with the comb Jepp had used on me. "Moranu bless you," I exclaimed, nearly leaping from the bed and snatching it from him. "How did you know?"

"I noticed you wanted one last night. Earlier this morning," he amended with a wry grimace that melted into a broad smile. "That was some night."

"It was," I agreed, pausing in my combing to give him a kiss. He sat in the bolted-down chair, poured himself something that steamed, and watched me work at the tangles—something much more difficult to do than it looked. Maybe I should try shifting… unease curled in my gut at the thought. *You've lost your nerve.*

"Come here," Marskal said. "You're making a hash of it."

"A hash?" I asked, but handed him the cursed comb.

"Kneel down here." He indicated the floor between his knees, and handed me the steaming mug when I did. Picking up the ends of my hair, he held them so that I barely felt the tugging. "Hash is a good way to eat leftovers—or trail food," he explained as he worked. "You kind of chop up everything and throw it in together. But it's also a metaphor for a disorganized mess."

"Ah. I'm not practiced at fixing hair messes."

"But not because you're accustomed to servants waiting on you."

"No." I laughed at the thought. "Because I could always just quickly shift to something else, then back to human form—and it would be fine again."

"Handy."

"Jepp commented the same—though she wanted me to figure out how to shift back armed and bristling with weapons."

He chuckled at that. "She would."

I sipped the brew in the mug, finding it to be some curiously strong sort of tea. Probably Dasnarian, as it smelled like the spiced oils Jepp had used. It was soothing to have him comb my hair—another kind of petting—and I relaxed into it.

"But you didn't want to try that today?" Marskal asked, too casually. "A quick and easy shift, and back again."

I shrugged and set the tea down, no longer so relaxed. My stomach didn't care for the spiciness. "Are we near the harbor at Nahanau?"

"Yes, about to pass the dragon guardians. And don't tense up—it was just a question."

"I'm not tense." But I could no longer sit still. I rose, took the comb, and handed him back the tea. To my surprise, the snarls had vanished as if they'd never been. "You did a good job. All those nieces?"

"You'd be amazed at what little girls get into. I'm the one they come to for help with the bad stuff that their moms will threaten to cut out rather than deal with."

"Always rescuing the baby birds." I said it lightly, teasingly, but he remained serious.

"If you extend my analogy about learning to use a sword arm again after an injury, then I'll point out that the warrior has to attempt to use it. Letting it hang there leads to atrophy."

Atrophy. What a horrible thought. "Whatever." I added an elaborate shrug.

"Not talking about it doesn't make it go away, Zynda."

"Talking about it doesn't fix it, either. I'll figure it out. It's my personal business."

He regarded me, sipping the tea. "There's food. Sit and eat." His eyes wandered over me, heating. "Though you might want to put on your gown first."

"Does my nakedness bother you?" I looked around for where the thing might have gone.

"Over there, on the foot of the bed. And no—I find it...rather wonderful that you're so unselfconscious being naked around me. I've never known a woman like that."

"Animals are naked. Sometimes it feels weird to me to wear clothes, particularly if I've been other a lot." I pulled the dress on and sat. "Better?"

"Not better, but less distracting." He handed me a slice of bread slathered in honey and a butter made from crushed nuts. "I'm less likely to drag you back to bed this way."

I raised my brows at him over the bread, the delicious honey much better than that bitter tea. After I swallowed, I licked the sticky stuff off my lips, his attention drawn and held there. "There's time," I purred.

He yanked his gaze up to mine, blew out a breath in a half-laugh. "Tempting, but we'd better get up top."

I shrugged as if I weren't disappointed, and slathered another slice of bread. "You have a lot of vigor—as much as any lover I've had." *More*, I conceded privately to myself. No sense making the man cocky.

He accepted that with a nod, an ironic glint in his eyes. "I am delighted to have done my part for the reputation of my mossback brethren."

"Oh you have. I'll be sure to tell all the Tala women. You'll have bevies wanting to try you."

His jaw hardened, amusement fled, anger in its place. "I don't want anyone else, Zynda," he said quietly.

I shrugged, elaborately, which irritated him more, and grabbed a piece of fruit. "Suit yourself."

"Is that how it's going to be?" He had on his remote face, but he was angry at me. Not that I cared.

"We discussed this last night. Earlier this morning," I amended with a saucy smile, but he didn't return it, so I got serious, too. "You asked what it would take to tame me. Well, the answer is that I can't be. You call me a wild thing and I am. I won't be domesticated and added to your collection of farm animals. Pet the tiger, if you like, but don't forget how easily she can bite your hand off."

"I'm not afraid of you."

"Maybe you should be."

"Why?" He stood, gathered up the last of his weapons. "You can't shift anymore, which means you won't be taking Final Form. All you have are your woman's claws and I've already been scored by those—and enjoyed it."

I clenched those dull nails into my palms, unreasonably enraged by that. "Don't you taunt me with this."

"With what? It's just a basic fact we might as well acknowledge. I'll have to report to Her Majesty that you've lost your ability to shapeshift."

"Don't you dare," I snarled.

He gave me a mock surprised look. "I have to. She needs to know, for strategy purposes. She's grown to rely on your shapeshifting abilities, so we have to plan around it. You have your magic, but we both know you're careful about how you use it. Maybe she can send to Queen Andromeda for someone else to help. Surely there are more magically gifted shapeshifters in Annfwn. Perhaps they can send a troop—that would be helpful."

I growled at him, momentarily incoherent.

He gave me an inquiring look. "Did you say something? I didn't quite get that."

Swallowing back the snarl, I managed a level reply. "I know what you're doing. And it won't work."

He finished off the tea, expression all reasonable. "What do you believe I'm doing?"

"Using your skills as a leader of men, seeking an emotional spur to get your wounded soldier not to be afraid of using his sword arm again."

"There's more involved here than just you," he said very seriously, stacking everything neatly on the tray. "I serve my high queen, first and foremost—something you've known all along, and should understand, as much as you go on about your devotion to your own primary loyalties—and we have solid evidence that her realm should expect an attack of unprecedented power and danger. That there might be shapeshifted sleeper spies already planted all over the Thirteen. It would be irresponsible of me not to inform Her Majesty of what I know. And what resources we can—and can't—rely on."

A sense of betrayal stabbed at me, all the more painful for being irrational. "I confided in you."

He grimaced, his expression softening, and he set the tray down, coming to me and stroking his hands down my bare arms. "I know you did, but this was never a secret. Even if you and I hadn't talked about it, I'd have observed the effects of your...encounter with the dragon and reported on them. It may be a point of pride for you, but—"

"It's not only pride." I jerked away from him, pulling the hair pin from its sleeve and winding up my hair before I reached for the door latch. Marskal had his hand on it, holding the door closed.

"Zynda," he said, close behind me. He pressed a kiss to my temple. "You're not alone in this. Talk to me. Let me help you. Or someone in Annfwn. Could someone there, a teacher or some such, help you recover your abilities?"

I wanted to drop my head against the door and weep. I wanted to turn and lean against him, let him enfold me in his arms and wipe the thoughts from my mind. I really wanted to fly, up into the sky and let all this nonsense bleed away. But that escape was barred from me, perhaps forever. Why hadn't Moranu warned me that I'd have to sacrifice that, too? Or perhaps she had.

Zyr could maybe help me, but I'd have to admit to my inability. He would gloat, too. I'd always been the better shapeshifter and in our various fights growing up, I had used that relentlessly to goad him. I supposed I'd deserve whatever scorn he wanted to return in kind.

"I don't need your help to go to my homeland," I replied, hating this feeling of weakness.

"But I'm offering my help," he said. "That's what loving someone means."

"Your love can't help me," I said, angry for no good reason. Maybe the meanness in my voice would get through to him. "A mossback couldn't possibly understand."

This time, when I reached for the latch, he didn't try to stop me.

~ 16 ~

THE *HÁKYRLING* MADE good time, passing the stone dragon guardians at full sail. Carved of the same black stone as the rocky prominences that protected the harbor, the immense sculptures seemed to rise out of the island, snarling and spreading wings to spring into the sky. They looked very much like Kiraka, only rendered in lovingly polished obsidian. Perhaps once there'd been a whole colony of those like her, shapeshifters who'd taken the final dragon form.

If so, that meant that choosing Final Form didn't necessarily mean the kind of extreme isolation Kiraka suffered. Perhaps she'd be less mean, and—let's face it, more sane—if she'd at least had companionship. I had no intention of reneging on my vow to take Final Form—if I ever managed to shapeshift again—but more than ever the prospect of the endless years ahead chilled me. Moranu take Marskal for his ill-advised love and making me think about having more. Bedding him had been a bad idea, which I'd known all along. I'd regret it, if it hadn't been so fantastic.

"Well, you look well-fucked," Jepp said, leaning hipshot against the rail next to me. "And I note the lieutenant bears a number of scratches and love bites. Did you at least leave the critical bits attached?"

Oh, to leap overboard and become a dolphin on the way

down. Maybe I'd leap anyway. "They're his bits to look after," I replied.

"Ho-kay," she drawled, turning to look at the rapidly approaching harbor also. "Most people, you know, are happier for a long night of excellent sex. Apparently with the Tala, not so much."

"It's only sex." I shrugged, then caught myself, remembering how Marskal commented that it meant I lied. Not that I was, but...ugh. Him with his mossback attachment to one truth. "You know how it is. A bit of fun to pass the time, blow off steam. Then back to the business at hand. Ursula will want to convene a council."

"We sent a crow ahead to warn them, so we can discuss and hopefully turn around quickly. And I know how it is, sure—but you've never been like that and the lieutenant certainly isn't."

"Regardless, it's none of your business." I seemed to be saying that a lot lately.

Jepp pulled one of her daggers, idly spinning it between her fingers, totally unconcerned that she might drop it in the ocean. I'd never seen her drop a blade. "See, there I think you're wrong," she said in a cheerful tone. "At least now I know which of you to warn about breaking the other's heart." She pointed her suddenly still dagger at me. "Be careful with his."

"I didn't ask him to fall in love with me," I replied, my irritation rising to a keen edge again.

Jepp's head whipped around. "He said that?"

I waved that off. "For now he thinks so. A fancy of the moment. It won't last."

Jepp snorted. "And here I always thought you were smart. You know, not book smart like Dafne, but... wise, or something." She gripped my elbow, making me look at her. "Since you don't see it, I'll tell you. Marskal is not a passing fancy kind of man."

I shook her off. "Nevertheless, I don't want it. Not his love or his heart. He can have it back."

She studied me. "You're not this cold. What's this about?"

"About? We're at war, Jepp. My people are dying by slow inches, facing ultimate extinction while Annfwn deteriorates. The temple of *Deyrr* wants to suck all the life from the world, and I'm to worry about one man's fascination with a woman he can't have? Let's keep things in perspective here."

"I don't know—you look pretty well had to me."

I returned her jest with a stern glare. "I mean long term, and you know it. Even if I didn't have responsibilities to my people, I'm not the woman for him." I hadn't told her about Final Form. The footloose and mercurial Jepp would likely react to that idea with horror, and I couldn't face that from yet another person. "Shapeshifters don't mate with mossbacks, for more reasons than that the Tala need babies."

She pursed her lips, then turned again to watch the harbor. A Nahanaun guard had lined up to greet us, and the ship had slowed, sailors crawling to furl the sails. "I saw some bad stuff in the Imperial Palace at Dasnaria."

"I know. I'm sorry for that, but—"

"Hear me out," she said in a mild tone that carried a razor edge. "I don't often wax philosophical, so you can do me the courtesy of paying attention."

I nearly laughed, but she looked completely serious, so I only nodded.

"I've never gotten to tell you all of it and I wouldn't, even if we had the time. Some things are too terrible to revisit, you know?" She turned her head to look at me, her dark eyes reflecting some of that horror. Maybe I didn't know. She lifted a shoulder, rolling off those memories, staring into the distance again. "I've never claimed to be wise, despite Danu's many lessons to ease me in that direction." She snorted at her herself. "But I'll tell you what, when the worst happened, when I felt so soiled that it was like a slime I couldn't wash off my skin, it was Kral who made me feel clean again."

"That's really lovely. I'm happy for you."

"I'm not done. Now Kral—he's no prince. I mean, he *is* literally a prince, or was, but he's an arrogant ass most of the time. He's stubborn and pigheaded and has a slew of messed up ideas about women. Still, loving him might be all that saved me. All that kept me from becoming someone who couldn't be retrieved."

She was quiet long enough that I thought I could be allowed to speak, although now I had nothing to say. I searched for some words that would sound right. "I'm glad he loves you. You deserve that, and it's good to see you happy."

Jepp glanced at me, impatient, eyes snapping with irritation. "You're not listening. It wasn't him loving me that made the difference. That's nice, sure, but—as you just said—not really a game-changer. It's me loving him that made the difference, that changed me, that allowed me to survive with my humanity intact."

That took me aback. Especially since she seemed to expect some sort of answer. "But I don't love Marskal," I told her.

She grimaced, shaking her head fatalistically. "Well, that, my Tala friend, might be a grave mistake."

URSULA HAD INDEED convened a council, and Dafne had

assembled her scrolls and maps, neatly stacked in front of her. We sat down immediately, Ursula asking Marskal to give the report, which he did, referring to Jepp and Kral to supplement details. He didn't solicit my input, nor did he mention my ... disabled state. No doubt he'd relate that to her in private, along with whatever other observations he'd gleaned while being my guard.

I tried not to let it bother me. Only pride, nothing more than that. But I felt surprisingly lonely. Both Jepp and Marskal were angry with me. I shouldn't care, but some part of me did. This must be how Kiraka felt, following her intuition to do the right thing for the greater good, and losing friendships, her only companionship because of it. Perhaps this meant I'd taken several more steps to becoming a dragon, myself. Maybe hardening the heart came before all the permanent external scaling.

Of course, I wouldn't be able to reach that final stage and save my people if I couldn't shift again. I needed to try. Though the prospect made my stomach twist, I made myself consider it, think through the steps. In that, at least, Marskal was right. Not thinking about it wasn't making it any better. Even if I died trying, it would be no different than if I'd died a week ago, looking from the larger perspective. Better, because now we had more information.

"Zynda, what's your opinion?" Ursula regarded me with that steady hawkish gaze that made it clear she knew perfectly well I hadn't been listening. I wasn't going to apologize or pretend.

"About what?" I made myself remain apparently languid, not bracing myself for questions about my abilities or my intentions.

They all looked somewhat exasperated with me, except for Marskal, who studied me with something like concern. I might believe that if I didn't know how we'd left things.

Kral stepped in. "Is it best if we take the *Hákyrling* back to monitor the barrier, fighting back any more incursions while you go to Annfwn? Or is there a way to search out the sleeper spies already inside? And is there a way to fight these things without your magic?"

I wanted to ask why I was going to Annfwn, then I caught Marskal's quiet look, and my mind caught up. He'd told them that's where I wanted to go. "Queen Andromeda, once warned, can likely strengthen the barrier, maybe even particularly where it crosses that peninsula. Until then I think we can only be alert to their presence—they'll look like normal animals to you—then chop into small pieces or incinerate." I shifted in my seat, the word alone bringing back phantom pain.

"I could go with them to the barrier," I said to Ursula. Maybe I could regain my shifting ability without having to face Zyr and take that blow to my pride. "I'd be useful there. My magic served to vanish the fish-bird flock."

Kral leaned on the table, intrigued. "Could you do that on a larger scale—or at a distance? Scour the peninsula, for example?"

I had to shake my head. "I couldn't affect anything outside the barrier, and I need a specific target. Like I needed to see and touch one of the fish-birds, first." It went against my grain to disclose such specifics about how my magic worked, and I really hated confessing those limitations.

"That wouldn't be good enough," Ursula confirmed, unnecessarily. "Any other advice on the barrier?"

I shrugged, irritated with her dismissal, disappointed with myself. "Stop crossing. The Star may be creating a kind of magic that they're exploiting. There might be more than one reason they're focusing on that region."

Jepp and Ursula exchanged looks. "It will mean suspending

efforts to help people get on the right side of the barrier," Jepp said. "And we have people on the wrong side."

Ursula nodded, resigned. "I know you speak of Dafne's man, Akamai. He knew the dangers when he agreed to go to Dasnaria. Communicating with him and restoring any others to their homes will have to wait for peace time. Right now we must plan for defense, against an enemy we can't see."

"Or attack," Kral put in, and—to my surprise—Harlan and Marskal nodded in crisp agreement. Kral laughed, sweeping a hand around the table. "This is the problem with putting women in charge. You instinctively think first about protecting the home and the babies. This is not a bad thing. It's in your nature. But every man knows the best way to defend his territory is to eliminate his enemies before they arrive."

"Remember the woman who sleeps in your bed?" Jepp said in a sweet voice, a brilliant smile on her face. "Think of her when you wake up dead tomorrow morning."

"Going to use those gnat stickers of yours?" Kral grinned at her. "I don't think so. Besides, you can't argue this. It's basic biology."

Jepp lost her smile and flashed a look at me. "I take it all back. Run while you still can."

Marskal's brows drew together and he gave me a glance I couldn't interpret.

Nakoa said something sharp and apparently Ursula needed no translation. She nodded at him. "I agree. Let's focus. As much as I never thought I'd say this, the Dasnarian general is correct about strategy, if not biology. And I'll accept that it's a personal blind spot of mine that I think in terms of defense first. We can't afford to wait for them to come to us—or rather to spring whatever trap they're laying for us. We will have already lost at that point."

Kral hooted his glee and Jepp rolled her eyes, muttering something. Ursula ignored them both. "Kral—if *Deyrr* is planning an attack, as they almost certainly are, will your brother the emperor support that? Are we looking at war with the entire Dasnarian Empire?"

All amusement and rancor fled from the table as Kral nodded, completely matter of fact. "Yes. Hestar would not pass up such an opportunity. And he has the arrogance to believe he can control the temple. Wouldn't you agree, brother?"

Harlan, not exactly surprised, regarded Kral a moment, then added his nod with a rueful twist of his mouth. "There can be no doubt."

"And I saw them," Jepp added. "A secret meeting between Hestar, the High Priestess, and Kir in the Imperial Palace. They were... indulging themselves." She swallowed hard, and Kral set a hand on the back of her neck, squeezing so she straightened with more spirit. For the first time I saw the decent man she'd insisted lurked inside his abrasive exterior. "They've been planning this for a long time, the emperor and *Deyrr*, and Kir is aiding them with inside information."

Ursula spread her hands on the table, regarding them as if she wished she could hold all of her realm in them, safe from attack. "My late, unlamented father would have been good at this. He was a terrible king, but an undeniably brilliant general." She looked to Harlan. "We could take our Tala ship and be the ones to monitor the incursion, while the others go to Annfwn. I'd love to be the first to greet Hestar, with the point of my sword."

"You can't be on the front lines of this war," Dafne said in a decisive tone. "We've had this argument before. You're the High Queen now, not an itinerant warrior. Your place is at Ordnung, ruling, creating and implementing the strategy."

"Like my father, you mean? The man built his castle next to the Wildlands, as close as he could to the foot of Odfell's Pass, because he regarded Annfwn as his enemy. He literally made his home on the front lines of his personal war. Why would I do otherwise?"

"Because you're not him." Harlan returned her glare with equanimity.

"That has nothing to do with—"

"And you already abdicated your role at the barrier by handing the Star over to Jepp," he continued.

"I'll happily give it back!" Jepp put her hand on her chest. "Somebody please take it."

Ursula and Harlan were still engaged in some silent conversation. Finally, she sighed, and threw up her hands. "One thing is sure, I am not my father."

"To return to the point, he did have Tala assistance," Dafne put in, and they all looked at me.

"Uorsin had Salena, yes," I said, feeling as if I stated the obvious. "You have all of the Tala, including our king and queen."

"Do we?" Ursula asked the question somberly, with insistence. I gazed back at my cousin, uncertain what she truly asked of me.

"Your fate is ours." I indicated Dafne's map of concentric circles. "We may be at the center, rather than the front lines, but we no longer have the safety we once enjoyed. It makes little difference if we save our future generations, only to give over their very souls to *Deyrr* to consume. I have my commitment to my role, but I feel safe in speaking for King Rayfe and Queen Andromeda in this."

She nodded at me, as if I'd just made her a promise. "Good. Thank you for that." She turned that uncomfortable attention away from me. "Kral, you were general of the Dasnarian forces," Ursula replied, "and I've been told your men are among the best. Was that job a sinecure or are you that good?"

Kral colored, his jaw tight. "I was given the appointment to keep me out of my brother's way, it's true—"

"He's that good," Harlan broke in. "A better strategist and leader of men I've never known."

Kral seemed truly taken aback, then shook his head slightly, as if clearing it. Jepp patted his arm and he covered her hand with his.

Ursula simply registered that, moving on. "Good, then I appoint you general of our forces for the duration of this war. Start planning our offense."

"You're so certain of my loyalty?" Kral protested. "It goes against my grain to question a gift of such power, but—"

"Shut up, Kral," Jepp said pleasantly. "We're sure of you, even if you're not."

"If only because he hates Hestar as much as anyone," Harlan commented.

"I know full well that the enemy of my enemy is not necessarily my friend," Ursula said, her gaze wandering back to me, "but in this, at least, I have no concerns."

I did my best to return her assessing gaze evenly, but my stomach twisted at the thought of what her doubts must be.

"Then we're decided," she said. "Jepp and Kral will take *Hákyrling* back to the barrier. Stay mobile. Dafne, you remain here with King Nakoa, implementing your spy plan to monitor the *Deyrr* incursion. Talk to Kiraka—don't start with me, we need her intelligence—find out if she knows of a way to identify these sleeper spies. They're shapeshifters and they're *Deyrr*. She might know. King Nakoa KauPo—you and your people remain our front line of resistance. I'd like to ask for extra ships and fighters to provide back-up to the *Hákyrling* until we get sufficient forces in place. Until then, anything you need, we'll find a way to supply. Same goes for you, Kral."

Dafne finished translating and Nakoa inclined his head in grave acceptance.

"Do you even have a standing navy?" Kral demanded.

Her flinty gaze shot sparks, but she pressed her lips over the retort she'd planned, the grimace turning rueful. "Not as such." She turned her speculative eyes on me. "But the king and the queen of the Tala do."

Oh, I couldn't wait to listen in on that conversation. Dafne and Nakoa had been conversing quietly in Nahanaun, and she held up a finger. When Ursula acknowledged her, she gave Nakoa a wistful smile, then turned to the group. "King Nakoa KauPo offers his assistance in creating storms to halt any invasions."

"Storms?" Ursula echoed. "I thought he just did rain." Nakoa regarded her with the black eyes of a dragon. Something clicked inside me, and I understood some of what I sensed in the coiled tension of the man—a storm about to break.

"He brings rain of all kinds," Dafne said simply. "I'm a witness. From nourishing rain to—" she glanced at him, asking a question in Nahanaun. She nodded, laughing lightly. "Yes, to a ship-sinking storm."

"That won't do us much good if he sinks the *Hákyrling* and his own ships," Kral groused.

"He can target them," Dafne replied. "Put the *Hákyrling* and our ships in the effective eye of the storm and sweep the rest away."

Kral grunted, fingering his beard. "Handy, that."

Ursula inclined her upper body in a slight bow. "More than handy. My gratitude for the offer. Thank you for the offer to go back to the barrier, Zynda, but if Annfwn is where you need to be, then you should do that. Harlan, Zynda, and I will sail the Tala ship back to Annfwn. Zynda, I have an additional agenda for you in that I hope you'll be available to help me parley with Rayfe and Andi, should it come to that. Marskal will, of course, be with Zynda."

"Why is Marskal of course with me?" I interrupted, and he gave me a long, unamused look.

"To continue to safeguard and assist you," Ursula replied without missing a beat. "You may be powerfully gifted, but you are not a warrior. You are a critical player in this, you're still recovering from a life-threatening injury, and I'm not taking any chances with you, so save your grumbling. After Annfwn, Harlan and I will continue on to Ordnung and see to ordering our forces. Kral and Jepp, whatever you can do to send messages on your status and needs. If Zynda is with us, perhaps she can fly to—"

Marskal stopped her with a subtle hand signal. Then he hadn't told her. She assessed the import in a moment. "Send Ove's crows, if you can. If not we'll relay via Dafne. Librarian—work on that, would you?"

"On it," she replied, making notes and giving me the impression she was carefully *not* looking at me.

Tired of it all, I spoke up. "I'm not clear on what you expect of me."

Ursula frowned, ever so slightly. "You said the Star could be creating magical permeability at the barrier. We also know *Deyrr* wants it badly. It's only smart—if thinking defensively—to get the Star as far from the barrier, Dasnaria and *Deyrr* as possible." She nodded to Jepp. "Time to relieve you of your unwelcome burden."

With a fist pump of glee, Jepp stood, dug the Star out from

under her leather vest, and dangled it on its long chain in front of me.

I took it, mostly because I couldn't resist its siren's call. Jepp had crafted a sort of wire cage around it, to attach it to the chain. Unlovely, but nothing could dim the radiance of the perfectly spherical topaz jewel. I'd only held it the once, after the high priestess cut it out of Ursula's stomach, but now as then, it carried a sense of depthless power and antiquity. Though flawlessly transparent, the center of the jewel held a deep opacity, a dark heart I couldn't see into. It seemed to hold an answer to a question I hadn't fully formed. Chasing after it only made it slide away, until I only looked into a topaz again. Realizing I'd been mesmerized, staring into the jewel for some time, I wrenched my gaze from it to find them all watching with similarly rapt expressions.

The insouciant Jepp recovered first, clapping me on the shoulder. "Well, that little display confirmed she's the one to have it. And Danu! Am I relieved to be rid of the thrice-cursed thing."

Feeling as if I were coming out of a dream, I frowned at them. "What am I to do with it?

"You're Salena's line, so I'm entrusting it to you to take it to the safest place possible—the Heart. That's what it's designed for, yes? The ultimate barrier against *Deyrr*. Also conveniently close to Andi, so she can retrieve it should the need arise."

But I couldn't get into the Heart, not without shapeshifting. My own heart clenched with physical pain and I looked to Marskal. He didn't look my way and the wires around the jewel cut into my palm. "I don't know if I can do this," I said softly to Ursula, almost a plea.

She cut me one of those steel-edged, expectant stares. "Better figure it out then. Danu knows none of us can do it. If nothing else, you can give it to Andi and she'll take care of it."

MARSKAL STAYED TO confer with—or report further to—his high queen, so I took the opportunity to give my ever-present guard the slip. By the time I made it out to the grand esplanade that led down to the beach, my fast walk had turned into a full-out run. At the last moment, I caught myself going in my usual direction, to my habitual beach where Marskal would know to look for me, and turned the other way instead.

I ran as fast as I could on the hard-packed damp sand where the waves had lapped. That, at least, felt something like exercising wings or fins. Not animal quiet in the same way, but the exertion lulled the anxiety, the insistent beat of doubt. My heart pounded, my hair flew behind me. Running at my maximum speed should shake any of Marskal's mossback spies.

I ran until I couldn't run any more. Until a stitch formed in my side and the edges of my vision went dim with exhaustion. Despite Marskal's diligent feeding, I wasn't up to full form. Especially not on a diet of fruit and honey. My human body needed protein to rebuild the muscle and bone I'd raided to make myself again.

Forced to stop, I flung myself into the sea, swimming out into the water. I swam well—as any child growing up next to the ocean did—but with nothing like the power of my other forms. Even if I hadn't already tired myself, I'd have to give up on going deep enough to see the brilliant sea life below. Winded, I floated a while, looking up at the endless blue sky also denied to me.

How did mossbacks live this way? Forever grounded, trapped in one form.

How could Ursula ask me to take the Star to the Heart when Marskal had informed her that I couldn't shapeshift anymore? The Heart could only be reached by a shapeshifter capable of many forms, shifting rapidly from one to the next. The Star lay heavily between my breasts, a reminder of my vows. I'd once been so certain that I could do this, that I could follow in Salena's brilliant footsteps, perhaps even outshine my powerful aunt.

Beware of overconfidence, little changeling.

Kiraka's words had been my first warning. No wonder she'd nearly knocked me out of the sky with it. Perhaps my unreliable gift of foresight had been speaking to me, telling me all along that I'd fail. I'd died, and maybe should have stayed dead. I was unnatural, an imbalance of nature. Who spoke to a goddess? That could have been my dying brain's hallucination, my will to live cobbling together rationalizations to spur me to resuscitate my own body.

Surely there are more magically gifted shapeshifters.

There were others. Zyr had plenty of ability, though he'd become prickly about the topic of ever leaving Annfwn again. The one time, with King Rayfe to rescue or abduct Queen Andromeda—depending on your point of view—had been more than enough of the land of mossbacks, he'd said. He never discussed his brief tenure as Uorsin's prisoner in the dungeons of Ordnung, but that refusal spoke volumes about what he didn't say aloud.

I only know you're not ready. Not even close to ready. Send another.

I'd died and I should have stayed dead. I certainly couldn't go on living this way, with nothing left to me.

There is loving and being loved. The voice seemed to whisper in my mind. Not the memories, not Kiraka speaking in my head. Moranu. I blinked open my eyes, crusted with salt, and gazed up at her moon, a waning fingernail in the dusky blue sky. A gentle smile.

All an illusion. I didn't have that. Marskal had admitted to loving me and I'd laughed at him and told him he'd get over it. Because I'd known that I couldn't love him back. Jepp had acted as if loving someone was a simple decision. I knew I no more had that ability than to shapeshift. Better if I hadn't come back. Better to sink into this ocean, a final swim.

But the cursed Star hung heavy around my neck, a reminder of all the responsibilities I couldn't fulfill. The final stone around my neck. I couldn't take it into the depths with me. I owed it to my friends to at least bring it back to them. Inexpressibly weary, I turned toward shore, swimming back.

I'd gone out so far. Much farther than was wise.

Farther than my body could swim, I suddenly realized, with atavistic, stark terror.

A wave slapped me in the face and I swallowed salt water, burning my lungs.

I tried treading water, my heavy limbs failing to respond. Going under, I sucked in more seawater. Not friendly on my gills, but searing my human throat. I struggled for the surface. Barely reached it. I gulped for air and took in more water.

I was drowning.

I couldn't make it. I'd die here, and take the Star with me.

Here was the moment of truth.

I had to shapeshift. A fish that couldn't drown. And I'd have to do so with enough skill to take the Star with me, and manifest it again.

I wasn't at all sure I could. At the peak of my abilities, that would have taken utmost concentration. Perhaps I could shift into a fish and take the chain into my mouth and carry the Star that way. Marskal's quip about giving me a rope to hold in my mouth came back to me and I choked out a sob of a laugh, swallowing more salt water, the surface a hazy distance above.

It was now or never. I couldn't let the will-sapping fear stop me. An easy form. Shift to a fish, grab the chain, swim for shore. Once I'd have done it with barely a thought. Easy. So easy.

Just do it.

~ 17 ~

Moranu's power filled me, stretching my bones, compressing. The shift took me and I leapt...

Panicked.

Like flying headfirst into a cliffside, I crashed back into human form.

I flailed, my lungs filling with water. The surface seemed impossibly far overhead, but I strained for it. So far away. I couldn't make it and I'd take the Star with me.

Irresponsible and arrogant. Incapable of love. How they'd all hate me. I'd deserve their loathing.

I loathed myself and it filled me like wet sand, weighing me down. I had nothing left to fight with.

Strong arms grabbed me, dragging me to the surface, pushing my face into the air and vising around my ribs. "Breathe!" he snarled.

I couldn't. He squeezed again, punching a fist up and under my sternum. I coughed up water, dragging in a burning breath.

"Keep doing that," Marskal ordered, changing his grip to under my arms, dragging me along as he struck out one-armed for shore.

"The Star," I croaked, trying to reach for the chain. I could give it to Marskal and be done with this onus.

"Be still, Moranu take you, or you'll drown us both. Just

breathe."

I concentrated on breathing, trying to be obedient and helpful, but the air dragged in sharp as knives, ragged and wet. It hurt. I was so tired of the pain. *You'll want to take the easy path. If you truly want this, don't take it. Choose pain.*

I'd thought my choosing was done, but apparently not. I'd still been taking the easy path. Avoiding the pain.

My heels grated against sand, Marskal cursing steadily as he dragged me ashore. In the shallows, he collapsed to his knees, shoving me onto my side and pounding my back. I coughed and vomited more water, unable to lift myself up. He reached under, bracing me with an arm, lifting and turning me face down so water flowed out of me. Waited for me to drag in a breath. Then repeated the methodical pummeling.

Until finally no more water came out, and I could breathe without undue struggle. Hooking his hands under my shoulders, Marskal dragged me the rest of the way out of the water, onto the dry sand still hot from the day. Then collapsed beside me. I stared up at the sky, most of the light fled from it, and even Moranu's moon smile had sunk beyond the peak of the volcano.

"Do you have a death wish?" Marskal finally asked, his voice gravelly and weary.

I rolled my head to look at him. He sat, knees up, arms folded on them, and forehead resting there. His long body curled into a shell and he no longer wore his leathers, boots, or weapons. He must have shed them to jump in the water to swim after me.

"How did you even find me?" I croaked.

He lifted his head, his brown eyes dark holes in his pale face, the baleful stare palpable. "You didn't make it easy, did you?" he accused. "You shook my people off your tail, so I had no choice but to follow in the last direction you were seen heading, and hope. If I hadn't made out your tracks here and there, I would have despaired. When I finally found where you went into the water—at least the general vicinity, because I missed it by half an hour and had to backtrack—I thought for sure I'd lost you forever." He laughed without humor, a rasping through salt-sore throat, and wiped a hand over his face. "You know, I thought to myself, 'Maybe she shifted. She just didn't bother to tell you and she's out there, being a dolphin or a fish, and she's fine. She'll emerge from the water, wading out like Glorianna born of the sea, with that beautiful smile, and she'll mock me for my worry.'"

"Marskal," I said, lifting a weary hand, but I couldn't reach him.

"That would have been all right," he repeated, harshly, glaring at me, "because it would have been far, far better than when I finally spotted you, so far out there, floundering in the waves. Seeing your head go under and knowing I couldn't reach you in time." He scrubbed his hand over his face again. Tears, not sweat or salt water.

"You did," I said, wretched that I'd brought him to this. "You did reach me in time. You saved my life."

"I've never swum like that in my life." He sounded wondering, as if he were talking to himself. "Nearly killed myself to reach you, and you don't even care."

That struck me silent and he shook his head, laughing that horrible harsh laugh again. "You asked me how long I've been in love with you. I think I've loved you from the first moment I laid eyes on you, that bright day you descended from Odfell's Pass. I'd never seen a woman who shook me to the bone like that, so beautiful, radiant with magic, and wild like a deer or an eagle. You never noticed me and it didn't matter. I watched you like I'd watch a sunrise, feeling that sheer astonished wonder at what a force of nature you are.

"How dare you," he said in searing accusation, all the worse for being spoken in a nearly voiceless whisper as he turned that baleful glare on me. "How dare you suicide?"

I opened my mouth, so salty, sticky with brine. The answer didn't come immediately. "I didn't mean to," I finally offered.

Making a scoffing sound, he looked away, clearly disgusted with me. "She didn't mean to."

"I didn't." I found some reserve in myself, enough to push myself up.

He didn't help, only watched my struggle. "You know, I would have gone on the same way, not telling you how I felt, never touching you, flirting with you, or asking to be your lover. I knew you were beyond my reach in every way. Until you weren't. You seemed so alone and you actually needed me. I thought if I let you know that you're not alone, if you enjoyed at least that aspect of being alive, then you might truly want to live again. And then this." He sounded so bleakly bitter—and betrayed—that my own heart thudded with sorrow.

"I didn't suicide," I insisted. "I never intended that."

"Lies," he said softly, the accusation sharp.

"I forgot!" I shouted at him, stung, unsure how to reach him. "I've never swum so far that I couldn't get back, never had no other recourse to save myself. I only needed to think for a while…"

"To escape," he supplied with a sneer.

"Is that so terrible?" I railed at him, raking my hands into my snarled hair and getting nowhere. I should cut the cursed stuff off if I was going to be stuck in this form. "I don't know how you do it, being trapped like this." My chest went tight. The seawater. Surely I couldn't be on the verge of sobbing. No descendant of Salena's would be so weak.

"Trapped," he echoed. Thoughtful more than angry and

contemptuous. "You say a mossback can't understand, and maybe I can't, but having one form isn't being trapped. You're not in a cage, Zynda, except one of your own making."

That made no sense at all. "I was trying to swim back. I realized I should, and then I realized I ... couldn't."

"What made you realize you should?" he asked, sounding idly curious.

Danger there. Some kind of bait I didn't dare take.

"Indulge me," he pressed. "I'd really like to understand what, in your puzzle of a mind, seemed important enough for you to try to make it back to shore."

"The Star," I admitted. "I forgot I had it with me and it would have been a failure if it were lost because of me."

He nodded thoughtfully, and I wished I could see his expression. Once I would have reached for a slight bit of shapeshifting magic to enhance my night vision.

"If not for that," he said, the same way he clarified mission details, "you would have given up and let yourself drown."

I wanted to deny that, but the lie wouldn't come. In those dark moments out there, I might have done exactly that. *The easy path.* Marskal was quiet, waiting for an answer, though he hadn't exactly asked a question. I rubbed my hands over my face, water dripping onto to it from the sodden hair I had no energy to wring out or deal with.

"When I left Annfwn," I said into my palms, "I thought I was going to be a hero. Like Salena. Did you know her?"

"No," he replied, no longer snarling with fury, but not exactly relenting. "I saw her a few times, when I was a boy in Ordnung Township, and later as a young man training at the castle. The mad queen. Even then, even so far gone, she was magnificent."

"She wasn't mad, not in that way. But she gave everything to her plan, sacrificed herself in a long, slow attrition. It ate at her, being unable to shift." Too close, there. "Never being able to return to Annfwn, shackled in marriage to that horrible man. He killed her in the end."

"I know." His voice held a world of regret.

"Anyway." I dropped my hands and gazed over the gentle water luminous in the starlight, so much kinder when it wasn't trying to drown me. "I thought I could do that, too. In my foolishness, I believed I could be as great—or even greater—than she. But I'm broken." My voice, too, broke over the word, a knife cutting me.

"You're not broken." Marskal sounded as if he were trying to be encouraging, but furious frustration with me ran beneath it. "You have incredibly powerful magic."

"That's not important. It's only occasionally useful. I'm talking about me. I am no longer a shapeshifter. *I* am broken."

"I don't agree on the magic, but as for shapeshifting, you simply need to recover, to try, to work at being able to—"

"I tried, all right?" I hurled it at him, even knowing he didn't deserve that. "When I was sure I was drowning, when I was desperate to live, I tried to shift and I *couldn't*. It's gone. Gone from me forever and I'm nothing now. *Nothing*." The sobs tore out of me, like a hatchling breaking out of its shell, ravenous and leaving the shards of my pride behind. Grief racked me, worse than coughing up the seawater, agonizing to my pitifully weak body.

I tried to curl up, but he was there. Yet again. Arms around me, lifting me onto his lap and wrapping himself around me. Safe. Warm. Protected. The memory came back of being the hummingbird carried in Marskal's hands, jolting as he ran down the mountain. I felt fragile like that again. Bird bones. I buried my face against his chest and wept as I hadn't since Anya's daughter died. Marskal cupped my head in his hand, holding me against his heart, murmuring words of comfort, of compassion and reassurance.

Finally I ran out. I might have drifted asleep, a broken bird cupped in the palm of his hand. When I opened my eyes, time had passed, but he sat unmoving, still holding me, though he must be exhausted, too. I stirred and he tightened his hold, not restraining, but cuddling me closer. Maybe he thought I still slept.

"I should have died," I whispered.

"You did die," he replied without hesitation, "and you came back. You had strong reasons to come back. Remember those and stop trying to die again."

I wanted to argue that I wasn't really trying to, but... I sighed and leaned into him, boneless and weary. "Yes."

"Yes?" He stroked a hand over my hair. "Will you promise me?"

That made me laugh. I couldn't even say why. A chuckle rumbled through his chest under my ear. "Some men want promises of eternal devotion from the women they love, it's true. I only want you to promise me that you'll try not to die. I might not survive it a third time."

"I can't promise you eternal devotion," I said, feeling that I needed to. Oh, honesty.

"I know." He didn't sound angry or even sorry. "I've never asked for that."

He hadn't asked for anything I wasn't willing to give. This much, I could. "I promise to do everything in my power to stay alive."

"Good." He kissed the top of my head. "You're not nothing."

I moved, suddenly restless, but he held me close, making a

shushing sound. "Don't try to escape. Listen to me. You are yourself. A woman of humor, intelligence, and an unmatched exuberant love of life and all the world. None of us love you because you're a shapeshifter. We love you for you."

"Even though I'm failing in my role, and you'll need to call in other Tala."

"I'm sorry I said that." His voice was indeed full of regret. "I *was* trying to push you, thinking that maybe anger would get you past the fear. A misguided attempt to help you. Plus you'd annoyed me."

"I did it on purpose, to push you away."

"I know that, too. In a better moment, I wouldn't have fallen for it."

I turned it all over in my mind. "I don't know how to have only one body."

He laughed a little, rocking me. "It's hard for me to understand, because I've only ever had one body, but you learn to make it into what you need. If you need to swim, to fly, to run—there are ways to do that as a human. Train the body you have. I'll help, if you want it. Though I still think you'll shapeshift again. Don't tense up."

But I had. The thought electrified and terrified me. "How can you think so?"

"Because you still have your other magic. And you still have your shapeshifter strength and speed. It's all there."

I shook my head. "Even partblood, non-shifters have that. Look at Ursula—that same shapeshifter strength and speed makes her a superior fighter, but she's never shapeshifted and never will."

"Never wanted to," he pointed out.

Which was true. Ursula clung to her mossback state with all the fear of those who dreaded change.

Like me.

"When I tried—out there—Marskal, it was life or death and I knew it. If that wasn't reason enough to push me past this… scar tissue or loss of nerve or whatever is wrong with me, what would be?"

He sat quietly, stroking my hair, snarled and wet as it was. "It wasn't a strong enough reason," he said after a bit. "Because you thought of yourself as already dead."

For some reason, the story he told me when I woke up came back to me. The warrior Morvared, who set everything to rights and then suicided, because he figured he was supposed to be dead. Marskal had dodged my question at the time, but suddenly I knew that he'd related that tale to me for this reason.

And, strangely enough, even though I had nothing else in common with that mossback warrior of old, the fact that he'd shared this feeling made me feel better. Not quite so broken.

"What will be a strong enough reason?" I asked.

Marskal moved, lifting my chin to look into my face. "There are lots of reasons," he said, and kissed me. The feel of his mouth, the taste of him, the sweetness of the desire coiling from him into me… it all felt so good and real and alive. And, yes, there was that love in him, like a soft blanket enfolding me. Maybe it was being so battered, but this time I accepted it with gratitude, letting his regard warm and fill me. Maybe my heart had cracked a little, because I felt something. Wanting and needing him.

The yearning rose up, too, and I wrapped my arms around his neck, sliding my fingers through his short hair, finding it sandy and sticky with drying salt. He tasted of the sea, too, and—deeper inside—of himself. I pressed into him, opening more and demanding more. He obliged, devastating me with the kiss, hands roaming over me with his own hunger. I didn't at all understand how he could want me—love me, even—when I'd been so awful, made him so angry, disappointed him so deeply. Breaking the kiss to breathe, I let my head fall back and he transferred his avid mouth to my throat, thrilling, fulfilling.

"I don't understand why you love me," I gasped, but holding on, so he wouldn't pull away.

He didn't. Instead he laughed, that darkly sensuous sound, licking up my throat, then finding my mouth again. "Maybe that's something else you have to figure out," he muttered against my lips, then dropped kisses on my cheekbones and closed eyes. "We should get you back. You need food and water."

"One track mind," I teased, not wanting to let go.

"Well, I need it, too." He eased me off his lap. "Somewhere on this beach are my boots, my sword belt, and a pack with food, if I can only find them."

Stricken, I contemplated him as he must have been, frantic, stripping off his weapons and boots and plunging into the sea to find me. I still didn't know how he'd seen me, or gotten there in time. I cupped his cheek. "I'm really sorry, Marskal."

He smiled slightly and turned his head to press a kiss into my palm. "Apology accepted. Don't do it again." He heaved himself to his feet, groaning, then held a hand down to me. "Think you can get up?"

I could, using the leverage of his help, but trying not to pull him down. The story of my life, lately. *No more self-pity*, I told myself firmly. Marskal was studying the darkened beach in each direction. Went a few steps and crouched, examining the sand. "This way," he said, nodding to himself. "I think it's not far."

"You can see in the dark?"

He took my hand, lacing his fingers with mine, leading me down the beach—which was also back toward the palace. "My night vision is pretty good, but I've practiced it, too. Yours isn't?"

"It is when I'm something nocturnal." The fear and grief stabbed at me, and I let it. No more fighting or denying it. "I used to be able to draw on certain keener senses," I offered. "Sort of a semi-shapeshifting."

"Useful. And explains why sometimes you looked like you had cat eyes. Or that night you came back from being the owl—your eyes and some of your face still looked like the owl."

I didn't know that. No one else had ever remarked on it.

"Aha. And I'm right. Here it is." He sank to his knees in the sand and I gratefully followed.

He snatched up the pack from his pile of things and extracted a flask, making to hand it to me. "You first," I said.

He raised a brow, but drank, then handed it to me. The fresh water tasted so sweet, soothing on my salt-scraped throat. "Fruit first or bread with honey?" he asked, rummaging through the pack.

"Any meatrolls?"

Shooting me a sidewise glance, he nodded, handing me one. I took a breath, not liking the scent, but determined to override the lingering hummingbirdness. Catching him watching me like I might faint or puke, I determinedly took a bite and chewed, telling myself the whole time that this was good for me. My stomach only barely rebelled, and I smiled at Marskal, even if it felt a little grim. "You shouldn't have to feed me—and I need to nourish this body properly."

He leaned over, sliding a hand behind my neck and kissing me. "I like feeding you. It's something I can do for you."

"You do everything for me. It's me who does nothing for you."

"That's not true." He kissed me, reverent, the love in him

humming through it. "You did suck my cock, after all."

The laugh snorted out of me, unlovely and graceless, but he didn't seem to mind, kissing me anyway, the kiss turning hungry. A hunger I returned in kind. With a reluctant sound, he eased off. "Finish your meatroll and drink more water."

"Yes, Mother," I replied, obediently eating.

"Is your mother like that?" he asked, casually curious.

"Badgering me to eat?" I thought about it. "Not really. You wouldn't know this, but eating has never been a … problem for me, before all of this."

"I did know that," he replied gently. "Remember that first night I brought you food? You ate like you were in pony form."

I laughed. "True. Speaking of—more meatrolls?"

"One more, then we're stuck with fruit and honey until we get back to the palace. I brought mostly that."

Thinking of me, even as I was trying to escape him. "Anyway, my mother's been dead for a while now."

He froze, looking embarrassed and pained. "I'm so sorry. I didn't realize."

I shrugged. "Why would you? But, my mother was…not warm? I mean, she was Tala, and so not like mossback mothers."

"Tala mothers abandon their children at birth?" Marskal nodded. "Figures."

I elbowed him. "Not like that, but we're a proud people. Don't snort like that. And Salena was her sister and my mom had only a few forms. I think… it bothered her, not to show as much ability, though her blood was as pure. And then Zyr—my brother—and I, we're more like Salena."

"Two of you then?"

"Three. I have a sister, Anya, as well, though she is more like my mom. Except not as fertile."

"Your mom had three children—that's amazing, given

what's going on, right?"

I nodded, making myself swallow the last of the meatroll. I didn't love it, but I already felt stronger for it. "More than that. She was pregnant at least a dozen times—if she kept count, she never said—and carried seven children to term. Only three of us survived to adulthood."

~ 18 ~

H E STARED AT me, face stricken and pale in the starlight. "Zynda... I had no idea. I'm so terribly sorry. And here I went on about my siblings."

"I didn't mind. I asked, remember? Our children have a high mortality rate—even those that survive birth and seem healthy. It's true of most every Tala you meet—we just don't discuss it with outsiders. Or, really, at all. With me, Zyr, and Anya, my mother found the right partners. We all three might even have the same father, since the blood matches worked."

"I'm understanding more now," he mused. "And your sister and brother—no children?"

"Zyr has fathered a few, he thinks, though none have lived that he knows of. The women...well, we've gotten to the point where the women keep to themselves if they're pregnant. Maybe they tell a few close friends, I don't know."

"They don't tell the fathers?" Marskal sounded aghast.

"Well, if they even know who the fathers are," I point out. "Some women try to keep track, but others don't. And then, if they do know, why trouble the men with the grief of losing a child?"

"Because." Marskal's patience sounded strained. "Because, Zynda, grief can be shared. People make each other stronger for sharing these things."

I shook my head. "That's a nice idea, but it doesn't work that way. Men and women fight over it, each accusing the other of having the bad blood. Some of the marriages, the grief and anger tears them apart."

"As when Salena's Tala husband suicided."

"Exactly." I shrugged, then hoped it was too dark for him to have seen it. "Anyway, if any of Zyr's children have lived—and the mother was sure of his fatherhood—she would have told him so our family could claim the child as part of our bloodline. And so other women would know he could produce a viable child."

"So much I didn't know."

"No one who's not Tala knows this."

"Thank you for sharing with me," he said gravely. "And your sister?"

I sighed, wondering if I could tell this. "She's carried one baby to term, but the infant ..." My voice went creaky at the end, and I couldn't get the word out.

Marskal heard it and moved next to me, putting an arm around me. I dropped my head onto his strong shoulder, not sure why I'd ever resisted it. "I'm sorry," he said. "You were there?"

I nodded. "Anya didn't want our mother to know. She was still alive then, but she'd had so much heartbreak with her own babies. So we went to another community up the coast when Anya began to show, and I stayed with her. To keep her company."

"To share her grief or joy."

I gave him an exasperated look, which he probably missed entirely. "With Anya it was more to nod while she moaned about feeling like a whale without getting to *be* one and to hunt down whichever exotic fruit juice she was currently craving."

"You're adorable when you're pretending you don't deeply care about someone. You were there in case the worst happened."

"I suppose that's so. We were—" My throat closed on it, but I powered through. "We tried to be practical. We knew better, but when she didn't miscarry, we were so full of hope. Anya had picked her lover very carefully, a man who'd fathered three viable children."

He stroked my arm, an easy up and down slide. "Hope makes things both better and worse."

"Worse," I replied darkly, the memory of those days like a stone in my belly.

"For someone so lighthearted in general, you have a strongly pessimistic side."

"Do I? I suppose we're all like that, the Tala. We live so close to death, to the loss of our entire people, that it kind of forces us into the other end, just to compensate. No one celebrates life like those in constant company with death."

I could feel him not commenting. "Just say it."

Marskal sighed a little. "It's not fair—but I was thinking that you, after your own brush with death, didn't compensate by celebrating life."

That sunk into me, and I was quiet, mulling that over. "You're probably right. I think—" I broke off, surprised at what I'd nearly spoken aloud.

"I'm listening."

"So you can report back," I had to point out.

He turned to me, raising my averted face with a finger under my chin, and kissed me. It felt like a promise, a vow. "I apologize for giving you that idea. You're right that I was trying to push you, but it was unfair to imply that I'd betray your trust. I won't say anything that you confide to me and that you don't give me permission to share."

"Isn't that a conflict of interest?" I teased him, but something about the moment made me breathless. And warmed me inside.

"Yes." He chuckled, then kissed me again and let my chin go, smoothing his hand over my hair. "At least Her Majesty understands putting personal loyalty above all else. Still, I don't look forward to the conversation."

"You don't have to do that for me."

"Yes, I do." He sounded resolute, unwavering. The Marskal I'd learned not to argue with so I didn't. "Say what you were going to, about celebrating life."

I twitched my shoulders, restless with myself. "It won't be a revelation to you. Normally my celebrating would have been shifting through all the forms I could, reveling in every perception of the world, all the ways of being and doing. Now that's lost to me, so it feels like there's nothing to celebrate." At least I didn't weep again, my voice as dull and lifeless as I felt.

"I'm sorry," he said, a world of understanding in the way he held me. "We don't have to talk about it anymore."

"No, I might as well finish. Anyway, Anya had her baby—a little girl, seemingly full of life—and I was so happy." Transcendently happy. Moranu take it, my voice broke again. "But she was... she was—"

"Not healthy?" he supplied gently, when I didn't finish.

I knuckled away the tears. Maybe this night of endless weeping would at least get it all out of me. "Not healthy," I agreed, laughing a little at the euphemism. So pleasant, the way non-Tala phrase things. "Sometimes a child is born part or mostly animal. Like they've partially shapeshifted in the womb. In this case, several different animals. Much of the time it means that their mind is distorted, too. Even if they live, which is rare, they are never able to care for themselves."

"She didn't live, Anya's daughter?"

I appreciated him calling her a daughter, instead of thing or worse. Their sideways use of language did help in ways. "She lived a few hours. Anya...she was hysterical, wanting to suicide, so we dosed her to sleep it off. And I took the baby and held her while she lived."

He was quiet. "I can't imagine how hard that must have been."

"I mostly cried." I laughed at myself, watery with it. "I thought I'd never weep again like that, but look at me tonight. She was so sweet. Powerful magic in her that I sensed. I hoped—again that word—I tried to help her, to coach her into shifting. If she could have taken a form that was *one thing*, you know, that might have..."

"Like you did, becoming the hummingbird."

"Yes. Only... most of the time, when we take that step, it truly is a last resort. Almost no one ever comes back from that animal form. But at least they live, and they become part of the family."

He huffed a laugh, then choked it back. "I don't mean to make light of that. I apologize."

"No." I nudged him with my elbow. "I want to know what you were thinking."

He shook his head a little, hugging me. "I was just imagining one of my siblings being the family dog, you know, or..." He made another choking sound. "It's terrible of me to find that funny."

I found myself grinning. "Humor in tragedy, yes? This is what I'm telling you—we joke and dance because the weeping becomes too much to bear. Speaking of family dogs, I'll confess something."

"I can't wait."

"I have this habit—a little game I play—where I imagine with my mossback friends what your First Form would be, if you could shift."

"I'm not sure I want to know."

"You? Wolf. Ursula, too, but a different kind. You'd be a timber wolf, mostly a loner, alpha when you need to lead the pack. Mostly you prefer to roam on your own."

"The lone wolf, huh?" He sounded somewhat consternated. "I'm a cliché."

"No. Not that. Never that." I turned in the circle of his arm, cupped his scratchy face in my hands and kissed him. "Thank you for talking me through this."

"It's what people do," he murmured against my lips.

"And I like that you can laugh, even at terrible things."

He smoothed the hair back from my face. "I like the way you laugh, too. That first time I saw you—you were laughing. You were riding beside Dafne, the sun shining on your hair, the breeze blowing it around your face, and you laughed at something. I don't even know what. But you looked so excited and alive."

"I was excited," I said, remembering that day. "Leaving Annfwn. At last going on my great adventure. I thought I was going to do heroic things. Looking back on that day, I see myself as a foolish girl, full of naïve ambition. I was going to save the Tala, and I've barely managed to keep myself alive."

"I don't think you're being fair to yourself."

I shrugged. Then laughed. "I thought our relationship was that you chewed on me and I pretended not to care. Now you're reversing things?"

He slipped his hand behind my neck, holding me there for a kiss so fierce it made my head swim. Then he leaned his forehead against mine. "I'm not pretending. And if you need me to kick your ass to help you do what you need to do, I will."

"I don't know," I whispered. "It all feels so huge. I don't know what I need."

"Think about it then." He was silent for a bit. The water made soft lapping sounds and a night bird called. "This is something I've been thinking about. If the sleeper spies might be people forced into animal form by the Practitioners of *Deyrr*— would that be similar to what you're talking about, coaxing an infant to shapeshift?"

"I hadn't thought of it exactly that way, but maybe that was in the back of my mind. I've never heard of anyone being forced to shapeshift—only helped into their natural inclinations, but..."

"But the two might not be separated by much?"

I sighed. "It's turning out that a great deal of what I thought was distantly separated might not be so much."

"I'm glad to hear you say that." Marskal's voice was so warm with feeling—with that impossible love he nurtured for me— that I didn't correct him to say I hadn't meant the two of us. Besides, he might be right about that, too. Something else for me to ponder.

"Marskal?"

"Yes, quicksilver girl?"

I laughed a little. "Do we have to go back to the palace tonight?"

He shook his head, lips brushing mine as he did. "Not unless you're still hungry. Both ships leave on the dawn tide and we need to be on board ours. Otherwise...well, we're all accustomed to you disappearing and turning up at the last moment. They'll assume I'm with you."

I wasn't sure how I felt about that. So, I focused on the relief that we could stay outside a little longer. "Did you mean it, about sleeping outside—I mean, would you be all right with sleeping right here?"

"With you? Anywhere."

"Good." I reached for the laces of his shirt, and he stopped me, hands closing on my wrists.

"What are you doing?"

"Getting you naked," I replied, very reasonably, I thought.

"We're not having sex tonight."

"No? I seem to recall a deal where I get my way this time. Bed or no." I stopped his sigh with a kiss, drawing him into it, delighting in his rapid arousal despite his half-hearted attempts to fend me off. Getting my hands inside his shirt, I hummed in pleasure at the feel of his skin, nipping at the strong edge of his jaw when he broke from the kiss.

"Zynda," he said, gripping my shoulders and setting me away from him. "You almost died just now."

"I'm feeling better," I purred. "And you were the one to chastise me about celebrating life." I slipped his hold and, moving faster than he could stop me, ripped his shirt off.

"I'm going to run out of shirts, you minx." But he was laughing as he scolded me, tumbling me onto my back, pinning my wrists by my head, a knee between my thighs. I struggled, but couldn't break the hold this time.

I narrowed my eyes at him. "Have you been practicing Dasnarian wrestling tricks?"

"The Hawks and the Vervaldr have traded a number of useful techniques, yes," he replied.

Lifting my hips, I rubbed my sex against his hard thigh where it pinned my groin. "Those Dasnarian men, so clever."

"Don't start." He closed his eyes a moment, mastering himself. "You and I need to talk."

"Oh, Moranu, save me from mossbacks! We've *been* talking.

Sex now. No more nattering." I strained up to reach him with my mouth, but he kept reared back, expression set. Never had I longed more to shift form and take him by surprise. He'd find himself wrestling the tiger and we'd see how his Dasnarian tricks worked then.

"This is important," he insisted. "Lie still. We need to talk about babies."

That did it. Few topics could more immediately dull my lust. But I still wasn't discussing it. "If that's how you want to be, let's go back to the palace."

His voice gentled, but his grip didn't. Not a stupid man, by any stretch. "I didn't think of it before, because the women in the Hawks all use certain herbs to prevent babies. It was careless and stupid of me, but I made an assumption. Our conversation tonight made me realize... Zynda, could you get with child, being with me?"

I shrugged as best I could, which wasn't much. "Unlikely, as you are a mossback. And I'm probably not fertile. If I ever have, I miscarried before I knew about it." On any other night, I could have made it sound like I didn't care. Not this one, not with so much jumbled emotion already.

Marskal unbent enough to kiss my forehead. "I'm sorry. I didn't think."

"It doesn't matter." Though, of course, it mattered. More than could be voiced. "Anyway, you needn't worry about being saddled with a partblood child."

"Why not?" He sounded careful. "Are you taking precautions?"

I nearly gaped at him, then had to laugh. "Haven't you been listening? No Tala tries *not* to have babies. If I get with child by you, it would be a goddess-gifted miracle."

He still didn't release me. "Would you tell me?"

Dangerous territory here. "Let me up."

He considered it, then shook his head. "No. I want a straight answer."

I sighed and turned my head. "I've tried to tell you I'm not the right woman for you—and not only because of Final Form. Tala and mossback ways don't mix. Even if I don't take Final Form, I could never be exclusive to you. Shapeshifters sleep around in part to find a compatible mate in the hopes of making a child."

"I'll worry about that part later. You're saying no, you wouldn't tell me."

"Fine. That's a no, I would not tell you." I relented a little. "Maybe, if I were sure you were the father, and if ..." I had to take a deep breath. "If the child survived the first couple of years, I would maybe bring them to visit you."

Stony silence met that. This is what comes of honesty.

"You say that like we wouldn't be together."

I laughed, tossing my head in the sand, ignoring how he glared at me. "This is all academic if I take Final Form."

"But not if you don't. Why couldn't we be together in that case?"

"Maybe I'd be sleeping around, looking for a compatible father."

"This is if you quickened with my child, then we could be together and you wouldn't need to look at other men."

The possessiveness in his tone made me both tingle and want to kick at him. "Where would we be together?"

"There's no longer a barrier around Annfwn. If you want to live there, I'm willing to do that."

"You would *not* fit in."

He set his jaw. "You can't know that."

"You've never even been there."

"Wrong—I traveled through Annfwn with Her Majesty to board the Tala ship to come to Nahanau."

"Marskal! I met you there and I know perfectly well that you were all blindfolded and escorted through in the middle of the night."

"I've still been there," he replied, obstinate as an ox.

I blew out a long breath. "Can we maybe not argue about where we'd theoretically live if we—against all probability—decided to continue this affair, assuming I don't take Final Form, if—again, against all probability—I, who am likely infertile, should conceive a child with you, an incompatible mossback?"

He considered that, then laughed a little, shaking his head. "You have a point."

"Thank you. Can I be allowed to move now?"

"Not yet." But he bent down to kiss me, seductive and sweet. Oh yes. Much better. "I want you to promise me something."

Here it was. I braced myself.

"Promise me that if you have any idea that you're with child, you'll tell me."

Moranu save me. And him. "What if I don't think it's yours?" I asked bluntly.

But he didn't flinch. "Even then."

"Why?" I asked it plaintively. "It makes no sense."

"It makes sense to me. I want to know, to be there for you."

"You wouldn't be able to do anything."

"Shh. Leave that to me." He kissed me again, coaxing now, increasing the fire. I moved him, but to no avail. "Promise," he murmured.

"Fine. Though it will never happen, I promise to tell you if I think I'm with child—*if* we are still in contact."

He hesitated slightly, then nodded. "I'll take it."

~ 19 ~

"*YOU LIED TO ME.*"

My eyes snapped open. I lay naked in Marskal's arms, his sleeping breath warm on my shoulder where he wrapped up close around me. Amazingly, my jolt to wakefulness didn't transmit, because he continued to sleep deeply, his arm and thigh draped over me, surprisingly heavy for a such a lanky man.

Of course, I wasn't at all sure how either of us had slept through an enormous dragon landing on the beach and settling down a snout's length away. Though my heart hammered in panic, I made sure to appear outwardly languid.

"*Good morning, Kiraka,*" I thought at her. The sky remained dark, but dawn scented the air. Soon the horizon would pinken and we would have to head for the harbor anyway. Detained by dragon would be an unassailable excuse for tardiness, however. "*In what way did I lie?*"

"*Ah, now I know you must be kin, however distant. You do not quibble over whether you lied. You only wish to determine which lie I detected.*"

"*Makes it easier to give you an intelligent reply anyway.*"

She snorted, steam billowing from her nostrils in the cool predawn air. Marskal stirred, then tensed. I put a hand on his arm around my waist. "It's all right for the moment," I murmured. "She and I are talking."

"This never happens with the mossback girls," he muttered into my hair—making me laugh—but stayed still. Which was good, because Kiraka had continued speaking in my head and I didn't want to screw up because I was talking to them both at once.

"You claimed the man wasn't your lover and he clearly is." The dragon had a tone to her voice I couldn't quite decipher.

"He wasn't then. Now he is. Time has passed and our relationship changed." It had changed, it occurred to me, and not only because of sex.

She seemed to mull that over, the twin puffs of steam reminding me of the older nobles at Ordnung, puffing on their lung-healing herbs over wine after dinner. *"Time."* She sighed the word through my mind, an endless loop of shuffling scales. *"It becomes difficult to track. Centuries pass in moments. Moments endure for years. If you wish to become a dragon, keep that in mind."*

My heart hammered so hard, I felt sure Marskal would feel it through the press of our bodies. *"You will show me the way then?"*

"Can you shapeshift?"

I resolved not to quail before the question. *"I will soon. I'm working on it."* There. I would make that be true.

"If you can learn, I will teach you."

At last. I should have felt exultant. Shaman would rejoice. And yet... I felt a strange sorrow.

"However," she said. *"That must perforce come later. I have considered the matter and I've decided on the gift I require."*

"What can I give you, Lady Dragon?"

"Release the other dragons. I need company. And they'll be helpful in the war."

"That might be a compelling argument. I have to tell you—after you... attacked me, my people are less than enthusiastic about having more of you around."

"Convince them," she replied with airy disinterest. *"One would think I've provided you with sufficient motivation."*

"I only know for sure of one other."

"Start there."

"Any suggestions for how?" I'd have no local barbarian king to sexually kindle the magical connection. Amusing that the method sounded relatively convenient.

"This would be your problem," she replied with acerbic emphasis. *"You were there when I awoke. Do the same thing."*

I mentally sighed, but suppressed it. *"Understood."*

Then, silently as she must have arrived, she slithered back into the sea. For a few moments, her dorsal spines showed, like a school of sharks, then she disappeared entirely into the mist.

"It's safe now," I said. "I think."

Marskal let out a breath and rolled me over, pulling me close. "I've been awakened by a man standing over me, lowering a mace to bash in my brains, and it didn't galvanize me like waking up to see *her* breathing smoke on you."

"It was steam."

"Oh, well then." He laughed and kissed me on the forehead. "No need to have worried."

"Kiss me for real." I lifted my lips to him.

"My mouth is stale from sleep. Let me rinse it."

"Do mossback girls care for such things? I don't." I slid my thigh between his, stroking against his erection. "Remind me I'm flesh, Marskal, and not ash." Cheating a bit, to play on that, but it worked. With a sound of concern, he kissed me, tasting not stale—whatever that might mean—but like himself. A flavor I was beginning to know well and miss when I didn't have it.

I reached between us and gripped his shaft, sliding up to tease the sensitive head, and he groaned in my mouth. "Temptress," he muttered, pulling half out of the kiss. "We should get up."

"An hour until the sun touches the horizon," I said. "Plenty of time. And I need you."

His huff of a laugh was part groan. "Half an hour, if that. This old soldier has something of an internal clock, too."

"Plenty of time," I repeated in a velvety tone, rolling him onto his back and holding him at the right angle to be sheathed in me. He threw his head back with a groan, clenching his teeth over it, neck muscles taut and enticing, so I bent to lick and nibble at them.

"Bless Moranu, woman," he groaned. "Warn a fellow next time."

"I like taking you by surprise." I sank my blunt teeth most satisfyingly into the thick muscle on the side of his throat, loving having him fill me there, too, and dragged the woman's nails he'd mocked down his naked chest. His hands vised on my hips.

"Play nice," he warned.

I let go of his neck and straightened, rolling my hips to torment him another way. Lifting the mass of my hair—which, ugh, I was definitely cutting off at the first opportunity—I arched my back. His gaze dragged over me and he slid gentler hands up to my breasts, cupping them and thumbing my nipples, making me purr.

"So lovely," he murmured. "Your eyes almost glow in this light, bluer than the deep sea."

"Very good petting." I rocked my hips lazily, lowering my lids at the waves of pleasure from having him so deep inside me.

He caught his breath, hands tightening on me. Narrowing his eyes, he caught onto my game. "We don't have time to draw this out."

I clamped my inner muscles on him, making him shudder. "What are you going to do about it?"

"You should know by now not to dare me." With that, he flipped me onto my back. I shrieked with surprise and laughter, losing my breath, then gasping for it as he impaled me. Without a pause he thrust into me, establishing a fast, hard rhythm. I wrapped my legs around his narrow hips, cupping his face and feathering my thumbs over his cheekbones. His face ridged with arousal and fierce determination, he still turned his head to kiss my palm.

A hard blade of toned muscle, he stroked against my softer body, spearing me with his unrelenting thrusts. Until, completely unmoored, I had to grab onto his shoulders, as I unraveled in the best of ways—coming apart in the steadfast circle of his body.

AFTER A BRIEF swim to clean up, we walked down the beach to the harbor at a fast clip. Glorianna's rising sun crested the flat sea, spilling pink and gold over the sky and water. Marskal eyed it then me.

"We're going to be late."

I shrugged, maybe exaggerating it a little. "The Tala don't care for—"

He clamped a hand over my mouth, tucking my head under his arm and rubbing knuckles on my scalp. "Don't say it," he warned.

I slipped his hold, skipping away and laughing. Because I felt like it, I twirled, spinning in a dance and leaping through the shallow surf.

Marskal ran after me, grinning. "That's better."

I slid him a smile, cocking my head. "Why did you think I was lonely? Before."

He considered me, clearly debating his answer. He'd put on the remains of his shirt, tucking the ragged ends together inside his fighting leathers, but it still showed. Along with the vivid bite mark on his neck.

Mine, some animal part of me purred.

"I don't know," he finally replied. "A feeling? Maybe I was wrong. But you just seemed... alone. I knew you felt alien among us, and that you missed Annfwn and being around other Tala."

"How did you know those things?" I wondered. I'd certainly never said. Rarely even contemplated that. The old me hadn't liked to dwell.

"A look in your eyes, maybe. Even when you were in a group, laughing and talking, there was this look to you, like you felt alone." He cracked his neck, rolling it off. "Might have been my own fancy."

"No." I almost didn't say more, but he deserved the more. "I think you were right. I was lonely and didn't know it." Or, I supposed, I had known it, but had seen it as practicing for Final Form, not as something I could change. Feeling a little shy for no good reason, I took his hand. I shouldn't have hesitated, because he laced his fingers with mine, holding me in a reassuringly strong clasp, and giving me a warm smile.

"Tell me more about my eyes."

He arched a brow. "More petting about how beautiful you are?"

I laughed, swinging our joined hands. "Not that—though I like that—I mean how they look different sometimes. I'm thinking about something."

"Hmm." Now his brows drew together in thought.

The beach had ended at the great rocky spur that tumbled down from the mountainside to curve out into the water, forming one arc of the harbor, so we cut up to the path through the trees. We were nearly there. I found myself looking out at the higher view of the ocean, the sky bluing. *No running away,* I told myself.

As if reading my impulse, Marskal squeezed my hand, not tethering, but reassuring. "It's like when you looked at the Star in the Council yesterday," he said. "And kind of how your magic looks—your eyes take on a slightly different shape, and have a similar light in them." He studied me, gaze roving over my face. "It's both obvious in my mind's eye, and simultaneously difficult to put into words."

"That's all right. That much helps." I wasn't sure what I'd do with the information, but I'd think about it. The path took us onto the long pier, where both ships waited at the end, tugging on their ropes, sails partially furled. We'd been sighted, shouts passed along, and last-minute preparations accelerating. Marskal didn't let go of my hand, though, and I didn't try to shake him loose.

Ursula waited aboard the Tala ship, in intense conversation with Dafne. She lifted a hand to acknowledge us, but didn't pause otherwise. Jepp stood at the foot of the gangplank up to the *Hákyrling,* emanating impatience. Closing the distance, she seized me in a hug.

"I'd already prayed to Danu to smite you if I missed saying goodbye because you dallied." She gave me a fierce smile, her dark eyes damp. How could I have imagined she was angry with me? "Kral is about tear my hide off with his determination to be heading out already."

"What's involved in smiting?"

She laughed and hugged me again, pressing a kiss to my

cheek. "I have no idea. But now you don't have to worry. Be careful. I'll miss you."

"*You* be careful," I replied. "Don't take chances."

"Me?" She grinned, pulled a dagger and spun it. "I'm the definition of careful."

"I'll pray to Moranu to cover what Danu misses then."

"I appreciate that." She'd gone abruptly serious, bowing to me. Then she gave Marskal the Hawks' salute and bowed again. "Lieutenant. I know you're always on alert, but…" She flicked a glance at me.

"Understood," he said gravely. Then pulled her into a hug. "And stop saluting me. Though if you get yourself killed, I'm kicking you out of the Hawks."

"What?" she demanded. "No wake, no big party extolling my virtues? I'm owed that!"

He shook his head. "Nothing. Unmarked grave. So no heroics."

"Danu take it," she growled, but her eyes had an even more marked shine. "I'm done with the two of you." She turned to climb the plank, not looking back.

Dafne finished with Ursula and started down toward us. Marskal darted up to assist her, as the pitch of the ship on the waves gave her already rolling walk an unsteady cant. She hung onto him with a grateful smile and they chatted on the way down. Who knew what about.

She looked me over. "You look like a pauper's daughter, all big eyes and ragged clothes. You'll be happy to know that Jepp and Kral transferred your things onto the Tala ship, so you can change." She held out the box she carried. "This I hoped to put directly into your hands."

The wooden box that held the map-sticks. I took it automatically, but searched her face. "Are you sure you want to entrust these to me? I can't shapeshift anymore."

She studied me seriously. "You will. And besides, Kiraka told me to give them to you. They're meant for a shapeshifter to use and you're going to the land of shapeshifters. The Tala will make better use of them than I ever could."

"Thank you."

"I hope it works for you." She cast a glance at Marskal and away. "Final Form, if that's what you decide. I'm sorry that I was angry. I was mostly hurt that you didn't trust me enough to tell me the truth."

"I'm sorry, too." All these muddy mossback emotions and relationships. I needed to navigate them better. "It wasn't that I didn't trust you."

She smiled slightly. "Or rather, that it wasn't me specifically who you didn't trust."

I nodded, throat oddly tight. Maybe that lurked at the heart of Tala caginess. Trust wasn't part of my makeup. Something else to learn to change. I handed the box to Marskal, who had a thoughtful expression, and hugged her.

She held onto me, then stepped back, making a face. "Eyew. You're all damp and sandy." She glanced at Marskal. "You, too. I don't even want to know what you two were doing all night. And morning. Lieutenant, I should mention that your things are packed up and on the ship, also. That shirt might need to be retired for polishing the deck."

He grinned at her. "It has sentimental value."

She slid her gaze to me with a knowing smirk, one that covered deeper emotions. It struck me suddenly that Jepp and I were leaving her here again. This time she wanted to stay, and was secure in the happiness of her circumstances, but still—it had to be reminding her of that abandonment, with the *Hákyrling* already pulling out.

"I can only imagine," Dafne was telling Marskal. "I'm terrible at goodbyes, so I'm going to pretend you're going off on a jaunt and will be back soon."

"Dafne," I said, before she could go. She turned back, wiping the tears off her face. And I realized I didn't know what I wanted to say. Something to make her happy. "Your daughter," I said, breaking my superstition against speaking of the unborn. I gestured to Dafne's swollen belly. "She's healthy and full of magic. I can feel it."

Fresh tears welled from Dafne's eyes, and she dashed them away impatiently, smiling through them. "I weep at the least thing these days," she said. "Thank you. That means a great a deal to me." She hastened off, very nearly at a trot.

Marskal put a hand on my back, guiding me up the gangplank. "Well done," he murmured. "And lightning didn't flash out of the sky."

I made a pig snorting sound at him, and he laughed. A good sound.

WE MADE IT out of the harbor quickly, the light Tala ship leaping through the waves, and soon we were surrounded by open sea. A pod of dolphins—the group I'd played with, I thought, though it was hard to tell from human form—followed along for a while, making me long to join them.

Because I needed to keep to my resolve to at least try to lift my wounded sword arm, after we cleaned up, I took myself off to a private corner of the deck. I considered the form, remembering how it felt, testing the sensation of anticipated joy and freedom. How it might feel to leap overboard and be one with them.

But, like a saboteur in the dark, the twisted fear grabbed hold, phantom pain riddling my body. The sensation of running full speed into a wall made my head ache. Apparently lifting a wounded arm hurt. I sank to the deck to rest, lifting my face to the sun, and imagining the breeze blowing over it meant I flew through the sky.

"Making any progress?" Marskal asked, running a hand over my hair and dropping beside me to sit cross-legged. He'd stopped me from cutting the nasty mess off, sitting patiently with a comb and oil after I bathed, working out the knots in short order. Baffling to me.

"How did you know?" I asked, eyeing him. He gleamed with sweat. Having stripped down to an old shirt and short pants, he'd been sparring with Ursula, Harlan, and a few other Hawks. Then, after Ursula and Harlan retired to go over strategy, Marskal and the others continued running drills. Also baffling.

"I saw you watching the pod of dolphins and guessed. It's one of your favorite forms."

The man observed far too much. "Are you ready to take on the sleeper spies and Dasnarian forces single-handedly?"

He gave me a cocky grin. "Bring 'em on."

I sat back on my heels, considering. "Tala children drill in shapeshifting, like you do with your Hawks. Practicing over and over like that."

He regarded me calmly. "Could be a good path to pursue. I'd certainly do something like that with an injury—go back to basics, warm up again with simple exercises, rebuild strength and flexibility."

I laughed at him. "You make everything sound so simple."

"I'm a simple kind of guy," he said, picking up a lock of my hair dashing itself across my face and winding it around his finger.

"Now who's lying?"

He smiled easily. "Not a lie so much as an…" He tugged me closer, searching for the word.

Obligingly, I kissed him. "Oversimplification?" I offered.

"Nicely played. We'll go with that. So, do you want me to help you with your exercises? You'd have to teach me shapeshifting basics."

"And share Tala secrets?" I replied archly. "Never! But my brother Zyr does teach the children. I'm thinking of asking him."

"Good idea. Will he be nearby?"

"When we get to the cliffside city this evening?" I patted his cheek. "Oh, my darling mossback, *everyone* will be there. Prepare to be overwhelmed."

"Do I have to be blindfolded this time?" He looked distinctly unhappy about that, and I paused to mull, as I hadn't thought about it.

"Well, Ursula and Harlan won't be. Everyone else will stay aboard the ship until they travel to Ordnung. That's been the usual protocol. I'll make a case for you, so no."

"Do you have that much power?"

I raised my brows at him. "I am of Salena's line."

"So… yes?" He tugged me into a kiss again. "I like a powerful woman."

I laughed, enjoying this playful side of him, the easy calm before the storm. "Keep that in mind when my family are interrogating you about everything in the world."

"They'll be there, too?" He'd gone still, arrested by some thought.

"When I said *everyone*, I meant it."

"How do you plan to introduce me?" he asked, very casually.

"As Marskal, I thought. Or do you prefer 'Lieutenant'? Maybe you have a family name I should include."

He gave me a long look. "That's not what I meant, and I think you know it."

"I don't think I do know. Does it matter?"

He didn't reply immediately, studying the lock of hair wrapped around his finger. "No. No, I suppose it doesn't."

"Marskal," I said softly. He lifted his gaze to meet mine, his face that remote mask that meant he hid what he felt. He'd used it before so I wouldn't know he loved me, I realized. Now he covered something else. "I'm not practiced at this, and I'm not teasing when I say I'm not like mossback girls. If you want me introduce you a certain way, then you have to tell me."

His mouth quirked, eyes roving over my face. "Sometimes I can't tell if you're teasing me or being brutally honest in your tricky Tala style."

I kissed him, lingering over the taste. "Can't all of that be true at once?"

He laughed at me. "Only you." He took a breath. "I want you to introduce me as your lover—or whatever name is appropriate for what we are to each other."

I looked into his steady brown eyes. They opened into that love now, hiding nothing, asking for more. "My brother Zyr will not be kind if I do that."

Marskal's mouth firmed. "I can handle myself."

He could, too. I believed that now. "All right, lover," I breathed against his mouth, kissing him again. "Want to find a private place with me?"

"Yes," he replied, real happiness in his eyes.

It surprised me, how much I liked that I'd put it there.

~ 20 ~

WE SAILED INTO the cove at the foot of the cliff city of Annfwn just as the sun set. The four of us gathered at the rail, watching the white, flower-draped cliffs rise taller and taller as we approached.

"It still amazes me that we can get here so fast," I commented.

"You saw the maps," Ursula replied. "Without the barrier, it's a fairly short distance by straight line from Annfwn to Nahanau." She gave me a wry grin. "We just sent you the long way around last time. You can blame your king for that."

"It's unbelievable," Marskal breathed, sounding awed as I'd rarely heard him. Except maybe talking about seeing me for the first time, which pleased my vanity excessively. "And I'd expected a great deal."

Seeing it as he must be—and having been away long enough that I drank in the sight, too—I took a moment just to enjoy the beauty of my homeland. Even with the sun angled so low, the water shone with a crystalline purity, retaining hints of the shining turquoise of daylight. The white sand beaches stretched in each direction, bordered by verdant, fruit-bearing trees at either end. Farther to the north would be my clan's enclave, but I hadn't exaggerated my certainty—confirmed by the staymach messengers—that they'd all be in the cliff city to greet us.

Staymachs in bird form had been flying back and forth for the last couple of hours after we'd been sighted, carrying messages. Among the instructions for visitors, they'd surprised us by directing the ship to sail directly into the cliff city cove, rather than to one of the harbors up and down the coast where the Annfwn navy was kept.

My friends and family would be curious about why I hadn't flown ahead personally, as I invariably would have in the past, and anticipating their questions was knotting my stomach. My hands tightened on the rail, and Marskal ghosted a caress over one, noticing, as always. I let out the breath that had wanted to snarl in my lungs and focused on savoring the sight of Annfwn.

Most Tala lived in the cliff city, which rose in tier upon tier, cut deep into the sheer wall. Roads for carts and narrower walking paths wound in and out, passing under arches and balconies, all embedded with jeweled tiles and draped with flowering vines. On the beach, Tala thronged—in human and animal form—building bonfires and setting up feast tables. In the middle tier, awnings of bright silk shaded the wares of merchants and artisans, and just beyond them the council halls blazed with light. They were ready for us, both for the negotiating and the celebrating.

Perhaps Moranu had given me this gift, of one last evening with my people, just to enjoy life. I took Marskal's hand, still near mine on the rail, grateful that he'd reminded me of this. He laced his fingers with mine, but had a distracted smile. He shook his head, gesturing with his other hand at Annfwn. "I can't quite take it in. I understand more now, how you feel about this place. It's a paradise like none other."

"It's ridiculous that you couldn't see it when we passed through before," Ursula groused. "And I don't like my Hawks being confined below, as if they'll somehow sully the place by looking at it." She tossed me an annoyed glance and I shrugged, making it extra languid.

"Take it up with King Rayfe and Queen Andromeda," I replied. "I don't make the rules."

"Except you have all that power," Marskal murmured for my ears alone, making me laugh.

"Speaking of rules, why does Annfwn keep a standing navy?" Harlan asked, leaning around Ursula. "This has long puzzled me. The barrier only dropped a year ago—why invest in building and maintaining so many ships when they could sail only a few hours before having to turn around?"

I smiled easily and held up my palms. "Just in case."

Ursula pounced on that. "In case of what?"

"Attack?" I suggested.

"Attack from what quarter, though?" Harlan persisted, Ursula nodding along. Perfectly matched, those two predators. "Uorsin was Annfwn's greatest enemy for the last three or four decades, and he was on the other side of the mountains. What attack did you anticipate from the sea?"

I laughed a little. "You're asking me as if it was my idea. I have no idea what the reasoning was."

"But you knew about it," Ursula said, gray eyes keen.

I glanced at Marskal, who still stared at the beauty of the vista ahead, giving me no clue what they were driving at. "I knew we had ships, yes."

"And how did you think of them?" Harlan asked. When I blinked at him in confusion, he clarified. "Did you think of them as a fishing fleet, for example?"

"Oh no! We prefer to catch fish ourselves. Much more fun."

"So, if not for fishing, then…" He prodded while Ursula watched me keenly.

"I don't know." I threw up my hands. "It's tradition. We

have tournaments with them. Not having ships would be... wrong."

They nodded at each other in satisfaction, as if they'd won a sparring match against me.

"Told you," Ursula said.

"No," he countered mildly, "I suggested it first."

"I'd thought of it already, though."

Harlan shook his head. "Doesn't count unless you say it."

Marskal finally tore his attention from the cliff city. "You're thinking it was part of the original strategy by the founding Tala—embedding in the culture the tradition of keeping a standing navy, in anticipation of attack by *Deyrr*, knowing it would come from the sea?"

Ursula nodded, a pleased smile on her face. "You always see clearly, Marskal."

I huffed in annoyance. "But nobody's ever said that."

"They wouldn't," Ursula explained, "because it's not something you see when you're inside a culture. Especially for a people as ... fluid as yours in terms of governance, making something like keeping a defense against an ancient enemy that could be easily forgotten part of honored tradition—"

"With regular tournaments," Marskal inserted.

"Right. And tournaments—it makes having the navy a part of life, rather than some edict."

I laughed at them all. "I don't know. It seems far-fetched to me."

"Look at your capital." Ursula jabbed a finger at it. "I know you don't call it that—I still think it's imprecise that 'Annfwn' refers to both the cliff city and country."

"Like the Kingdom of Avonlidgh and Castle Avonlidgh?" Harlan asked with a pleasant smile.

She scowled at him. "I didn't name that one, either. Still,

when I first came to Annfwn, I didn't understand how it could be so open, so without any way to close it off. The walking paths go right past homes with unenclosed balconies and windows. One dwelling might lead directly into another. Rayfe gave me some balderdash about animal territories and mutual respect, but—"

"Which is accurate," I inserted. "The Tala are much more aware of territories and personal space than you mossbacks are. We don't *need* locked doors because we're smart enough, and have enough sensitivity, that we'd never invade another's space unwelcome."

She stared at me in consternation, and Harlan laughed, smoothing a big hand over her short hair. "She's got you there. But that wasn't your point. To be fair, I felt the same, that first visit. Now, however, I see the same thing you do."

"See what?" I looked back at the city, the cliff now towering over us as we closed on it, brilliantly lit in violet, tangerine, and fuchsia by the setting sun.

"It's a fortress as far as attack from the sea," Marskal said in his matter-of-fact way. "Access to the lower tiers can be easily cut off by destroying those ramps and rope bridges." He pointed to them. Notice how the lower tiers have no doors and windows?"

"To keep them cool," I said. "They're mainly for food storage."

They all nodded in satisfaction. These warriors all loved the game of picking apart strategy.

"Those tunnels we slid down," Harlan said to Ursula, sharing an intimate smile with her, "they could be used to drop nasty surprises or fighters on an invading force."

"The balconies, too," she replied. "See how that first tier juts out farther? They'd both create a ceiling to anyone trying to climb, and provide convenient platforms to drop rocks and worse on attackers."

I narrowed my eyes on the balconies she spoke of. Those were shared, open to anyone to use, particularly for snacking on treats gotten from the street vendors. "Those are for dining and dancing," I said. "Musicians play there."

"In peace time, sure," Ursula replied, and put a hand on my shoulder. "We're not criticizing, cousin. Quite the reverse. The Tala have been exceedingly clever and I was too dense to see it before. Everything is geared toward resisting the onslaught of your true enemy: *Deyrr*."

"You have it in your secrecy, too," Marskal said, tucking a strand of hair behind my ear and smiling when I frowned. "Most of your Tala secrets aren't that critical—except that you have a habit of not trusting information to anyone. It's ingrained in you to conceal strategic information from an enemy, to be ready for *Deyrr*, whether you know it or not."

Trust again. I regarded him in bemusement and he gave me a gentle smile, as if he already understood the inside of my heart.

"And we are *not* the enemy," Ursula declared, leveling her hawkish gaze on the cliff city again. Her dark red hair gleamed with the dying rays of the setting sun, which also outlined her sharp, determined profile. "Which I'm going to take up with Andi—and Rayfe—immediately. We have too many enemies outside our barrier to be playing these coy games within it. Time to trust each other already."

I smiled back at Marskal, Ursula's words echoing in my mind.

ANNFWN DOESN'T HAVE a pier like the harbor at Nahanau—nor was the cove as deep as the harbor there, so we had to leave the ship anchored farther out. I'd teased my companions that they'd have to swim—the Tala sailors already had, diving or flying off as soon as they'd made the ship fast—but the staymachs had told me that Andi and Rayfe were sending a small boat so the distinguished visitors wouldn't have to soak their clothes.

Probably a good thing as everyone had donned the best clothes they had with them. Ursula had even conceded to wearing a gown, though she refused my offer of a lighter Tala-style silk, muttering about feeling naked in the thriced things. Her crown, a simple gold diadem that swelled to an upward point over her forehead, set with three of Salena's rubies in a staggered line, to represent the three goddesses, the topmost cut to resemble Danu's star, rested on her brow, shining like a beacon.

A little staymach, in the form of a pretty pink songbird, sat on my shoulder chirping. Marskal—stirring my blood with his handsomeness in the Hawks' formal uniform—examined it with curiosity. "It's more intelligent than a typical songbird?" he asked.

"Yes, though songbirds have extensive and complex memories for the songs they sing. It makes them good for carrying memorized messages," I explained. I held up a finger and the bird hopped onto it. "Here, you take him."

With a look of bemused wonder, Marskal held out his index finger and the little bird hopped onto him, singing a series of trills. A delighted smile creased the man's face, with none of his usual reserve in it. He glanced up at me, the sheer pleasure lighting his eyes. "What is it—he—saying?"

"It's not really like that. It's more like I hear the thoughts in his head, than that the song means anything."

Marskal nodded in understanding. "Like with Kiraka."

"I hadn't thought of it that way." I studied the bird, thinking. "It's the same and not. Like the difference between listening to birdsong and having a giant condor sit on you and peck a hole into your brain."

Marskal laughed. "Has that happened to you?"

"No," I replied primly. "But I have a vivid imagination."

He caught me around the waist, the little bird squawking and leaping to his shoulder in an indignant flutter. "And you are vividly beautiful, just like your home," he said against my temple, kissing it. "I've realized why you always smell like flowers. It's Annfwn, in your skin and in your blood."

"Stop that, you two," Ursula commanded. "Have some dignity—the skiff is here."

"You're in Annfwn now," I replied cheerfully. "Dignity doesn't exist here."

She would have retorted, but Queen Andromeda and King Rayfe had arrived. He leapt from the boat, flashed into the shape of a raptor, then landed on the deck and shifted back to himself and leaned over the rail to give the queen a hand over from the rope ladder. I ignored the painful stab of envy at his casual shapeshifting. They were in formal regalia also, deep Tala black, and even wearing their crowns, too, albeit far less rigid and fancy than Ursula's.

"King Ray—" Ursula had inclined her head and began her formal request for entry to Annfwn, but Queen Andromeda launched herself at her sister, nearly knocking the taller and stronger woman over with the force of her embrace.

"Oh, skip that, Essla!" she cried, clinging to the high queen, dark hair rising around them and swirling with the force of her magic and strong emotions. "You nearly died! How could you do that to me?"

Ursula, clearly bemused and seeming uncertain where to put her hands, awkwardly hugged her sister back. Harlan watched her, amused, and not helping in the least, even when she looked to him appealingly. It made me feel a little better about my awkwardness with strong emotion to see Ursula also struggle with it. Perhaps we shared that trait.

"I'm fine, Andi," she said, finally relaxing into the embrace and rocking her sister. "I'm really fine. It's all right. I would never leave you."

Queen Andromeda at last released her fierce hold, though only far enough to grasp Ursula's forearms. "Promise."

"I already promised. And look, here I am." Ursula said it gravely, with all the certainty in her.

"Yes. Well." Queen Andromeda blew out a shaky breath, then glanced back at King Rayfe, who broke his stern expression to nod at her, mouth curving with affection. "I promised Rayfe I'd be dignified, but that flew out the window with the hatchlings."

He stepped forward and offered her his forearm, which she took. "Not dignified," he corrected. "The Tala don't care for such things. I—" he broke off, glancing at Marskal who seemed to be suffering a precipitous coughing fit.

I shook my head at the man. Always so reserved and then one little joke puts him over the edge. "King Rayfe. Queen Andromeda." I bowed deeply. "Greetings to you."

"Welcome home, Cousin." Queen Andromeda gave me a light embrace, kissing me on each cheek. She smelled of the flowers of Annfwn, as Marskal claimed I did, making me suddenly and fiercely homesick. Which made no sense as I was already home. "We're so proud of all you've done."

"Done?" I echoed, feeling as if she'd thumped me between the brows.

"Representing the Tala," King Rayfe added with a smile and a nod of recognition. "Your exploits have been much discussed and celebrated."

"Not only did you save the Star from the high priestess of *Deyrr*, you saved my sister's life." Queen Andromeda took my hands and squeezed them. "Nothing less than what I would have expected of Salena's blood. My mother would be so proud of you."

Unexpectedly choked by that, the words rose in my throat to explain what had happened to me, how I no longer carried on the proud tradition, but my moment's hesitation was enough that they moved on, discussing logistics with Ursula and Harlan, ordering priorities. It gave me long enough to catch my breath.

A tug on my hair and I glanced at Marskal, watching me quietly. "Steady?"

I nodded, realizing I was. Ursula and Harlan were climbing down the rope ladder to the skiff, she bitching about her long skirts. Queen Andromeda still had an echo of laughter in her smile when she looked to me. "Will you shift to meet us on the beach?"

And, just like that, I lost my equilibrium again. Moranu bless him, Marskal stepped in. "I've asked the Lady Zynda if she'd stay in human form and translate for me."

King Rayfe frowned. "You're going ashore? I thought it odd enough that you're on deck, but…"

"I vouch for him," I said, and they both relaxed.

"If I have to climb down that thriced ladder," Queen Andromeda said to her husband, "especially in this getup, you have to also." With a good natured grin, he helped her over the rail again and quickly followed.

"I take back any remarks I might have made that cast aspersions on your power," Marskal said, his tone so deliberately admiring that I threw him a look. He raised his brows at me. "What? The king and queen of the Tala immediately accepted your word without question."

I rolled my eyes at him, then went to the ladder. "Because I vouched for you."

"What does that mean, exactly? Shouldn't I know the rules?"

"Just stick with me and you'll be fine."

His hand drifted down my back and patted my bottom. "An assignment I can enjoy."

AFTER THE SHORT row to shore, all chance for conversation ended. As soon as we set foot on the sand of Annfwn, I was whirled into embraces, kisses, and impromptu dances. The king, queens, and Harlan strode off to the lighted council chambers, having settled on business first, but Marskal stayed with me. Apparently—likely after her sister's emotional greeting—Ursula had decided I wasn't needed to help parley. Hopefully it would stay that way.

It was good to be home.

And any time I looked up from another breathless conversation, or spun out of a hug, Marskal was there at my shoulder, a quietly bemused smile on his stern mouth. Next I looked, he held a mug of wine, flicking suspicious glances at it, then scanning the jubilant crowd, watching for danger. I sashayed over to him, borrowed the mug, took a long drink of Annfwn's flowery wine, and handed it back with a smile. He warded me off with upraised hands. "You keep it," he raised his voice over the music.

"Don't you like it? It's just wine. No one will poison you."

His mouth quirked in a half smile. "I'll keep on the alert just the same, thanks."

"Always on guard," I teased.

He tugged on a lock of my hair. "Yes."

I lifted the mug again, but it flew from my hand. And I went crashing to the sand, the huge black panther rolling me several lengths toward the water, teeth at my throat. I shrieked—mostly surprise, but also infuriated—which was a mistake because Marskal dived into the fray, sword drawn and swinging in a lethal arc for the cat.

"Marskal, no!" I yelled, which fortunately stopped the downward strike, especially since I then dissolved into laughter as the cat had me pinned, licking my face raw with its raspy tongue. "Gah! No, stop!" I pushed at him ineffectually. "I mean it, Zyr." I managed a much sterner tone, mostly because Marskal still stood over us with sword in one hand and short blade in the other, looking murderous.

The panther leapt off of me, kicking me with a spray of sand, and became my brother. His eyes, sparkling with triumph and merriment, shone blue even in the twilight, and his hair hung nearly to his knees. He put hands on hips and sneered at me. "The time among mossbacks has made you into a wimp! Once I could never have surprised you like that. Why didn't you shift?"

That pang of misery stabbed at my heart. I'd wanted to ask Zyr for his help, but hadn't gotten around to envisioning how that conversation would go. Marskal held out a hand to help me up, but I ignored it, struggling to my feet on my own. Zyr observed with a dark look that he pinned on Marskal.

"Why is this mossback here, blades drawn?"

"She vouched for me," Marskal replied evenly, sheathing his blades but not losing his ready edge. "And I drew my blades to protect her, as it's my honor and duty to do."

Zyr laughed, heartily, throwing back his head. "Zynda doesn't need anyone's protection, much less a mossback's."

I winced a little, hearing the derision in his tone, quite sure I'd once said it the same way. I finished shaking the sand out of my hair and slipped my arm through Marskal's. "Be nice. He's my lover."

Zyr laughed. "For a night, yes?"

"No." I hesitated over how to explain what even I didn't understand. "More than that."

Zyr's angled black brows lowered, as if he were the panther still, putting back its ears and sizing up his pretty as he looked Marskal up and down. "Really?" He drew out the word dubiously. "I'm not seeing it. He can't possibly be compatible."

I glared at him. "My apologies for my brother's rudeness. Marskal, this is Zyr. Zyr, Lieutenant Marskal, leader of the Hawks, the high queen's personal guard. Don't mess with him."

"Clearly your time among the mossbacks has degraded your sense. What in Moranu are you thinking?"

"I'm thinking that my sex life is my business and that I thought you had better manners than this."

"This is stupid, even for you."

"Don't speak to her like that," Marskal said, voice tight.

Zyr threw him a viciously irritated glance. "Stay out of this, mossback. If you need a female on your arm that badly, I can round up a few more shapeshifter girls for you—maybe you'd like to try a few more of us, broaden your sampling of the exotic."

"Zyr!" My brother could be an ass, but this was excessive, even for him.

"What!" he yelled back in the same tone, slipping into Tala. "This isn't like you. Why are you letting him act like he owns you? Don't you know who this guy is? He was at Ordnung. He killed, imprisoned, and tortured us. Whose side are you on, anyway?"

Marskal gave me an inquiring look, sensing the aggression easily. I translated and Marskal studied Zyr, then said in Common Tongue, "I thought you looked familiar. You were captured at the Assault of Ordnung, weren't you?"

"Caught, but not held," Zyr snapped back, showing his teeth, which retained a hint of the panther's fangs.

"Fought, but honorably," Marskal replied evenly. "It was my duty to defend Ordnung. And I never tortured anyone."

"Bah!" Zyr flipped a hand at him. "You all look alike."

"Zyr," I intervened. "That stuff is history. We won our queen. King Rayfe brought Queen Andromeda home and—*and*," I said more loudly when he made a scoffing sound, "our king and queen signed a treaty. Marskal is not the enemy. None of them are and we have a *real* enemy to fight together."

He growled, low in his throat. "He's not good enough for you. Look at him. I could take him apart in a moment."

Marskal pulled away from me, relaxed in that perfectly alert and ready way of his that meant his attention had gone into precision fighting mode. "Care to test that theory?" he invited.

"Happily," Zyr replied, grinning in a way I knew well. He wasn't playing.

"No," I said. They both ignored me.

"Are you confident enough to set your blades aside?" Zyr asked in a lethally soft voice.

Marskal smiled at him, not at all friendly. "Sure. If you don't use fangs or claws."

They circled each other, assessing.

"Don't do this," I commanded.

"Stay out of this, Zynda," Zyr snarled, "and don't use your

magic to help, or I'll know your mossback truly is too weak for you."

Marskal caught my eye, an opaque glance, but a speaking one. He wouldn't take kindly to my interference.

"Your blades. My fangs and claws," Zyr declared.

"Done," Marskal replied, drawing his sword and long dagger.

~ 21 ~

ZYR FLASHED INTO grizzly bear form, roaring mightily and lunging with lightning speed. A massive paw bigger than Marskal's head swept through the night, razor claws gleaming. Terror burst through me, chilling my blood. But Marskal dodged, coming up and under, sword slicing the underside of Zyr's foreleg.

He roared, moving fast, catching Marskal on the hip with his claws. Marskal winced, but leapt back out of the hug that might have crushed him. I stood back, the need to shift, to fight, pounding in my temples. If Zyr killed Marskal, I'd—

But Marskal turned the tables, spinning behind the bear to hamstring him. Zyr fell in a howl of pain and rage. Marskal followed in with a wicked sweep of his sword, the short blade poised for a killing strike. If he killed Zyr, then—

Zyr flashed into the cat, springing up with elastic grace. Marskal didn't hesitate, adjusting his defense instantly. I'd seen him fight the fish-birds, but he'd been on the defensive, protecting me. Now he went on the attack, as vicious and hard-edged as any fighter I'd seen. Nothing like Ursula's enhanced speed, but as fast as Jepp, and stronger. He used the length of the sword to advantage, wielding it one-handed to keep Zyr well back.

Frustrated, Zyr sent up a ululating wail that sent a scree of warning down my spine. He swiped at Marskal in fury, catching his paw on the keen edge for his trouble. For his part, Marskal looked calm and cool, despite the blood I could scent on the air. He fought with meticulous intelligence, outmaneuvering the cat.

Zyr leapt and Marskal raised his short blade to impale—and Zyr became an eagle mid-leap, dodging the blade and raking Marskal's cheek with his talons. Marskal lost no time, wheeling and bringing the sword in an arc that cleaved the eagle's wing.

Zyr crashed to the sand with an avian scream. I realized I had my hands at my throat, as if keeping myself from screaming also. Marskal advanced, on guard, but with concern in the lines of his body. I relaxed, as I should have from the beginning. As I should have trusted. Marskal would no more kill my brother than he'd hurt me. Family was everything to him.

"Enough?" He asked the eagle, speaking to him as a man, remembering as he always did with me that he spoke to a person, not an animal.

Zyr flicked into human form, now wearing only short pants, and clutching his arm though it had healed when he shifted. Marskal would have remembered that, too, going for debilitating wounds to maim his shapeshifter opponent, knowing he could heal from it. Zyr glared at him. Then burst out laughing.

"Moranu, that hurt!" He added a few more curses, then flexed his arm, checking that it moved cleanly. Marskal straightened from his crouch, sheathing his blades. Then extended a hand to help Zyr up.

"Truce?"

Zyr shook back his hair, flicking me a look. Then shrugged. Taking Marskal's hand, he yanked with shifter speed and tumbled him to the sand. "Truce," he agreed. "Well fought. Zynda—bring the wine, would you?"

I took a deep swallow to settle my nerves. Apparently mossback and shapeshifter men shared certain bewildering behaviors. Snagging a skin and two more mugs, I brought them and settled into the sand with them, making a point to the triangle.

"Are you bleeding badly?" I asked Marskal, filling a cup and handing it to him first.

He grimaced. "Not too much, but if you have a Tala healer handy, I wouldn't say no."

Zyr surveyed him. "We can round someone up for you. I don't know why you people aren't easier to kill, with the way you can't heal yourselves."

Marskal returned the look steadily, much the same as he studied me, I realized. "Maybe we work harder to learn to fight well, because we know we can't heal midfight. We do heal ourselves. It just takes longer."

Zyr laughed. "All right, I'll grant that." He narrowed his eyes. "But are you implying I don't fight well?"

I tensed, ready for them to go at it again, but Marskal grinned easily. "You fight very well—but you fight like an animal. If you fought like a man in animal form, I wouldn't have been able to beat you."

Zyr growled a little and I summoned my magic. I'd had enough of standing by and watching them beat on each other. But then he laughed, drinking deeply of his wine. "Maybe you can give us pointers, mossback."

"I'd be happy to," Marskal replied. "We're allies after all. Your strength is my strength."

"Allies in what—sharing trade goods? Our food goes over the pass and you send back *things*," Zyr sneered the word, but without menace.

Marskal glanced at me. "Things might get bad, Zyr. There is a foreign enemy, called *gelyneinioes* in the old tongue, called *Deyrr* by the mossbacks. They're using reanimated animals to penetrate the barrier. Maybe people forced into shapeshifting."

Zyr stared back at me, appalled, but also with a glimmer of recognition.

"Have you been seeing anyone like that?" I asked.

He nodded, draining his mug. "The king and queen will hear about this?"

"Yes, Ursula is telling them now."

"They might put it together without me, but I'll remind them of a few incidents," Zyr replied, a faint frown for the news.

"We appreciate all intelligence on this," Marskal put in. "You know far more about this that we do, obviously, so we'll rely on you for help."

Zyr studied him, then glanced at me. "Well, he's interesting. And he's a decent fighter. Still, Zynda, a mossback? Is he that good?"

"I'm sitting right here," Marskal said, and Zyr flashed him a rakish smile.

"As if you didn't try for one yourself," I replied to Zyr with relish. I'd been saving up this tidbit, and he deserved it, after taunting me about Marskal. "Though Dafne turned you down, didn't she? Poor, rejected Zyr. I bet that stung."

Astonishment gave way to chagrin, then humor. "She told you, huh? Yes, that tasty little librarian turned me down. Once. But I haven't given up. Is she with you?" He craned his neck, scanning the laughing, dancing throng on the beach.

"She married the King of Nahanau," I informed him. "She's a queen now and out of your league—but then she always was or she wouldn't have turned you down."

"You are never going to let me live this down, are you?"

"Nope." I grinned at him. "How the mighty have fallen. Struck down by a mossback girl, too."

Even Marskal laughed at that, then looked between us. "You

look remarkably alike."

"Womb companions," Zyr replied.

"Twins?" Marskal clarified.

"That's your word for it," I replied. "We don't have the concept so much, since womb companions might have different fathers. But Zyr and I look enough alike that we likely do have the same father."

"Moranu shield him in her shadows, whoever he may be," Zyr added cheerfully, refilling Marskal's mug and springing to his feet. "Here, have a drink. There's food over there. I'll get a healer to come over. Come on, Zynda. Enough of terrible futures. Let's play for a bit."

I resisted Zyr's tugging hands. "No, I'll stay here a while longer."

Zyr only grinned at me. "Don't be silly. This party is dead boring. Let's go *play*."

He didn't have to emphasize it like that—I knew what he meant. "That's all right, I—"

"What in Moranu is wrong with you?" Zyr demanded, all humor fled again.

Marskal, following along just fine, apparently, though we'd lapsed into the Tala tongue, put a steadying hand on my knee. "I think Zynda would prefer to stay at the party a while longer. There are many people here excited to see her."

I threw him a grateful look—marked contrast to Zyr's scowl. He paced a tight circle, and I could imagine his tail lashing. Then he stopped and leveled a long stare at me. "What's going on with you? This is more than your lust for the mossback."

My heart sank into my gut. I'd have to tell him. "I can't..." I started. And stopped. This wasn't how I'd imagined talking about it.

"Because of *him*?"

"No!"

"Then *why?*" Zyr threw up his hands. "Why won't you just—"

"Because!" I screamed it at him, venting all the frustration of standing helplessly by while they fought, and clenching my fists. "Because I can't shapeshift! I'm done. I'm broken, and I'll never get it back."

ONE ADVANTAGE OF having a grand weeping fit, as I had the night before—I seemed to have spent all my tears. I'd worried I might break down telling Zyr the awful truth, but I didn't. Other than a little shouting—and Zyr and I had always lost our tempers with each other—I didn't do too badly.

He, however, was completely stunned. He shook his head. Stared at me. "What?"

"I know you heard me just fine."

Zyr looked to Marskal and back to me, then sat heavily again. "Explain."

So, I did, as concisely as I could. For all his mischievous charm and temperamental nature, Zyr listened very well when he decided to. Finally he raked his hair out of his face, and looked to Marskal. "You. You carried her down the volcano as a hummingbird and hand-fed her sugar water."

Marskal nodded, eyes going to me. "I did what needed to be done."

"Well, I'm an ass," Zyr sighed.

"Do you hear me arguing?" I said, trying for sass, but he only shook his head at me, seeming weary. At least he wasn't pitying me.

"Zynda." He took a breath. "You shouldn't have been able to do that."

"I know."

"I mean, *no one* has been able to do that, ever," he insisted.

"Zyr. I *know*," I ground out.

He stared at me, as if he didn't know me. "I mean, it's not poss—"

"Zyr!"

He held up his hands and grinned. "Yeah, yeah—couldn't resist. Turns out my sister is some kind of heroically gifted shapeshifter sorceress. All the girls will want to try for my babies now."

"As if they don't already," I retorted, but he only smiled happily, waggling his eyebrows.

"True, Moranu bless them." He sobered. "What are you going to do?"

"I don't know," I answered, honestly, the misery returning.

Zyr hugged me. "Don't worry, gruntling. I'll always be your brother."

That made me a little weepy after all, and I nodded, sniffling.

"I realize I'm the mossback here," Marskal said, "but she's alive and healthy—isn't that cause for celebration?"

Zyr blinked at him. "Well…" He looked back at me. "I mean, yes, better she's alive than dead, but…" He closed his mouth, looking pained.

I shook my head. "I've tried to explain. He doesn't understand."

Zyr shrugged, elaborately, and I saw myself in him. "How can they?"

From the corner of my eye, I saw Marskal set his jaw against a comment. Good man. "You were going to ask him for help," he prodded me, in a tight voice.

Zyr's eyes opened wider. Moranu take it, after Zyr's reaction I'd decided not to ask. If he'd thought he could help, he would have said that right away. Instead he'd commiserated. He knew as well as I that I'd lost the ability forever.

I took Marskal's mug, which he still held, untouched, and took a long drink. "Never mind, Zyr. It's all right. I'd just kind of thought that..." I couldn't finish past the regret lodged in my throat.

"I *am* the best teacher," he asserted, brow furrowing. He drank from his own mug thoughtfully. "I don't know. It depends on why it's gone."

I rolled my eyes at him and laughed. "Oh, thank you for that brilliant insight."

He pinched me. Or tried to—I was too fast and wise to his ways, ducking him easily.

"You're still fast," he observed.

"And strong as ever," Marskal added. "I think it's still in her."

Zyr gave him a long look. "Do you, now? You have a good eye. Hmm." He stared at me so ferociously I began to get restless.

"Let's forget about—"

"Meet me in the morning," Zyr interrupted me, rising to his feet. We did likewise, Marskal putting an arm around my waist. "I'll cancel the children's classes and we'll try."

"Zyr, I don't—"

"We'll try," he repeated. Then grinned and tossed back his hair. "Even the mossback thinks you can. Don't be such a gruntling."

"I am not a gruntling."

"Uh huh. Look like a gruntling to me." He turned to survey the party. "If we can't play, I'm going to find me a mossback girl and find out what's so wonderful about them. I think I spotted one with a long braid the color of sunshine."

Only Zyr could have noticed that while harassing me. Ursula must have gotten her way with letting the others off the ship, which—why had I ever doubted it? "Karyn. She's Dasnarian. And a virgin saving it for marriage, as is the way of her people. You won't be able to seduce her."

Zyr grinned at me. "Challenge accepted!" And he went off, whistling along with the musicians.

"Are you all right?" Marskal asked me, turning me to face him and holding me by my shoulders.

I mustered a smile. "That actually went better than I feared."

His lip curled and he shook that away. "I hate to imagine what you feared then."

"I know it's hard for you to understand, but this is about who we *are*."

"And pride," he added.

"I won't argue."

"A miracle." He grinned, then kissed me before I could retort. A kiss that quickly went deeper and hotter than I expected.

"It could be it goes back to this thing," I said when I could speak again, "that you were all talking about on the ship. Maybe it's conditioned. The only useful Tala is a shapeshifter."

"But you have those who can't."

"Yes. And they are... lesser." It bothered me that I'd always seen it that way. "Anyway. If anyone can help me, Zyr can. And we'll try in the morning. Can we not talk about it anymore tonight?"

"Of course. Besides, you have a welcome home party to attend."

I surveyed the crowd with some dismay. "I'm not sure I'm

up for more conversations. And you need a healer."

"It's a shallow set of scratches. He barely nicked me and it's stopped bleeding for now. I wouldn't worry about it except that I'd prefer to be in top form."

"Always the protector."

He nodded, crisp and serious, then gave me the Hawks' salute, fist over heart and bowed deeply. "My job, Lady Zynda."

I laughed and he grinned at me. "How about dancing then?" He asked.

"Dancing?"

"I believe I owe you." He lifted my hand and kissed the back of it, a courtly gesture. "If my lady would favor me with a dance."

I had to laugh. "You know it won't be like at Ordnung's court."

He cocked his head at the Tala dancing in wild swirls of silk and flying hair, weaving among the torches and bonfires. "I'd noticed. But good thing. I didn't exaggerate when I said I don't dance. I'm really not good at it—and in the court at Ordnung I'd never presume to dance with a highly ranked lady such as yourself."

Winding my arms behind his neck, I snugged up against him, moving sinuously. "You're an excellent lover; dancing should be just the same."

"Think so?" he murmured, then kissed me.

"Yes. Let's stay here. Keep it smooth and easy."

"I can do that."

I let myself sink into it, moving with the music and taking him with me. He followed along, hands moving over me, becoming part of the dance as he caressed my curves, stroking over the silk and making his own patterns with each part of me I offered. I held on to him—as I'd gotten in the habit of doing, though I couldn't make myself worry about it in that moment—leaning against his strong chest, drifting on the sweet waves of music, Marskal's loving hands, and the scents of the redolent night-blooming flowers of Annfwn.

For the time being, I forgot about my vows and what the future held, and just savored the moment. In my heart, I soared.

IN THE MORNING, I rose and pulled on the dress I'd already treated badly by almost drowning in it. I could hardly do more damage to it. And I left my hair pin on the window ledge. I'd be going back to the childhood basics of shifting, which meant that—if I did manage to shift—then Moranu only knew what I'd be wearing, if anything, when I returned to human form.

Looking out the open windows of the balcony room, I watched the sea take on its distinctive turquoise color as the sun rose over the cliffs above. Even this borrowed room in the royal house felt closer to sleeping outside as any I'd ever been in. Using the comb Marskal had made sure was placed in my trunk brought over from the ship—the man was forever prepared, taking care of mundane details—I worked the few snarls out of my hair.

Maybe I was getting better at the chore. Which was a good thing, if I ended up trapped in human form, but the thought still depressed me. Not a good thing, as I needed to concentrate on an optimistic perspective for working with Zyr.

I turned to find Marskal watching me from the bed. With hands folded behind his head, his arm muscles showed off his masculine beauty, along with his furred armpits and chest, his tanned skin dark against the white sheets. His cuts—a bit more than scratches—had been easily repaired by the healer and he was back to fine health. Tempting to crawl back in and indulge ourselves some more.

But even I could recognize that opting for pleasure over the pain ahead would be taking the easy path.

"I might be a while," I said.

He dipped his chin, unsurprised. "Take your time. Whatever you need to do."

I laughed a little, both of us acting like this wasn't a deciding moment for me.

"You can do whatever you like. Explore. If you want anything—food, drink, something that catches your eye—just tell them my name and it will go on my account."

With a strange smile, he huffed a laugh. "Now I'm the kept man, lying abed while my lady goes off to manage her business, but promised whatever treats I wish to occupy me until she returns."

"I didn't mean it that way." The trial ahead must have been making me emotional—although I seemed to be a ball of emotion these days—because I felt oddly stricken by that. I wasn't any good at this thing with Marskal, whatever it was.

He held out a hand to me. "No, that was my fault. A bad joke. Come here."

I sat on the edge of the bed, taking his hand and holding on, probably too tightly. I didn't care.

"I'll need to check in with Her Majesty," he said, all matter of fact, his standard planning approach. "My bets are that she and Harlan will head to Ordnung today. I'll find out if there are updates on her plans and strategy. I'll also report on our progress, which means I'll have to tell her what you're up to."

"You'll tell her that I'm working with Zyr on regaining my

abilities."

He nodded, perfectly neutral, just another part of the plan. "Yes. And I'll let her know that we'll send messages on our next steps. If you're wanting to go to Windroven, we'll need her permission and to smooth the way with Queen Amelia."

I let out a breath, not letting it be shaky. "All right."

He squeezed my hand and let it go. Then tangled his fingers in the ends of my hair. "I can come with you, if you like. I just assumed that this needed privacy. Tala secrets and all," he teased gently.

"And concentration," I agreed. Then I kissed him, wishing I could linger over it. "But thank you for offering. Will you do something for me?"

"Of course." He said it gravely, and it felt like he was telling me he loved me.

I pulled the Star on its chain over my head and gave it to him. "I need you to keep this for me."

He enclosed it in his fist, but watched me with sober brown eyes. "I will, but shouldn't you have it with you? You're its guardian now."

I shook my head, my hair sliding over my bare arms. "I'd have to set it aside while I attempt to shift, as I can't be sure of taking it correctly with me and bringing it back again. Better for you to keep it."

His fist tightened, along with his jaw, though he didn't otherwise move. "Is this that dangerous?" he asked softly.

I shrugged—then stopped myself. He deserved an honest reply. At least what was most true in this moment. "Yes. It's possible I'll manage a partial attempt and muff it up."

"And die, is what you're saying."

I held his gaze. "That could happen. If it does, I don't want you to think badly of me, that I didn't tell you the truth."

He sat up, slowly, and set the Star on the bed next to him, then enfolded me in his arms. I leaned into him, and we sat like that for a long few moments. Finally he kissed my temple. "Thank you for your honesty," he said in a rough voice. "But I'm finding it very..." He dragged in a breath. "I don't want to say goodbye, and I'm feeling like I should. Just in case."

"No—don't." I pulled back and framed his face in my hands. He had on that remote expression, the one that covered strong feelings. "With this kind of thing, intention matters. Thinking of the best outcome will help. I wouldn't have even given voice to the worst outcome, if not for..." I ended with a shrug, unable to do otherwise.

"If not for the sensitivities of your mossback lover," he finished for me with a wry grin. Then he sobered, searching my face with grave eyes. "Is it worth it, Zynda?"

A rush of emotion whirled through me, so much threaded into it, sucking me under and spinning me out that I almost couldn't answer yes or no. Maybe he read it in me because he took my wrists in his hands, holding them tight.

"Is it worth risking your life to get this ability back?" he pressed.

I shook my head. "I honestly don't know. But there are more important considerations at hand than my own life—and those things require me to do my utmost."

He nodded once, hooding his gaze as he released. Then he picked up the Star and looped the chain over his head, the topaz glowing tiger-gold over his heart. "I'll keep this for you then."

"Thank you. Ah, if necessary, give it back to Queen Andromeda. I trust you to do that," I added.

He smiled, but with a haunted look in his eyes. "I'll give it back to you when I see you later today."

"That sounds good." I smiled and stood, shaking out my

hair, resisting the urge to wind it up with my pin. If—when—I returned, I'd want it. "I will see you later."

"Zynda."

I looked back to see him still sitting in the bed, the sheet barely draped around his hips.

"Remember your promise to me," he said, with grave insistence.

Confused, I frowned at him. "Even if I were with child, I wouldn't know by now. Most likely."

He shook his head a little, with that huffed laugh. "Not that one—though I'm glad you remember it. The other one."

I promise to do everything in my power to stay alive. I had sort of forgotten that one, as irrational as it was. Oddly like the promise Queen Andromeda had extracted from Ursula, however. I suppose these are the sorts of promises people who love each other make. I wasn't at all certain how I'd wound up making so many promises to Marskal.

"Oh, right. Yes." I nodded. Because he seemed to expect something more, I added, "Everything in my power."

He enfolded the Star in his fist, holding it there, close to the Hawks' salute, but different. Somehow intimate and just for me. "I'll wait for you."

~ 22 ~

ANNFWN BUSTLED WITH activity. Many Tala have First Forms that are crepuscular, so they wake up hours before dawn, busying themselves with their projects before taking a long midday nap. There are, naturally, nocturnal types, but they tend not to live in the cliff city. Those sorts prefer to live more in the wild, forming communities in the forests or more remote cliffs and meadowlands, according to their nature.

The royal residence sits near the top of the cliff. After the discussion of the day before, speculating on the strategy against attack from the sea, it occurred to me for the first time that this could be the safest location for the king and queen. More practically, it meant I could use the household back paths up to the training arena on the flat top of the cliff.

I had been there only rarely since my own childhood lessons, having had little reason to go there. I'd been a proficient shapeshifter from my earliest days and hadn't had to take lessons for very long, as I'd quickly surpassed the skill of my teachers. But my feet knew the way and the chalky dirt felt familiar on my bare soles. Sense memories awakened in me, along with the sight and scent of the periwinkle blossoms that bordered this trail at the top in the hot sun, and the sound of the waves lapping the sand far below, and I suddenly and viscerally remembered being that girl again. So alive and full of magic. Zyr and I running up the cliff trails, changing form along the way, always challenging each other.

It had all seemed so easy and simple then. No dread or fears of the future. No complications. No pain. Only the joy of shapeshifting and being alive.

Maybe that's what Marskal meant by needing a better reason. Or Moranu by saying that it wouldn't be all pain, that there was loving. I'd loved shapeshifting once, before I'd had to use it to save my life. Connecting with that feeling again could be the path I sought.

Optimism coursing through me that this could work, I rounded the last curve, the walled arena in sight ahead.

Where the Shaman of Moranu blocked my path.

Shaman is wildly unkempt, even by lax Tala standards. Working with magic has bleached his hair white and darkened his Tala blue eyes to almost black. For the most part, the deeper blue or gray a shapeshifter's eyes, the purer his blood. But there's something about the immersion in the rites of Moranu that deepens the color, too. The waning to the new moon. Shaman espouses a purity of intention in shapeshifting, which means he doesn't bother with vanities like unsnarling hair or manifesting with clean garments when returning to human form.

Shaman also has forsaken his name as belonging to the frivolous world, so though I'd known him all my life, I knew him only by his title. Shaman wore furs, a combination of many sewn together. His dark hair fell in knotted ropes around his shoulders, braided with carved stones significant to Moranu, along with teeth, claws, scales, and feathers. All of it, including the furs, I knew came from his various animal forms—during rites in which he cut off parts of his animal selves before returning to human form. Sacrifices to Moranu always curdled some deep part of me in horror. In his costume, though, I now recognized an imitation of Moranu as she'd appeared to me, in her endless shifting.

The full moon silver disc of his office rested at his collar-bone, and the Sword of Moranu rode at his side. He'd come when I asked, to crown Ursula as high queen in the name of Moranu, and had also performed the mate binding on King Rayfe and Queen Andromeda, consecrating them to their roles as leaders of the Tala and to each other.

"Zynda." His voice carried the resonance of wind-tossed forests and a storm at sea, giving me shivers. "I'd expected you to come see me. Though not as this," he added, disappointment in his eyes. "I expected perhaps too much."

"I'd been planning to come see you," I said, "but I hoped to solve a small problem first."

"I am not interested in your problems." Shaman said, lined face stern. "Only in your solutions to the grave fate awaiting the Tala. Did you meet with the dragon or not?"

"I did, Shaman."

He studied me, seeing into me, face dark. That dread, ever present since the incident, as Marskal put it, coiled up like a cobra spreading its hood.

"The dragon is called Kiraka," I told him. "I don't know if she's one mentioned in your histories." He didn't offer any response. Not that I'd expected or hoped for it—he never revealed what sources he drew his information from. "She was able to speak in my mind with clear words, and could hear what I thought to her."

He didn't say anything, but the sense of heightened alertness intensified. If he'd been in mammalian form, his ears would have pricked. I picked my way through my own words, knowing I couldn't avoid the pit at the end, but the cowardly part of me wished to.

"I put our plight to her. She was critical of our ancestors' choices to expand the Heart to allow us to live inside the barrier."

He stirred, then stilled himself. I continued under his remorseless regard. "In the end, she agreed to teach me to take the Final Form. However, she—"

"Then why are you not returned as a dragon?" he demanded, mouth contorted in outrage. "While you fritter your time away, dallying with a completely inappropriate mossback lover, our babies are dying. With every moment you waste, we lose countless lives."

"I..." It all felt too huge to explain. And what had made sense only last night no longer did.

"You were not so selfish when you left Annfwn. Your time among the mossbacks has changed you. And you of Salena's purest blood. She would be ashamed of you."

I felt it keenly in my bones, how Salena would be ashamed of me, of my many failures. A shapeshifter who couldn't shift. Queen Andromeda had said Salena would be proud, but this felt so much easier to believe. Shaman's lip curled in scorn as he surveyed me. And all of this without telling them I might not even be able to shift into Final Form, even if I satisfied Kiraka's other condition.

Setting my jaw—a gesture I must have learned from association with Marskal, as I didn't recall ever doing it before—I forged on. "Kiraka first tested me. Now she requires a gift, so I set out to deliver that to her."

"And that is..." Shaman asked, though more of a demand than a question.

"She asked me to free her dragon kin from the volcano under Windroven." I wanted to laugh at how simple I made it sound, Shaman would not appreciate the irreverence.

Shaman scowled at me. "Windroven is not Annfwn. It is none of our concern."

I snapped my mouth shut on the retort that *he* could go tell Kiraka as much in person and find out her opinion on the matter. "Regardless, we are the beggars and that is what she requested."

"What was the test?" Shaman asked, eyeing me keenly. Could he see it in me, how I'd been broken and barely pulled myself back together?

"Personal," I replied. The most personal challenge I'd ever had to meet. I had no desire to open it to his scrutiny.

He didn't like that. Shaman chewed on his lips. "You will go back to Kiraka," he decided. "Tell her we will send other acolytes to free the dragon, if she will send you back in Final Form."

Oh, that would go over brilliantly. I barely contained my snarl. "I will not," I replied, as evenly as Marskal might, though I surprised myself with my disobedience.

Shaman pulled his power around him, the air thickening to the oppressive levels of a thunderhead about to strike lethal lightning. With a shiver of astonished relief, I discovered he didn't frighten me. I'd been immolated by a dragon and survived. A mere shaman of my own people could barely scratch that agony. I stared him down, feeling my own magic settle around me like a cloak. Just as Salena had always looked to me. For the first time, I thought of my powerful aunt as a woman like myself. Perhaps she'd pulled magic around her like this because she'd felt this way, too. Perhaps she, too, had needed the comfort of a strong defense.

"The will of Moranu is that you obey me," Shaman intoned.

"I don't think so," I answered him, giving him an easy smile. "At least, She didn't mention you during Her visitation with me."

I stunned him with that. Shaman grunted, closing his hand over his silver disk of office, lowering his lids. After only a moment, his eyes snapped open. They were midnight black and full of stars.

"So be it," he said, and in his voice, I heard a resonance of Moranu's. "Do what you must. We await your return in Final Form."

With that, he turned and walked away. Then he paused, and looked back. His black eyes glistened with emotion, and in that moment, he was only a man. One who carried a weight of grief. "So be it," he repeated. "But... so much rides on this and you are the only one. Come back as soon as possible."

"NO. COMPLETELY WRONG." Zyr's criticism flayed my already flagging confidence.

I pushed the hair off my sweating face, inexpressibly weary. Every cell of my body seemed to throb, as if I'd been trying to tear myself apart from the inside out.

Zyr wiped his face also, the midday sun beating down on us. He was covered in dust, also grimy, also exhausted. We'd been working for hours and I hadn't budged from human form. As set in place as any mossback ever was.

"You're going about it backwards," Zyr said—unnecessarily as that much was painfully obvious—bristling with frustrated impatience. For the first few hours he'd maintained his sunny teacher's calm. He'd coaxed the most intransigent children into finding at least First Form. That I'd pushed him past his patience spoke volumes. Putting fists on slim hips, he glared at me. "You're overthinking! And you know better. You of all people know that this is instinct, underneath thought. Stop trying so thrice-cursed hard."

"And how in Moranu am I supposed to do that?" I'd meant to snap back at him, but I only sounded tired and pitiful. I sat back on my heels, tired of kneeling in the dust, like some mossback child pretending to be a pony. We'd switched to trying for that form when my least attempt at First Form sent me into near paralysis with terror.

"How did you always do it?" he demanded. "You were the one who never needed lessons. You're a better shapeshifter than I am. I don't understand this."

"I don't understand it either and I don't know how I did it before. I just... did."

You've lost your nerve. Jepp's flatly pragmatic diagnosis whizzed around my mind in dizzying circles, like the hummingbird I might never be again. Just that thought brought out a fresh outbreak of cold sweat, dripping down my ribs to soak into my already saturated dress.

With a sigh, Zyr dropped to the dust beside me. He put his head in his hands, then looked at me, blue eyes dark with compassion and weariness. "I think that's part of the problem. You had so much innate talent that you never had to learn or practice. Shapeshifting was always so easy for you. Now you're trying too hard and entirely the wrong way."

I set my teeth. "Then what *is* the right way?"

"I've been trying to show you but it's like you can't hear me," he snapped back.

"I'm trying to hear you!"

We glared fiercely at one another, then he put a hand behind my head and leaned his forehead against mine, as we hadn't done since we were little kids.

"I can't help you," he finally said. "I thought maybe I could, but whatever is blocking you is something I can't undo. I'm not sure anyone can. For what it's worth, I think your mossback lover is right—it's still in you. You're not like the kids with barely enough of the right blood. I can sense it in you. You're practically bursting with magic wanting to move you into different forms, but you're..." He shrugged.

My skin crawled with the need to shift, my blood burned with it, so I believed him. But lots of those who could never shift felt the same. It drove them mad, too. "Don't call him that," I said, rather than half a dozen other replies. "His name is Marskal."

"Attached, are we? How mossback of you."

"Oh, shove it. I'm not in any mood to have you chew on me."

"Just pointing out the obvious, sister dear. You can't have anything long term with him, unless he's willing to love you from afar while you confine yourself to shapeshifter men of adequate bloodlines long enough to get with child. I suppose you could fuck him while you're pregnant. That could be fun."

I glared at him, then saw through his harping. "Ah, did Karyn turn you down? *Two* rejections from mossback women. No wonder you're bitter."

He glared back at me, sulking. "Virgins. Meh. These mossbacks have too many rules. Anyway, you're trying to change the subject. Which is you, who can't change. Funny, huh?"

"I have to," I snarled at him, completely unamused by his games. "I have to take Final Form."

He gazed at me, serious now. Surprised. Maybe a little horrified. "You've been working with Shaman? I thought you gave up that idea."

"I'm the only one. Unless *you* want to do it."

"No, thank you. Even if I were good enough, I wouldn't. 'Only one.' That means nothing. There's no predestination. No one swooped down at your birth and declared that you would be the one to save the Tala. I should know—I was there, too." Zyr grinned at me, but it lacked its usual sparkle.

I smiled back, also weakly. "If not me, then who?"

He shrugged, elaborately. "Maybe Stella, when she grows up. Or one of King Rayfe and Queen Andromeda's kids."

"I don't think we have the luxury of that much time. Queen Andromeda can't take the Final Form—we need her more as queen."

Zyr stood, waiting for me to do the same. No offer to help me up like Marskal would. How quickly I'd become spoiled. "We've waited centuries—what's another few decades?"

"Maybe the end of us."

"Yes, well." Zyr stared out at the sea. "Maybe it's meant to be. If you believe in fate and the working of the goddess's hand, then you also have to believe that Annfwn and the Tala—like all things—are meant to come to an end. Everything dies, yes? We die, our bodies dissolve, and new beings grow from the fertile earth. We learn that first as children. Like the moon, we wax and wane."

I nearly said those last words along with him. My frivolous flirt of a brother had it right—and the truth had been coiled in everything I'd gone through—the fate of the Tala and Annfwn mattered far less than the rest of the world as a whole. I had to try, but maybe my time among the mossbacks had changed me. My world had grown bigger.

"Thank you," I said, hugging Zyr with fierce gratitude.

"But I didn't help," he said, surprised, but holding on.

"Yes, you did."

"Where are you going?"

"To see the queen."

"Better clean up," he called after me, "you look like a sweat-soaked, dusty gruntling."

I made a rude hand gesture, smiling to myself when he laughed.

MARSKAL WASN'T IN our room when I went to clean up. He wasn't the type to hang about with nothing to do, vows to wait for me to return or not. The sun had slipped to mid-afternoon, and it belatedly occurred to me that it would have been a long day for him of worrying about me. A strange responsibility for me to have. I'd never asked him to care about whether I lived or died, but it seemed that doing what I could to make that easier for him was the price I paid for all the caring he gave me that bolstered me through this.

So I washed quickly, including my hair which took far too long. If it wouldn't disappoint Marskal so, I'd have cut the lot off by now. But I used the hair oil and comb he'd left out for me, and it wasn't as grueling as in the past. The oil worked really well, smelling of a flower I didn't recognize.

Meanwhile, I called on a staymach to search for him, coaxing it into bird form and sending it to look. That sort of magic took so little effort, like the shapeshifting used to. Before I met the dragon. *Whatever is blocking you is something I can't undo.* Had Kiraka done something to me? Or the goddess, Herself? No—because I'd shifted after meeting them, first to the hummingbird, then back to human. Though I didn't exactly recall doing either, just that red haze of agony that made me wince away from remembering.

Glumly, I considered Jepp's harshly concise assessment. I'd lost my nerve. The only one blocking me was me, and I had no idea how to undo it.

Fear is a powerful force. More than I ever knew. But then, I'd never had much to be afraid of before.

Marskal turned out to be on the beach, drilling and sparring with the other Hawks, Karyn, and some Tala shapeshifters. The latter surprised me, but they seemed to be enjoying the game of using weapons, so I supposed Marskal—and perhaps Zyr—had cleverly convinced them to treat it like play instead of work. I watched them in glimpses as I wended my way down the walking paths, pausing here and there at a balcony to observe.

They were shifting into animal forms—darting, leaping and flying about in dizzying patterns—then returning to human with a weapon in hand, attempting to surprise a Hawk, strike them, and shift back in time to duck retaliation. They'd been at it for some time by the look of it, both shifters and mossbacks seeming to find the game quite hilarious. Karyn looked to be using arrows with some sort of blob on the end that made them bounce off harmlessly, but left a telltale dye mark behind.

Not wanting to distract them, I made sure to descend to the beach from the angle that Marskal faced, walking so he would spot me from a ways off. I knew the moment he did, by the way he straightened, then relaxed again, though he didn't pause in his running commands to the fighters.

He studied me as I approached, nothing obvious, but the heat of his assessment warmed me. Once I was within earshot, he called a halt, giving everyone a break. With happy shouts, humans shed clothing and dashed into the sea, chasing after the shifters who'd beaten them there, needing no such considerations. Unlike the Hawks, male and female alike, who stripped bare with no concern for modesty, Karyn kept on several layers of underdress.

Old habits die hard, I suppose.

Marskal opened his arms to me and I slid into them, enjoying the simple groundedness of human contact and his unconditional welcome. I sighed, realizing that I felt right again for the first time that morning. All those jumbled feelings, the demands and failures—none of it mattered with him. We could just *be* together. He expected nothing of me, not even that I return his love, and I began to be aware of what a gift that was.

He didn't ask questions either, seeming happy just to hold me and lightly comb his fingers through the long fall of my hair. Finally I lifted my head and he smiled at me.

"You smell good."

"That oil you left for me. I don't know what it is."

"An import from Elcinea. A thing I found in the market and thought you might like. Priced dearly, but bought with my own coin." He raised his brows. "I'm not exactly a pauper."

I laughed, unutterably pleased that he'd thought to buy me a gift. "Elcinean perfumes in the Annfwn market—how things have changed."

"Good changes," he said. "It's good for us all to be blending like this."

"Oh yes. Shapeshifters have to embrace change." I managed a smile, even through the awareness that I was a shapeshifter who couldn't change. "That looked like an interesting exercise." We turned to watch the erstwhile trainees frolicking in the surf, Marskal sliding his arm around my waist.

"Productive, too. I've gained an insight or two from you, and Zyr, on how to both add Tala talents to our forces and motivate your kind." He gave me a wry half-smile. "You're not the sort for regimented discipline, but given a challenge to your trickster natures and you can't resist."

"You think you know me so well."

"I've made a serious study of the topic. I ought to."

We stood in comfortable silence for a bit, as if we had no greater concerns than watching happy people at play. A few shapeshifters in dolphin and sea turtle form were giving Hawks rides through the surf. Karyn stood hip-deep in the water, experimenting with the swells, but apart.

Finally, I let out a breath. "It didn't work." Oddly, it didn't hurt too much to say so.

He tightened his arm. "I'm sorry."

"So, it's good that you're training other shapeshifters. We'll need them."

"Yes, we undoubtedly will. But we need you, too. I need you."

"I know that it probably makes you happy," I ventured.

He pulled back enough to give me a strange look. "Why would I be happy about something that makes you so miserable?"

"Because it means I can't take Final Form."

He turned me, putting his hands on my shoulders, very serious. "Zynda, I love you. I want to be with you, yes, but I could never rejoice in you losing such a profound part of who you are. That was never what I meant about taming you. I only wanted to find a way past your claws."

Moved, I swallowed down the emotion that rose in my throat. "Well," I said, as lightly as I could, "now I don't have any, so you're in luck."

He smiled, barely. "Quicksilver girl, you have claws enough to shred the entire world if you wish to."

I looked at him and he returned my stare, calm and unshakeable. "I have to go talk to Queen Andromeda, and give the Star to her."

He nodded, let me go, and dug the Star out from under his vest. Holding up the chain in a circle, he waited for me to bow my head so he could slip it over. Then he lifted my hair out from under the chain, arranging my hair and the jewel as if it mattered how I looked.

"Do you want me to come with you?"

I shook my head. "Better if not. But it shouldn't take long."

"Meet you in our rooms for a quiet dinner then? I'll make arrangements."

I cupped his cheek and lightly kissed him. "That would be very nice."

~ 23 ~

B ECAUSE I WASN'T expected, I waited a bit on the public
balcony outside the council chambers. The king and queen
were closeted with various advisors, but would expedite meeting
with me, the page informed me. As Marskal had predicted,
Ursula and Harlan had left for Ordnung early in the day, riding
hard and fast with only a small escort of Hawks.

Various friends and relatives said hello as they passed and
spotted me, but none asked me any hard questions. A group of
cousins who'd been at the party the night before stopped to
gossip. One, a younger woman named Sey, pulled me aside.

"Anya sends her love," she said, raising her brows. "She's
upcoast and asked me to tell you."

Ah, then Anya was pregnant again. I wished I could ask how
far along Anya was, but that would be bad luck, if Sey even
knew.

"I just came from there and I'll go back. The countryside is
lovely," Sey added.

I squeezed her hands. "Give Anya my love. I'm glad you like
the scenery there."

Sey shrugged, elaborately. "I have nothing better to do. But
she wanted me to ask—Anya seems to think you might be
bringing something with you, to *help*."

I resisted closing my eyes against the pain and guilt. Anya

knew I'd planned to take Final Form. Unlike Zyr, she'd been all for it. But then, Zyr didn't have to face losing his babies. Perhaps Marskal had a point about us not sharing this pain with the males.

"Tell her I don't have it yet, but I hope to soon."

Sey glanced over her shoulder at the other cousins, watching us curiously. She leaned in and lowered her voice. "Soon," she emphasized. "And if you do have something… well, obviously we all want it."

"I'll do my best," I replied, keeping my voice steady.

She shook her hair back and smiled with sunny cheer. "Best news!"

They moved on and I was regathering my equilibrium when I saw Karyn trudging up the winding road. I had no idea where they'd quartered the Hawks, but it was no surprise that Karyn would pass by. There's really only one way up and down the cliff—not counting vines, tunnels and side paths, because they all begin and end on the main road. She had her head down, eyes on her feet. Hopefully Zyr had not been unkind to her.

I called out. "Karyn!"

She jumped, as if caught doing something wrong, flinching and swiveling her head. I waved a hand and she relaxed somewhat, smiling half in relief, half with suspicion, and came over to me.

"Lady Zynda," she said, curtseying deeply.

"You too?" I teased, laughing. "Has Marskal been at you?"

"My lady?" Her brow furrowed and she braced, as if for a reprimand.

"Plain Zynda is just fine. I have no rank. The Tala don't care for—" I caught myself and rephrased. "Other than our king and queen, we're all on equal footing."

She remained puzzled, but her concern faded. "It's so different from Dasnaria," she confided. "I apologize. I don't know what I'm doing most of the time. This." She waved a hand at the people passing, the road, a troop of children who thundered past, some on bare feet, the rest on hoof. "I can't wrap my head around it."

How would Marskal handle this young woman? Gently and with firm calm, no doubt. "I'm sure it's odd to be around magic and people who shapeshift." There, I said it without undue emotion.

She looked surprised, eyes widening. They were a lovely blue, like the summer sky, her thick gold lashes a striking contrast. No wonder she'd caught Zyr's lustful attention.

"Not that!" She blushed. "Apologies. I didn't mean to speak so forcefully. I only meant that, yes, that is strange, but in a gorgeous, wild way. It reminds me of home, which makes no sense, since my family estates are nothing like this." She gazed about, bemused.

"What did you mean?" I asked, trying to be encouraging.

"Oh! I apologize. So much to take in. I meant, wandering about like this on my own, no one telling me what to do or where to go. Unprotected."

"You have your knives, and your bow." I indicated the weapons she wore. "You're very good with the bow, and Jepp mentioned she'd been training you on the knives and you have a deft hand."

"Yes." She blushed deeper. "Everyone is so kind. I'm sure I don't deserve it. I'm sorry—I don't mean to imply that I'm unhappy."

"I never thought that," I said, feeling oddly gentle with her. I'd never heard anyone apologize so many times in one conversation. "It's good to have some wandering time. See the sights."

"Is it?" Her expression crumpled a little, though she forced on a smile. "I know I'm privileged to be here. It's just that—it's funny. All those years I longed to see the world, to do more, even though I knew I never would. And now I can and I find myself wishing someone would tell me what to do. I was so grateful when Lieutenant Marskal called us to training. Now he gave us free time and I'm... I don't know what to do with myself."

I wanted to laugh, but she might take that wrong, so I kept it to a smile. "Would you like a suggestion?"

"Oh, yes, please!"

"Follow this road another loop, then keep going south on the side path. The orchards are there. That might feel more familiar—though I'm sure the trees and fruits are very different."

"How did you know my family estates had orchards?"

Because Jepp told me, but it didn't seem polite to mention we'd discussed her, so I ducked answering. "Feel free to pick any fruit that appeals to you. No one will mind. None of the orchard keepers speak Common Tongue, I'm sure, but they'll know you're a visitor and be welcoming."

She ruefully brought her waist-length braid over her shoulder, yanking on it. "I stand out, I know. I keep thinking I could find a dye and darken it."

"Oh, don't do that!" I ran a finger along the interwoven coils. Like silk, and so much of it, the braid as thick as my wrist. "It makes you exceptional, yes, in an interesting way."

She frowned. "I'd rather not draw attention. There's this one man. Tala. And he's very persistent."

"Zyr?"

Astonished chagrin flooded her delicate face with more color. "I'm sorry! You know him."

"My brother," I admitted. "He spoke of you. He's quite smitten."

"Oh no!" She clapped her hands to her cheeks. "I'm so sorry. You've been so kind and I didn't mean to give offense. I'm so—"

"Karyn." I said it crisply. Gentle wasn't working with her. "You gave no offense. My brother *is* persistent. He's also an ass, but he's not a brute. If you don't want him to pursue you, tell him so in no uncertain terms."

"I can't do that." She sounded aghast, all that color fled, leaving her pale.

"You can. The only one getting in your way is you. You're not in Dasnaria any longer, so stop apologizing for yourself and start doing what *you* want to do."

She gaped at me and I realized I'd forgotten to be encouraging when I abandoned gentle. Apparently Marskal's forte wasn't mine. No big surprise there. Just then the page called my name, and I was out of time to find words to reassure her.

"I have to go and meet with the king and queen, but we can talk later, if you like."

"Oh no!" Her face flooded with color again. It must be dizzying to feel so much. "I'm so sorry I kept you."

"You didn't—but you did just apologize again."

"I'm sor—you're right, Lady Zynda." She curtseyed. "I'll attempt to do better."

"Zynda!" One of the councilwomen spotted me as she walked past. "They're waiting for you."

"I must go," I said, though Karyn had caught the import of the words, if not the content, already curtseying, offering additional apologies, then fleeing, spots of color high on her fair cheeks.

The councilwoman stared after her, then shook her head sadly. "It's terrible what happens to these younglings who are mistreated. They escape one prison and, terrified of being free, they construct another of their own making, telling themselves they're safe, when in truth they're only more thoroughly trapped."

I hastened into the council rooms, my mind whirling with the councilwoman's words. Though she hadn't meant them for me, they hit some bruised part of myself, making it throb. Setting it aside, I slipped into the otherwise empty rooms, finding the king and queen deep in conversation, foreheads nearly touching. King Rayfe had a long lock of Queen Andromeda's hair looped around his hand, reminding me of Marskal. An obsession not limited to mossback men, perhaps.

Hearing me, they looked up and smiled in welcome. They gestured me to a set of chairs on a side balcony shrouded with flowering vines. Open to the air and yet private. Playing monkey-see, monkey-do with Marskal's approach to things, yet again, hopefully with better success this time, I reported the way he would, laying out the situation and making my request. But when I pulled the chain holding the Star over my head, Queen Andromeda received it with a wince.

She exchanged a long, grave look with King Rayfe, then turned back to me, her gray eyes stormy. "First, let me offer my empathy with your troubles," she said softly. Her Tala remained oddly accented, but she'd gained much fluency during her time in Annfwn. "As you know, I never shapeshifted until I married Rayfe." She touched his hand and heat palpably flowed between them. "And then not until I struggled with it. I sometimes think I never would have found the key to that particular lock if my mother hadn't left me a … token, to help me along."

"You would have," King Rayfe said, entirely confident. He lifted her hand, turned it over and kissed her palm. "You are Salena's daughter, you have the mark, and there is nothing you cannot do."

She rolled her eyes, in a very mossback way, and it made me smile to see it. "He's impossible," she whispered loudly to me, as if he couldn't hear. Then she turned solemn, the sense of storm gathering around her. Unlike Shaman's, hers felt like the sort that brings a soaking rain, gathering to linger for days. "However, I cannot do as you ask. We've already discussed it, as Essla brought this up, too. I cannot go to the Heart. Not now."

I felt my jaw slacken with the drop of my heart and hopes. "Cannot?" I echoed.

She shook her head and Rayfe held her hand. "I can't." She arched her brows in emphasis. Then added. "As I came to it late in life, the healers have strongly suggested that I avoid shifting."

"Not avoid," Rayfe corrected, completely intransigent. "Do. Not. Attempt. To. Shift."

She started to roll her eyes again, stopping when he squeezed her hand and stared her down. "I'm not going to attempt it. I promised, didn't I? You don't have to go all alpha male about it."

"I'm King of the Tala," he reminded her implacably, but a smile ghosted over his mouth.

"Who could forget?" she muttered.

I understood then, the byplay about climbing the ladder onto the ship, and what they couldn't—rather, wouldn't—give voice to. She must be with child, and far enough along for hope to begin to grow. Seeing my dawning understanding, she dipped her chin, a slight acknowledgement that spoke volumes.

"Because I came to shifting late, they think it's best if—"

"Have determined absolutely that," King Rayfe corrected.

"My love," she said in a sweet voice. "If you interrupt or correct me one more time, I'm moving up the coast for the duration, like all the other Tala women do."

His jaw tightened, deep blue eyes flashing. "I would find you and drag you back."

"You could try," she promised airily, but the sense of impending storm thickened. She returned her focus to me. "It will be months before I can go to the Heart. That is unless—"

"Don't speak it," King Rayfe and I said at the same time, making her look between us.

"I'd never have guessed the Tala are so superstitious," she commented, making him glower at her, far from amused.

"It's less superstition than living in the thick of magic all our lives," I supplied. "You learn to be careful of your thoughts and expectations because they have a tendency to get picked up by the magic."

Her face cleared, eyes thoughtful. "That makes a lot of sense, actually. Thank you for that *clear* explanation."

"I explained it," King Rayfe ground out and she cast a frustrated look at him. I was only happy that I'd recently practiced by explaining to Marskal. Perhaps trusting, and not keeping every bit of Tala lore secret, got easier with practice. Most everything did.

"You only think you explain things." She held up a hand, stopping him as she'd stopped me. "At any rate, Essla is unhappy with me, too, as she'd hoped I'd strengthen the barrier at the point of incursion. Arguably, the fate of so many is more important than this one." She rested a hand on her belly, ignoring our wince. "If thoughts and expectations are important, then this is *my* way of ensuring good luck," she said with considerable asperity.

King Rayfe hesitated, then put his hand over hers, meeting her gaze. "Nothing is more important than you are."

"Now that's not true," she replied, but everything about her softened. "Annfwn needs me, after all." She dragged her gaze from his and pinned me with it. "You'll have to find someone else. I'll give whatever permissions are needed, or if there are rites…"

She trailed off as the king and I both shook our heads. "There is no one else," I clarified.

"All those cousins, the traditions of Salena's line." She frowned at us both. "You led me to believe there are others. There's Stella."

"Not for years," King Rayfe said with regret. "Stella must grow up and, as far as others… well, I didn't want you to feel too much pressure."

Her slackened jaw firmed, gray eyes going stormier. A hint of ozone and her hair stirring in an invisible wind. "It can't be all on me. I have to risk shifting. The world is bigger than me and Annfwn. Don't start with me." Her voice cracked like lightning striking too near, but King Rayfe didn't flinch. His own considerable power gathered around him.

I stood. "No, it isn't all on you, Queen Andromeda. It's on me. This was my charge, for more years than you've been queen, and this is my failure."

Her storm receded, sun breaking through clouds, and she bit her lower lip, sympathy in her eyes. "It's not a failure, Zynda. We all can only do our best. I spent years of my life feeling that I'd failed everyone in everything. I did my best to hide from that, to be invisible." When King Rayfe took her hand again, she let him, though she shot him a look that made me think all wasn't forgiven so easily. He grinned at her ferocity. Difficult to imagine this woman who scintillated with so much magic, as invisible.

"I learned otherwise," she said to me, her tone full of import, as if she'd heard my thought. "I'll keep the Star for you. We're alert now to these sleeper spies, so we'll be on guard. It will be as safe here as anywhere."

"Thank you," I said, then bowed. "I hope that I can help you, ensure the best possible outcome, when I return."

King Rayfe gave me a long look of dawning understanding, but Queen Andromeda gave a puzzled laugh. "That's a lovely thought, but that responsibility isn't yours. Don't take on too much of the world, cousin. But do give my love to Ami." She stood. "And give her this for me."

She hugged me, softly, but with so much warmth in it that I nearly teared up. What a tenderhearted mess I'd become. Andi pulled back a little, but still held onto me. "A lot of that was for you, too."

~ 24 ~

"SO, TOMORROW WE leave for Windroven," Marskal said, pouring us both more wine. At least he'd gotten the really good stuff for his coins. He'd plied me with plenty already—along with the flowers, candlelight, and an amazing assembly of all my childhood favorite foods. He seemed to find it amusing that he'd only had to mention my name to the various vendors and they immediately packaged up something with no further prompting. I suspected his coins—gold ones stamped with Ursula's hawkish profile, newly minted from her father's personal and considerable treasure hoard, it turned out—were highly sought enough, both for their value and novelty that he'd likely overpaid considerably.

Not that I'd say so, since he seemed boyishly delighted to have surprised me. And I'd enjoyed the deliciously amusing, if eclectic, meal—and being romanced. Having my head swim delightfully with wine and his masculine attention helped mitigate my fretting.

He shoveled the rest of the lemon candies onto my plate. "Those things are foul. I don't know how you can stand them."

"An acquired taste, perhaps."

"We're not that far away," he continued. "With the barrier down, I figure we could even cut through the mountains north of the Crane Isthmus. We never made it that far south on our expedition." He flicked a mischievous glance at me when I made a face for Ursula's spying efforts. "But if we went down the coast of Annfwn—even catch a ride in a boat, maybe—it would be a pretty short diagonal across to Windroven. Part of the world I've never seen, too."

I had to smile for his enthusiastic wanderlust. "Not in human form, I wouldn't want to try it. The mountains there are lower, but full of boggy willow bottoms and sinkholes."

"You've been there then?"

"Flown over, mostly." I gathered up the wistful pain and tucked it away under practicality. "I haven't walked it, but I'm reasonably certain that going on foot would take forever."

"Didn't King Rayfe take Andi that way after their wedding on the battlefield at Windroven, though?"

I raised my brows. "How did you know that?"

"We tracked them for a while, when we believed it might be possible to get her back. But we couldn't keep up." He grimaced ruefully for the failure.

"They were on staymach and shifter horses—you would never have been able to. Even so, they still skirted settlements and took a circuitous route. Via Odfell's Pass and down would be faster for us. No pursuing enemy to avoid." I gave him a sweet smile.

He ignored the jibe, nodding. "Just the two of us, and a couple of good horses, and we could still be there in two days. Three at the outside."

"It's not a pleasure jaunt, Marskal."

He shrugged that off. "I'm looking forward to time alone with you, regardless of the purpose of the journey."

"We won't be alone long, nor will it be quick, if you get embroiled in goings-on at Ordnung," I pointed out.

He grinned back. "No, we'd avoid the castle for that very

reason. Her Majesty isn't expecting us, so we'd go around. From the stories, it didn't take long after you all landed on Nahanau to free Kiraka."

"Except that Nakoa knew what he was doing, magically speaking."

"You have more magic than he does, you understand shapeshifter ways, and you've seen the ritual before. I have confidence." He said it so casually, methodically finishing the fresh crab morsels, that it gave me a shiver. No exaggeration there. "Maybe Kiraka can advise you, if necessary."

"I don't know if I can talk to Kiraka over that distance."

"Bring some staymachs with us—no reason they have to stay here, is there?"

I regarded him with some consternation. We'd been so long in the habit of insularity in Annfwnn that I'd grown barriers around my thoughts, as well. With magic so widely dispersed now, of course the staymachs could come with us. The one I'd coaxed in to bird shape had been visiting regularly anyway. They tended to get attached that way. No doubt I could persuade it and maybe a few others to come along. Ones who liked to be horses would be ideal for multiple purposes.

"So long as Kiraka decided not to have them for a snack."

Marskal's eyes sparkled with humor and he opened his mouth, then closed it with an odd twist.

"What?"

He shook his head slightly. "An inappropriate joke I thought better of."

I could follow his thoughts well enough by now to guess. "About me already being her snack?"

He regarded me steadily. "I wasn't sure if you'd find it funny."

I grimaced ruefully. The day a Tala couldn't laugh at herself would be lusterless, indeed. Perhaps I'd been taking myself far too seriously. All this wounded pride and arrogance.

"Ursula might not be thrilled to have another dragon loose," I said, and picturing her expression made me laugh softly. "Though Queen Andromeda seemed to know where we planned to go."

"I didn't get to tell you yet, but Her Majesty gave us permission." He assumed a narrow-eyed steely glare, tightening his lips in an uncanny imitation of Ursula, saying, "If Ami will let you near her precious volcano, and you can release the dragon, then do it. Things can hardly be worse. At least we know they're not *Deyrr*'s creatures."

I laughed in truth, and his eyes sparkled with mirth. "I had no idea you could imitate her so flawlessly."

"Long familiarity," he commented drily. "And if you ever let on, I'll take revenge."

"You could try," I retorted, aware I echoed my queen and not minding.

He lowered his brows and reached across the table, taking my hand again in a firm grip, his eyes hot. "Is that a challenge? You know how I feel about challenges."

A zing of arousal shot through me and I tugged at our joined hands. He tightened his, not letting go. In fact, he started pulling me over the table toward him. Not ready to be controlled that easily, I simply crawled up onto the table, stalking toward him, not caring that I knocked my empty wine glass over.

"You think to taunt the tiger?" I purred.

"Taunt?" He went very still, which should have warned me, but I underestimated his reflexes. In a flash he dashed the dishes, candles and all from the table and toppled me onto my back, pinning me by the wrists and trapping me with the lower half of his body.

"I've been practicing my wrestling moves," he informed me.

I twisted out of his hold and he neatly recaptured me, this time with both my wrists in one hand, stretching them over my head so I lost leverage. "Several of the shapeshifters were helpful today in teaching me how to bypass your particular kind of strength."

"Which shapeshifters?" I demanded, testing his strength, struggling more for the fun of it than really trying to break his grip. I could if I wanted to. Maybe.

"Jealous?" he teased.

"No," I replied, winding my legs around his narrow hips and locking him into place. "Because they all know you're *my* mossback."

"Am I?" he breathed, eyes gleaming with reflected candle-light.

I would have offered more, the words I knew he wanted from me, but I didn't like to lie to him more than came naturally. Instead I flexed my thighs, tightening on him, while arching my back so my breasts thrust up enticingly. "You seem to be captured, so yes."

He stretched my wrists higher, leaning over me and firmly cupping my breast through my silk gown, then tweaking the turgid nipple so I gasped. Already so primed with wanting him. "I think I'm the one who's caught the tiger by the tail."

"That sounds unwise to me," I warned, but it came out breathless.

"I'll be the judge of that." His gaze raked over me. "I believe you owe me this one." Hooking his hand in the neckline of my silk gown, he tore it down the middle—making me gasp—and baring me to the waist. "Oh yeah," he growled. "I see why you like that. Works for me, too."

With that he fastened his mouth on my breast, sliding his

free hand between us to cup my sex in a grip so fierce my eyes rolled back in my head. I cried out, impossibly climaxing immediately. All the frustrations, anger, grief, and sorrowful rage of the day welled up and out of me. He drove his fingers into me, teeth and tongue savaging each breast in turn, and I writhed under him screaming out my physical pleasure and emotional pain.

When he let go of my wrists to use both hands to finish ripping my gown off me, I followed him up, kissing him with all the blocked savagery in me. He got his pants open without breaking the kiss, pulling my hips to the edge of the table to open me for him. Breaking our connection only to position his cock at my opening, he slid into me without resistance, I'd gone so slick and needy. His turn to groan, losing all of his practiced wariness in the sheer pleasure of being inside me. I could feel the echoes of it in him, reveling in the face he wore only for me.

He opened his eyes, gazing steadily into mine, hands gripping my hips, my arms draped around his neck. My hair and silk gown flowed behind me like a cloak, the room shadowed in the twilight, all but one of the spilled candles having guttered out. Our mood shifted in harmony, the fierce need of moments ago transforming into something achingly sweet.

Moving in me, he gazed at me with a kind of wonder, brown eyes lustrous with it. "Zynda," he murmured my name, his love and exquisite pleasure all singing through the way he voiced it.

I kissed him, taking that in, feeding on it. Maybe no longer so worried about the way he sustained me. In turn, he seemed to drink me in, the lazy strokes turning urgent. Hands fisting into my hair, he gripped me tight, pouring himself into me as I dissolved. As he went over the edge, he whispered my name and declaring his love, over and over.

I SENT MY staymach bird to fetch Zyr in the early morning. He arrived, sleepy-eyed, hair tousled, and decidedly grumpy. He glared at us balefully. "What? I have a tasty female in my bed and I don't want her to wander off."

"You seduced Karyn?" I asked with some surprise. Zyr had worked a miracle in that case. Impressive, even for him.

He gave a dry laugh of disgust. "That one? No—I'm leaving her to her search for true love and the perfect husband."

"Ah, too bad," I said, not believing him for a moment. "I like Karyn. She might be good enough for you."

Zyr squinted at me. "You can't be serious."

"One thing I've learned is that I haven't always valued the things that came easily to me." I shrugged, making it extra elaborate because Marskal had that glint of humor in his eye. "Anyway, I want you to have this."

Zyr took the wooden box from me, weighing its heft in his hands dubiously. "Now I know you are mossbacked beyond retrieval, to give me a big, heavy *thing*."

I punched his shoulder. "It's a shapeshifter thing. Open it."

He opened the lid and extracted a map-stick, holding it up to the growing light and eyeing it. Then he fastened a deep blue eye on me, sharp with perception. "Quite the feel to this."

"Yes," I agreed, beyond pleased that he felt it, too. "It's a map. You can carry it in talons and compare it to the coastline below. The ancients made them."

He whistled long and low. "Clever. We should have thought of this. Do we know where they're maps to?"

"One is Nahanau. I know because I tested it. The others...

maybe N'andana."

Carefully, he put the map-stick away, closing the lid and tucking the box under his arm. He acted nonchalant, but his eyes burned bright with fascinated curiosity. "I'll bite. Why do I get this gift?"

"Because you can shapeshift." I held up a hand when he opened his mouth. "And Dafne is hoping we can find N'andana. She has her reasons, ferreted out of her many texts in the library at Nahanau. She'll be in touch with instructions."

"Will she?" Zyr licked his lips. "Is her husband one of the understanding types, or—"

"Not." Better cut that off right now. "Don't cause a political incident or Cousin Ursula would have your head."

Zyr scoffed. "I could take her."

"But not both of us together," Marskal inserted meaningfully.

Zyr grinned. "Could be fun, though."

"Be kind to Karyn," I told him. "It's not easy, you know, to be among people who aren't your kind, where you don't understand the customs. It can be lonely."

Zyr cupped the back of my head, leaning his forehead against mine. "You can always come home."

"I know. I've missed you."

"I've missed you, too." Zyr tossed back his hair. "Have fun releasing the dragon. Try not to get immolated again."

I laughed. "I'll do my best."

WE RODE OUT on our staymach horses, a staymach bird on each

of our shoulders. Marskal glanced at me with some concern. "I'm glad you got to say goodbye to Zyr, but sorry that you didn't get to see your sister, Anya."

"That wouldn't have happened regardless. She sent her love, but she wasn't available."

"What does that mean? In plain words, not Tala euphemisms, please."

I slid him a sideways look. My mossback could certainly entrench on odd issues. "That she's gone upcoast to finish carrying to term and have her baby." It felt odd to put it so baldly to him, but he'd demanded clarity and Queen Andromeda's words about the Tala being superstitious on the topic lingered with me.

"What?" He started to rein up, his horse resisting and sticking with mine. "Don't you want to go see her? We're not in that much of a hurry."

I shrugged. "Even if I did, it would take too long to find her, as she won't want to be found. She wouldn't want to see me, given that I didn't bring good luck last time."

He pondered that, a deep line between his brows. Finally he shook it off. "Maybe I'm thinking of things differently. I'd be worried about my sister dying in childbirth and that I'd regret not seeing her before that. But that must not be a concern—only that the baby might not make it."

"Oh, Anya could die, too. That's how we lost our mother, so that's always a strong possibility. Childbirth is particularly dangerous for a shapeshifter woman if a healer isn't close enough. After labor, a woman might not have enough energy to shift and heal, particularly because she'll have been out of practice."

He gave me a queer look. "And that doesn't bother you?"

I shrugged. "Whether I see her first or not won't change the outcome."

"Sometimes I don't understand you," he said under his breath, but I had no trouble hearing it. Oddly, it pained me. Though of course he didn't. We might have found common ground, but our different cultures and races created a gulf between us. Something I shouldn't allow myself to forget again, no matter how much pleasure and respite he gave me. Love doesn't guarantee compatibility.

To cover it, I gave him an easy smile. "That's because I am not like—"

"Stop staying that! Being Tala has nothing to do with it." He waved a frustrated hand at the dwellings around us. "I've seen your people—they live in big families, just like we do. This is about you. Don't you care about anyone—*need* anyone?"

I fumed over that a few moments, annoyed that he'd gotten under my skin. I'd never pretended to be anyone other than who I was. "I warned you that loving me wasn't a good idea."

"That's not an answer."

"What answer do you want from me? I don't have one. I am who I am. And when you said you loved me, you also promised that you wouldn't bother me with it."

He set his jaw, staring ahead. "I said that a long time ago, before we became lovers. Before I thought there was any chance we would. I'd been awake for three days and nights, nursing you back to health and could maybe be given a little room for exhaustion and delirium. Besides." He cut me a sharp look. "You were a hummingbird at the time. I didn't expect to be held to the letter of it later."

"Is that meant to be an excuse? Because I know perfectly well that you've always talked to me as myself, no matter what form I wore."

He considered that, losing some of his frustration with me in the surprise. "Of course I do. Is that unusual?"

I snorted. "For a mossback, definitely. It was one of the first things I noticed about you. You always talked to me as a person, even when I was an animal."

"I didn't think you noticed me at all."

I waved that away. "When I did."

"Uh-huh." He had a particular smile on his face, no longer annoyed at all, but actually looking terribly pleased. Smug, even.

"What has you looking like the winner of I Eat You?"

He burst out laughing, the staymach bird on his shoulder spreading its wings in a flutter. It had grown larger since picking Marskal as its perch, and browner. He reached up and stroked its head with a finger, smiling slightly when it leaned into the caress and cooed. He'd better not be thinking he could manage me as easily. "What in the three is 'I Eat You'?"

"A game. I forgot you wouldn't know." Blurting old things out in my irritation. Being with Zyr stirring up childhood memories. "Two or more shapeshifters shift simultaneously, and whoever has the form that could eat the others wins."

"Wouldn't everyone just become the dragon or the tiger?"

I smiled archly. "Well, not everyone *can*."

"Ah." He nodded knowingly. "And the canny shifter doesn't tell anyone all the forms she is able to take."

"Now you're catching on."

He gave me a slow, intimate smile, one that reminded me of how he'd looked holding me the night before when we were fused together, him so deep inside me he'd felt like he'd always been a part of me. A flutter ran through me and I didn't know how he could do that with a single look.

"I'd like to think so," he said.

A long time later I realized that he'd successfully ducked answering my question. Too much time around the Tala. He'd begun to pick up my tricks.

WE TRAVELED QUICKLY, the staymach horses much faster than regular ones. Which meant the weather chilled considerably over a short space of time. I shivered as we ascended through the forested foothills that rose above the flat cliff tops, and Marskal called a halt. He dismounted and rummaged in the packs he'd put behind my saddle. To my surprise, he pulled out the cloak I'd worn when I first left Ordnung with Jepp and Dafne. It had been winter then.

I'd been so long in lands of summer warmth that I'd forgotten about cold weather. Before the barrier expanded, it would have stayed Annfwn-warm all the way to Odfell's pass. Since then, the circle of warmth retreated before the colder air of the mountains. Slipping from the saddle, I let Marskal wrap me in the warm cloak and pull up the furred hood, though I didn't need that much yet. He buckled the clasp, adjusting the fur around my face, and smiled at me, something wistful in it. "You look particularly beautiful in this—the white fur frames your black hair and blue eyes." He kissed me, lingering over it. "And lips as red as freshly spilled blood."

"Marskal!" I thumped his shoulder, laughing. "That's hardly romantic."

The corners of his eyes crinkled with mirth, but he kept a sober expression. "That's mossback romance."

"I'm certain it's not."

"Oh yes. You'll learn to love it. Here, might as well put your boots on now. We'll hit snow soon."

Bemused, I let him slip the fur-lined boots onto my feet and lace them up. Running my fingers through his short hair, I commented, "I forgot that it would be winter. And you, ever prepared—I can't believe you packed all of my stuff."

"You don't have much of it, and I'm accustomed to preparing quickly for long journeys. It's second nature. But I'm surprised you forgot about the seasons—not long ago you traveled to Ordnung in the dead of winter there to bring Her Majesty the news of Dafne."

"Yes, but in animal form. It doesn't feel the same. Human form doesn't adjust nearly as well. Or maybe it's because I can't adjust to it like I can—could—choose the animal to suit the climate."

He glanced up at me thoughtfully. "Seems like if you could choose an animal form, you could change the human form."

I laughed. "You and Jepp are so much alike. I don't think it works that way. Like, my animal forms are—were—always the same. If I shifted to the pony, I would have the same coloring."

"You don't have to keep reframing to past tense." He laced his hands for me leg up to the back of my horse again and, because I liked the courtesy, I took the assistance.

"I think I do," I replied. "Accepting and coming to terms with who I am now."

"It's an interesting conundrum," he said, after he'd mounted and we'd moved on. "That implies that you're not really creating the form but sort of slipping yourself into one that's already there."

I nodded. "There are some who think that way." So odd, to be discussing this with him, but I'd begun to relax into it. "That's part of why no one really agrees on whether a pregnant woman should shapeshift. If she's simply moving her mind, her consciousness into a new form, what does it matter?"

"But you said once that a shapeshifter trapped in animal form could have a child in that shape."

I raised my brows. Of course he'd remember everything people said. Such a good scout and spy. "Yes, but was she pregnant before she shifted or impregnated in that form?"

"You don't know?"

"How could we? If she's in animal form, no one can ask."

He thought about that. "Queen Andromeda clearly believes it's better not to risk it."

"She has a great deal to risk, including King Rayfe. If she were to die, we'd lose both our king and queen."

Marskal glanced at me. "Because he loves her that much?"

I sighed. Mentally said a prayer to Moranu that she wouldn't mind yet another secret revealed to the mossbacks. "Remember how I said their bond was different?"

"Of course."

Of course. "It's literally different—their lives are magically wedded together. King Rayfe asked a shaman to seal their marriage with a blood bond. Their life forces are tied to each other."

He scanned the trees, turning that over. "Since the wedding itself?"

"The ritual was invoked during the ceremony and completed on their wedding night. It's partly sexual." I smiled when he shook his head sharply.

"I don't need that image in my head," he said. "So, even if we had caught up with them, it would have been too late."

"Exactly."

"Does Her Majesty know that?"

I laughed. "No. Not many Tala even know. You can imagine the strategic value of that information."

He quirked a smile. "A fascinating people, the Tala. You

either have virtually no bond with your lovers or one unto death."

I started to object, then shrugged. "I suppose that's a fair enough assessment."

"So, High Queen Salena…"

"Married Uorsin according to your ways, not ours. Her own vow—and vision of the future—kept her sealed to him. Nothing more."

He pondered that and we rode quietly for a while.

~ 25 ~

B Y THE TIME we reached the pass and the demarcation where the barrier had once been, the horses forged through knee- and even chest-deep snow, slowing us considerably. Belatedly realizing I could be useful, I summoned some of the staymachs who lived as shadow guardians in the canopy and gorges to clear the trail ahead of us. Marskal startled at seeing them converge, angling his horse to shield mine and drawing his sword.

I laughed and he shot me a glare. "Quiet! Something's here."

Explaining what I'd done, he somewhat sheepishly resheathed his sword, muttering that I might have told him. "You looked terribly gallant, though," I replied.

He raised a brow at me. "Now you don't mind me guarding you?"

And I realized I didn't, though I didn't tell him so.

With the paths cleared all the way through to the fort above Castle Ordnung, we made excellent time, though the late winter sky darkened early.

"I don't see how we can avoid stopping at the fort," he noted with a frown. "Which will mean soldier's gossip and they'll no doubt invite us to share the evening meal, and then want us to stay the night."

"We have to sleep somewhere," I pointed out. Even my

preference for sleeping outdoors failed in the face of the freezing temperatures.

"True, but I was hoping to make it down to Ordnung tonight."

"I thought you wanted to avoid time-wasting embroilments at the castle, too."

He gave me a sideways look, oddly hesitant for my steadfastly confident soldier. "I do. I meant the township."

"The township?" It would be easier than answering questions at the castle, I supposed. "That could work. We could stay at an inn."

He scrubbed a hand over his face, then squared his shoulders, giving me a steady look. "What I mean is, I'd like to visit my family. Just to stop in for the night. I haven't seen them in some time and... well, you might not understand, but—"

"I understand," I interrupted in a gentle tone. "Just because my ways are strange doesn't mean I don't understand the desire to see the people you love. It's clear even to me that you love your family."

"I didn't mean to imply that," he said quietly, brow further furrowed.

I saved him groping for more of an apology. "Don't be concerned. I'm not at all offended. I don't mind staying at an inn while you see your family. As long as there's a fireplace," I amended. "And maybe some fur blankets."

"No, no." He shook his head, the color high on his cheekbones not from the cold, but...embarrassment? Not my stalwart mossback. "I'm doing this badly. I'd like to visit them because I'd like you to come with me. To meet my family."

Oh. *Oh.* My own face flushed, which made no sense. I laughed, to cover it. "But will they want to meet *me*?"

A strange expression contorted his mouth before he

smoothed it to impassivity. I'd hurt him, carelessly, and laughed while doing it. Would I ever get better at this?

"That's not the point," he said in a neutral tone. "I love you and I love them. It's perfectly natural for me to want the people I love to know each other."

I swallowed back my sigh. And the urge to explain—yet again—that I was no good at this and that I wouldn't be around long enough for them to know anyway. But what could it hurt to pretend? Marskal had been good to me. Better than I'd been to him. Truth be told—and look at his influence on me, that I should be doing all this honest introspection—I'd been happier and more at peace with him than ever before in my life. Considering how difficult these last days had been, that was particularly noteworthy. I owed him more than my life.

I could pretend to be his—whatever the mossbacks called it—for an evening. How hard could it be?

So I gave him an enthusiastic smile, made even easier when he lit up to see it. "Sure, I'd love to meet them. And I can help with avoiding the fort."

He looked dubious. "I think it's better to keep the staymachs away, other than the ones with us." He offered his finger to the bird who'd taken refuge inside the warmth of his leather cloak, stroking its coyly offered neck. Spoiled little thing. Marskal clearly had a talent for charming all the denizens of Annfwn.

"I won't use staymachs." I let my smile curve into mysterious when he looked puzzled. "You'll see. But be quiet. We don't need to be absolutely silent, but avoid speaking unless absolutely necessary."

I pulled a shroud of deflection around us, and we trotted past the patrols, lookouts, then the fort itself—neatly avoiding them all without setting up an alert. When we'd passed out of earshot, Marskal raised his brows in question and I nodded that we could speak.

"*That* is how the Tala snuck up on Ordnung so easily!" The words virtually exploded out of him. "It's been killing me all this time that none of the Hawks' scouts or Ordnung's guard spotted anything. You can turn invisible."

"Not exactly invisible." I had to correct him, though his astonished enthusiasm made me laugh. Sharing Tala secrets turned out to be fun, too. "It's more of a distortion. Especially if someone doesn't know to look for you. I made us seem like more snow and forest, the horse's hooves sounding like normal creature movements in the woods. Another Tala could spot us easily, but…"

"But mossbacks are dense like that," he finished, shaking his head ruefully, but his canny eyes showed that his thoughts were working. "Could you teach a mossback what to look for— carefully selected scouts, maybe?"

I considered it with some amusement. "Probably. But aren't we supposed to be all friendly allies now—why would we be sneaking Tala past your Hawks?"

He grinned. "Force of habit there, I suppose. Though…" He stared into the distance, thinking, then turned his gaze back to me. "Could that be similar to the magic *Deyrr* used to sneak up on our ships, when the high priestess attacked Ursula?"

"Oh." I turned that over with some surprise. "That hadn't occurred to me."

"That's been bothering me, too," he confessed, with a wry grimace. "A spectacular failure on my part."

I hadn't thought about that, how Marskal would have taken his failure to protect Ursula personally. "Aren't you the one telling me I can't be responsible for everyone?"

He tipped his head in acknowledgement. "Ah, but that *was* literally my job. If not for Tala healing, my high queen would have died." His expression had gone bleak, an aching insight into the valiant heart behind his usual remote façade.

I should've said something comforting, but he was the one good at that. "People die," I said, knowing while I said it that it wasn't the right thing. "We can do everything right and they still die. That's the way of the world."

I expected a caustic comment about my Tala-born insensitivity, but he only pursed his lips, then nodded. "Fatalistic," he commented, "but inescapable." Then he flashed me a grin. "But don't hold it against me if I go down fighting to stop it as much as possible."

Catching his humor, I laughed. "Well, you wouldn't be the man I—" I caught myself, aghast at what I'd almost said. A flip remark and I'd have let him think our time together could last beyond this short sequence. "My mossback," I finished, blowing him a sultry kiss in the hopes that he didn't catch the slip.

He barely noticed even that, deep in thought. "And these sleeper spies—what if they have similar abilities? We have to start thinking ahead. Kral is correct that we've been on the defensive for too long. If we're going to win this war, we need to do more than react." His attention focused on the path ahead. "Riders approaching. It would be convenient if you could—"

"Already done," I replied. I'd never dropped the distortion, as it was one of those tricks that was just as easy, if not easier, to simply leave in place than take down and put up again.

"It doesn't drain you?" he asked.

I shook my head. "No—it takes some concentration and a bit of energy to put it in place, but then I can leave it indefinitely."

"Interesting," he commented, then didn't say more because we went quiet to pass the group of Ordnung guards heading up the hill. Marskal watched them with a bemused smile, no doubt picturing Ursula's annoyance at their obliviousness to our presence. Then we stayed quiet, passing more and more people as the path wound down to the main highway below the castle. Full winter evening dark had fallen, sparkling crystalline chill, and Ordnung's white towers reared against the night with dramatic and cold ferocity. Ursula's flag flew beside the one for the Thirteen Kingdoms, showing the High Queen had returned to be in residence. The windows blazed with light to match the torches on the battlements, chasing away every shadow.

Ordnung had always struck me as a sterile, uncomfortable place. A massive fortress rather than a home. But with my new perspective, I saw the ways in which it echoed Annfwn's white cliffs. Had Uorsin somehow intuited something of how Annfwn looked? Or perhaps Salena had coached him in the design, in the early days of their marriage when he was still flush with triumph of the war she'd won for him. Either way—his or hers—the implicit longing for a place neither would ever see made my heart hurt, as if I'd suffer the same loss.

It shouldn't because I would see Annfwn again.

"What's that?" Marskal asked, making me wonder if I'd muttered that aloud. I shook my head, smiling to show I was fine, and pushed my hood back. I needed the cold air to clear my head. We passed the castle gates and entered the township proper, bustling with activity still. Marskal nodded at me and I dropped the distortion. Time to be seen again.

Almost immediately a young boy bolted up, automatically grabbing for the reins the staymach horse didn't have. "Uncle Marskal!" he shouted, hopping from foot to foot instead. "You're home!"

"I am, indeed, young Robbie," Marskal replied gravely. "Would you tell your grandmother that—"

"I'll tell *everyone*!" Robbie shouted, turned, and bolted off at top speed.

Marskal gave me a chagrined smile. "My second oldest sister's fifth child. He hit the ground running at birth and has never paused since."

Five children. I marveled at it. And Marskal had said he was one of six siblings, five of them here in the township, with two to seven children each. And the boy was telling all of them.

"How many people will I be meeting?" I tried to sound casual, but it must have come out plaintive enough that he reached over, offering his hand. More to reassure him that I wouldn't bolt like his impetuous nephew, I took it, the horses snugging together so our knees bumped.

"Don't worry about remembering names," he said. "And thank you for doing this. I know you're indulging me."

Was that a bad thing? I wasn't at all sure. I smiled easily. "It will be fun."

He laughed, throwing his head back to release the hearty sound. "Ah, the lies my lady tells. If I didn't know her so well, I might believe her."

I yanked my hand away, turning up my nose like a court lady at Ordnung. "I can't imagine what you mean. And you ducked the question—how many?"

He scratched his chin, mentally counting. "Possibly… thirty-five? I can't remember when Alisa's baby was due. Might be thirty-six now."

Attempting to maintain a languid pose, I nodded. "All in one… house?"

"Yes," he said very seriously. "We walled up the windows so we could stack bunk beds against the walls. That way we can fit in four to six people per room."

My jaw dropped in horror. I could still stay at an inn. Or, I had my furry cloak. I could sneak out and—

Marskal's gasp of laughter caught me mid-thought and I whipped my head around to find him pointing at me, eyes leaking tears he was laughing so hard, albeit nearly silently. "The... look on... your face," he panted out.

I curled my lip in a snarl. "You are *not* funny. And I was so nice to you in Annfwn! Oh, help the poor mossback fit in. It will all be so strange to him... But do you return the favor? No."

He attempted to sober himself, nodding somberly. "You're absolutely right. It was totally unfair of me to—" A strange snorting sound escaped him as the laughter overtook him again.

"You're impossible," I informed him. Where had my stoic and quiet mossback gone? "And you're not paying attention. We're leaving the township behind."

"I know where I'm going," he replied easily, as if he hadn't been choking with laughter a moment before. We turned down a lane, passing into more open country again. "See up ahead? That's my parents' home. Only they and one sister and her husband live there—though they are the ones with seven kids. Mom and Dad help with that brood."

I blinked at the enormous sprawling house at the end of the lane, spilling with light, the double front doors wide open. People were going in and out, including three children who sent up a shout and dashed toward us.

"The rest live in various houses around the property," Marskal continued, watching me carefully now. "There's a lot of land."

"I thought your cowardly grandfather gave up your lands."

A grin broke across his face. "You were listening."

I waved a hand at him. "I was bored."

"Her Majesty gave the land back to us," he said, a look of pride and nostalgia on his face. "We were lucky in that it hadn't been broken up much. This close to the castle, the farm and barns were mainly used to supply Ordnung, run by staff. Everyone is still in the process of fixing it up again, some living in houses on the land and in town, both." He gave me a slight smile, wistfulness in it. "I have a cottage of my own, on a very pretty piece of land. We can sleep there tonight. I'd love for you to see it. I think you'll like it."

"Does it have windows?" I asked, adding extra asperity, because the way he talked about the place made my heart twist uncomfortably.

"It does." His smile widened. "And I'm fairly handy as a carpenter. I'll add more windows, and skylights and balconies. Whatever you need to feel comfortable."

"Tonight?"

"Well, obviously no—but if we come back here."

This had gone far enough. "Marskal," I said, hating the forbidding sound in my own voice. "I don't want to be unkind to you, but this simply can't—"

My timing was terrible. As it seemed to be lately. The pack of three children reached us, jumping up and down and breathlessly telling their uncle several different pieces of news at once. He dismounted to walk with them, picking up the smallest and notching her onto his hip, casting me a wry smile as he showed her how to pet the bird that had hopped back up to his shoulder, and trusting me to guide the horses in.

We walked them nearly up to the front doors, people and light pouring out and down the steps. So many children, all belonging to one family. Most of the people fortunately swarmed Marskal first, but a young man with a wide smile and Marskal's eyes came to help me unstrap the packs. "I think we can make room in the stables for these," he said, though he sounded dubious. "We weren't expecting Uncle Marskal tonight."

"He wanted it to be a surprise," I replied. "But no need." With a thought I gave the staymach horses, and my bird one, free rein to choose their forms. I left Marskal's bird as it was, since it seemed to be a big hit amongst the youngsters. They all morphed into snowy owls—a good choice for foraging on a cold winter night.

I turned back to find the young man blinking at me, and all of Marskal's rowdy family gone silent. Then they sent up a clamor of noise, throwing questions at both of us. Marskal held up his hands, calling for peace from the assault—though he was laughing—and came to me, taking my hand and leading me forward, up to an older couple. The man looked like Marskal might in a few decades.

"Mom, Dad," Marskal said, "this is Zynda. She's a Tala sorceress and shapeshifter, and much of this is unfamiliar to her," he added, raising his voice so they all could hear, "so I expect everyone, even Shanna, to be helpful and pleasant." He gave the girl who'd climbed up to his hip and now held the bird a stern look, but she only giggled.

Then *I* was swarmed, people taking my hands and even hugging me, giving welcome. I got asked if I was hungry half a dozen times, so it clearly ran in the family. Once again, Marskal came to my rescue, declaring that all of this could happen indoors, did they want me to freeze? He retrieved me to lead me inside, while everyone else fell into a hubbub of conversation about who was to do what next.

"Why did you say I'm a shapeshifter?" I hissed at him.

"Because you are," he replied evenly. "Shanna, be careful with that bird. It's a living creature, not a toy. And I want them to know who you are from the beginning. No secrets." He slid me a look.

"You mean *what* I am."

"They're a lot to take in, I know." He squeezed my hand. "Again, I really appreciate you doing this. We'll just stay a bit, eat, and then we can go to my house and sleep."

He looked so happy, utterly relaxed, and for once not constantly scanning for danger, that I couldn't begrudge him any of this. Aware that I'd be making a statement, I cupped his cheek and kissed him, rewarded by the pleased sparkle in his eye. "I'm good. Enjoy your family. Don't be concerned about leaving. The Tala love to eat and talk all night, you know."

A woman with brown hair, brown eyes and a serious expression just like his came up, holding an infant wrapped in blankets. The child was red-faced and screaming, waving impotent fists in the air. "Uncle Marskal—your newest niece, Iris." She gave me an apologetic smile. "I'd hoped to settle her down, but she's in a mood tonight and nothing will appease her."

"Nothing?" Marskal asked, taking the baby, blankets and all, from his sister. "Ah, sweet Iris, let's see what we can do to improve that cranky mood." The little girl fell silent, her eyes going big as she stared at Marskal, wrapping her tiny hand around the finger he offered, as he carried her off into the other room.

"We call him the baby whisperer," the woman confided, brown eyes crinkled with affection. "I was desperately hoping he hadn't lost his touch. I'm Alisa and I don't expect you to remember that. Let me take your cloak, and do you want to take off your boots? It's not a house rule—just if you'd be more comfortable. Oh! Look at all that black hair. It's very nearly blue when the light hits it just right, matching your eyes. I've never seen such deep blue eyes. You're so striking. Do all Tala look like you?"

I caught my breath from her dizzying blast of questions, then laughed. She smiled with me, dimples in her round cheeks.

"I know—I talk too much and too fast. Lars, my husband, is forever saying, 'Lise, if you'll pause to take a breath, I might answer one of your questions.'" She closed her mouth significantly and waited.

"I will take off my boots," I said, "and yes, I look like most Tala."

"Though more beautiful than most, I'll bet." She winked at me, dimpling more. "Marskal always did have an eye for the pretty ones." She took my boots and set them by the fire to dry, then came back and took my hand. "We're exceptionally pleased to meet you and welcome you here. I want to say it now, in case we forget to later. It's so very special to us that he brought you to meet everyone."

I wasn't at all sure what to say back, and I searched for an appropriate reply, but she twinkled at me, dropped my hand, and gestured to the kitchen. "You're overwhelmed and I'm going on too long. Let's get you something to eat and a quiet spot to sit in."

As good as her word, Alisa installed me in a big chair by the fire, with a plate of food and a mug of some sort of spiced, warmed wine. She also herded all the children away from me—Moranu bless her—telling them they could ask questions later. Marskal sat at a table, surrounded by children of all ages, still holding the now sleeping baby cradled in one arm, and shoveling food into his mouth with his free hand, in between answering questions. He moved so he could see me, raising an inquiring brow when I first sat, then nodding when I smiled at him.

Alisa took my cleaned plate and refilled my mug of wine, leaving me to sit in peace when I said I'd prefer it. After a bit, however, Marskal's mother came out of the kitchen area with her own mug of wine and took the chair opposite me. A glance at Marskal told me he'd observed and had half risen, but his father put a hand on his shoulder, saying something that had Marskal looking interested. I began to suspect a conspiracy.

His mother sat with a relieved sigh and a weary smile, smoothing her skirts and drinking deeply. Her gaze over the rim observed me with canny alertness, however. Though a pale blue, her eyes reminded me of Marskal's habitual suspicion.

"There now," she said. "It's lovely to assemble a big meal when one's boy comes home, but it's a lot of work to do at the last moment. Smart of me to have five daughters to pitch in." She winked at me, exactly as Alisa had. "Call me Merry, by the way," she said. "Marks will have told you not to bother memorizing names, but mine you should know, don't you think?"

Not sure how to reply to that, I gave her an easy smile. "He did tell me that. How did you know, Merry?"

"He always does." She chuckled, a sound like the fire logs cracking. "Every one of his friends he brought round, he'd tell 'em so. You're the first girl he's brought home, though. Do you plan to marry him?"

~ 26 ~

I CHOKED ON my wine, then set it aside so it wouldn't happen again. "No," I said, quite definitively. I'd pretend for Marskal, but only so far.

"No?" She pursed her lips. "That means he hasn't asked you."

"That means I have no intention of marrying your son."

She frowned at me. "Well, that's just silly. My son is the best of men. He'd have been married long since if he hadn't been so determined to hold out for the right one." She considered me. "I can see why you fit his standards, though. Marskal never was satisfied with farming, with the regular girls hereabouts. Always wanting to travel, always saying there's more to the world."

"Marskal is the best of men," I agreed, picking the safest part of her speech to respond to. How had Marskal come to be so quiet, coming from such a garrulous family?

"Of course he is." She nodded sharply. "Tala, are you?"

"Yes." A simple, safe answer. One she already knew.

"And a shapeshifter. That means you can become an animal. More than one, some of you can, I hear. How many can you do?"

"Several," I answered, the old, habitual answer coming back to save me. So much easier than explaining.

"Hmpf. So, my grandchildren by you could be shapeshifters,

too?"

"I think you have plenty of grandchildren already," I pointed out, with some acerbity.

To my surprise, she threw her head back and laughed. "That I do, dearie, that I do, but there's always room for more—in my heart and in my home. And you'll do, too. I see why he likes you. Not just a pretty face with an exotic pedigree. You'll do me a favor, will you?"

"All right," I answered faintly, feeling ten steps behind the conversation.

"I want you to—hello, Marks honey." She took Marskal's hand as he came up, still carrying the sleeping infant. "I was just getting to know your lady love here."

"I see that." He sounded wry, but he bent to kiss her cheek when she offered it. "Which is odd because I distinctly remember asking you to leave Zynda be."

She waved that off. "I'm your mother and I know full well you'll be gone by morning. I'm taking my window of opportunity."

Marskal gave me a rueful smile his mother couldn't see.

"Now, Zynda, I was saying—with all your magic, I'm counting on you to take care of my son. He's a wonderful warrior, but reckless at times.

Marskal closed his eyes with a pained expression, shaking his head slightly. I had to laugh. "Marskal is the least reckless mossb—man I've ever known," I said with perfect honesty. "He's forever prepared, careful, and alert. An excellent fighter. I trust him with my life. Which he's saved several times."

"Has he now?" Merry looked pleased, beaming up at Marskal and squeezing his hand, still holding him captive. "I like to hear that. Well done, my boy." She gazed at him, face full of love. "A mother's fear never goes away, you know," she said to me. "You think it will, once they're not so tiny and fragile, but it doesn't. You'll see. You learn to live with it and manage the best you can. Help your mother up, dear."

She stood, not needing his help at all, crossed over to me and kissed me on the top of my head. "There's my blessing, Tala girl, not that you need it. Next time you come through, stay a little longer. You kids!" she called out. "Get yourselves in the kitchen and help with clean up, or I won't say where I hid the pudding."

Marskal hipped onto the arm of the chair I sat in, studying my face, his own expression chagrined. "I'm really sorry. I'd hoped to head her off, but I got distracted."

"Your father," I agreed. "I believe it was a team effort."

He winced. "I should have predicted that, instead of hoping they'd give you some room for a one-evening visit."

"They love you," I replied, realizing it was true. That it was something I could easily see in all of them. "I don't mind a bit of interrogation. Now I know where you get it."

"A strike to the heart. Nicely played." But he smiled at me, catching me peeking at the baby. "Do you want to hold her?"

"No!" I said it too forcefully, one of the other sisters looking over. "I mean. I'm not good with babies. She'll just start wailing again."

He was watching me with those quiet, too-knowing eyes. "She won't die, Zynda."

"I know that." But did I? So much fear in me. Where had it all come from? I opened my arms. "Fine. But the moment she cries, you're taking her back."

"Deal," he replied, with a slight smile, setting the baby in my arms.

She was warm and soft, squiggling a little and then settling again, opening her perfect little mouth in a yawn, then subsiding again. Tangled emotions rose up in me, chewing with little teeth. I looked at Marskal, feeling helpless against the tide of it all. "She's really beautiful," I said. "Perfect."

He stroked my cheek. "Maybe it wasn't fair to bring you here, but I wanted you to see this. To feel what it's like to be part of something."

I leaned into his hand, his touch and the weight of the baby in my arms bringing up far too much in me. There I was, the mermaid stranded on dry land, full of longing for what I could never have. I'd never thought I'd envy the mossbacks anything, but this simplicity had a lure to it I hadn't known about. Marskal saw it all as this simple, and it... just wasn't. Even without the ability to shift, I remained at least half other.

"Marskal," I whispered. "We have to—"

He laid the finger over my lips, smiling sadly. "Don't say it. Not tonight. For this evening, let's just be. We're having pudding and putting the kids to bed. Then we'll break out the good liquor and maybe have some dancing. Or we can go to my place and sleep, if you're tired."

I swallowed back my words and fashioned them into a smile. "Liquor and dancing sounds good. You know how we Tala like that."

He kissed me, a hint of fervency in it. "I do know that. And I love that about my quicksilver girl."

WE STAYED UP late, drinking the good stuff and dancing to the fiddle and drum music played by another of Marskal's sisters and her husband. Then Marskal took me to his cottage. It was small, yes, but set next to a still pond that gleamed in the starlight. Moranu's moon had gone nearly to new, and her dark power flowed through me as I leaned back in Marskal's arms, listening to his low voice describe his plans for the place.

He'd been thinking about possible solutions for where we'd live—a place in Annfwn and maybe one nearer Ordnung, too. The pond wasn't anything like the ocean, but the River Danu ran past the far boundary and we could dig a channel from it to make it into a lake deep enough for me to swim in. We could summer there and then travel over the pass to Annfwn for the winters—or even sail to Nahanau. The kids would love that.

Just tired and drunk enough not to argue, I let him paint the picture for me. One night of pretending, I'd promised after all.

We made love in his bed. The one his mother promised me another sister made sure had fresh sheets, before she kissed me on both cheeks and wished me a good night's rest. I'd had it in my mind that we shouldn't, but I didn't have the heart to hold him off, he was so happy to have me there. And the night wasn't yet done.

The next day would be soon enough to begin the inevitable separation.

I fell asleep with my head tucked into my place on his shoulder, the taste and smell of him in my human senses as keen as in any form. I'd remember it forever.

A shout awakened me, and I startled. Marskal. He shouted again. Afraid and in danger.

Without thought, I slipped into tiger form. Claws at the ready to fight and defend.

Then realized where I was. Marskal's bed. Creaking beneath my furry weight.

So easy, that shifting. As if it had been right at my fingertips. And simple to shift back. Marskal shouted again, struggling against the sheet, trying to punch. I didn't know what to do. So I kissed him. On the cheek. Then, when he stilled, on the mouth.

I felt it when the nightmare loosed its hold, when he relaxed, then kissed me back.

"Zynda," he murmured, and curled himself around me. I stayed that way for a while, listening to his breath deepen and even out. Then I slipped out of bed, pulled the jeweled pin from my sleeve, and used it to wind up my hair.

HE FOUND ME out by his pond in the morning, wrapped in my fur cloak and watching Glorianna's sun gild the mirror of it with rose and gold. Soft hills covered in new snow rolled white and pristine around. In the distance, cows lowed, harmonizing with people's voices, an occasional door slamming. I couldn't see any of them, but Marskal's family was all around.

"You woke early," he commented, handing me a cup of hot tea.

I smiled at him as I took it, not saying I'd never gone back to sleep. That slip into tiger form had been so natural, so easy. Like before. And yet, I didn't yet want to tell him. Soon enough something would disturb the glassiness of the pond and the white of the hills, but I wasn't yet ready to throw the rock.

"Breakfast at the big house still all right with you?" he asked. When I nodded, he held out a hand to help me up.

AFTER A BREAKFAST as hearty as the dinner the night before—with Marskal conscripted to feed two toddlers, while Shanna, Robbie and several other children asked me one question after another—we said our goodbyes. To please the kids, I summoned the staymachs with more flourish than necessary, coaxing the horses into one black with a white mane and tail and one white with black. My own bird I suggested into a more exotic palette and it obligingly manifested in a larger size, with rainbow bright coloring.

The kids applauded with glee, which at least satisfied the ones who'd hoped I'd shapeshift for them. Marskal—and surprisingly, his mother—put an end to their pleas, saying they were being rude. I found myself tempted to shift, just to play with them a little. I could give them pony rides, do aerial acrobatics as a falcon, or show them what a real tiger looks like.

Marskal's nieces and nephews made me want to share the joy, rather than doing it only for my own pleasure. A new perspective for me, that before shapeshifting had always been about pride and pleasing myself. But I needed to try again on my own, not with an audience. I had no idea what had let go in me, that the wall had crumbled away. Maybe just time, like Marskal had claimed all along. Maybe the dark of Moranu's moon. Maybe something else.

Most of all, I wasn't sure how to tell Marskal.

"You've been quiet," Marskal observed after we'd been on the road a while. The paved highway Uorsin had created made for even faster travel and we wove through the steady flow of carts, riders, and walkers with ease, heading south for Windroven in fair weather.

I laughed. "Coming from you, that's saying something."

He gave me a crooked smile. "Now you know why—with my family, I never could get a word in edgewise. I finally went for being quiet and listening as the better part of valor."

"Ah." That made sense. "It all comes together for me now."

With a self-conscious shrug, he returned his gaze to the road, back to his relentless scanning for danger. "For better or worse, they made me who I am."

"They're good people," I said softly. "I'm glad you took me there."

"Yes?" He glanced at me, checking for honesty, then smiled in earnest. "Good. When I—after Uorsin fell... You know, it was days and days of dealing with the aftermath of Illyria's black magic. She was gone, but her living dead remained." His face had gone cold and bloodless, the gaze he focused on the road ahead haunted. "So many people I knew—friends from the guard, from town. Guys I'd grown up with and girls I'd kissed. She'd made them into her puppets and we couldn't do anything but chop them into the smallest pieces possible and burn them. The pyres lasted for days and that smoke smell..."

He shook his head. "I thought I'd never get it out of my head. I tried to tell myself that they weren't *them* anymore. That our spirit or whatever makes us alive and ourselves, that it was gone and just this magic moving them around, but even then I knew." He blew out a long breath. "We did what we had to do, clearing Ordnung and the township of every last one, every stinking vestige of her magic."

"Did you lose any of your family?" I asked carefully, realizing I should have thought to ask before.

"Miraculously no. They cleared out early, mostly because I was able to send them a message when we fled Ordnung, and Harlan did me the favor of passing the word for his Vervaldr to look the other way when they slipped past the barricades. I was lucky that way—as so many weren't. But I thought I might never be the same again, that I'd never be able to break open the shell

I put around my heart to get through those days. I needed something of normal life, of beauty and love so badly."

Things fell into place for me. "And you first saw me right after."

He gave me an odd look. "I suppose that's true. Maybe a couple of weeks later, but that's not my point. Before that, I went home. That's when Her Majesty restored our lands—one of her first acts as High Queen—and she sent me home. All of us who'd been on pyre duty were given leave to go home for a few days, those of us who had a home close enough to Castle Ordnung.

"My family can be a pain, but being around them, working on the house and the land to get it livable, farmable again—picking out and fixing up my cottage—it gave me something of myself back again. That's what I wanted you to experience last night. I thought it might help."

"Thank you," I said, as gravely as I could. Yet another gift he gave me. "I think it did help."

"I wanted you to know, too," he continued, watching the road, "what they mean to me. You tease me about taking responsibility for everyone, but that—them, other families like them—that's what's good in this world, worth fighting for. The thought of those *Deyrr* creatures coming there again—." He broke off with a sharp shake of his head.

"Is that what you dreamed last night?"

He slid me a sideways look, rueful. "Sorry about that. And yes—I dreamed of dragons scouring the farmland, incinerating the children and you. And I couldn't reach any of you. No need to interpret that one."

Guilt and regret filled my heart. He shouldn't suffer such things because of me. "You don't have to come with me to free the dragon. I'm all right on my own."

His face set into annoyed lines. "Don't start down that path again. You need me to protect you. What if one of those sleeper spies—"

"We need to end this thing between us," I broke in. "I should have said so earlier. You could have stayed at Ordnung and I could have gone on my own to Windroven. In fact, you could still go back. You should go back."

He actually looked amused. "We both know that's not happening, even if I hadn't vowed to Her Majesty to guard you through to the end."

"Fine," I bit out, not surprised, but still annoyed that it hadn't been so easy. "But anything personal between us is over with."

I'd expected hurt or anger, but he laughed. "Good luck with that."

I glared at him. "I guess it would be too much to ask you to respect my wishes in this."

He looked over, studying me. "Did my family seem that terrible? Or is this about your terror of maybe bearing your own child and having to watch them die?"

My heart snapped closed, choking me. "I never said that."

"You didn't have to." His gentle brown gaze held compassion. "I understand the things you don't say. And I know you love me as much as I love you, so you haven't fooled me."

The cold air made my teeth ache and I realized I'd been staring at him in open-mouthed shock. I shook my head slowly. "I'm not in love with you, Marskal."

He grinned, apparently greatly amused by this entire conversation. "Yes, you are. You might not say the words, but you show me all the time. It's in your eyes right now. You just don't know that's what you're feeling."

"*You* don't know what I'm feeling," I shot back.

"Have you ever been in love?" he asked.

"No." I said it triumphantly, certain I'd made my point.

"Exactly."

I scowled at him. "You are making no sense."

"Sure, I am. If you'd been in love, if you had experienced love, then you'd know that's what you feel for me. As it is, you've been writing it off to passion, or flirtation, or whatever. The real problem is your conviction that we can't be together."

"I think we can't be together because we're nothing alike! We come from different worlds and we'll go back to those different worlds. I will never be like one of your sisters, happily tending the farm and making babies for you to play with and whisper to sleep."

He raised his brows at me. "With all your observational skills, you'll have noticed I'm not a farmer."

I set my jaw. "I've explained over and over that if I don't take Final Form, I'll have to find a compatible father. Shapeshifter, not mossback."

"You need to outbreed and you know it," he shot back. "More inbreeding will only exacerbate your problems. Your chances of viable babies go way up with me. Ask any expert in husbandry."

"I'm not a broodmare," I said through gritted teeth.

"Then why do you claim your decisions are based on that? If you didn't view yourself that way, the argument that I shouldn't father your children wouldn't even come up," he reasoned.

Something about that phrase gutted me. *Father your children*. It made me *want* in that horrible, famished way. The mermaid longing for land. "I've told you over and over, I probably can't even have children," I said, willing my reply to be as rational and even as his.

But he glanced at me with eyes full of understanding. "I

know and accept that. But if you can have children, I want to be the one to father them. And if you can't, I can provide you with many nieces and nephews to love. And we could adopt children to raise. Wars make orphans and there will be plenty who'd benefit from a loving mother like you."

I wanted to cry. To scream at him. To throw him to the ground and pummel him or kiss him silent. "You've come a long way from seducing me into considering you as a lover for one night to demanding to be the only father of my children."

He regarded me seriously. "That's true. You've changed me. And you've given me reason to hope, so…" He shrugged and grinned at my consternation. "You can't ask me not to hope, when being with you has made these the best weeks of my entire life. I'm greedy. You've given me more of yourself than I ever expected, and now I want even more than that. I want it all and I want forever." He ignored my black look. "Also, I've been thinking—remember Dafne's circles on the maps? My family has been in this region for generations. I'm as connected to any of this as she is. I think it's not only possible, it's likely that I am compatible."

I gaped at him. I couldn't seem not to. "You've been thinking about this ever since."

He nodded solemnly. "We're a good fit. You can't deny that."

"I can deny it!"

He laughed, surprising me, shaking his head in amusement. "True or false: admit it. You're in love with me."

Caught like that, I couldn't summon the lie. It would have been easier to drive him away, tell him that I'd lost interest. Cut this thing between us off cleanly and neatly. Though it was far too late for neat. And though it would be easier to drive him away, to play a game and make him angry, I couldn't do it. Gone was the person I'd been, who could pretend that truth and lies were mutable, just another part of the spectrum. Which left me only bitter honesty.

Time to tell him and break his heart. *That* would be his forever.

"I can shift again." There, I said it. Made it real.

He gazed at me in astonishment, then with such sincere joy that my heart shuddered under the pressure of it. "What? When?" He asked. "You didn't tell me!"

He made me smile, even with the heartache. "Last night, when you startled me awake. I thought you were in danger and slipped into tiger form for a moment without thinking."

"You were defending me." He had a pleased quirk to his expression, a knowingness that bothered me.

"I wasn't thinking," I repeated, realizing as I said it that I'd failed to make a good argument.

"If you say. I knew you'd never really lost it. It makes sense that you simply needed to relax and allow it to come back to you naturally again." His smile radiated such pride and love that I had to look away.

"You're not thinking this through," I told him softly, holding his gaze, and his smile faded. Such was my effect on him. I hated that we had to do this.

"Final Form, you mean," he replied after a long moment.

I looked at him and he returned my gaze soberly. "Yes. Once I free the dragon under Windroven, I'll go see Kiraka and take Final Form. It's time for us to accept the inevitability of a goodbye."

He was studying me. "I've been thinking about what you said, about the completion of cycles, and how *Deyrr*'s reanimation of creatures takes them outside of that. And how you don't like to use magic to do anything that interferes with that cycle."

I frowned at him, not understanding the direction of this argument. "So?"

"So, it occurs to me that Final Form breaks that cycle. Why is that all right with you when the rest isn't? By becoming the dragon you'll make yourself immortal and unable to bear children. That's not part of the cycle of life."

"It's not the same thing."

"Isn't it?"

I shrugged him off. "Besides, this is for the greater good. It's not about me and my personal happiness. I'm taking Final Form. Nothing will stop me."

He studied me, contemplating. "Dafne is a companion to Kiraka, keeping her sane and with some of her humanity, you said."

"That's how I understand it," I replied warily, not sure where he was going with this.

He nodded, that decisive gesture. "Then I'll go with you. I'll be your companion."

"What? No."

"Yes. I've been thinking about this."

"You've been thinking about a thrice-cursed lot of things."

"Yes, this is important to me. You are important, so I've been thinking through all the possibilities. You'll need someone to be your human companion if you take dragon form. Who better than the person who loves you better than anyone in the world?"

"Anyone but you!"

He narrowed his eyes at me. "You don't mean that."

"I do mean it. You have a life to live. I know you want children to add to that horde of a family of yours." Thinking of Dafne's swelling pregnancy, how perfect little Iris had fit just so in my arms, irrational jealousy filled me. "And if you think I'd forgive you taking a wife and happily impregnating her while being my friend and human companion, I wouldn't."

"You'd incinerate my wife?" He tried to sound aghast, but the corners of his mouth quirked with delight.

I'd trapped myself, revealing too much. "I won't have to do that as you'll be off on the farm bedding her in your little cottage. I won't have to see it." Ugh, but the image was far too vivid in my mind. The thought of another woman in his bed, sleeping wrapped in his scent and arms did make me want to breathe fire.

"I don't think you'd put it out of your mind so easily," he said, still looking pleased, as if he could read my thoughts as he claimed to. "You'd know and you'd hate it, thinking of me with another woman, living the life you could have had."

As always, he was right, but Moranu take me if I'd admit it. "You're wrong. I won't give you and your boring mossback life another thought after I become the dragon."

"Liar," he said, grinning.

I didn't know how to deal with him, how to make him see. I growled, feeling the tiger wanting to rise up.

Marskal held out a hand, expression going serious. "Don't upset yourself. I'd never leave you. I don't want another woman, ever. You've spoiled me for mossback girls. I want you and I'm staying with you. I love you, no matter what form you wear."

"Marskal," I said hopelessly, "you can't give up your whole life."

"You're giving up yours. You expect I'd do less?"

"It's not the same. I'm sacrificing for a greater good; you'd be doing it for me, and I'm not worth it."

He dropped his hand, face going stern with determination. "Don't tell me what you're worth to me."

"This was always my plan," I said, holding my voice as

steady as I could. "I never expected more than that. Never expected…" To fall in love. That was this tangle of emotion. Moranu take the man, he was right.

He knew it, too, easily filling in what I hadn't said. "I love you, too," he said quietly. "That's not a tragedy. It's a gift."

"A gift I can't accept."

"No? Remember who gave it to you."

When I frowned, puzzled, he smiled. "A goddess is guiding your steps. I'd be careful of thwarting Moranu's plan."

Having had enough of him and his certainty, I let go. Not reaching, but slipping down. Taking falcon form, I let the fur cloak drop away and took to the icy blue sky.

Taking refuge in flight and not thinking about anything at all.

~ 27 ~

I CIRCLED ABOVE, watching Marskal ride the one horse, leading the other, my staymach bird on one shoulder, his on the other. He'd bundled up my fur cloak neatly on the saddle, riding along in his direct, unhurried way. I'd considered flying ahead to Windroven. I could have been there and gone before he reached it. If freeing the dragon wasn't too difficult.

That, however, would be the coward's way out. I'd run from our conversation, but I was done escaping all the time. If I was going to take Final Form, then I needed to embrace every consequence, good and bad, that came with it.

Besides, I missed him.

Marskal spotted me, his face lifted to watch my descent. He held up a leather-clad arm, so I landed on it, careful not to pierce his flesh with my talons. Looking into my eyes, he caressed my head with a gloved finger. "Welcome back, quicksilver girl," he murmured. "Good flight?"

I hopped off his arm, landing on human feet and summoning a fur cloak and boots to wear also.

Marskal raised his eyebrows. "Nice trick."

As if nurtured by the time of disuse, my shapeshifting ability did indeed feel as if it had grown. A vast reserve of power awaited, like a reservoir deep beneath the earth. It made me wonder if Kiraka had intended that, priming me for the shift to

Final Form.

"I still think you're impossible," I told Marskal.

He smiled easily at me. "Likewise. See how well suited we are?"

I shook my head at him in exasperation. "You can stay with me until we release the dragon. Then we part ways."

"No," he replied. "Hungry? My mother packed lunch."

I huffed at him, but I let him feed me anyway.

THOUGH WE DIDN'T send our staymach birds ahead—as I hadn't thought there would be anyone there to understand their mind messages—Queen Amelia and her consort, Ash, were awaiting us at the castle gates, clearly alerted by the Avonlidgh watch. The castle, built into the volcanic rock of the high peak, reminded me oddly of the carved dragons at the Nahanaun harbor, entwined into their perches. There was no peak or crater as at Nahanau, but sulfuric smoke lingered in the wintery air, a distinctive odor I remembered well, and ash sifted with the occasional flurry of snowflakes. The rumbling I heard might be the sleeping volcano—or dragon—or could be the violent surf dashing itself on the cliffs below.

As we made the last turn up the narrow road that climbed the old volcano, we easily spotted them. Queen Amelia looked like a lavish hothouse flower against the winter-bare rocks, in her elaborate pink gown, a fur-trimmed cloak in a deeper shade over it. With her hood thrown back, the wind off the ocean caught her famous rose-gold curls, that the poets called the color of sunrise, grown much longer now. Ash, a step behind her and dressed in deep green, stood as still as the Sentinel stones we'd sailed through months ago.

"The last time I did this," Marskal murmured to me, "we brought her husband's corpse home. The day was just as bleak."

I cast him a narrow glance. "I hope *you* aren't being superstitious now."

His eyes crinkled at the corners. "Of course not. Mossbacks don't care for such things."

Because I wanted to stick my tongue out at him, and even I wouldn't do that in front of a queen, even one not mine, I studiously stared into the distance, ignoring his chuckle. As one we dismounted, walking the last few steps. Marskal bowed to Amelia. I inclined my head in respect. The poets call her Glorianna's avatar and, while Ami looked nothing like Salena, she carried her mother's shapeshifter magic in her blood, too— which manifested in her unearthly beauty. In contrast, Ash's scarred visage revealed little of his Tala partblood, but his apple-green eyes were those of a healer.

I acknowledged him, too, belatedly wondering if he had enough mind magic to read the staymachs. Something to find out.

"Cousin Zynda," Ami said in her musical voice. "Lieutenant Marskal. Come in out of the wind." We followed them into the inner courtyard. "I understand you're here to rid me of vermin in the cellars," she continued.

"Ah, you received some letters then?"

"From Dafne ages ago and now Her Majesty sent one only yesterday, commanding me to render all assistance and not to be a brat about it. Verbatim." Her lovely mouth twisted in wry humor. "So here I am, graciously rendering all assistance. I should tell you, though, that the rumbling has subsided considerably since the Feast of Moranu. Maybe the dragon went back to sleep?"

I didn't know, but small hairs of foreboding rose on my skin. I reached out with my magic, sensing the presence of dragon that felt like Kiraka, but couldn't discern more. "We'll find out."

"Go ahead." Ami smiled prettily. "But I'll be put out if you wreck my house. What do you need?"

I glanced at Marskal who returned it blandly. Up to me, then. "I just need access to the depths of the volcano, I suppose."

"We need access," Marskal corrected. "And I can find my way through the lower tunnels, Your Highness, if we have your leave to go where we may."

Ami smiled at him, so radiantly lovely that even the stoic Marskal looked dazzled. I suppressed a snicker at his expense. "That's right, Lieutenant," Ami said. "I recall you and some of the other Hawks whiled away the time during my lying in by exploring the tunnels."

He bowed again. "We did, and—"

A small furry shape hurtled out the doors to the inner castle, followed by another. One resolved into a little girl with curls like her mother's, but in Tala raven black. She threw herself at me, climbing me like a tree, small fingers digging with clawlike tenacity, shrieking, "Auntie Andi! Auntie Andi!" The other remained a small black cat, but—not to be outdone—climbed my other side with actual claws, ending perched on my shoulder.

Ami lost all regal bearing and gasped in maternal horror. "Stella! Astar! That is *not* your Auntie Andi. Get down immediately and greet your Auntie Zynda appropriately."

Ash stepped forward, ready to assist, though Marskal only grinned at me, no help at all. "Stella—what have we discussed about licking people?" Ash said sternly.

For Stella was indeed licking my cheek, snuffling happily, while Astar purred in my ear. "That's all right," I told him. "This

I actually know how to handle." I threw Marskal a significant look, but his grin remained undimmed.

Turning my head, I sniffed Stella's cheek and licked her in return, sharing her scent, murmuring to her in Tala and sharing some baby thoughts with her, as I would with a staymach. Her eyes widened and she stuck her little finger in her mouth. With a pang, I realized Anya's daughter might have been just like Stella, the magic of the mark thick in the air around her. My staymach bird that had taken wing in startlement circled her head, and she immediately focused on it, drawn by its magic.

"Would you like to play?" I asked. "Must be good and stay in human form." She transferred her intense deep blue gaze to me and nodded. "Hold out your finger," I said, the warm memory of teaching Marskal the same catching me unexpectedly. I looked his way to find him watching me with sensual intensity, no doubt remembering also. Setting Stella down, I showed her how to hold the bird, and nudged an image into her mind of how to exchange pictures with it. A very simple child's game.

Her brother dug his claws into my shoulder, feline eyes glinting entirely the wrong color. We'd have to work on that.

But I rubbed whiskers with him, giving him the same greeting, and he relaxed his claws, purring. I gave him a little suggestion, promising that he could play with the staymach, too, if he'd take human form. He shivered into a toddler again. Naked, but that could be fixed with more practice. Reaching for Stella's staymach, he screeched like a cat, and I had to firmly remind him of manners. He quieted, wide eyes just like his twin's, and put out his finger for the bird Marskal offered, so they'd have one each.

I smiled gratefully, and gave Astar the same instructions. Both twins put their heads together, murmuring to the staymachs and showing them to Ami and Ash.

"Now who's the baby whisperer?" Marskal murmured, brown eyes alight with quiet mirth. He nodded when I raised my brows. "I know they call me that."

"Well, I might not know babies," I replied, "but I know how to herd unruly shapeshifter children. See what a narrow escape you've had?"

"I don't want to escape," he replied in that making-a-vow voice. "I want that."

I made a sound of frustration. "It's never going to—"

"You're hired," Ami said, swanning over and waving her hands at me in wonder, interrupting our hushed exchange. "Stay here forever. I command it. Ash—disarm the lieutenant. They're never allowed to leave."

"If only," Ash fervently agreed.

"True," Ami sighed. "The Tala nurses Andi sent hated...well, *everything* here so much that I let them go home. We've yet to find a new nurse capable of keeping Willy and Nilly from escaping at every turn, much less shifting into something new every week."

"Must run in the family," Marskal noted blandly, and I glared at him, making no dent in his good cheer whatsoever.

Ami laughed, a sound like sunshine made musical. "We do have some information you might need. So, in return for ridding me of an unwanted dragon and taming my beastly children, we can at least fill you in and feed you before sending you into the bowels of the volcano."

Marskal leaned in, murmuring into my ear, "See? It's not just me and my family."

OVER DINNER, WE told them about the sleeper spies, a topic Ursula's missive had alluded to, but hadn't detailed.

Ami and Ash exchanged a long look, and he cleared his throat. "We've had them here," he explained. "That's what we planned to tell you."

A chill—which had up until then been adequately fended off by the roaring fire in the stone fireplace big enough for Marskal to stand upright in—ran across my skin.

Marskal put a hand to his blade, scanning the shadows as if something might leap out at us. "What happened?"

"Various creatures," Ash replied. "Mostly a twisted sort of wolf. All as you describe. Mindless, but with some sort of ability to hide themselves until they attack."

"That's the other reason the Tala nurses went home," Ami put in, a wrinkle in her pert nose. "They called the creatures evil shapeshifters—and a lot more in Tala that I couldn't get them to translate—and refused to stay. They left though the rest of us were snowbound. Suffice to say we had an interesting Feast of Moranu."

Ash took her hand and kissed her fingertips, green eyes full of meaning. "Good with the bad, yes?"

She blushed, prettily, as she did everything, but she had a determined set to her chin. "The best ever." She said it like a vow.

I looked away from it, catching Marskal's knowing gaze.

"We've killed all the ones we've found," Ash continued, his scarred face sobering. "But I'm certain there are more. The tunnels are so narrow, it never made sense to me to take more men down there. I didn't see how we could kill enough of the creatures to justify the men we'd lose. It was easiest to wall off the tunnels. I'm having the men unblock a passage for you while we eat. Since we closed them off, we haven't seen any more of the creatures. Still—I sometimes think I sense them, like a strange scent on the air."

"You're a Tala partblood, yes?" I asked.

Ami glared at me and opened her mouth, but Ash squeezed her hand and smiled. "Zynda doesn't mean it as an insult. Yes, I am. With sufficient shapeshifter blood magic to heal, but not to shift."

I examined him with that inner sense I seemed to have gained. "You came to it late in life, or you would have. I'm sorry."

He gave me a funny half smile. "Don't be. I'm happy in my skin. Grateful for the life I have." His gaze wandered to Ami again and softened. "More than grateful."

"I mostly ask because I think shapeshifter blood can detect them," I said. "I feel like I can smell them, too—only it's not exactly a scent."

Ash nodded slowly, eyes hard again in his corrugated face. "Same. Also, there's something else. I've been working with various groups to locate Tala partbloods in hiding, especially escaped convicts."

"I know something of that. King Rayfe and Queen Andromeda are committed to repatriating all of our partbloods."

"Yes." He looked grim. "But they're disappearing before we can get to them."

"Disappearing?" Marskal asked.

Ash shrugged. "We get word of one or more. Our people go to meet with them—we've been having good luck at making contact and drawing them out in the recent past—but then they're gone without a trace." He raised his brows at me. "Others have mentioned a strange scent."

"Moranu preserve us," Marskal swore.

Ash dipped his chin. "I couldn't have said it better."

WITH NO REASON to delay and feeling the press of *Deyrr*'s stink, I resolved to descend into the tunnels that night. Marskal, of course, came with me.

"You don't need to." I tried yet again. We'd long since passed the storage cellars—along with the guard stationed at the narrow, unbricked opening—and entered corridors carved by lava flow rather than the castle's builders. The heat grew steadily, thick and humid, the hiss of vapors combining with the roar of the surf on the other side of the rock walls.

"Don't start," Marskal replied, evenly and without inflection. Though his sword remained sheathed, he'd drawn his heavy knife, carrying it at the ready in one hand, a torch in the other.

"Are you going to stick the dragon with that knife?"

He met the mocking gaze I tossed over my shoulder with grim severity. "If necessary."

"You know I can't save you if—"

"Oops," he cut in. "That counts as starting. Don't. How about you share your plan instead?"

I sighed, which he ignored, then twisted up my hair, pinning it in place as we walked. The oppressive, moist heat was truly unbearable. "I remember the feel of the magic spell on Nahanau when Nakoa used the connection with Dafne to wake Kiraka. I ought to be able to replicate it. This dragon has been on the verge of waking longer. If not, I have another idea that might work."

"What do you think it means, that the volcano has been quieter?" Marskal asked.

"I don't know," I replied, troubled by that, too. "I hope a

sleeper spy hasn't gotten to the dragon."

Unsurprised, Marskal nodded, grim. "That's my fear also."

I followed the sense of dragon, indicating the direction and Marskal finding the appropriate tunnel. Until we reached those deeper than any he'd explored before, twisted channels with narrow openings we had to crawl through.

We emerged into a somewhat bigger chamber, large enough that the torchlight didn't penetrate the shadows, and the stink hit me. I held up a hand to signal Marskal. He immediately thrust the torch into a crevice, and drew his sword, too. All at my slightest gesture of warning. Love quick-punched me, an emotion I didn't have time for.

All was still for a moment, the only sounds the gasp and hiss of the venting gases. I wasn't at all sure what had alerted me; perhaps I'd imagined it. The torchlight flickered, as did Marskal's eyes, darting as they scoured the gloom.

"There," he whispered, pointing his sword and taking a half-step forward. As if summoned, a massive creature leapt from those shadows, snarling with rage, reeking of death. With a speed belying its size it juked around the sphere defined by Marskal's reach, fangs bared. Going for my throat.

I dodged with shapeshifter speed, slipping into tiger form, while Marskal spun on its flank, stabbing it in the side of its shaggy neck with his sword. The blow should have felled—or at least staggered—the beast, but the creature didn't so much as pause as it stalked toward me, ripping the hilt from his hand. Marskal frowned, nonplussed, as the wolf-thing prowled forward, the sword still lodged in its hide. Then his usual determined visage snapped into place and he advanced again, armed only with his big dagger.

I growled deep my throat as I instinctively backed away, my tail lashing with feline rage. *Don't let the instincts overwhelm you*, I told myself, mindful of Marskal's advice to Zyr to fight with the mind of a person. Oh, but it felt good to be the tiger, to rend and tear, to be powerful again. With a roar I leapt at the creature and we tumbled together, jaws snapping, claws slicing.

Its teeth found my shoulder and I yowled with pain. Without thought my rear legs pulled to my abdomen and I raked down, eviscerating the squirming monster. Putrefied innards and black ichor spilled from the wound, but the creature continued to fight. Its claws sliced my flank. I barely felt the wound as I tried desperately to grapple the beast. It was no use, the creature was too much larger, too much stronger than I was.

But it didn't have to be. With a burst of will I summoned the form of an elephant. Toppling the creature with the sudden shift, I pinned it under my massive gray foot. As if we'd rehearsed such tag-teaming, Marskal dashed in, grabbing the sword protruding from the wolf-creature's neck and, with a deft motion, severed its spine.

But it didn't stop struggling. Just as the pieces of those fish-birds had kept fluttering grotesquely on the deck of the *Hákyrling*. I reached down with my trunk and, avoiding its snarling head, wrapped around its thick neck and pulled, decapitating the writhing horror. It stared at me with mad eyes, jaws continuing to snap voicelessly—and for a moment I imagined I saw a human being trapped inside that monstrous form. Appalled, I gave into my instincts and squeezed with all my might. The bones crumbled, pulping under my grip. I released the disgusting mess and allowed myself a victory trumpet.

Coming back to human form was a relief, if only to shed the disgusting ichor. Marskal, his blade still impaling the beast's chest, assessed me. "You took some hits."

"Healed by shifting back," I assured him. "And at least—"

"Watch out," he warned as he used his off hand to push me to the side. The half-crushed carcass of the headless beast was attempting to rise. With four efficient strokes, he severed each of the legs at the knee. The claws continued to sheath and unsheathe.

"These...things, they don't die easy," he muttered. "This one seems neutralized, if not exactly dead. We should probably burn the remains. Do you know what they are?"

"Nothing natural. Definitely stinks of *Deyrr*, but the magic is different," I told him. "Like the shark. A variation. But a fortunate one for us. I have this. Stand back."

He withdrew his blade and circled behind me. I applied the magic I'd prepared, vanishing the still-moving remains of the beast.

"Onward?" Marskal asked, cleaning his blade.

"Yes, though I'm afraid of what we'll find."

"More of the same, I'm guessing," he replied.

AN ACCURATE GUESS. We killed five more of the creatures, all of them monstrous, though none in exactly the same way. Each continued to battle despite a multitude of mortal wounds; only dismemberment worked. Each focused on me, ignoring Marskal unless he interposed himself. Which he insisted on doing, ignoring my arguments.

Over time, the relentlessness of their assaults began to wear on us. We pushed through the fatigue, but each attack was more difficult to repulse than the last. The third beast scored a bite on Marskal's leg, slowing him. The fifth nearly took his eye, but he deflected with his forearm at the last instant, taking three deep gashes there from the creature's claws. Nonetheless, he steadfastly refused to leave my side. I comforted myself that Ash could heal him at the end of all this. We went deeper—and something brushed my mind. Like Kiraka, but... sleepier.

"Who—Kiraka?" The awareness sharpened. *"My love, are you here?"*

The keen-edged excitement in the mind, the excruciating leap of hope, nearly ripped out my already tender heart. Despair and resolve were my companions. Hope only made me hurt and I couldn't handle any more pain. I was too weak.

"No. But I'm a friend. And I know Kiraka. She sent me."

"Kiraka! Where are you?" The mind-voice was thready, as if hoarse from disuse, and clearly confused—like talking to one very old and not seated in reality. The volcano rumbled, fires roaring somewhere off to my right. The heat became unbearable. Sweat rolled down Marskal's face as he watched me for cues, utterly calm and focused.

"Kiraka is awake. She bids you wake, too."

"Kiraka is awake. Kiraka is awake." The chant sounded almost childish, and I hesitated to feed the growing hysterical urge to move that emanated from it. The volcano rumbled again, the stone floor of the tunnel shuddering so I staggered sideways, caught by Marskal's steady hand. "Her Highness will be angry if you wreck her castle," he observed. "Work on releasing the dragon without that part, okay?"

I had to laugh. "I'll see what I can do."

"See? Kiraka, I can't see you. I hurt. I can't move. Where are you? Kiraka!" The volcano roared. Or was it the dragon? The thing off to my right that had been venting gave way with a collapse of stone rubble.

"Remember the babies," Marskal said calmly. "Your kin.

Protect them."

We should have evacuated them. Why hadn't I thought of that? My heart fluttered, hummingbird speed, stressed and needing to escape. "We have to get out of here," I breathed.

Marskal's hand closed on my arm. I wondered wildly what he'd done with the knife he'd held. He caught and held my gaze, torchlight and shadows leaping wildly across his face, his brown eyes steady as earth. "Handle it. You know shapeshifters. You have this."

Something thumped, a huge tail hitting rock. "I have to see him, look him in the eye."

"Go," he replied. "I have your back."

"Kiraka!"

"Here, I'm here," I mind-whispered, soothing, adding images and feelings like I would for the toddlers or for a staymach.

"Kiraka..." He crooned the word, ages of love and passion riddling it like venting tunnels of lava. *"I've waited all this time. I was so afraid that..."*

"Don't be afraid. All is well. Kiraka is awake. She's waiting for you. Where are you?"

"Here. But it's so dark. I want out. I'm trapped. These things. Who trapped me?"

"You're inside a volcano where you went to sleep. Remember going to sleep?"

"No."

"That's okay—I'm here to help. The memories will come back."

I followed the call of his voice, wending my way through blind passages, picking over rockfalls. Then we stumbled into a cavern that hadn't seemed to exist a moment ago, and there was the dragon. We faced a ruby eye more than twice our height. An enormous tail thrashed, rocks rattling from the ceiling. The dragon tried to lift his head, but dropped it weakly again.

Wrapped around his gleaming silver scales were nearly a dozen long, fetid tendrils, festooned with pulsing suckers. Each tentacle led back to a malignant lump on the dragon's back, a huge tower of decaying flesh.

The stink of *Deyrr* was nearly unbearable.

"He needs our help." I had to swallow down my sympathetic horror at the sight.

"How do you know it's a male?"

"He's been talking to me. But he's not... entirely sane."

"You say that like you think Kiraka is." He grimaced when I didn't smile. "I'm not surprised, given the nightmares the poor bastard must have been having. How do you want to go about this?"

"If we can cut those tendrils off of him, I can vanish them. I don't want to try it with them attached. Then we can deal with that...whatever it is." I gestured toward the main mass on the dragon's spine.

Marskal nodded grimly, stepping forward. I put a hand on his arm. "You're wounded. Are you up for this?"

"Let's finish it and get out of this place."

Tentatively, we approached the nearest of the vile growths. It stretched from the nexus on the dragon's back all the way along its neck, terminating just below and behind the gargantuan red eye. The scales where the suckers attached were mottled and discolored, flaking away. One of the suckers quivered, like a suckling baby might, and I had to suppress the urge to retch. I reached out, wanting nothing more than to pull the abomination off the lustrous scales of the dragon.

"Wait," cautioned Marskal. I stopped, and Marskal stepped forward. He worked his dagger between the tendril and the dragon and began to pry. The sucker began to spasm, and Marskal grunted with exertion. He put a leg up on a scale for extra leverage, and gripping the blade with both hands, pulled. The cords in his neck stood out, his muscles straining. Finally, after an interminable moment, the sucker released and that segment of the tentacle had a slight droop to it. The scale it had been draining flushed with sparkling silver, already beginning to look healthier.

We shared a look that was a mixture of satisfaction, triumph, and exhaustion. We could do this, but it would take time. Then a horrible screech split the air. Had I been in animal form, I might have been deafened. As it was I merely clutched my ears. All over the dragon, the tendrils unwrapped themselves, withdrawing. The pillar of decaying flesh on the dragon's back moved. Two glassy eyes opened. As I stared into those cold, malevolent orbs, a cetacean memory thrust itself into my consciousness: *kraken.*

"Down!" shouted Marskal as a tendril whipped towards my head. Instead I shifted to my falcon form, soaring above the flailing limb. Marskal stood his ground, resolute, a castle withstanding a siege. As a tentacle flew toward his head he sidestepped and swung his sword, the momentum of the incoming attack adding to the power of his slice. Ichor splashed from the severed appendage and the kraken roared in anguish.

With the behemoth distracted, I stooped for one of its alien eyes and was satisfied to feel it burst under my talons. Too late, a tentacle curled up to protect its ruined organ, pressing into the eye socket. Three more shot up, attempting to snare me. I banked and dipped, a small target for the huge beast, but one of the suckers caught my wing, dragging me down.

I went weak, my magic and life force draining away. Shifting without thought, I took cobra form. My brilliant gold scales were too slick to provide any purchase to the grasping suckers and I slithered free. The serpent instincts clamored to run and hide, but I forced myself to stay, to turn and sink my fangs into one of the whirling tendrils, pumping my venom into it.

No luck. The thrashing didn't slow. I shifted again, becoming a crocodile. I released my bite and snapped down again, cleaving the limb. Two more tentacles darted toward me and I became a hare, bounding over one and under another.

Unlike the wolf-creatures, the kraken treated both Marskal and me as a threat. Part of me worried for him, but despite the limitation of a single body he moved in a graceful and complicated dance, weaving around each whirling tentacle as it came for him and inflicting telling blows with regularity. He seemed at one with his sword, existing completely in the moment. Perhaps Final Form would give me something of that thorough self-knowledge, that complete and steady cohesiveness.

Although he had his back to me, he seemed to sense my gaze. "Don't worry about me," he grunted even as he leaped over a tentacle attempting to sweep his leg. "I've got it distracted. End this."

I looked back to the head of the kraken. Between Marskal and I, we had severed four of its tentacles and half blinded it. The remaining eye was the most vulnerable point on the creature. Taking grizzly bear form, I roared and loped forward. Three tentacles smashed into me and my essence began to drain again, but my momentum and terrible strength carried me through. The kraken turned, slicing its gargantuan beak at me, attempting to snap me in two. But my ursine form was too powerful for it and I twisted free, sinking my teeth into its remaining eye, digging my claws into the socket for purchase. As I spat its repulsive ichor from my maw, its remaining limbs reached for me, but I shifted to heron form and flew above its reach.

Blinded, it flailed helplessly as Marskal meticulously severed each of its remaining appendages, then hacked off its beak. It seemed a long time before I felt strong enough to return to human form and dissipate the still-flailing pieces of the kraken with my remaining magic.

THE DEED DONE, Marskal sat heavily on a rock outcropping, mopping sweat and gore from his brow. "We should go eat and rest," he said. "Come back later."

"What if those things come back? Or the wolf-creatures. I still smell them, lurking in the back caverns." At least they were too afraid to attack.

"Do you have enough magic to finish?" He asked pointedly. "You've gone pale. And I don't know how, but you look thinner."

The relationship between my shapeshifting and other magic had changed. The one somehow fed the other, drawing on my physical form, though I wasn't entirely sure how. I'd have to practice with it, except that changing to Final Form would likely alter everything again. "I think I can do this," I said.

I approached the sleeping dragon and Marskal followed me, sword at the ready. As ever. I leaned palms against the softly scaled hide, like and unlike Kiraka. So much cooler. That couldn't be good. But he grew more silvery in color with the giant parasite gone. Marskal stroked the dragon, too, tentative at first, then with more confidence. He glanced at me, a half smile on his mouth.

"Why is he a different color than Kiraka?"

"I don't know," I murmured thoughtfully, letting my magic

tendrils wind in with the dragon's sleeping mind. "Maybe each individual is different. Reflects who they were as people, perhaps."

"Then you will be a deep, sapphire blue," Marskal replied in the same soft tone. "Like your eyes always are, no matter what form you wear. You'll be beyond beautiful."

My heart tore itself a little at the words, at the sorrow in his voice. But I didn't reply. I found the spark of consciousness deep inside, calling to him as I'd tried calling to Anya's daughter to shift. Coaxing him to hear as Zyr had tried to do with me, showing the path.

The dragon rumbled and stirred. Then lifted his head and opened his eyes. Silver light filled the room. He blinked at us. *"Out,"* he thought at me.

"Yes," I answered. *"Follow us."*

MARSKAL KNEW THE way to the cliff openings onto the sea, so he led while I followed, encouraging the dragon all the while. Sea spray blew in the cave opening, blessedly cool on my overheated skin. Shifting had helped me, but Marskal had no such recourse. Still, he continued on, uncomplaining and undaunted.

We'd been in the tunnels all night and now the sun rose behind the volcano, casting her rays on the turbulent winter sea. At the sight of it, the dragon leapt forward—and, reacting with warrior alertness, even exhausted and injured, Marskal pulled me into a crevice, protecting me with his body as the dragon thundered past, narrowing himself to snakelike slimness, then billowing into full form, his wings snapping open. He flew out and up, trumpeting his freedom, as the sun sparked off of his silver scales in the all the colors of fire.

So beautiful. We'd done it.

Marskal was watching the dragon fly with a rapt expression, Glorianna's sun gilding him with loving fingers of rosy light. He belonged to that world, not to Moranu's shadows. It was time for us to say the final goodbye. The sea churned below, reminding me of my true nature, eternally divided, fighting myself. It would be worse, being the dragon. I knew it in my bones. But it would also be inescapable. There would be no turning back. In time I'd forget that I'd wanted anything else.

His gaze snapped to my face, as if he'd heard my thoughts. I cupped his beloved face in my hands, each line around his mouth and in the corner creases of his eyes a map of all his travels and battles. I kissed him, for the last time, and he returned it with ferocity, wrapping his arms around me with a groan. Our tongues tangled, flavors mingling, and I pressed myself against him, groaning with the longing to stay just like this forever.

But I wrenched myself out of his arms. "I have to go."

He nodded. "Then let's go. With you able to shift again, we can take the diagonal across the mountains. You can get us through the swampy parts."

I was already shaking my head. "Faster still for me to fly. I'll go to Kiraka." Before I could weaken and change my mind. "This is goodbye. You're absolved of your duty."

His jaw clenched, the fire in his eyes not all from the sun. "Don't try that nonsense. You know this has never been about duty for me. And you won't be able to dismiss me so easily."

Not easily, no. Nothing had been more difficult, not even straining to shift. *There is loving and being loved.* "You're right. I'll never forget you." I took a breath, finding it hurt, my chest so tight. "I do love you."

He smiled, caressing my cheek. "It's so good to hear it, at last."

I pulled away from him. "And because I love you, I can't let you give up your life." I pulled the jeweled pin out of my hair and gave it to him. He clutched his fist around it, knuckles going white. "Go find your mossback girl and have many babies. But don't give it to her. Save it for your daughter, maybe. Or just keep it, and remember what we had."

"Zynda," he said, voice ragged, face ravaged. "Don't do this."

"It's done. Don't try come after me. You won't be allowed into Annfwn, so don't even attempt it. If you love me, you can let me go. That's why I'm doing this. For you. Have a good life."

He grabbed me and hauled me up against him. I should have been able to dodge him, which meant I didn't really want to. He kissed me, deep and drugging.

I wanted to resist. I really did. And yet I couldn't find it in me. He fisted one hand in my unbound hair, holding me tethered to him. I'd been prepared for the other being our last kiss. This one caught me off guard, sneaking beneath my skin. The immediate prospect of losing him forever had me clinging to him, savoring these last moments of flesh to flesh. Once I took the Final Form, I'd never feel him again. The thought made me want to weep and rage. Instead I poured it into the kiss, longing rising in me and escaping in a long moan of despair.

"I know," he murmured, soothing me even then. "We'll figure it out. Let's go up and eat, get some sleep. Then we'll talk"

I looked at him, setting the image of him in my memory. "Food and rest don't solve everything, my love."

He opened his mouth, and because I knew I'd never win an argument with him—never had, never would—I became the seabird slipping out of his arms. A sharp pain stabbed at me. Not heartache, but the loss of a feather he grabbed and plucked out.

Let him have it.

I winged out of the cave, into the sky. Putting the rising sun at my back, I headed to Nahanau. And Kiraka.

~ 28 ~

I FLEW DIRECTLY to Kiraka, not stopping in Annfwn or at the
palace in Nahanau. Having learned my lesson with Marskal, I
didn't dare try to say goodbye to anyone else. It was too difficult,
and I wasn't that brave. Once in Final Form, I'd change my
name and no one would know it was me. I'd vanish as if I'd died
in truth. I hadn't been back to human form since I'd shifted in
Marskal's arms to escape his grasp.

Kiraka watched me circle in, wearing falcon form. She lay
sprawled across her meadow, blinding gold in the sun. I searched
carefully with my falcon's keen sight for any glimpse of Dafne or
anyone else nearby—one reason I'd chosen the form.

Seeing no one about, I landed and shifted to human form. A
stiff breeze off the ocean caught my hair, whipping and tugging
it. My heart shifted in my chest at the sensation, and I suddenly
missed Marskal with a desperation bordering on panic. Steam
billowed from Kiraka's nostrils, but I felt no fear. In fact, I'd
almost welcome it if she incinerated me again. I didn't care
anymore if I lived or died.

Do you have a death wish? The pained way Marskal had voiced
that question came back to me, and I knew it would hurt him
terribly if I died. I needed him to go on living, to be happy, and
make babies with some pretty mossback girl and... irrational and
angry jealousy flared up. I wasn't capable of that kind of

generosity, so no thinking about that. Just picture him happy.

Once I was the dragon, I wouldn't care so much.

"It doesn't work that way, you know, little changeling." A whisper of dry humor, steam hissing over coals.

"Hello, Lady Kiraka," I spoke aloud, since there was no one to overhear. "I've satisfied your terms. I've freed the dragon under Windroven. I've survived your tests and challenges, and am ready to take Final Form."

"How many forms do you have?"

Here we were. I stood on the precipice. "I have one hundred and forty-seven forms."

"Good. Show me."

I became the hummingbird. First Form. Forever associated with Marskal and his strong, loving hand. Then I became a white seabird. And a raven. And an owl. All the birds I knew. Then into the four-legged creatures. With a vast well of replenished power, I showed off my many forms—all but the aquatic ones, as I had no desire to suffocate.

I ended up back as myself, wearing the gown I'd used to bring with me by default. No hair pin. I'd left that with Marskal. I hoped he would give it to his daughter someday. Along with a feather from a white seabird who flew away with a broken heart.

"The conditions are satisfied. Here is the knowledge."

It slid into my mind, so simple. As if I'd always had the form. In a way, perhaps I always had. It had been one of Moranu's shifting faces. And it would be my last one. Forever.

I want forever, Marskal had said, with that bright and burning conviction.

I sank to my knees, crumpling under the weight of my dread and turbulent emotions. Had I ever felt so much before Marskal? I didn't think so. He'd awakened something in me that wouldn't sleep again. As if I'd lived in a hibernation of my own all these years, believing myself free when I was only alone. If I'd been so free, why had I always felt such a need to escape?

Only with him had I lost that constant search for the opportunity to flee.

I hadn't been trapped, I'd found a home.

Just when I had to give it up, forever.

"I warned you the price would be higher than you could imagine then."

I wiped the tears from my face, uncertain if the voice had been Moranu or Kiraka.

It didn't matter.

Slipping the tethers to my human form, the body Marskal had caressed and loved so well, I reached for Final Form.

~ 29 ~

I FOUND HIM slogging through the mountains well inside the Annfwn border. Of course, the stubborn man. How he'd made it so far, so fast, I had no idea.

He rode one staymach horse and led the other—still in the complementary black and white coloring I'd given them. Amazing that he'd persuaded them to continue to serve him. But then I knew well how persuasive my mossback could be.

My dragon wings cast a vast shadow as I soared low, surprised and yet not to find his face turned toward me, studying my descent with a fixed, narrow-eyed stare. He knew me. My heart, a larger, stronger one than I'd ever had before, raced with more than flight.

True to the promise, dragon form preserved all my intellect, which meant I still retained every human emotion. Perhaps more, because the sight of Marskal's face turned toward me made me feel the love for him with excruciating immediacy. I'd come to see him first, of everyone who loved me. He deserved that much. And I'd made him a promise.

I folded my wings, landing in the chilly marsh water with a sigh of pleasure. Being a dragon was hot, and any cool had become a treasured treat. Marskal raced the horses toward my landing, hoofbeats thundering like the steaming blood through my immense scaled body. He halted the horse in a spray of mud and gravel. Exhaustion lined his face, and made circles under his eyes. I'd done that to him, and yet he still chased after me. He swung down, strode forward, then stopped.

"Zynda." He spoke my name in wonder and satisfaction. "I was right. Deep, sapphire blue. Even your eyes. I'd know you anywhere."

I hesitated, terribly afraid of what might come next. But he loved me. More, I loved him. That had changed me, in more ways than I'd known.

Marskal approached closer, relieved joy relaxing his face. "You came back. You changed your mind. I haven't changed mine," His voice shook with deep emotion. "Change the staymachs into birds and we'll go to Annfwn. You'll let me stay with you—be your human companion."

Taking a breath—oddly, finding it more difficult than the reach to Final Form, or rather, not Final Form at all—I let go, and became myself again.

He staggered back, face going white. But only for a moment. Then Marskal had me in a grip so fierce not even my shifter strength could break it. A strange sound came out of him, part laughing, part gasping for air. He reared back and cupped my face. "What sorcery is this?" he demanded.

"I forgot something," I said. Not the right words, but at least I'd managed to speak. I would have to get used to remembering that I couldn't think my words as in dragon form. I shook my head. "I mean, no. Moranu, no. You will not be my human companion. I'd have to incinerate every female who made eyes at my handsome, stalwart mossback, which means we'd run out of women before long. Not a good idea."

"I don't understand." His hands flexed on my face, ran down over my arms. "How are you back from Final Form? I saw you as the dragon."

"Yes, well, it turns out that Final Form is not so final." I laughed, raggedly, and wiped the tears from my face. I hadn't even realized I'd been crying. "It only happens after centuries in that form, and then only if the shifter decides to stay in it and not shift back. Kiraka just never bothered to tell me that, because she wanted to test how much I'd give up."

"You gave up everything," Marskal whispered, pain in his eyes.

"Yes. And it was the hardest thing I've ever done. Except maybe for this. Marskal, do you love me still—even after the way I left you?"

He cracked a weary smile. "Oh, I'm pissed about that, but I still love you. I'll always love you."

"I love you, too." I said it and it felt good. Right and beautiful and part of life. "Is the offer still open?"

His brow cleared, but his eyes crinkled in question. "Which offer?"

"Everything. Will you father my children, and protect them and me? Can we live in your house near your family—I will want that lake—and in Annfwn, too? I'll need to be there a lot of the time, but maybe—"

He stopped my words with a long kiss, the relief and delight vibrating through him. I clung to him, immeasurably reassured to find he could still be my ground and my center. Gathering the fall of my hair in his hands, he held me close. Encircled in his arms, but not trapped. And we kissed each other as if we'd been apart for centuries.

As if we'd never part again.

"There's one more thing," I told him.

He laughed and kissed me. "I don't care what it is. This is more than I ever hoped for."

"I have to tell you," I insisted. "I promised."

Going still, he searched my face. "You stayed alive."

I laughed. "That, too. But the other. It's very early, but shifting to dragon form—recovering my shifting—it's given me new insight into my body. I discovered something."

I took his hand and laid it over my belly, watching the delighted wonder fill his face. "Don't get too excited," I warned him, feeling breathless.

"Too late," he whispered, reverence in it. He cupped the small life in his big hand, just as he'd once held and preserved me.

"I don't know what being a dragon will do," I continued doggedly. "And I have to do that. So it could—" I put my hand over my mouth to stop more words. Marskal gently pulled my hand away and kissed me.

"Thank you for telling me," he said against my mouth.

"I'm so afraid," I answered.

"I know." He slipped a hand into my hair and drew me against his chest. His heart thundered under my ear, and his scent filled my senses, bringing me home. "We'll get through it together. I will love no less for a short life than a long one— none of it can break me. And it won't break you. Look at you." His smile filled his face. "You're a fucking dragon! You'll be the most spectacular mother under Moranu's gaze."

I laughed. "Only you."

"Only us," he replied, kissing me with such tenderness my heart nearly stopped.

"I want forever," I breathed against his mouth.

He laughed, all the music of life in the sound. "As my lady desires."

"Want a ride?" I asked him, batting my lashes.

"Yes. But if you drop me in the water, I'll take revenge."

"You can try." I stepped back and flashed into dragon form.

Marskal unstrapped the packs from the horses and I clutched them in my talons. The staymach horses became birds, circling my head joyfully. Marskal climbed onto my back.

"Ready!" he called.

With the strong clasp of his thighs close against my skin, I spread my wings and took to the sky.

The story continues in the next of tales of The Twelve Kingdoms and The Uncharted Realms:

THE ARROWS OF THE HEART

July, 2018

ABOUT JEFFE KENNEDY

Jeffe Kennedy is an award-winning author whose works include novels, non-fiction, poetry, and short fiction. She has been a Ucross Foundation Fellow, received the Wyoming Arts Council Fellowship for Poetry, and was awarded a Frank Nelson Doubleday Memorial Award, and recently received the Rita® Award for paranormal romance.

Her award-winning fantasy romance trilogy *The Twelve Kingdoms* hit the shelves starting in May 2014. Book 1, *The Mark of the Tala*, received a starred Library Journal review and was nominated for the RT Book of the Year while the sequel, *The Tears of the Rose* received a Top Pick Gold and was nominated for the RT Reviewers' Choice Best Fantasy Romance of 2014. The third book, *The Talon of the Hawk*, won the RT Reviewers' Choice Best Fantasy Romance of 2015. Two more books followed in this world, beginning the spin-off series *The Uncharted Realms*. Book one in that series, *The Pages of the Mind*, has also been nominated for the RT Reviewer's Choice Best Fantasy Romance of 2016 and won RWA's 2017 RITA® Award. The second book, *The Edge of the Blade*, released December 27, 2016, and is a PRISM finalist, along with *The Pages of the Mind*. The next in the series, *The Shift of the Tide*, will be out in August, 2017.

She also introduced a new fantasy romance series, *Sorcerous Moons*, which includes *Lonen's War*, *Oria's Gambit*, *The Tides of Bàra*, and *The Forests of Dru*. She's begun releasing a new contemporary erotic romance series, *Missed Connections*, which started with *Last Dance* and continues in *With a Prince*.

A high fantasy trilogy taking place in *The Twelve Kingdoms* world, *The Lost Princess Chronicles*, is forthcoming from Rebel Base books in 2018. In 2019, St. Martins Press will release the first book, *The Orchid Throne*, in a new fantasy romance series, *The Forgotten Empires*.

Her other works include a number of fiction series: the fantasy romance novels of *A Covenant of Thorns*; the contemporary BDSM novellas of the *Facets of Passion*; an erotic contemporary serial novel, *Master of the Opera*; and the erotic romance trilogy, *Falling Under*, which includes *Going Under*, *Under His Touch* and *Under Contract*.

She lives in Santa Fe, New Mexico, with two Maine coon cats, plentiful free-range lizards and a very handsome Doctor of Oriental Medicine.

Jeffe can be found online at her website: JeffeKennedy.com, every Sunday at the popular SFF Seven blog, on Facebook, on Goodreads and pretty much constantly on Twitter @jeffekennedy. She is represented by Sarah Younger of Nancy Yost Literary Agency.

JeffeKennedy.com

facebook.com/Author.Jeffe.Kennedy

twitter.com/jeffekennedy

goodreads.com/author/show/1014374.Jeffe_Kennedy

Sign up for my newsletter here.

jeffekennedy.com/sign-up-for-my-newsletter

Titles by Jeffe Kennedy

OTHER FANTASY ROMANCES

A COVENANT OF THORNS

Rogue's Pawn
Rogue's Possession
Rogue's Paradise

THE TWELVE KINGDOMS

Negotiation
The Mark of the Tala
The Tears of the Rose
The Talon of the Hawk
Heart's Blood
For Crown and Kingdom

THE UNCHARTED REALMS

The Pages of the Mind
The Edge of the Blade
The Shift of the Tide

SORCEROUS MOONS

Lonen's War
Oria's Gambit
The Tides of Bára
The Forests of Dru

CONTEMPORARY ROMANCES

MISSED CONNECTIONS

Last Dance
With a Prince

CONTEMPORARY EROTIC ROMANCES

Exact Warm Unholy
The Devil's Doorbell

FACETS OF PASSION

Sapphire
Platinum
Ruby
Five Golden Rings

FALLING UNDER

Going Under
Under His Touch
Under Contract

EROTIC PARANORMAL

MASTER OF THE OPERA E-SERIAL
Master of the Opera, Act 1: Passionate Overture
Master of the Opera, Act 2: Ghost Aria
Master of the Opera, Act 3: Phantom Serenade
Master of the Opera, Act 4: Dark Interlude
Master of the Opera, Act 5: A Haunting Duet
Master of the Opera, Act 6: Crescendo
Master of the Opera

BLOOD CURRENCY
Blood Currency

BDSM FAIRYTALE ROMANCE

Petals and Thorns

OTHER WORKS

Birdwoman
Hopeful Monsters
Teeth, Long and Sharp

Thank you for reading!

48826349R00239

Made in the USA
Middletown, DE
28 September 2017